Girls From Da Hood 16

Girls From Da Hood 16

Racquel Williams, Na'Cole, and T. Friday

www.urbanbooks.net

Urban Books, LLC
300 Farmingdale Road, N.Y.-Route 109
Farmingdale, NY 11735

Summer Fling in New York Copyright © 2025 Racquel Williams
Thot Girl Summer in Chicago Copyright © 2025 Na'Cole
Thot Girl Summer in Detroit Copyright © 2025 T. Friday

ISBN 13: 978-1-64556-753-0
EBOOK ISBN: 978-1-64556-754-7

First Trade Paperback Printing January 2026
Printed in the United States of America

10 9 8 7 6 5 4 3 2 1

This is a work of fiction. Any references or similarities to actual events, real people, living or dead, or to real locales are intended to give the novel a sense of reality. Any similarity in other names, characters, places, and incidents is entirely coincidental.

Distributed by Kensington Publishing Corp.
Submit Orders to:
Customer Service
400 Hahn Road
Westminster, MD 21157-4627
Phone: 1-800-733-3000
Fax: 1-800-659-2436

The authorized representative in the EU for product safety and compliance
Is eucomply OU, Parnu mnt 139b-14, Apt 123
Tallinn, Berlin 11317, hello@eucompliancepartner.com

Girls From Da Hood 16

by

Racquel Williams, Na'Cole, and T. Friday

Summer Fling in New York

by

Racquel Williams

Prologue

"Naomi Coleman," the commentator yelled out my name, and everyone started clapping.

I stood up, grabbed the tail of my gown, and sashayed my way up the stairs to receive my BS in nursing.

"Thank you," I said as I accepted my diploma. I turned and smiled as I made my way off the stage. As I looked up, I saw my boyfriend of three years standing there beside my daddy. It was a great feeling, not because I was graduating, but more so that my two favorite guys in my life were here cheering me on.

"I'm so proud of you, baby. You did it." Jerome kissed me on the cheek when I met up with him.

"Thank you, my love. I couldn't have done it without your support and all those late-night study groups."

"Yeah, that's true, but you did, and you deserve all the praise. C'mon, let's get out of here. You know Mr. Coleman is eagerly waiting for you."

"You're right." We held hands and made our way out of the crowded room and into the hallway. I could see Daddy standing there holding a bouquet of roses in his hand. I let Jerome's hand go, and I ran into my daddy's arms. As old as I was, I was still Daddy's little girl, and I didn't care how anyone felt about it.

"Darling Naomi, congratulation; you did it. You make yo' old man proud." He wrapped his arms around me tightly.

"Thank you, Daddy, for being there and for paying this hefty nursing school tuition. I couldn't have done it without you."

"Well, I'm glad you didn't just eat my money, but you made good use of it. Now, if I could only convince you to go to medical school, you could be the very first doctor in the family. I'm sure Jerome would love that. Ain't it, Jerome?"

"Ha, oh, I'm sorry, sir. I was busy checking some emails."

"That's what I'm talkin' about. Jerome is always on the grind. Imagine both of you being doctors . . ."

"Daddy, stop, please. Let's get out of here. These heels are killing my feet." I took Daddy's hand and started walking toward the exit.

Once I reached the car, I quickly slipped into a pair of Gucci slides, which felt much better. I wasn't sure what the plans for the evening were, as Daddy told me it was a surprise. I got into the car with Jerome, and he pulled out behind Daddy's SUV.

"Hey, babes, do you know what Daddy has planned?"

"Are you trying to get me give up the surprise, darling?"

"Who me? Noooo . . . I was just hoping you would give me a little hint." I flashed him a flirtatious smile.

"Well, my love, you know Mr. Coleman is a man of many surprises. Let's just wait and see what he manages to pull off."

"I guess so . . ." I pouted.

After about twenty-five minutes of driving, we ended up in Snellville, down a long stretch of road. The houses were huge with neatly kept lawns. I could tell it wasn't your average neighborhood, and I couldn't help but wonder what we were doing in this area. I knew there was no use questioning it, so I kept calm and enjoyed the scenery.

Daddy pulled into the driveway, and Jerome followed and parked. I noticed about five to six other cars parked on the property.

Daddy hurriedly walked inside the house, which was strange to me, but I remained quiet. I got out of the car, straightened my clothes, and followed Jerome to the door. The only thing was that he stopped and knocked.

"Come in," a voice hollered.

Jerome stepped in, and I followed him closely behind.

"Surprise!" everyone yelled in harmony.

Bright lights flickered, and balloons were everywhere. I put my hands to my face as I tried to hide my excitement. The room was filled with family and friends rushing up to me, giving me hugs and congrats. My heart was full of happiness to see that the people that I loved were here to celebrate my special day with me.

After all the excitement died down, we all sat down to eat dinner. Daddy went all out—shrimp, lobster, steak, alligator meat, just to name a few that were on the menu. I ate so much that I felt like I was going to burst out of my tightly fit Angel Brinks dress. I also drank two glasses of red wine, which made my head feel heavy. This was what you called a party, and I was grateful to my daddy.

"Can I get y'all attention? I know y'all full and probably ready to hit the road, but I got something to say." Daddy clicked a fork against a glass to get all our attention. Everyone got quiet and stared at him, trying to see what he was about to say.

"First, I want to say a big thanks to all you guys who came out to celebrate this day with my daughter. I appreciate y'all. Most of you should be getting bonuses this year." Everyone started clapping loudly. Most of these people were his employees who had become family.

"Quiet down, I ain't done yet. Come up here, sugar." He waved for me.

Oh God, this man must not see that I was barely keeping my eyes open. I knew it was an order, so I got up and slowly walked over to him. He placed his arm around me.

"Baby, I know I said it a million times, and I'ma say it again. You make yo' old man very proud, and if I could give you the world, I would. So, while I figure out that part, here are the keys to yo' brand-new house."

"What? House? Me?" I looked at him for confirmation.

"Yes, this is all yours, honey, and oh, that's not all. Here is a paid vacation for you and your girlfriend for a week in New York. I know how much you talk about visiting, so here is your chance." He handed me an envelope.

"Oh my God, Daddy, thank you. Thank youuu." I wrapped my arms around him as the tears fell from my eyes.

Chapter One

"Bitch, I wish you would hurry the fuck up before we miss our flights." I turned to my bestie, Yash, and yelled as I made my way through the cluttered airport. We were already late checking in for our Delta flight, which was leaving from Atlanta Hartsfield Airport to JFK in New York.

"Girl, I'm trying, but these damn heels are holding me back," she yelled while she struggled to keep up.

I took a quick second glance back at her feet and almost burst out laughing. It wasn't funny, but I couldn't believe this bitch really slid into some six-inch stilettos to get on a flight. She must know how long the walk was to some of these gates, but she'd learn today. I shook my head as I headed down the stairs where the trains were located.

"Girl, I need a fucking drink. Why the hell this place got to be so big?" Yashira complained as she caught her breath.

"Hmm, it wouldn't be so hard if you had worn some flip-flops like the rest of us regular bitches do. But, nah, you got to be the bad and boujee bitch. Now, look at you, feet hurting and shit."

"Fuck off. I ain't never been yo' average bitch, and I damn sure ain't goin' start acting like one now," she shot back.

I looked at her and rolled my eyes. This bitch was extra as fuck, but I loved her, and this behavior wasn't new. "Uh-huh, now picture, Miss Boujee walking around with those big old bunions all over her toes."

"Go to hell, bitch. You sound like a hater." She burst out laughing, and I joined in the laughter.

A few seconds later, the train pulled up, and we climbed aboard. We were getting off at E gate, so I glanced up to see where we were. We had a few more stops before it was time to disembark.

We got to our stop, got off the train, and then had to walk up another set of long stairs. Even though I had on a pair of Tory Burch flat sandals, my feet started to get tired. All this damn walking was also beginning to get to me. I was hoping that our gate was the closest one, but soon realized it was almost at the end. We finally made it and were able to relax a few minutes before it was time for us to board our flight.

Yash sat beside me and was still behaving as if she were dying. I shot her a look. "Bitch, you are extra as hell."

"You call this extra; you just wait until I get to New York. Shit, I'm going to be talking just like them niggas. You goin' think I was born up there," she said in her best New York accent that she could muster up.

Before I could respond, the lady announced our boarding over the intercom. I jumped up and gathered my things. I was very excited about this trip and grateful that Daddy booked it for us. Once he disclosed it was for me and a girlfriend, the choice wasn't hard to make. Yashira had been my best friend since middle school, and we always talked about going to New York together.

Our relationship had taken a rocky turn over the past few months when another friend of ours told me that Yashira shouldn't be trusted, and I should just watch her. I tried to inquire why that friend said that, but she was hushed about it. Me, being the friend that I was, went to Yashira and asked her why Tameka would feel the need to tell me that. Yashira made a big deal out of it and told me to fuck myself. We didn't speak for a while until the party, the day of my graduation. I wasn't going to lie. I felt happy when I saw her in the crowd. After things calmed down, we spoke, and she apologized to me. We both accepted that we handled the situation wrong and decided to put it behind us. Now, here we were, going on the trip that we always wanted to take. I was hoping we could get our relationship back on track, even though at the back of my mind, I couldn't help but wonder what Tameka was referring to when she made that statement.

I must've dozed off, but I woke up when the pilot made an announcement over the intercom that we should get ready for landing. I sat up and peeped out the window. Excitement rushed all over me as I couldn't wait to see what the hype about this city was all about. I had heard about niggas with big dicks and lots of money. Not saying those were bad, I was just curious to find out what else the great Big Apple had to offer.

"Girl, you're finally up. All that damn snoring." I looked over at Yashira.

"You a damn lie. I don't snore. I was tired, though. I had to get a little rest up, so I can get my party on tonight."

"I hear that. I can't wait to hit the bar either. I'ma be getting back-to-back shots. I ain't goin' be no good to myself tomorrow morning."

A few minutes later, the plane landed. I gathered my things and waited for the people in front of me to exit the flight. We followed and got off. Again, Miss Boujee couldn't keep up 'cause her feet were hurting. I stopped and stood there, shaking my head at my dear friend. She was still struggling. "Why don't you take off the shoes?"

"And go barefoot? Yuck, this floor is filthy."

"Yeah, but we are never going to make it out of here at the rate you're going." I walked off.

"Bitch, I'm trying. Let me hold on to you."

I looked at her and could tell she was in some serious pain. I took her arm and supported her down the ramp. Thank God the walk wasn't long, so we got our bags and walked outside. I wanted to get a rental, but I heard it was easier to move around in New York using Uber or Lyft, so we decided to do that instead.

Outside was busy, and vehicles were everywhere. It took awhile to get a taxi. Every one of them seemed to be packed. I finally spotted an empty cab and waved to the driver. He drove up, and we loaded our baggage into the trunk, then got into the car. I pulled up the address on my phone and read it off to him. He didn't speak English too well, so he had difficulty understanding us. As much as I wanted to snap at him, I used the little bit of Spanish that I learned in college to read off the address to him. Finally, we were able to leave the congested airport.

Daddy booked us into the Hilton in Midtown Manhattan. As soon as we pulled up, the bellboys helped us unload our luggage into the lobby. Everyone seemed so friendly and made us feel welcome. After we checked in, we headed to the elevator and walked to our room.

My eyes lit up like stars on a dark night when I entered the room. Daddy really outdid himself with this one. The room was a massive suite with a living room area, two large beds, and a couch. I placed the suitcases down, threw my purse on the bed, and headed to the balcony. It was a sight to see up from the twelfth floor. People and cars were everywhere. Tall buildings surrounded us. This was what the hype was about. This city was lit, and I was ready to explore every bit of it for the next five days.

"Bitch, this is dope as fuck. I can't wait to hit the party scenes," Yash yelled out as she joined me on the balcony.

"You and me both, but listen, bitch, we're in an unfamiliar place, so we need to be aware of everything around us. No matter what, we got to look out for each other."

"I got you, boo, but you know I'm the one that always gets drunk first, so that means you have to look out for me, bitch."

"See, that's exactly what I'm talking 'bout. You can't be the only one enjoying yourself. We are here together, so we have to look out for each other. *Comprende, chica?*"

"I hear you, boo boo. I'm about to lie down for a few. Get my energy up for later on. I heard this city doesn't sleep, so I plan to be up all night."

She walked back into the room and left me standing, taking in this beautiful scenery. I shook my head and smiled. She was the wild one, and being in this fast city wasn't going to help. I just prayed that we could enjoy ourselves and head back home in one piece. I promised Daddy I would be careful. . . .

Chapter Two

Naomi

We had dinner at a nearby Friday's. It took about an hour just to get a table. By then, I was famished. We ate, drank red wine, and chopped it up. We were equally excited to see what the nightlife was all about. After dinner, we headed out to stroll the place and see what they had going on. We saw a few bars, but the lines were stupidly long, and after that long wait for dinner, I didn't have it in me to wait any longer. We continued walking until we came upon one that had no line, so we stepped inside. Looks could be deceiving 'cause it was full of people inside. There was barely any room to stand, much less breathe comfortably. We made our way through the crowd and headed up the stairs. I was hoping it wasn't as packed as the downstairs. Luckily, there weren't that many people, and there was a balcony that overlooked the city. I took a quick glance at the scenery. The music was blasting, and I saw a few dudes standing around while chicks were all over the floor, showing off their grinding skills.

We found a comfortable spot to stand up without anyone bouncing into us. After a few minutes, we headed for the bar. There was a long line, so we joined and waited. I was eager to get some alcohol in my system and eager to get my dance on.

"Look, bitch, ever since we walked in, that nigga been eyeing you," Yashira whispered in my ear.

I shot her a weird look. I was shocked 'cause if a nigga was looking at me, I didn't see him.

"Girl, what you talking 'bout?" I inquired.

"Don't look right away, but it's that nigga standing at the bar with the Gucci glasses on with the red Psycho Bunny shirt."

I waited a few seconds, then slightly turned my head. I didn't want to be obvious, so I slowly looked around the bar. My eyes made it to the bar, and there was a dark-skinned nigga standing there, looking in my direction. He was the only one in a red shirt, so I assumed that was who she was talking about.

I couldn't see clearly from where I was, but the little that I could see let me know that he was cute, but nothing else about him seemed interesting.

"Girl, that boy ain't worried about me. He probably in here with his bitch, plus I'm in a committed relationship and ain't checking for no other man."

"Ha-ha, bitch. Please don't tell me you think that Jerome is really committed to you."

"Oh my God, Yash, are we going to do that in here? I understand he ain't yo' cup of tea, but please respect our relationship."

"Bitch, whatever. I only tolerate that motherfucking boy 'cause you my friend. All the times I just wanted to run up on his ass. He is lucky I love you and don't want no drama between us. But the day that he violate you, I'ma be on that ass."

"Well, thank you, friend. Now, drop it. We are here to enjoy our vacation and spend up Daddy's money."

"Yeaaah, you're right. That's the vibe right there."

By then, the line had moved up, and we were up next to order our drinks. I tried my best not to glance over to where this mysterious man was standing.

"What can I get you?" the bartender quizzed.

"Let me get a shot of Grey Goose with pineapple juice." Then I turned to Yash. "What you getting?"

"Umm, let me get Henny on the rocks."

I opened my Gucci purse and took out a crisp one-hundred-dollar bill to pay the tab, but before I could do that, I felt someone grab my hand.

"Drinks is on me, beautiful," this stranger said while he stared me down.

I snatched my arm away quickly. "I appreciate it, but I got my own money." I still managed not to make eye contact with him.

"What she really mean is we appreciate it." Yashira stepped in and snatched the money out of my hand.

I opened my mouth to say something, but no words came out. I looked at her, then turned my attention to this short, athletic-looking stranger. "Thank you," was all I managed to squeeze out.

I grabbed my drink and walked away from the bar. I didn't look back to see what was taking place behind me. We found an empty table and decided to hang out there. I made sure my back was toward the bar and this stranger.

"Bitch, are you crazy? That nigga is fine as fuck," she exclaimed as she took a sip of her drink.

"I don't care about him being fine. For all I know, he can be a serial killer or something. I know you heard all the stories about chicks getting kidnapped by strangers."

"You watch too much damn ID channel, chick. Hello, this is the *real* world, and we are in New York City, where dreams are made. You better listen to Jay-Z and Alicia. Bitch, you are making us look bad. Shit, he might even have a friend that I can scoop up for myself."

"Do you hear yourself right now? Thirsty much?" I took a sip of my drink while trying to bring my anxiety down a little.

"Bitch, fuck being thirsty. I'm ready to be fucked. Shit, the right nigga ain't even got to touch me. I'll be busting all over his ass just by him breathing on me."

"Oh my. Why do you have to be like this? What happened to my nice, quiet friend?" I took a quick glance around, trying to see if anyone was listening to our conversation.

"Girl, that's when I was young. I'm a grown-ass woman now who knows what she wants and won't waste a minute getting it. You can keep acting like the Queen of England, boring as fuck, and you will leave this earth never experiencing what a good fuck is like. That pastor son you're with isn't fucking you the right way, or else you wouldn't be uptight. Hmm. God gave you some sweet pussy between your legs, and I promise you, it deserves some good ole fucking."

She caught me off guard with that statement. I spat my juice out all over my shirt. I grabbed a napkin quickly and tried to wipe off my clothes. I was too embarrassed to look around, hoping no one saw that. "Bitch, please, shut the fuck up."

"I'm sorry, boo boo, but you need to hear the truth. You are too uptight. You need to live a little."

Even if I wanted to go back and forth with her crazy ass, I couldn't. I was still trying to catch my breath from laughing so hard. A few seconds later, a waitress walked over to our table with a few more drinks on the tray.

"We didn't order that," I looked at her and blurted out.

"The gentleman at the bar ordered them for you guys." She placed the cups of liquor on the table.

I looked over to the bar, and the same dude waved at me while smiling. I reluctantly waved back. I had to give it to this dude. He was very persistent.

"See, bitch, I told you that nigga has eyes on you."

"Uh-huh, whatever," I acted nonchalantly.

"Tell him thank you," Yash chimed in.

I sat there, looking and thinking if I should even take a sip of this drink. What if he spiked it? I wasn't naïve to believe that it couldn't happen to us. Before my thoughts were complete, Yashira picked up her glass and started drinking. Oh well, I decided to follow suit, hoping I wouldn't regret it. I took the first sip with precaution, then waited a few seconds to see if there would be a side effect, but nothing happened. I guessed I was being paranoid.

After the second round of drinks, my muscles were relaxed, and I wasn't feeling as uptight as I was earlier. The DJ was playing some dope music, which made it hard to sit still. I was feeling myself, or should I say the liquor—whatever it was—and it boosted my confidence. I jumped up and started dancing slowly at first. I didn't want to bring too much attention to myself, so I stayed close to the table. I wasn't the best dancer in the house 'cause these New York chicks were showing off their best skills. But I didn't let that deter me. I knew how to shake the round, phat ass that I inherited from my mother, so I leaned on the table and did just that. I was so into myself that I didn't notice that someone had walked up to me. "Can I join you?" I heard the voice echo in my ear, causing me to jump and pause instantly.

I turned around quickly to face Mr. Persistent. We were so close to each other's face that I could smell the alcohol reeking off his breath, but it wasn't a turnoff. It was appealing, and something about him was pulling me closer. Without notice, he moved his mouth closer and placed his lips on mine. He kissed me, and instead of me slapping his face off for assaulting me, I leaned forward, grabbed his head, and kissed this man that I just met in front of everybody. It took a second for my brain to catch on to this erratic behavior, and then I pulled away.

"Oh my God. I'm so sorry. I didn't mean to." I started looking around. Everyone was still minding their own business except Yashira. She was laughing and clapping. I could strangle this bitch right now for not helping me out of this situation that I'd gotten myself into.

"Ain't no need to be sorry, love. I should be the one apologizing, but truthfully, I'm glad I did that. You felt what I felt. You can't deny it. I'm Trini. What's your name, love?"

"Naomi, and Trini, is this normal for you to walk up on a strange female and push your tongue down her throat?" I squeezed out, still blushing from embarrassment.

"Nice to meet you, Naomi. I can tell you're not from here. Where are you from?" He skipped over my statement.

"Atlanta. I am so sorry. I never did anything like this before. Oh my God." My face was flushed, and I wanted to run away, but my feet felt like they were glued in that one spot.

"You need to relax, ma; we're both grown here. Plus, your lips tasted like sweet honey from my country, and damn, they softer than a baby's ass." He licked his fine set of lips.

"Damn, you couldn't think of something more appropriate to describe my lips?" I burst out laughing.

"I could have, but you got the picture. From the moment you walked in, I was drawn to you. Your looks is flawless, and your spirit is fearless. How long are you going to be in the city?"

"A few days, and sorry, Trini, thanks for the compliments, but I have a man."

"Listen, love, I have no interest in yo' man and . . ." He grabbed my left hand, stared at my fingers, then let it go. "I don't see no ring on yo' finger, so that mean whoever he is, he not too serious 'bout making you 'is wife."

"You know nothing about my man, and not every woman is interested in being married either. So, before you go assuming shit, you can ask me," I snapped a little more than I wanted to.

"Chill out, love. I'm speaking on my observation. Anyways, kill all that. Let me get yo' number. I would love to take you out, show you my city."

My head was screaming "Hell nah," but something inside of me was going in the opposite direction.

I looked over at Yashira. She was eavesdropping the entire time and was nodding her head yes. I knew I shouldn't be doing this, but he was cute, he was appealing, and I was curious. I read off my number to him and watched as he stored it on his phone. He wasted no time 'cause my phone started ringing. I was pretty sure it was him. I saw the strange number, so I pressed ignore right away.

"That's mi number. Mek sure you locked it in." He spoke in broken English.

I could tell that he wasn't American. I concluded that he was either Jamaican, Barbadian, or Trinidadian. Whichever one it was, his accent sounded sexy as fuck.

"Okay."

"A'ight, love, be safe out here," he warned, then turned to walk away.

Once he left, I could breathe normally again. I watched as he made his way back to the bar, where a group of niggas started greeting him. I let out a long sigh of relief. But my relief was short-lived because seconds later, chaos broke out in the bar.

Pop! Pop! Pop!

We dropped to the ground as gunshots rang out. People started running and screaming over the loud music.

"Oh my God, what's going on?" Yashira yelled as she huddled beside me under the table.

"I don't know." I started crying. I reached over and grabbed her, hoping that we wouldn't end up dead. I was trying to think, but my brain froze. Next to us were some other girls, and they were screaming for help. I could tell another one was on her phone, talking to a 911 operator.

Pop! Pop! Pop!

Another round of gunshots rang out. This time, the music was off, so it was loud and clear. I heard niggas yelling and bitches screaming. I kept my head down 'cause I was too afraid to lift it and look out.

It was a nightmare all around us. My heart was racing, and all kinds of crazy thoughts were running through my mind. The place got quiet again, and people started running. I jumped up, grabbed Yash's hand, and dashed for the stairs. People were everywhere, so it wasn't as easy to move quickly. When we reached the stairs, we saw a dead body. I tried not to look, but I could tell it was the DJ lying there in a pool of blood. I glanced around and saw a door that read exit, so I dashed that way, hoping to get out. We got to the door, but couldn't move because people had stampeded and blocked it. I flung off my heels while trying to figure out a way not to die up in this place.

Someone grabbed me by the hip. I swung around and looked. It was Trini. I tried to wrestle out of his grip, but his firm hold on me made it impossible. "Let me the fuck go."

I was confused. Here this nigga was, snatching me up. Was he trying to kidnap me? Was this his doing?

"C'mon, B. I can get you outta the private entrance. Either that or you can stay here and die," he yelled.

I heard his words, but I didn't know if I could trust him. Why was he doing this?

"C'mon, bitch, let's go," Yashira yelled at me.

He quickly shoved us in front of him while he tried to open a side door behind the bar.

The door was locked, so we watched as he knocked.

"Who that is?" a voice echoed.

"Yo, it's Trini. Open the door, dawg," he commanded.

The door popped open, and we ran inside with him. We headed down the stairs and outside the building. No one was back there, which was weird 'cause all those people were trapped inside.

"I ain't going farther until you tell me what the fuck is going on." I stopped and forcefully pulled my hand away from his.

"What the fuck, yo? You see the bomboclaat bwoy them shooting up the place? You want stay here, or you want to get the fuck outta here? Choice is yours, but I'm getting the fuck outta here."

It was only then that I saw that he had a gun in his right hand. I was conflicted, and my thoughts were all over the place.

"We going with you," Yash concluded.

He ran over to a black Audi that was parked and instructed us to get in. Reluctantly, I got in the backseat while Yash got in the front. He pulled out with so much speed that he broke the gate. He didn't stop. He sped in the opposite direction from the club. A few blocks down, we drove past a line of police cars making their way in the direction of the club.

So much was going on too fast. I couldn't think clearly. I took my phone out of my purse and dialed Jerome's number. The phone rang out until his voicemail kicked in. I rested my head on the windowsill, trying to get the stale air that was blowing in, while the tears flowed. I felt disappointed when he didn't pick up the phone. I knew if nothing else, his voice would help calm me down.

I tried calling him a few more times, but there was still no answer, so I placed the phone back into my purse.

I was feeling tipsy and scared from all that had happened back there. I couldn't help but wonder how many people were dead. My stomach turned just thinking about it. This could've easily been me or Yashira. How would our family deal with *that* news? I let the window down some more, but the smell of the garbage on the streets only made it worse.

"You need to pull over," I yelled out.

"What? You got to pee?" Yash yelled back.

"No, I need to—"

Before the words could finish coming out of my mouth, I started vomiting all over myself, and even though I tried, his beautiful white leather seats didn't escape the nasty onslaught.

"She's vomiting. Pull over," Yash yelled over the music.

He pulled over instantly on a side road. I jumped out and continued throwing up my insides all on the sidewalk.

"Damn, you good?" he inquired while he rubbed my back.

My body tensed up as I felt violated by this stranger, but my head was spinning, and I wasn't in the best shape to check that shit. Plus, that rub felt good and soothing.

"Look in the truck and grab me that bottle of water."

"Here you go," Yash said, handing the bottle to him.

"C'mon, love. Use this and wash out your mouth."

I did as I was told and rinsed my mouth before I got back into the truck. The stench of vomit serenaded my nose. All I could think about was how tired and sleepy I was.

My phone kept ringing, and at first, I ignored it. My head was throbbing like I had been hit by a ton of bricks, and I was scared to open my eyes. Whoever it was calling wasn't easing up, so I forced my eyes open. I blinked a few times before I could focus. The room was dark, which was great for my eyes, but I suddenly noticed it wasn't the hotel but someone's bedroom. I started panicking. I threw off the blanket that was covering me and sat up in bed. I was in a room, but whose fucking room I had no idea. I looked down at my clothes. I was no longer in the clothes that I had on last night. Instead, I was in a large T-shirt with a Trinidadian flag plastered on the front.

I searched my mind, trying to remember something—anything, but I was drawing a blank. Tears started rolling down my face. My thoughts were interrupted again by the ringing of the phone. I reached for my purse that was nearby. I took it out and realized it was Jerome calling. I started to answer, but I stopped. What would I tell him when I had no idea where I was or what the fuck I had done?

He called four times, but I refused to answer the phone. I knew he was probably pissed as hell, but that was something I would just have to deal with later on. After the calls stopped, I decided to turn off the phone completely. I knew that I would have some explaining to do, but fuck it. He was receiving a dose of his own medicine. There were times when I used to call him, and his phone would go unanswered, and his favorite line was, "I was sleepin'," so I guessed I could run that back on him, and it shouldn't be a problem.

Seconds later, someone knocked on the door. "Come in," I yelled out.

I held my breath as the door opened. I wasn't sure what I would be faced with. After all, I had no idea whose house this was and why I was here in the first place. I tried my best to stay calm.

"Good morning, beautiful," Trini said while displaying his set of pearly whites that were more visible in the daylight.

"Good morning. Where is Yashira, and is this yo' house?"

He was standing there in only his boxers and his bare chest. I should be focused on his face; however, instead, my eyes traveled from his well-toned biceps to the package between his legs. I wasn't usually this bold, but my eyes were laser-focused. This nigga was blessed down there. I started daydreaming about getting fucked by this nigga. I bet he could fuck me in all different kinds of positions.

"You're finally awake, bitch," Yashira said as she popped her head in the room.

I felt so embarrassed. I wondered if he noticed what was going on. I quickly regained my composure.

"Yeah, I'm up," I refocused and replied.

"Bitch, you was drunk as hell last night. Vomiting and all." She looked at me and burst out laughing.

Now that she mentioned that, my memories of the night rushed back to me immediately. Oh my God, I remembered the chaos at the club and how I feared that I was going to die.

"Why didn't we go to the hotel?" I shot both a dirty look.

"I decided that you were in no shape to go to the room, so I brought you to my crib. I hope it's okay."

"He right, bitch. Plus his crib is so much nicer than the hotel. No offense to your daddy, but you have to see the rest of the house. It is hugeeee," she emphasized.

She was making me nauseated by how she was behaving in front of this dude. I kind of felt embarrassed and was curious to know what he was thinking.

"So, Trini, did you find out how many people died last night?"

"Shit, my bwoy tell me that a few cats from Bronx got hit, and a female and the DJ, Benny, got killed."

"Oh, wow. Is it always like this at y'all clubs?"

"Nah, but you know how it is in the streets. Niggas got beef, so when they see one another in the club, then it's whatever."

I looked at him as he spoke about this as if it were business as usual. I could tell he was a street nigga, and this was just another regular day of business for him.

"Wow. I just want to make it back home in one piece. If this is how y'all get down out here, I am ready to go back home now. I'ma see if I can change my flight." I reached for my phone to turn it on again.

"No, the hell you not, bitch. You acting like niggas ain't getting killed all the time in the A. This ain't no damn different. We are here to celebrate, and that's what we going to do. So, get yo' ass up, boo, and get yourself together."

This bitch was starting to irritate me to the core. She was definitely acting weird around Trini, and it was becoming sickening. It was like she was trying to get one up on me all the time.

"All right, ladies, I'm going to give y'all some time together. I ordered breakfast, so it should be here shortly." Then he walked out of the room. My eyes followed his well-kept body and long locs flowing down his back.

She looked back in the hallway, then closed the door behind her. "Bitch, this nigga here is paid outta the ass." She gleamed with excitement.

"Okay and what?" I quizzed nonchalantly; I was really trying to figure out what she was getting at.

"Bitch, what I am saying is you better play your cards right. Shit, I bet he will take us on a shopping spree out here."

"Girl, you need to chill the fuck out. Right now, you are behaving like a chicken that's running around with its head chopped off. We don't know this nigga from a can of paint, but you let him take us to his house. What if he had his niggas here and raped us?"

"*Excuse* me? Bitch, *I'm* not the one who got drunk and didn't know how to act. I was sober the whole damn time. So, before you start judging me, boo boo, check yourself. I made sure you got here and made sure you were safe."

I guess she did have a point there. I should be grateful that she made sure we were safe.

"You're right, and I was wrong for coming off at you like this. I just wish we had gone to the hotel room instead of coming here."

"Yeah, well, now that you're awake, I guess we can leave."

I could tell that she was still feeling salty for the way that I came off on her, and I couldn't blame her. I just didn't like how she was behaving in front of dude. This would blow over, though. She was my bestie, and this little fight wasn't going to break our bond.

"Come on, ladies, the food is here." Trini knocked on the door, then yelled out.

We both walked out of the room and followed him into the dining room.

Chapter Three

Yashira (Yash)

Some of us bitches were born to get it out the mud, and then, there were the bitches who were spoon-fed. This was the only way to describe my bestie, Naomi. We grew up as friends, but it was no secret that her daddy was a big boss in Stone Mountain. They lived in the big, three-story house while we lived in the rented house down the street. They shopped at Saks Fifth Avenue like we shopped at Macy's and JCPenney. I could go on and on, but I would come off as a jealous, hating-ass bitch instead of the supportive friend that I knew I was. It was our vacation in New York, courtesy of her rich daddy, and honestly, I was happy 'cause I had heard so much about the Big Apple but had never been there.

Last night was one for the books. First, they got the shooting in the club. Then next thing you know, this bitch was throwing up all over the place. I was so fucking pissed off and embarrassed, to say the least. Little Missy Prissy couldn't hold her fucking liquor. If it was up to me, I would've left that ho on the sidewalk. Her daddy would have to send one of his people to find her. I couldn't, though, 'cause dude was there and so damn attentive to her, which made me feel jealous as hell.

I was the one who suggested that we go to his crib. 'Cause her ass was drunk and passed out, I felt like this was my chance to get at this nigga. After all, I didn't see what the fuck he saw in her.

I had a nice, round ass that clapped when I walked, and my CC cups stood firm. I had a honeycomb natural beauty, and I never had to wear makeup, unlike her. You would never catch her without her face beat to the gods, like she always said. Half the time, she looked like she was making a casket appearance. My pussy was tight, and I could fuck better than her. Don't ask how the hell I knew that. I just did.

So, last night, after her ass went to bed, I decided to stay up with dude. He was smoking some high-grade and drinking Henny. This was my kind of party. He was playing reggae, and we were chilling. I thought everything was good, so I reached over and rubbed his leg. Instead of this nigga reciprocating the feeling, he shoved my hand away. This angered me. How dare he turn me down like this. Feeling neglected, I got up and walked into the room that he gave us. Naomi was asleep, so I lay at the edge of the bed, texting my boo until I fell asleep.

When I got up, she was still asleep, so I quietly walked out of the room. Trini was sitting in his living room, watching sports on the television. As soon as I spotted him, I started to walk away, but he stopped me.

"Aye, B, come here real quick."

"What is it?" I quizzed while I folded my arms.

"I just want to apologize 'bout last night. I figured you was drunk, plus I wouldn't want to take advantage of you."

"It ain't no issue. I had too much to drink, so I overstepped my boundaries. Aye, can we just keep this between us? I wouldn't want to hurt my girl's feelings."

"Yeah, sure. Ain't shit happen anyways." He turned his focus back on the TV.

"Right." I shrugged, but deep down, I was feeling salty as hell.

I took a seat on the couch opposite him. This nigga thought he was slick, talking about ain't nothing happen anyway. I guess that he felt like shit was great, but he'd learn soon enough.

I pulled my phone out of my pocket and logged into IG, trying to catch the latest news. I knew after the BET awards last night, social media was jumping, and boy, was I right. They were roasting Yung Miami's ass 'cause she stood up there holding a sign for Diddy when that fool didn't even acknowledge her. Shit, I knew I'd been dumb a few times, but I always made sure I got paid.

After an hour passed, I decided to go check on Naomi to see if she was up. I sure didn't come to New York to be cooped up in no house, so I was sorry she had too much to drink, but she needed to wake her ass up. I wanted to see what these stores were hitting for. Shit, my sugar daddy sent me a few hundred to spend, so I was ready to grab some new clothes.

Chapter Four

Naomi

We sat at the table with breakfast in front of us, but I wasn't hungry, so I forced myself to take several bites of the pancake. I was still feeling crazy, and this headache was starting to become unbearable.

"Do you have any pain medicine?" I turned to Trini and asked.

"Shit, I doubt it, but I could run to the store and grab you some."

"No, I wouldn't want you to do all that. I'll just grab some on the way to the hotel. I need to go so that I can take a shower. I appreciate this shirt, but it doesn't fit too tightly." I smiled at him.

"My bad. You had vomit all over your outfit. By the way, is washed and dried. I laid it on the bed for you."

"Oh, really? You're such a sweetheart. Why are you being so nice to me?"

"Shawty, I told you, I'm digging you. These little things don't mean nothing if I'm trying to make you my woman." He continued eating.

"She can't be yo' woman. She already got a nigga in Atlanta," Yashira blurted out.

The food that I had just swallowed almost stuck in my throat. I reached for the glass of pineapple juice and quickly took a few sips. It washed down the food. After getting myself together, I looked at Yashira and shook my head. I was shocked to say the least.

"What? Did I say something wrong? I mean, I know you're in love with Jerome, so I was just telling him not to waste his time. I mean, I know you was too scared to tell him."

I had some words for her ass, but I decided to wait for later. I just flashed a fake smile, then took a few more sips of my juice.

"Shit, I ain't worried 'bout the nigga that she has back home. I know what I bring to the table, and if she gives me the chance, then she'll see that ain't no competition," he boasted.

I wasn't sure if it was the island accent or the level of cockiness, but this nigga sounded good as fuck. The sound of his voice hypnotized me, which sent chills up my spine.

I wanted to laugh out loud about what he just said, but I could see from the look on Yashira's face that she was shocked. That was *exactly* what her ass got. It was *my* business and *not* hers to tell.

After moments of silence around the table, it started to feel uncomfortable. My headache hadn't eased up any, and I needed to get a hot shower, plus lie down for a while.

"Well, thanks for breakfast. I'm going to get dressed so I can head to the hotel."

I got up and took my plate with me. I made my way to the kitchen and started washing it.

Trini walked up to me and whispered, "Love, you ain't got to do that. I got it."

"Well, it's done."

I turned around, which probably wasn't a good idea. My mouth watered as I stared at his naked chest. His arms were strong and well-defined.

"Listen, I can tell that you like me. Stop fighting the feelings, B."

"Boy, I have no idea what you talking 'bout," I lied and tried hard not to show different.

"Boy? Ha-ha. I'ma grown-ass man, and you're not a good liar. I could tell that you feeling a nigga, but you scared. Shit, it might be 'cause of that nigga back home."

He took a few steps closer to me and grabbed my face. We started kissing. I could feel his hard dick pressing down between my legs. That T-shirt that I was wearing made it accessible. He held me tight and passionately kissed me. It felt good, so I didn't fight it. Instead, I welcomed the refreshing feeling. The thought of me having a man back home never crossed my mind. I was living for this moment only.

"Uh, ummm, excuse me, y'all." Yashira cleared her throat, then spoke.

This bitch just *had* to walk in and interrupt a great moment. I was startled, so I quickly pulled away.

"I didn't mean to interrupt y'all little session. Was just putting my plate in the sink."

"You're good," I said before I pulled away from Trini.

I walked out of the kitchen, feeling a little embarrassed. Here I was, pretending like I didn't like dude, but was caught red-handed with my tongue down his throat.

I walked into the room and quickly put on my clothes. I was grateful that he was considerate enough to wash them for me. In my eyes, he was an okay dude.

The door pushed open, and Yashira walked in. "Bitch, what was that back there?"

"What you talking about?"

"Don't play stupid. All along, you pretend like you don't like dude, then all of a sudden, you making out with him in the kitchen."

"If I'm not mistaken, last night you was the one pushing me to give him my number, so why, all of a sudden, do I feel like you trying to sabotage it?"

"I'm not trying to sabotage shit. Last night, I was tipsy, so you can't hold that against me. I just don't want you to lead him on, knowing we leave in a few days. What if Jerome finds out? Then what?"

"How he going to find out? We are the only ones here. Girl, chill out. You acting like I'm a little-ass girl. I'm grown as fuck, and I'm in New York, and what happen in New York stays in New York, right?"

"Bitch, I think that was a saying for Vegas. You right, though. You're grown, and it's your pussy, so pop it if you want."

"Thank you, baby," I replied sarcastically.

"Hugs."

"Of course, you know you my best bitch."

We exchanged a long, tight hug. I was happy we made up for all this catfighting we were doing. We were here to celebrate my accomplishment, and that was what we were going to do.

After Trini dropped us off at the room, I wasted no time jumping into the shower. He did his best to clean me up last night, but nothing beat this Dove body wash and the hot water beating down on my body. I pulled out a little pair of shorts and a tank top. The weatherman said New York weather was going to be scorching hot the entire week. I was happy that I brought clothes that would be suitable for this kind of weather.

As I sat on the bed lotioning, my phone started ringing. I looked at it, and I knew that I had to answer.

"Hey, babes."

"Yo, where the fuck you been? I been calling you."

"Ummm, I been sleeping, and why is you coming at me with that tone?"

"Don't turn this shit on me. From the time you got to New York, I ain't been able to reach you. You all on social media posting but ignoring my calls. What the fuck really going on? Was you laid up with another nigga?" Jerome yelled in my ear.

"There you go with yo' accusations, but when *I* do it, I'm insecure. Listen, like I said, I was sleeping. If you don't believe me, ask Yashira."

"That lying-ass bitch? She ain't goin' do nothing but lie for you. I'm telling you, don't fucking play with me. I'm out here staying faithful to you, so I better not find out that you doing no snake-ass shit," he warned.

"You can go straight to hell, Jerome. I ain't doing shit, but if you continue accusing me, I might start throwing this pussy on another nigga that talk to me like he got some sense. As a matter of fact, I'm about to hang up. Don't call me back until you learn how to talk to me properly."

"Naomi, don't ha—"

I didn't wait for him to finish his sentence before I disconnected the phone. Then I blocked his number before I threw the phone on the bed. I planned to unblock him later, but for now, he needed to learn how the fuck to speak to me. We had been together a little over three years, and his ass had never talked to me like this. I didn't know what the fuck got into him, but he needed to check that shit before he found himself alone.

"Girl, who was that? You sounded pretty heated," Yashira quizzed as she walked out of the bathroom with a towel wrapped around her.

"Girl, who else?" I shook my head in disbelief.

"Jerome. What's his problem now?"

"Girl, talking 'bout he been calling me and ain't no answer."

"No, the fuck he ain't tripping like that. How many nights have you called him and no answer? The one time you did it, he having a nervous breakdown. It goes to show you that niggas can't handle the same hurt that they dish out."

"Girl, fuck him. I hung up and blocked him for now. I ain't never give him a reason to doubt me, so I don't understand what he going off for. I ain't going to allow him to spoil my fun."

"I don't blame you, and I won't allow that either. He just in his feelings that you took a trip without him. He be a'ight." She went on to get dressed. "Enough about that nigga. What's the plans for today?" she asked.

"Well, I was thinking that we could hit the stores, get some shopping done. I heard they got some of the hottest stores up here."

"Bitch, you know I ain't got no money like that unless we going to Chinatown to cop some of them knockoffs they got. One of my girlfriends told me they got some of the best. They so good that you can't tell the difference between them and the authentic."

"Girl, quit playing so much. I rather shop in a no-name store and grab some regular stuff than go buy some fake, China knockoff."

"Sorry, love, you know some of us ain't that fortunate or have Daddy Big Bucks to pay our way through life. I don't see the difference 'cause most of the shit is made in China anyway," she shrugged.

"Listen, Yashira, I know you don't mean no harm, but I'm tired of you reminding me that Daddy be helping me. Truth is, I bust my ass, just like y'all, and I don't ever sit around, waiting on Daddy's money. Am I lucky that I have a parent who looks out for me? Hell yeah, but I don't sit around and ask for no handout."

"Girl, relax, you ain't got to make no whole speech. Ain't nothing wrong with spending Daddy's money. Shit, I wish my dumb-ass mama did fuck with a nigga with money. My ass would've been paid too. Shit, but it's too late for all that."

It really irked my soul when anyone mentioned Daddy's money. It was like they wished I was in the same boat as them. After hearing it so much, it got irritating. I was trying not to ruin our trip, so I dismissed my thoughts.

"Forget 'bout all of that. Let's see what these stores have to offer, and no, we are *not* going to Chinatown. See, I got my own card." I dangled the Navy Federal Platinum Card that had twenty-five grand on it. I'd never used it before, so now was the perfect time.

"Oh shit. Lemme get my clothes together." She grinned from ear to ear.

I placed the card back into my wallet and put it back into my purse.

We took a cab to the Village. I've heard many stories about how dope their stores were. As soon as we exited the cab, I realized this was a whole different level of shopping. Stores were on both sides of the street, making it hard to pick which one to start with. It really didn't matter. I just walked into one, and we started shopping. They had nice things, and the prices weren't extra high. I was able to grab a lot of stuff, from clothing, purses, boots, and accessories. I also made sure Yashira grabbed her some stuff.

Once I paid for everything, I spent over ten grand. We had multiple bags, and our poor little hands were tired. After we shopped, we stopped at one of the spots where food was served and grabbed us some hot dogs with cole-slaw. You couldn't tell we were not from New York 'cause we fit right in.

I was full, and these bags were making it hard to move around anymore. "Let's grab a cab. My arm's killing me." "Shit, I was thinking the same thing. I never knew I would ever say that shopping made me tired, but I'm tired as fuck," Yashira exclaimed.

On the ride to the hotel, Trini was on my mind. There was something about him that I couldn't shake. He was so different from Jerome. Maybe it was because he was a street dude, and Jerome wasn't. I was shocked at myself 'cause I was never drawn to dating a street dude before now. Shit, I knew it was only lust, plus, in a few days, I'd be going home to the love of my life. I couldn't wait for us to get married and start our life. I knew I was nothing but 24, but we'd been through so much in these three years, everything from him taking my virginity to sticking by me through nursing school. Jerome had been there for me. That was why it bothered me so much that he was carrying on like this. I guessed he was just nervous because this was our first time really apart from each other.

The cab came to a standstill, and Yashira touched my arm. "Girl, come on. What you doing, daydreaming?" she asked as she exited the cab. I grabbed my bags and followed behind her.

"Bitch, you are the bestest." Yashira jumped on me and started hugging me.

"Damn, you a'ight? You almost knocked me over." This was weird. I'd never seen her this happy before.

"In my whole life, nobody never took me shopping and let me get what the fuck I want. You're the only one." She began tearing up.

I sat on the bed and removed my shoes. "Look, girl, I know your life been rough, and I'm sorry. We are friends, and you know I always try to help you as much as I can."

"Naomi, I love you like a sister, and I swear I would never do anything to fuck us up. You and your family have shown me so much love over the years. I don't know what I would do without y'all," she cried.

I got up, walked to her, and sat, wrapping my arms around her. "Look, we are family, and we are always going to be here for you. Now, we are here to enjoy ourselves, so dry these damn tears."

"I know, I know . . . I just got so emotional when I see all the things you done bought me. Just know I'm forever grateful, and I love you, man."

"I love you too, baby. We are locked in for life. . . ."

As soon as those words left my mouth, I remembered what Tameka had said about not trusting her. Not a day passed by that I didn't think about that. I even thought about asking her again while we were here, but after seeing her this emotional, maybe it was best to leave it alone.

Shopping was the therapy that I needed. I skimmed through all the things that I purchased earlier and was very pleased. I loved Lennox Mall and all, but I felt like I got some better-quality clothing for a decent price. I even managed to grab two Polo shirts for Jerome and two for Daddy. There was no way I could visit New York and not bring something back for the ones I loved.

The sun was still beaming outside even though it was well after 5:00 p.m. It made it hard even to get back out there. I stepped out on the balcony, just trying to take in some more of the beautiful scenery.

"That's where you at. What we eating for dinner tonight?" Yash asked as she joined me on the balcony.

"Girl, I'm still full from eating that hot dog I had earlier."

"Naomi, bitch, that was *hours* ago, andddd some of us bitches have to eat more than one meal per day to survive.

We can't live on air alone like somebody I know." She pointed at me, then started laughing.

"Bitch, I catch the shade and sent it right back. I was thinking maybe we can grab some Chinese food and kind of chill tonight . . ." Before I could finish my sentence, her phone started ringing.

She looked at it, and I watched as she pressed ignore.

"Well, that sounds good to me. We can grab a bottle of wine and watch a movie like old times. I miss those days."

"Aweee, yes, me too. But you know I got that new crib and all, so you will be over all the time."

"Ummm, not if Jerome has anything to do with it. I swear that boy do not like me at all."

"Why do you say that?"

"I notice the dirty way he looks at me whenever I'm around. I thought probably you was telling him what we talked about."

"No, I haven't noticed, but it's my house, and Jerome can't tell me who to have over. Don't forget he has his own place."

Her phone never stopped ringing and was starting to get annoying. "Girl, whoever that is must really want to talk to you, huh?"

"Girl, it ain't nobody important." She rolled her eyes before she walked back into the room.

Something strange was going on. Why didn't she answer the phone? My suspicions were getting the best of me, and I didn't like that. I tried to shake those crazy thoughts I was having. I decided to head back in, and she was locked in the bathroom. I assumed she was on the phone. I decided to lie down and browse social media.

A few minutes later, she walked out, smiling from ear to ear, before she noticed I was in the room.

"That must be some sweet shit you just heard?"

"Huh? Oh, that ain't nothing."

I could tell she was either lying or unwilling to share what was going on. So, I decided to quit prying. Either she was fucking a new nigga that she didn't want me to know about, or some other dumb shit. Either way, I decided to keep an eye on her.

Chapter Five

Yashira

This ho really went out and spent all this money on clothes and shoes? I was shocked at first, but then it hit me. Why was I worrying about her and the coins she was spending? I got more than five outfits, and let me tell it, they were not cheap, either. Once she gave me the go-ahead, I went wild, picking up the most expensive clothes. I also got me a Tory Burch leather purse for $1,200 and matching sandals for a good $550. A bitch had never had no shit like this before, so I was happy as hell.

I was really starting to enjoy my trip as she was making sure I was good. The only thing was, I was missing my boo thang back in Atlanta. I had tried my best to keep him updated on what was going on in New York in text messages since I couldn't really be on the phone like I wanted to.

Shopping was very exhausting. The sun was very hot, and I was feeling tired. I decided to strip down to my drawers and bra, so my body could cool down before I hopped into the shower. My phone alerted me that I had a video call coming in.

This boy play too damn much, I thought.

Busy, I'll call you later on, I texted him.

Busy doing what? he texted back.

I loved this man, but sometimes, he could be very persistent. I decided to go on the balcony and get some fresh air, hoping that he would ease up and wait for me to call him later.

Naomi and I started talking, and the phone started ringing once again. I didn't have to look to see who was calling 'cause it was my very special ringtone. I silently wished he would quit already.

I heard a text message come in between calls, so I diverted my attention to the message.

Call me now, or I will send this to your friend's phone.

Seconds later, a pic of me, butt-ass naked, came through.

My eyes popped open, but I caught myself. I walked into the room and headed straight to the bathroom. I knew he wasn't serious and that he was just trying to get my attention, so I called his phone.

"Hey, my love," his voice echoed in my ear.

"What are you doing? I told you now wasn't a good time."

"I don't give a fuck 'bout alladat. I want to hear my baby's voice now, not later."

I smiled hard as fuck when I heard him referring to me as his baby. It took us awhile to get to this level, and I loved every bit of it.

I couldn't talk for long, so I spent a few minutes on the phone with him, just to calm him down some. When he was satisfied, I said goodbye and exited the bathroom. That man was doing something to my soul. I couldn't wait until we were officially a couple.

Chapter Six

Naomi

It seemed like when you were enjoying yourself, the time seemed to move along much quicker 'cause we had been here three days already, and it was almost time to head on back home.

We had breakfast in the hotel for the first time, and then we went for a walk. There was so much to see that I was afraid that we wouldn't have enough time to see everything. I love it here. My only issue was the traffic. It was horrible from what I saw. I guess if you lived out in the suburbs, it would be much easier.

"Look, let's get some ice," Yash patted me on my shoulder and said.

It was hot, and that was a great idea, so we stopped and grabbed two before we continued our sightseeing and stroll of New York.

"So, how is things going with you and Jerome?"

"It's not going," I laughed.

"Then you all haven't talked since that fight?"

"Yash, to be honest, I don't know what's going on with him. I guess I'll find out when I go home."

"Even though I don't really like him, I think he loves you. He probably just missing you."

"I don't have no doubt that he loves me, but is that how you show love?"

"Bitch, I'm the wrong one to ask about love. I never experienced that kind of sweet, mushy love before."

"Really? You could've fooled me. I saw how you was smiling yesterday after you took that phone call in the bathroom. I figured it's that young, exciting love. The kind that has you feeling all fuzzy inside."

"Girl, what you talking about? That was my cousin, Trina, I was talking to. I wish it *was* a nigga."

Again, I could tell she was lying, but I had no proof. "Well, your Mr. Right is out there somewhere," I said, then sucked some more of my icee.

"Yeah, he probably with Mrs. Wrong and not sure how to end it." She shrugged.

We continued making our way through the crowded streets of Manhattan, heading back to our hotel.

I walked over to the fridge and grabbed me a bottle of water. Then I opened it and started drinking. This heat had me feeling dehydrated even though I constantly drank fluids.

"So, Madam Lady, what are we having for dinner to-night?" Yash quizzed as she flopped down on her bed.

"Umm, Trini was saying that he wants to take me out on a date," I replied.

"Really, so you just goin' to leave me by myself?"

"Nooo, he said he was going to ask his homeboy, Josh, if he wants to join us, so we can all go."

"So, when were you going to tell me this?"

"Bitch, you were in the shower earlier when he texted me."

"Oh, okay. Well, I guess that's fine. I hope Josh ain't no broke-ass nigga or ugly 'cause I don't do ugly niggas."

"Well, we just have to wait and see what Josh looks like."

"Bitch, if this nigga ugly, I'm cutting the date short. There's no way I'm going to sit there and pretend."

"Oh my God, bitch, you wouldn't do that." I burst out laughing.

Even though I was laughing, I knew that bitch was dead-ass serious. I prayed Josh wasn't no ugly nigga 'cause this bitch was going to embarrass all of us.

After I finished dressing, I let my hair down and applied my makeup. It was hot outside, so I didn't put on much foundation. I would hate to start melting in front of this nigga. The thought alone made me cringe a little. I quickly dismissed the idea and prayed for a drama-free day.

"How do I look, bitch?" She spun around in front of me, flaunting her outfit that clung to her body as if it were designed just for her.

"You look goodddd, bitch. Josh goin' fall in love with that badass shape."

"Thank you. Yeah, if he cute and have some money, I might give him a little taste of this sweet pussy."

"I hear that. Just make sure you use a condom. You don't want to end up pregnant."

"Bitch, I'm on the pill; plus I wasn't talking about fucking him. I just want him to bury his head deep inside this love nest."

"Bitch, he goin' want to do more than that."

Before I could finish speaking, my phone started ringing. It was Trini letting me know that he was downstairs. I jumped off the bed and grabbed my Chanel purse. I was feeling fuzzy on the inside and was eager to see him again. It had been a minute since I felt like this behind a dude. So, it was scary, but I was enjoying every bit of it. I took one last glance in the mirror to make sure not even a hair was out of place. This thirty-two-inch raw Indian weave that I was wearing was giving me that Ethiopian queen look and screaming, "She's a *bad* bitch."

"Come on, chick. Let's see what these niggas have planned for us." I cut off the lights, then headed out the door.

"Bitch, don't you forget what I told yo' ass. If this nigga is ugly, I'm leaving yo' ass."

"Ha-ha. Chill out, friend. I bet his ass fine as fuck. He might fuck around and be cuter than Trini."

"Well, friend, let's hope so 'cause if not . . ."

The elevator stopped, and we stepped out. Immediately, I noticed Trini standing in the lobby. A dude was standing beside him, whom I assumed to be Josh. As I walked closer to them, I examined him from head to toe. I let out a sigh of relief. He was fine as fuck. He was of Indian descent and was dressed nicely.

"Hey, guys," I greeted them.

"What's good, love?" Trini reached in and gave me a hug, slightly rubbing on my ass.

"So, is this your friend?"

"Oh, my bad. Ladies, this is my homie/brother, Josh. Josh, these are the ladies that I was telling you 'bout."

"Hello." I kept it brief and simple.

"Hey, I'm Yashira. Nice to meet you. Whew, I'm glad you ain't no dusty-ass nigga 'cause I had my mind made up to run back upstairs," she blurted out.

This bitch was sounding so ghetto and rude right now. I wished the ground could've opened up and sucked me in. That was how embarrassed I was feeling.

"Damn, love, I'm glad I'm what you expect. Nice to meet you."

"Let's go, y'all. I have reservations made, plus I'm hungry as fuck," Trini said before he walked off. I ran up behind him, holding his hand.

I could hear in his voice that he was irritated, but tried his best to play it off. I wanted to pull this bitch to the side and check her, but it wouldn't make the situation better. Plus, I didn't want to show my ignorant ass in front of Trini. We ended up all riding in Trini's truck. The air was tense at first, but then they started talking in the backseat, so I felt relieved. Usually, Yashira wasn't this rude, so I wasn't sure why she was portraying herself to be someone she was not.

Trini cut on the music while weaving through New York traffic. I would say this was the worst, but being from Atlanta, the traffic was similar. It took us forever to get to the restaurant, but once we arrived, I would say the stress was worth it. I'd heard New York bragging about City Island and how great their food was, so I was ready to find out for myself.

The food was good, and the mood was right. I could tell those two were vibing and seemed to be all into each other. So, I decided to focus on this fine-ass nigga in front of me. After dinner, they walked off to one end of the pier, so me and Trini finally got some privacy together.

"Thanks for dinner, hon."

"No problem. I wanted you to get a taste of my city. I know what happen at the club the other night kind of put us in a bad light. But there's so much more out here for people who want to enjoy themselves and stay out of drama."

"Yeah, that was frightening. I'm happy that you came back and grabbed us. If you didn't, only God knows what could've happened to us. That's scary as hell. I think I'ma chill off y'all clubs."

"It ain't always like that, B. It's just these young cats that got beefs. They know they goin' see one another in the clubs if nowhere else. Enough 'bout them though. I'm tryin'a see what's good wit'cha."

"What's good with me? That's a broad question," I said, smiling.

"You know what I peep about you?" He took my hand into his.

"What is that?" I asked mischievously.

"You like to play games, and it's cute and all. But a nigga serious and shit, plus, it ain't like you live out here. What you got left, a few more days?"

"I'm a grown-ass woman, sir, and I don't play games. However, you just keep saying you like me. I mean, any nigga can like a woman. That doesn't mean shit."

"I hear that. A nigga who risk his life to come back in and get you out of a club . . . Not just that. I cleaned you up that same night and made sure you was safe. I would say I made my intentions very clear. Or wait, what you want me to do? Grab a big-ass rock and drop on my knee?"

"I guess you have a point there. I just don't know. As Yash told you earlier, I got a nigga back home."

"Look, woman, I don't give a fuck 'bout that nigga out in Atlanta. We are two grown people, and that nigga ain't got to know shit that went down between us. I'm really digging you, and I would love to get to know you more."

"You mean to fuck me?" I got straight to the point while I stared him down.

"Let's be clear. It's a must that I'm going to run up in that pussy, but I want more than that. I want to get to know you beyond some fuck shit."

His words were clear as he stared into my eyes when he spoke. My pussy was on alert and started shifting around in my Victoria's Secret hiphuggers.

"I hear you, love . . ." My words trailed off as he started kissing me. His hand trailed off, massaging my breast. Electricity traveled through my body as our bodies moved in unison. He used his other hand and stuck it inside my panties. By now, juice was flowing out of my body. He slowly inserted his finger. I took a long exhale while I savored the feeling. I started grinding on his fingers while he twirled them around, sending me to the highest level of ecstasy.

"Y'all ready?" Yash said.

It was an embarrassing moment. He got caught with his hand in the cookie jar. We couldn't do anything but burst out laughing.

"Let's finish this at the crib," he whispered in my ear.

"Uh-huh." I was still trying to recover from the excitement he had given me a few minutes ago.

After we got to his crib, we sat around with them, drinking while they smoked. The liquor wasn't helping the situation. It was making me hornier, and honestly, I was ready to get my back beat out. While they talked, I took my phone out and texted him.

"Meet me in the room."

I watched as his phone alerted him. His face lit up as he read the text. I knew I had his attention, so I smiled and got up. I walked out of the room without saying a word, hoping he would follow shortly.

I went to the bathroom and washed my face. Then I went to the room that I was in earlier. I was tipsy, and my clothes were only making me hot. I started stripping off, down to my birthday suit. When the door pushed open, I used my hand to cover my breasts since I wasn't sure who was behind it.

"Oh, damn . . . You dead-ass serious, huh?" he quizzed.

I didn't need to answer 'cause he also started stripping. That nigga was fine, but butt-ass naked, that nigga was fine fine, and that dick was thick and a good size. My mouth started watering as I started playing with my clit in front of him. I usually wasn't this bold, but I saw something that I wanted, and the alcohol pushed my confidence all the way up. I sat on the bed while I parted my legs, so he could get a good view of what lay beneath. He smiled and licked his lips while he started slowly massaging my clit. I pulled him down to me. All that playing with my pussy was cool, but I wanted more. I wanted to taste that long thing between his legs. It was even prettier when it was hard. Whew. I could barely contain myself.

I reached my hand down and gripped the most beautiful, dark chocolate dick that I had ever laid eyes on. I took a few seconds, just admiring it before I used my hand, massaging it all over. The feeling was overwhelming. I could feel it all the way in my guts. I could tell he was enjoying himself 'cause he let out a few soft groans. In my mind, this pretty motherfucker belonged to me, and I was going to make sure it was pleased in the best way.

"Go ahead, taste it, love. It won't hurt you," his voice coaxed me.

That was all the motivation that I needed. I parted my moist lips and guided it over the tip of the dick. His dick stiffened up as soon as my wet lips made that connection. I started off slowly by licking the tip, using my tongue to force its way into the tiny opening. I felt his body tense up further. My moist lips parted and guided his head into my mouth. It made his dick stiffen even more. Then I went in for the kill, taking the entire dick all the way into my mouth until it touched the back of my throat. His groans started getting louder and louder, which excited me even more. He tightened his grip on my weave and began to move my head up and down. That didn't deter me any. I moved my neck up, down, and all around. I made sure his dick was covered with enough spit, then I would make sure the sound of my slurping and sucking was less than subtle. Truth was, I never sucked a dick like this before, so I was excited and made sure he enjoyed this. My pussy was happy as hell 'cause it was leaking like a broken fire hydrant.

After about twenty minutes of making sweet love to his dick, his veins enlarged. I fixed my mouth so I could receive the pure juice that was about to shoot out. The warm, thick dick juice spilled into my mouth and down my throat. It was coming full force. I almost choked.

I didn't move a muscle, though. I swallowed every drop, and then I sucked on his dick, trying to draw out the last little drop that was lingering inside his dick. He stood up, snatched my ass up, and forcefully threw me down on the bed. I was lying on my back, my legs spread wide apart, and his head was buried deep in my pussy. I screamed out uncontrollably as he devoured me, and I mean that shit respectfully. He wasn't shy, and I could tell he was very experienced when it came down to the art of pussy eating. He was so far in my pussy that juice was all over his face. He pinned me down on the bed with no room for me to move around. This nigga sucked my pussy so good by exploring every inch of my petite body. I was trying not to scream any louder, but he was making it hard to do so. It was painful but sweet at the same time. I couldn't do anything but bite down on my bottom lip until I tasted blood. This was my first experience getting my pussy eaten so fucking good. I couldn't deny the feelings much longer. I just burst into tears.

"Oh my God. Help me, God. This is so, so . . . Stop, please," I begged as my legs shivered. I couldn't hold it in anymore. Finally, my body gave in. My pussy juice started flowing out of my opening. That didn't deter him. He sucked harder and faster until I was dry, and I literally mean dry.

As if he were just getting started, he lifted my legs in the air and sank his big, black, pretty dick all into my soul. The pressure was hitting me, and I thought about running, but there was nowhere to run to. He had me pinned down under his weight. My head was banging on the headboard while he placed my legs on his shoulders. He slowly thrust in and out of my pussy, which had gotten wet once again. He stared into my eyes as he made love to my pussy. It seemed as if he were looking inside my soul. He knew exactly what he was doing. He had me in a sexual trance, and I couldn't escape it at all. I knew then I was in big trouble . . . *very big* trouble.

"Aww, fuuck!" I screamed and turned my head, trying to escape his stare. My pussy lips wrapped around his dick as he continued to reach deeper and deeper. Then my body started shivering hard as if I were having seizures. He gripped my legs tighter and thrust all the way in. I felt my climax coming, the orgasm building in my thighs. My chest heaved. My mouth hung open, becoming dry.

"I-I-I com—" Before I could get the words out, I exploded all over his dick.

"I bet you glad you come, huh?" he quizzed with a smile plastered all over his face. I tried to respond. I wanted to tell him that this was the best dick I ever had, and he was making my pussy happy, but even though my mouth was open, the words just wouldn't come out. Instead, tears just continued flowing down my face. That shit felt like he was massaging my whole body and spanking the right places at the same time.

"Whose pussy is this, B?" he quizzed.

"It's yours, daddy," I lied.

I mean, it really wasn't his, but the way he took control, it was his for this moment.

I lay in Trini's arms, on his chest, after we both washed off. He had fallen asleep, but I was still up. This was my first time cheating on Jerome, and I was feeling horrible. I remembered all the times I'd accused him of cheating, and here I was, lying butt-ass naked in a nigga's bed. This sex I had was one of the best, and I loved it, but it was wrong on so many levels. I closed my eyes, trying to drown out the negative thoughts and just enjoy the moment at hand.

Chapter Seven

Yashira

I was feeling tipsy, not really drunk, but I pretended like I was drunk. After Naomi and Trini left the room, we started to make out on the living room couch. I was really shocked at how much I was feeling him 'cause I was in love with my man back home in Georgia.

Josh was easy on the eyes and was very appealing. I tried my best to ignore him, but I couldn't. Also, I listened to how they spoke about money; I could tell these niggas were paid. Fucking this nigga for free was my intention, so my mind started wandering, and then a bright idea popped up in my head. I mean, these niggas had it like that, so spending a few grand shouldn't be an issue for them. I almost chuckled at the thoughts that were running around.

"Let's go in the room," I suggested.

"Yeah, let's do that," he agreed.

We were all over each other as we walked into the room next to where Naomi and Trini were. I locked the door behind us as we continued making out. Even though sex wasn't in my plan, I wouldn't mind getting some head from this fine-ass nigga. I quickly undressed and lay on the bed with my legs parted, revealing my neatly trimmed pussy. He looked at it as an open invitation, so he quickly undressed. The lights were off in the room, so I couldn't really see what that dick was hitting for. But I wasn't worried. The way he talked, I bet he had that nine and a half between his legs.

He got on the bed beside me, and we started kissing. He started fondling my breast, and I reached for his dick so that I could massage it. When my hand felt his dick, I became confused, so I reached again. Surely my mind must be playing tricks on me, so I started kissing him harder and massaged his dick, so that it could get hard. Even though I couldn't see it, I could tell this nigga's dick was little as fuck. I thought about pushing his ass off me, but I held off 'cause he had my pussy wet. He slid his fingers between my legs, and I started moaning, quickly forgetting about what I just discovered. I grinded on his fingers as he worked my pussy. He started kissing all over my breasts, and I was feeling great as fuck. I tried pushing his head down lower. I mean, all that mouth he had, I wanted to feel what the tongue was hitting for. He resisted, though, which made me more confused.

"Yo, B, what you trying to do?" He stopped kissing my stomach and asked.

"What you mean? My pussy on fire, so I want you to eat it."

"What the fuck you just say?" he asked in a higher tone.

I was thrown off. This nigga was acting like I was speaking a foreign language. All I was asking for was some head.

"Look, chill out. All I was asking for was to get some head, nothing more."

"Look, bitch, I don't know what kind of nigga you used to, but I don't do that shit. Plus, I just met you. All I want is to stick this big dick in your pussy."

His audacity hit me in the face. The soft-spoken nigga that was cool as a cucumber was no longer here. Instead, it was this hard-ass, little-dick nigga talking shit to me.

I sat up in bed and gathered my thoughts quickly. "Look, nigga, I don't know what kind of bitches you are used to, but I'm from motherfucking Atlanta, and you better learn how the fuck to talk to me. Matter of fact, fuck you and this little-ass, soft dick. I had bigger and better."

I tried to get out of bed. I didn't care if Naomi was busy or not. I was ready to get the fuck out of here and go to the hotel. My plan wasn't working, so I was ready to go.

"Bitch, lay yo' ass down. You ain't goin' no-mother-fuckin'-where. Ha-ha. What you say, this dick little? Let's find out what this little dick hitting for," he said while he flashed a devilish grin.

"Boy, get the fuck away from me with yo' stupid ass." I shoved him hard.

He jumped to his feet and grabbed his pants. The room was dark, but I could see the gun that was pointed at my face.

"Yeah, like I said, bitch, you ain't going nowhere. Now, drop to yo' knees and suck on this li'l dick," he ordered with venom in his voice.

I couldn't believe what I was hearing. But I could tell this nigga was serious. I wanted to scream or dash out of the room, but I was afraid of what he might do to me before I could escape.

"Come on now, bitch," he yelled while he pressed the gun up against my head.

I did as I was told. By now, tears were falling out of my eyes. I took the limp, li'l dick in my hand and reluctantly brought it to my lips. I started licking it until it got hard. The goal was to speed up the process. So, I started massaging his balls while I bobbed my head up and down in a circular motion. I wanted this fucker to hurry up and bust. But the more I sucked, the harder his dick was getting. He grabbed my head and pulled it closer to his dick. It was making it difficult for me to suck his dick properly 'cause he pushed it all the way to the back of my throat. I felt like I would throw up, but that would probably just anger him more. I did the best that I could while I silently cried.

"Aargh, shit. Yes, bitch. Suck this li'l dick. Ha-ha," he teased and laughed out.

I felt so humiliated and low, but I continued doing what I was ordered.

"Oh, fuck, bitch. That shit feels good. Aargh, yes. Oh shit, I'm 'bout to bust." He grabbed my head tighter and forced his dick in farther. I felt his veins getting larger, and his dick stiffened, so I tried to shift my head. But this bitch-ass nigga snatched my head and held it down as cum shot out of his dick and into my mouth.

I tried to spit it out, but some spilled into my throat, forcing me to vomit all over the carpet.

"Bitch, why you did that fa?" he yelled.

As soon as he released my head, I bolted for the door. He ran up behind me, but I was determined to get away. I started screaming at the top of my lungs. "Help, help. Trini, help me," I screamed.

They both ran out of the room and stopped when they saw me. The nigga had caught up to me with his gun in his hand.

"Yo, what the fuck going on out here? You good, B?"

"No, this nigga raped me," I said while I collapsed into Naomi's arms.

"He did *what?*" Trini yelled out.

"This bitch lying, my nigga. She just mad 'cause she tried to throw her old stanking-ass pussy at me, and I turned her down. All I wanted was to get my dick sucked, and the bitch did it," he shrugged.

Trini looked at me, I guess waiting for my confirmation of what the nigga was saying.

"This bitch-ass nigga lying. He held the gun to my head and forced me to suck his dick. Where my damn phone, so I can call the police? Where is my phone?" I released myself from Naomi's embrace and headed toward the living room, searching for my phone.

"Yo, hold up, B. Leave the police out of this. If what you saying is true, I'll handle this myself."

"Yo, my nigga, we bros. You goin' believe this old ly-ing-ass, country bitch that you just met?"

"Man, shut the fuck up right now. I can't have the police coming to my crib."

"All right, my nigga, but don't believe a word this bitch says. The bitch calling a bluff right now. I bet she ain't calling no police."

"Nigga, shut the fuck up. Come here, B. Come talk with me real quick." Trini took my hand and walked me out to the balcony.

He asked me to be honest with him about what really went down, so painfully, I described the entire situation that went down, but I lied. I told him the nigga stuck his dick into me, making the story more believable. After all, rape was rape, no matter if it was oral or not.

"When I told the nigga that I'm going to tell you what happen, he was like, 'Fuck that nigga. He a bitch anyway and not going to do shit about it.' The way he was talking, it was as if he got some kind of secret beef going on with you. Trini, I know that's supposed to be yo' homeboy and e'erything, but you need to be careful. He might be plotting on you." I started crying harder, so he could un-derstand how deep and serious this situation was.

"Listen, B, I know you upset, and I swear I'm sorry about this, but you can't get the police involved. Without telling too much about my business, I'm a real heavy hitta in these streets, and the police ain't no fond of that shit. 'Cause of that, I can't afford to bring no heat to my crib. What can I do fa you, so this can go away? And don't worry 'bout that nigga. I'm going to make sure I take care of him myself."

The tone of his voice was serious, and the look that was plastered all over his face screamed he was *serious* about everything he was saying. I thought long and hard on what he said about what he could do for me.

"What do you mean, what can you do for me? You mean like for me to stay hushed about what your friend did?" I wanted to understand what he was talking about so that there would be no misunderstanding.

"Look, B, I'm a busy man, and I got some shit to handle. So, what's the price so all this can go away, and you can go back home?"

"Well, I mean, the nigga raped me, and there's no price on that violation. So, I don't know, Trini. . . ."

"E'erybody got a price. Think about it and let me know."

Without another word, he opened the screen door and walked back into the living room. I followed closely behind him. I knew then that I had that nigga right where I needed to have him. I already had a figure in my head, but I needed to let him sweat some. That nigga was paid, and I planned on being a paid bitch courtesy of this nigga.

Chapter Eight

Naomi

I sat on the couch with my hands massaging my temples. I couldn't believe what was going on right now. How could a beautiful evening turn to shit in the matter of a few hours? I was angry as fuck that this nigga violated my friend. I sat there thinking all kinds of crazy shit that I wanted to do to him my damn self. I tried to listen to what Trini was saying to her, but the door was closed, and I couldn't hear a damn thing. I started biting down on my well manicured nails, trying hard to calm my nerves.

The door opened, and I jumped up. Trini seemed irritated as he walked through the door. I tried to ask him what was going on, but he shrugged me off and made his way through the house.

"You all right? I'm so sorry this happened to you. It's all my fault. If I hadn't wanted to chill with Trini, this wouldn't have happened to you. I swear I can call Daddy. You know he'll be on the first flight up here without a doubt."

"I thought this nigga was cool. I mean, how would I know he was a fucking rapist? I feel so humiliated right now. I just want to go," Yash said.

"I understand, baby, but you know with rape, you need to get to the hospital, so they can check you out and get some swabs of his semen. This nigga violated you, and he needs to pay. What did Trini say to you?"

"You know this his boy, and they goin' stick together. I want to call the police, but he talking 'bout he don't want the heat at his crib."

"So, he want you to keep quiet about a rape? This nigga done lost his gotdamn mind if he thinks this just going to go away. Where the fuck he at?"

I walked away from her in hot pursuit of Trini. Fuck what this nigga was talking about. If she was scared to call the police, my black ass was going to call them for her. I was the one who invited her to New York, and I was the one who had her coming over here.

"Trini, Trini, where you at?" I yelled while walking through the crib.

I didn't see him, but I heard loud talking coming from a door behind me. I walked over and opened it. It was the stairs that led downstairs. The voices sounded louder, like they were arguing. I stepped on the first stair, then tiptoed down farther. I got almost to the bottom of the stairs when I heard sounds that sounded like gunshots and spots of light. My mind was telling me to run upstairs. Instead, my dumb ass ran toward where the sound was coming from. There Trini was, standing over Josh's bloody body. I froze in place, trying to make some sense of what I was seeing. It took a second for Trini to notice that I was standing here. We locked eyes before he rushed over to me.

"Don't touch me. Did you just kill him?" My voice trembled as I burst into tears.

"Yo, babes, what you doing down here? You not supposed to see this. I'm sorry, babes, but this nigga straight violates your girl and then talk shit on top of it. I don't get down like that. I got a moms and sisters. The last thing I need is for a nigga to violate them like this."

"You didn't have to kill him. That's what they have police for. You can't just take someone's life and then try to explain your reasoning behind this. Now, what's goin' happen? You prepared to go to jail?"

"Nah, I ain't going to jail. You the only one who saw him down here, and I hope you won't say shit. You know the law. They might try to say you an accomplice to this."

"Don't put me in this shit. I wish I had never met you. From day one, you fucking trouble. Oh my God, what have I gotten myself into?" I shoved him away from me.

"Do you really mean that? So, you regret what we shared?"

"What we shared? We fucked. That's what it was. Now, I find out you a cold-blooded killer. You could've killed me. I need to get the hell out of New York. I need to go home."

I turned to leave. I tried not to look at the dead body on the ground. A few moments ago, I hated that violator nigga and wanted to kill him my damn self, but now that he was dead, I started feeling pity. He didn't deserve to die like this.

"Stop, B, listen. I get it. You feeling scared and angry at me right now. But this nigga deserves what he got. Me and you, that's a different situation. Everything we shared is real, and even though we just met, what I feel for you is genuine."

"You're a murderer. How could we ever be together? I've never ever gotten even a speeding ticket. Let me go." I tried to wrestle out of his tight grip.

"Forget what you just saw. Listen to what your heart is saying to you. Fuck that nigga that you have back home. This is us, B. Don't fight it. You could end up regretting this. Give me a chance to show you I'm much more than a street nigga. I can be yo' nigga, the one that make you happy. The one that make your pussy beat like a drum."

I heard his words, but my mind couldn't stop thinking about that dead man on the ground a few feet away. Tears continued pouring down my face. I just needed to go. My mind was clouded, and I couldn't think straight.

"I just need to leave. I won't say anything to anyone, but I can't be with you. I'm sorry."

I'm not sure what I was apologizing for, but I needed to say whatever so that I could get me and my friend out of here in one piece. God knew what he might do to us if he thought that we might talk.

"Listen, you can stay with me until you leave to go back home. I promise, you will be safe with me."

"Thank you, but I need to get my girl back to the hotel. I just don't want to be here."

"Okay, I understand. Can I trust you not to mention this to anyone, not even your girl upstairs?" He stared me in the eyes with his dark, charcoal eyes. I looked down at the gun that he was still holding in his hand.

I just stood there, shaking and feeling scared. What was this he was asking me to do? I was not a criminal. *I can't do this,* I thought.

"Promise me, B . . . You got to promise me. If not, you can go down for this also."

This was him playing dirty 'cause he knew damn well I wasn't part of this. My brain was burned out, and my thoughts were all over the place. I couldn't go to jail. Oh my God, my daddy would be so embarrassed. I couldn't bring this kind of shame to them.

"If I promise you, can I go?" I continued crying.

"You got to mean it, B. Put it out of yo' mind, and no matter what, don't mention it to no one, and I mean *no one.*"

"I understand. I won't ever mention it." I tried fighting back the tears.

He hugged me tightly while he kissed my forehead. My body shivered as I prayed silently. Moments later, he finally let me go, and I dashed up the stairs. I ran to the bathroom, put my head in the toilet and started vomiting. I felt so sick inside. My palms were sweaty, and I was shaking. I knew I had to get myself together before I exited the bathroom. I washed out my mouth, then my face. I glanced in the mirror. My eyes were red, and I looked like I had aged a good twenty years since this morning. I wiped my face and walked out of the bathroom.

I went to the living room where Yash was sitting on the couch. She jumped up when she saw me. "I was looking for you. Where did you go?" I was about to blurt out some shit, but Trini walked in, so I stopped.

"I was downstairs talking to Trini. How are you feeling?"

"I'm still shaken up. Can we go?"

"Yeah, let me grab my things."

"I'll take y'all back to the room."

"We can grab an Uber," I blurted out while I headed to the bedroom to grab my purse and clothes.

"I insist, B," he said in a serious tone.

I wasn't going to fight with this nigga knowing what he could do. I headed to the room to grab my things. My mind was all over the place. I felt like I wasn't going to make it. I mustered up all my little strength so I could dress before I returned to the living room.

I got into the car and kept my head straight on the road. I tried my best not to glance Trini's way. I really didn't have anything to say to him. I was just happy we were out of that house.

Chapter Nine

Yashira

The entire ride back to the hotel was very quiet. I sat in the backseat, thinking and plotting. I knew we were supposed to leave New York soon, but I had no plan to go without my money. I was still playing with different numbers in my head. Shit, ten racks wasn't shit. I was leaning more toward twenty racks. Shit, after all, there was no price tag on freedom, and I heard they gave them numbers when it came down to rape.

My face lit up when I thought of all the things that I could do with twenty racks. Shit, CG Cosmetics had a special going on for a BBL, tummy tuck, and breast implants for fifteen grand. I could pay for that and still have five racks left over. I was feeling so excited that I didn't realize we reached the hotel until the car stopped.

Trini got out of the whip, and then Naomi got out. I could see him trying to hug her, but she brushed him off. That bitch was such a fucking lame. I had no idea why these niggas kept trying to fuck with her when she was nothing but a lame-ass bitch.

I opened the door and got out with my game face on. "Trini, give me your number so that I can text you the amount," I said loudly so she could hear me.

She looked at me. I could tell she was confused, but I didn't pay her no mind. The nigga read off his number, and I stored it on my phone.

After that, I walked into the lobby, and she followed behind. The elevator opened, and I stepped in. I was happy there were two other people in it 'cause it delayed any kind of questions that were bound to come.

We stepped off the elevator. She opened the door, and we walked in. I went to my bed and lay down, yawning like I was too tired, but this bitch didn't get the hint.

"Aye, what was that back there?"

"What you talkin' 'bout?" I pretended like I didn't know what the fuck she meant.

"You asking Trini for his number. What business you all talking about?"

"Oh, he didn't tell you?" I was shocked.

"Tell me what?" She looked at me with her eyes popped open.

I wanted to burst out laughing at the way this bitch was looking at me, but I held it in and gathered my words carefully.

"Well, he offered to pay me so that I won't report his boy to the police."

"And you going for that? That nigga violated you, and he deserve to be locked up."

"Well, I agree with you, but your man is scared and obviously don't want the police involved. I mean, I don't care about none of them niggas. You are the one who has a relationship with Trini. Oh, by the way, what you goin' tell Jerome when you get back to the A?"

"What you mean? It seems like you're more concerned about this nigga's feelings more than I am, and I'm the one fucking him."

"Bitch, I'm not worried about neither one of you's feelings. I'm just saying, since you come up here, you are behaving like you don't have a man back home. I mean, it's your life, so *you* figure it out."

"Girl, you sound real bitter right now. You know what? I'm not going there with you. You been through enough as it is, and if that's why you salty, again, I'm sorry that this happen to you."

"Girl, I'm good. That nigga gon' get his one day when Karma hits him. In the meantime, I'm about to text Trini so that he could come through with that paper. After all, it will help me deal with the hurt that I'm feeling."

"If I were you, I wouldn't take that money. That just show that a nigga can do what the fuck he wants, then just throw money your way, and it's all good."

"I'm not you, boo boo, so that's why it's not *your* choice. *I* was the one who was raped, *not* you, so it's *my* decision to make."

I was getting irritated that this bitch felt like this was her decision to make. I tried not to show my bitterness toward her, but I could no longer hold it in. I wanted the life that she had, and I was tired of playing the supportive friend while little Miss Rich Girl had everything she wanted and niggas falling all over her.

This money was going to help me get the perfect body that I wanted, and that would change the game for me.

Chapter Ten

Naomi

The next day was very quiet. Yash and I didn't say much of anything to each other. I was having conflicted feelings, to say the least. So much had happened since we came up here, and it wasn't good. I tried not to judge her, but we were all drinking last night. Could she have mistaken that he raped her? Oh my God, I felt so horrible thinking these things. But honestly, the person I grew up with had changed, and her behavior was very questionable.

This ho's attitude was getting worse by the second. I was trying my best to be understanding and supportive of her and the trauma that she experienced. However, I was shocked to find out that she was considering taking that money from Trini. How could she be so gullible? I was confused by her reasoning. This bitch wasn't thinking straight, but I saw that she was angry, and nothing I said was really getting through to her.

I needed to get some air. Being in the same room as her was making me claustrophobic. Too much was happening too fast. I needed a second to myself to process all of this. My phone started ringing. It was Trini, so I pressed ignore. I thought I made it clear last night that I wanted to be left alone. Plus, whatever business he and Yashira had, I wanted no parts of it.

I put my AirPods in and headed out the door. It was still early out, but I knew it was hot outside, so I didn't expect fresh air. However, at this point, any kind of air would do. I just needed to take a stroll and clear my mind.

I knew I'd been ignoring Jerome, but hearing his voice would definitely help right now. I waited until I got off the elevator. Then I called him. He didn't answer, so I called back again.

"Yeah," he answered in a groggy voice.

"Hey, babes. I miss you. I was hoping we could talk."

"Man, go ahead with all that. You been gone for days, and this is the first time you pick up the phone to holla at a nigga."

"Did you forget *you* the one who started a fight with me? I was giving you time to get yo' attitude under control."

"Really, shawty, you really think I'm green or something? Go ahead. Do what you been doing with the nigga you doing it wit'. I'm straight."

My eyes popped open when he mentioned another nigga. My heart started beating faster, but I figured he was popping his shit, trying to see if he could catch me in a lie.

"Boy, what the fuck you talking 'bout? I never cheated on you before, so why all of a sudden, you screaming this shit? Nine times out of ten, *you* the one cheating, and if that's what it is, just go ahead and say it without all this extra shit." I tried to sound convincing.

"Shawty, for real, what you want? I'm in the middle of handling some business."

"Really? So, I call you to talk, and this how you goin' act with me? I swear, you don't give a fuck how you treat me."

"Later, shawty—"

I was shocked at his behavior. I looked at the phone. This nigga clicked in my ear, just like that. My feelings were hurt, and I wanted to cry. Why was he behaving like this? I knew he could be an asshole at times, but he had never behaved like this before. I needed answers about why he was carrying on like this. I called him back, but he kept pressing ignore until he cut off the phone.

This only angered me more, but there was nothing I could do. I was ready for tomorrow to roll around. He had some fucking explaining to do. I knew damn well I didn't do shit to him, so either he just wanted to act like an ass, or there was another ho that had him feeling himself.

I cut on the music again and started strolling through the busy streets. New York was definitely a vibe. It was fast paced, and the atmosphere was dope as hell. They had all the big stores and the latest fashion. I remembered when I was younger. I used to say that I was going to move to New York when I got older. I took a glance around me. This didn't seem like a bad idea moving here. I was sure Daddy and the rest of the family wouldn't be too pleased, but it was my choice to make. I planned to give it some thorough thinking.

The sun was beating down on me, and the humidity made the air thick and muggy. I was sweating everywhere, even in my drawers, so I decided to turn back around. I hoped the tension with Yash had calmed down. I was trying to understand her pain, so I planned on not criticizing her for taking the money. Instead, I'd try to be as supportive as I could be, but if she kept pushing me away, then I would leave her the hell alone.

On the way back to the hotel, Trini popped up in my head. I knew I had told him that it was over between us, but deep down, I was missing him. That sex kept popping up in my head, even though I tried to forget about it. I needed to accept that it was a summer fling, and tomorrow, I'd be leaving.

I entered the crowded hotel lobby and made my way to the elevator. I looked forward to jumping in the shower and washing this sweat off me. I still needed to pack up my things so that I could be ready for my flight in the morning.

I reached the room and pulled out my key. I opened the door and entered the room. The lights were off, so I left them off. Maybe Yashira was sleeping, and I didn't want to disturb her. I removed my shoes and inched forward into the room. To my surprise, she wasn't in bed. *Hmmm.* Then I noticed the bathroom door was locked.

Okay, she was in the shower, so I decided to get out some clothes so I could take a shower when she was finished. I was digging through my suitcase when I heard her talking. I paused, then tiptoed to the bathroom door. I leaned my ear up against the door and listened attentively.

"Girl, I'm telling you these niggas are a fucking fool. I tricked them, and now, this nigga goin' give me twenty stacks just to keep quiet. Bitch, you can't tell me this ain't a quick come-up. A bitch is going to be paid . . . Shit, who thought sucking dick could be rewarding? That bum thought he was doing something. I guess I have the last laugh now."

I froze when I heard the words coming out of her mouth. I tried my best not to shift a muscle as she continued talking on the phone.

"Bitch, after I get this payment, I'ma give this nigga a break, then hit his ass up for another payment. What the fuck? I know he'll do anything to keep his homie out of prison and police up out of his business."

I didn't need to hear anything else. That right there confirmed that she plotted this whole situation, so that she could get paid. I felt sick in my stomach as Josh's dead body flashed across my face. This was so wrong on *so* many levels. I didn't have time to process everything 'cause she hung up on whoever she was talking to. I heard the toilet flush, so I carefully tiptoed back to my bed, grabbed some clothes, and pretended like I'd been tending to my own business.

The bathroom door unlocked, and she walked out into the common area. She stopped as soon as she noticed me.

"Hey, girl. I didn't know you was here. How long ago you came back?" she said in a friendly tone.

"I just came back a few seconds ago," I lied.

"Girl, my stomach was killing me, so I been on the toilet."

"Did you hear from Trini about the money?"

"Nah, not as yet. I plan on hitting him up in a few, though."

"What really happen in that room?" I shouldn't ask, but after what I heard, I really wanted to see if she was going to continue with the foolery.

"What you mean? I already told you that nigga raped me. What, you don't believe me?" She gritted me down.

I wanted to yell out, "Bitch, stop lying," but I remained quiet to let her think that I was believing the nonsense that she was feeding me. I didn't say, "I don't believe you, but rape is a serious situation that can put a nigga away for a long time. Y'all were drinking so . . ."

"Okay, *and?*" Her face got more serious.

"What you mean, 'and'? Is *that* what you really want?" Naomi asked.

"Listen, boo boo, you might've been dick dazzled and fooled by these New York niggas, but not me. That bitch-ass nigga violated me, and now, his boy wants me to keep quiet about it by paying me off. Guess what? I'm going to take this paper and haul ass out of this stinking-ass state, never looking back."

"I hear you loud and clear, but make sure you know what you doing. You take Trini money, make sure it's legit 'cause you don't know who knows who." I continued putting my dirty clothes in a small grocery bag before I placed it in one of my suitcases.

"Girl, go ahead wit' all that. Just 'cause that nigga got you wrapped around his pinky finger don't mean he nothing to fear. Matter of fact, let's just drop this. I told you what the fuck happened. It's either you believe the bitch you've known your entire life or believe a nigga that you just met."

I didn't know if it was the audacity of this chick, or it was me knowing that this bitch was a liar, but something was irritating my soul.

"You're right. It's your business, so I'll leave it the fuck alone."

"Thank you."

The rest of the evening was spent in quietness. She was occupied on her phone, and I watched television as I tried to calm my nerves. I felt so betrayed and angry. This girl and I had been friends—shit, more like sisters—and I had never seen this side of her. People warned me about her, but I didn't listen. I was usually a good judge of character, so how could I have been so wrong? I thought about that boy's body on the ground. He didn't have to die, but because of the lie she told, he lost his life.

I needed to get to Trini before he gave her that money. It was blood money, and she shouldn't get a dollar. I hopped on my bed and called his number. It rang out until the voicemail came on. She was on the other bed, so I couldn't risk leaving him a voicemail, so I decided to shoot him a text, hoping he would respond. I could understand if he didn't, 'cause I had been blowing him off.

I lay back down, hoping that he would respond. A few minutes later, my phone started to ring. It was Trini calling me back.

"Yo, B, what's good? If you calling me 'bout yo' girl paper, I already told her ass I was in BK handling some business, and I'll get at her soon as I come back in the city." Needless to say, he sounded very irritated.

"Nah, that's not why I called you, but I need to see you ASAP. This is very important."

"B, what's up with the change of heart? Last time I saw you, you didn't want to have anything else to do with me. Now, out of the blue, you urgently want to see me. What's *really* fucking good, B?"

"Just like I kept your secret, I'm asking you to trust me. Just meet me. I have something to discuss with you, and I can't do it over the phone." I tried my best to talk as quietly as possible while eyeing Yashira to see if she was being nosy.

She was busy on her phone, texting someone, probably talking about the money that she was so eagerly waiting on.

"A'ight. Gimme a hour tops, and I'll be there. Meet me in the lobby."

"Okay."

After I hung up, I wondered if I was doing the right thing. I wasn't sure, but it seemed like I had no choice. Trini needed to know the truth. If he decided to give her the money afterward, that would be on him.

I pulled out a minidress from Fashion Nova and a nice pair of thongs. I wasn't trying to get fucked, but anything could go down, and I wanted to be prepared. I took a long shower, trying to calm my nerves. Water had a way of cooling down our bodies and thoughts. After finishing, I stepped out of the shower and got dressed.

I walked back into the room and walked over to the mirror to fix my weave. I tried not to make any kind of eye contact with her, but that didn't work.

"Why are you acting strange all of a sudden?" she quizzed.

"What do you mean? You're doing your thing, and I'm doing mine. What seems to be the issue?" I shot back while I continued focusing on my head.

"Ha-ha, bitch, you know I know when you in your feelings. So, air it out. What, you mad that I'm taking the money from yo' little boy toy?"

"Listen, bitch. I consider you my friend, or better yet, my sister, but your business is your business. You made it clear earlier that I should butt out, so that's what I'm doing. Whatever you and Trini got going on is between you two."

"Hmmm, so where are you going? You all dressed up."

"I'm meeting Trini for drinks," I lied.

"For drinks . . . The nigga told me he was in Brooklyn, and now, you and him meeting up. This seems like game. Let's see how he feels when his boy gets locked up. I'm done playing wit' these niggas," she spat.

I had nothing to say 'cause going back and forth with her was going to make the situation worse. I made sure my weave was laid properly. Then I applied a little makeup and lip gloss and checked the time. It was twenty minutes to four, so I grabbed my purse and walked out of the room without saying another word. I decided to sit in the lobby and wait for Trini to arrive.

My phone started ringing, and I answered it. "Hello."

"Come outside. I'm pulling up now."

"Okay."

I stood up and walked out of the hotel. I saw his SUV two cars down, so I headed toward him. The traffic was bad, and there wasn't anywhere to park. I opened the door and got into the ride.

"Hey, you," I greeted him.

"What's good wit' you, ma? This sound urgent."

"Can we go somewhere private to talk?"

"What you have in mind?" he answered, but he was still being coldish.

"I don't know. This your place. Maybe somewhere to eat."

He didn't respond. He just kept driving. *Maybe this wasn't a great idea. Maybe I should've just stayed out of it*, I thought as he weaved his way through the congested New York traffic, and to make matters worse, it was rush hour on a Friday evening.

He pulled up at a diner in Harlem, and we got out. I followed him inside, where it was a nice layout and atmospheric with great ambience. I could tell this was his place 'cause the minute he walked through the door, everyone was showing him lots of love, like he was royalty. We got seated pretty quickly.

"What kind of restaurant is this?" I inquired.

"This is the best Trini restaurant in all of New York. If you want authentic Trinidadian food, *this* is the place to be," he bragged.

"So, are they food like the Jamaicans, curry and ox-tails?" I didn't want to sound ignorant, but I never had Caribbean food before.

"Well, not really. We eat a lot of curry like them. Some of our dishes are similar, but honestly, our shit taste way better."

"Oh, okay. What's on the menu?"

He waved for a waitress to come over.

"Hey, Trini, what *agwaan*?" she said in a thick accent while she shot me a strange look.

"Bring menu."

She walked away and returned seconds later, and handed us the menus. I curiously started looking at all this strange-ass food . . . Geera Pork, Pholourie, Aloo Pies, Saheena, Black Pudding, and a whole lot of other shit.

"They don't sell American food, like fried chicken, mashed potatoes, or fries?"

"I mean, they have fried chicken on it. Is that what you want?"

"Yeah, 'cause I don't eat all that other shit."

He got up and walked over to the waitress. I watched as they chatted, and she walked off into the back. He returned to our table.

"She's going to prepare what you need, ma. So, what was so important? Last time you saw a nigga, you made it clear that you were done, and you didn't want to see me ever again. What changed your mind?"

I looked around to see if I saw a waitress standing around. Before I got to talking, I needed to get me a drink or two in my system. I saw a waitress walk by, so I flagged her down.

"Yes, may I help you? What's up, Trini? You don't fuck with the kid no more?" She gritted him down.

I cleared my throat to break up their little monopoly and get me what the hell I wanted.

"Yes, may I help you?" she responded with an attitude.

"I need to order two shots of Grey Goose with pineapple juice."

"All right," she said in a low tone and sashayed off.

"What was that about?" Trini grilled me.

"What are you talking about?"

"You real smooth, you know that? I like that." He grinned.

I ignored his smart comment and just sat there with an innocent look plastered all over my face. A few minutes later, the waitress arrived with my drink and a drink for Trini. I figured they were so familiar that he didn't have to order. She knew what he drank. I felt a dash of jealousy overtaking me. I really had feelings for this nigga, and it showed.

I took a few gulps of my drink, trying to calm my nerves before I started talking. I tried not to make eye contact with him. After I started feeling the alcohol, I put down my phone and got ready for this much-needed conversation.

"Yo, B, your girl tripping out. Talkin' 'bout if I don't drop off the paper, she goin' call the police. Who the fuck this bitch think she's talkin' to? She must not know this my place, and I can get her wig peeled back. She lucky that I fucks wit' you, shawty, 'cause we would be having a whole different conversation otherwise." He reached for his glass and finished the liquor in one huge gulp.

"Listen, I need to talk to you about something."

"Shawty, you been saying that. If you got something to say, just spit it out." The aggravation on his face let me know he was angry.

"Earlier, I went for a walk, and when I came back in, I overheard Yashira on the phone talking to someone in the bathroom." I paused, still trying to figure out if I should continue. So, I gulped the remaining liquor in my cup.

"Okay and?"

"Boy, shut the fuck up wit' all that attitude," I said in a high-pitched tone.

He turned his head so hard, and I had no idea how it didn't pop off. Either he was shocked, or he was planning my funeral in his head.

"I overheard her telling someone that she set up dude."

"What the fuck you mean? My boy didn't rape her?" His nose started flaring, and spit flew out of his mouth.

"That's what I heard her saying. She was after the money all along."

"Yo, this unfucking believable. So, this *dutty, bloodclaat gyal* made up some sick story that my bwoy raped her? Oh no, Jah, Jah . . . I killed my nigga behind a fucking *lie?*" He started to massage his temples while he cussed under his breath.

I felt relieved getting that info off my chest, but I was nervous. What chain of events was going to follow? I just prayed that he would let it go, so we could head home and out of his life.

"Yo, before I pulled the trigger, my bwoy looked me in the eyes and tell me he didn't do that shit. He asked me to believe him 'cause I know him, but I-I-I didn't believe him. I *didn't* believe him. Oh, Jah, Jah. Yo, B, I'ma kill that bitch with my bare hands."

His hands were shaking uncontrollably as the tears fell from his eyes, dripping on the table. I reached over and took his hands into mine. I held them, and he squeezed my hands. For a few seconds, we spoke no words. We just held on to each other.

"Listen, boo, I'm sorry that this happen to you. I wish I could take it all away, but I can't. You just have to forgive yo'self 'cause you didn't know."

"Shawty, fuck all that. I killed my nigga and got rid of his body. How am I supposed to move from that, knowing he was innocent? How? Answer me that 'cause you seems to have all the fucking answers," he lashed out.

"Listen, I had no parts in this. I'm just telling you what I heard—"

Before I could finish my sentence, the waitress walked in with our food, but honestly, my appetite was long gone.

We spent the remainder of our time there in complete silence. Even though I was no longer hungry, I tried my best to eat the food. After all, he did put effort into getting me regular old fried chicken. I watched as he indulged in his native dish. It must be good 'cause he was eating like it was his last supper.

Dinner was over, and we got up to leave. On the way out, the one waitress from earlier approached us. "Trini, you a leave already? I thought me was going to get some time wit' you," she said in not-so-perfect English.

"Aye, gyal, chill out wit' all of that. Don't you see my lady friend here with me?"

"Who this Yankee gyal? You and I both know you might fuck them, but you don't love them." She turned her nose up at me and smirked.

She tried rubbing on Trini's chest, but he grabbed her arm and shoved her away. "Yo, B, get yo' disrespectful-ass away from me."

She stumbled and almost lost her balance. I smiled at her before I followed Trini out of the restaurant. He was speed walking, so I tried my best to keep up.

He got in his ride and slammed the door. I got in and sat down. "What was that all about?" my nosy ass inquired.

"Ain't shit. Shawty just don't know how to chill out."

"Y'all used to fuck or something? She seems to know what you like to drink," I stated sarcastically.

"Just drop it, a'ight? Aye, yo, what the fuck is yo' issues? You made it clear you 'ont want to fuck wit' a nigga, but here you are, acting all jealous and shit. Don't think I didn't notice that earlier. If you want the dick, just say it, and it can all be yours."

My face started turning hot pink. I was feeling jealous earlier, but I was unaware that he had noticed it.

"Boy, whatever. This dick seems to be around e'ery-where. What else can you offer?"

"Shit, I'm that nigga. If you want dick, lots of it, I got that. If you want paper, a nigga rich as fuck and can give you plenty of it."

"But can you give loyalty? I was born into money, so that shit don't faze me. My daddy had plenty of money and threw that shit at my mama, but guess what? She was *still* unhappy 'cause his ass don't know how to be loyal and keep his dick in his pants."

"Loyalty? You see this?" He pointed to a tattoo on his wrist. It read "Loyalty over E'erything."

"That shit don't faze me. I saw a nigga kill his right hand over a lie."

Oops, I shouldn't even go there 'cause it was over a fabricated lie.

"Listen, B, what's done is already done, but don't you sit up here acting like the fucking Angel Mary. What's loyalty? 'Cause from what I understand, you got a nigga back home, but that didn't stop you from getting that little pussy wet for me. It didn't stop you from riding my dick or letting me chew on your clit."

"Boy, fuck you." I hit him in his chest two times.

He grabbed my arm, preventing me from throwing any more blows. "That's what I'm trying to do. Let me taste that pussy real quick." He started licking his lips, sticking his tongue all the way out, teasing me. I couldn't resist. My pussy started throbbing, and I could feel my body reacting. I wanted him now, so I leaned over and started kissing him. All the anger I was feeling quickly disappeared.

Before you knew it, I was on top of him, in the restaurant parking lot, riding his dick while he sucked on my breast. I bounced my ass up and down, just like one of those music girls, making sure I squeezed my pussy muscles tight.

His dick was so long that it was touching the pit of my stomach. He took long, slow strokes while I was moaning out for mercy. "Oh, fuck, Trini. Oh Lord. Ohhhh Lord." He ignored my cries and grabbed my hips and started moving them up and down.

Seconds later, I felt his nut sack slapping up against my ass. The pressure intensified, and I moaned out louder. "Oh my God, fuck me." His dick was all the way into my soul, hitting every wall. He was so deep into me that we didn't hear the knocks coming from the window.

I eased my head off his shoulder to see a security officer standing outside of Trini's window. I was so scared that I remained in the position, afraid to move.

"Yo, what's good, Sicky?" He rolled down the window and asked.

"Yo, mi G, I didn't even notice it was you in there. My bad, bro. I'ma head back in."

I let out a sigh of relief when he walked away. I couldn't do anything but burst out a laugh.

"Sorry 'bout that."

We picked up right where we left off, but my nerves were shot. I started bouncing hard on his dick, and within seconds, he busted all up in me. I quickly got off him with cum dripping out of my pussy. *Shit,* I thought.

"Wait, here's some paper towels." He reached into the backseat and handed me the roll. I took some and started cleaning up myself. I was so embarrassed about getting caught by the guard, but the fuck was so good, my pussy was feeling happy.

After we finished cleaning ourselves off, he pulled out of the driveway. I felt relieved that we were leaving 'cause I didn't want to see that guard again.

"Listen, B, I'm digging you. I wish you didn't have to leave, not so soon anyway. I really see us together."

"My life is back in Atlanta; plus, I just graduated from school, so it's time to find me a job and move out on my own."

"Shit, you can work in New York, and I got two houses that you can choose whichever one to live at. Why do you want to run away from what we have?"

"What we have? We just met a week ago, and yes, I like you a lot, a whole lot, but we are strangers, and we both have different lives. It wouldn't work out."

"We are two imperfect people who can rewrite our story to become perfect. Give me that chance, and I promise, I can be that man for you." He reached over and grabbed my hand. He kept his eyes on the road while he rubbed it.

His words pierced my soul. He didn't know how much I wished it were this simple, but the reality was, my life was back in Atlanta. I gave Jerome three years of my life, and even though he had been pissing me off lately, I loved him and intended to spend the rest of my life with him.

Chapter Eleven

Yashira

This nigga sure was pissing me off. He was the one who offered the money to me. Now, suddenly, I felt like he was playing some kind of kiddie game. I lit me a motherfucking cigarette and took a few pulls while I paced the hotel room like a dope fiend.

This nigga was going to give me this motherfucking money one way or the other. I called his phone, but still, no answer. I knew that bitch was out with him, so either they were fucking or he was just ignoring my calls. But why would he, when he knew if I went to the police, I could bring him and his friend down? That nigga must wasn't loyal like he wanted me to think.

After I hung up for the millionth time, I jumped on Google to look up police precincts close to me. I copied the number, then made the call. This nigga was going to learn today. I was the wrong bitch to fuck with, but he'd learn fast.

"Hello, Midtown Precinct South. How may I help you?"

"I want to report a crime."

"What is your name, ma'am, and the crime that you want to report?"

"My name is Yashira Blackwell, and I was raped."

The nice lady went ahead to take the report about what happened. I was very precise, and I cried the entire time.

"I'm so sorry this happened to you. Give me your address. I can get a female officer to you immediately. She will assist in getting you medical, get some DNA off your clothing, and get this case going."

I gave her the hotel address and the room I was staying in. After I hung up, I got the underwear and clothes I wore, so I could give them to her. That should be enough evidence to make a case against that nigga. They thought that they played li'l old me, but let's see who was fucking who in the ass without lubricant.

About ten minutes later, someone knocked on the door. I walked over and looked out the peephole. Two uniformed officers stood there. I started rubbing my eyes, so the tears would start flowing again. Once they started, I opened the door.

"Miss Blackwell?"

"Yes, come in."

They entered the room, and I closed the door behind us. I was ready for the greatest performance of my life.

"We understand that you were raped earlier. We are sorry this happened to you, but we need to get a report about what took place. I know this might be difficult, but this can help us catch the perpetrator. Also, we need to get you to our hospital. An ambulance is on the way."

This bitch was doing too much now. I never told them I needed an ambulance. I just wanted to make a fucking report. I started telling my story again. This time, I made sure no holes were in it. I was aware that I might have to repeat this again, so I took my time recalling everything that went down.

"So, ma'am, do you have the name of the man who raped you?"

Fuck. I thought of every fucking thing except that. I searched my brain. He was introduced to me as Josh, but I doubted that it was his government. This was fucking embarrassing.

"Lady, I don't know his correct name, but his friend called him Josh."

"So, you don't personally know him?"

"I know him. Well, I only met him yesterday."

"You met him right before he raped you?"

I felt this bitch was being funny at this point, and it was pissing me the fuck off.

"I already told you. I met him through my roommate's friend. We went out to eat, we went back to his friend's crib, and the nigga raped me."

"You need to calm down, ma'am. My partner is only trying to get your statement correct. There's no need to be rude," the next bitch interjected.

"*I'm* the one who got raped, and y'all questioning me like *I* did something wrong. If I were a white bitch, would y'all be acting like this? Or would poor little Becky get assistance right away?"

"Ma'am, there's no need to play the race card here. You are the victim, and we understand that you're upset, but I need you to calm down and answer my questions. The district attorney will need all this info to secure an arrest warrant."

Even though I really wasn't feeling this bitch, I knew in order to serve these niggas a dose of their own medicine, I would need the cops on my side, so I swallowed hard and started answering the questions the best way I could. After about twenty minutes of talking and them writing in notebooks, it was over. Then I handed them the clothes, which they placed in a bag.

One of the officers' phones rang, and she stepped aside to answer it. A few seconds later, she walked over to me.

"The ambulance is downstairs; they are ready to transport you to New York Presbyterian Hospital."

"I never said I was going to no hospital. You got the nigga's name, got the clothes, and my statement. What do I need to go to the hospital for? I bathed, so there's nothing to find."

"I understand that, but we need to get a doctor to look at you. Plus, you don't know if he has any kind of STDs that might have been passed on to you."

"Listen, lady, I gave you my statement, and I'm *not* going to the hospital."

"Okay, it's your call. Here is my card. Give me a call if you remember anything else." She handed me the card and started walking off. Then she stopped. "Oh, do you by any chance have a picture of this fella?"

"Oh, I sure do," I said excitedly.

I walked over to my bed and grabbed my phone. I recalled we were taking pictures when we were out that evening. I quickly pulled up the pictures and showed them to her. I had some of all of us and two with just him.

"Are you a hundred percent sure this is the fella who raped you?"

"You keep asking me like my story is going to change. This is him."

"Send me the pictures to that number on the card. Oh, and we're going to need to talk with your roommate. Get her side of what happened. Do you know what time she's returning?"

"I don't know." I shrugged my shoulders 'cause what the fuck did they need to talk to that bitch for?

"Does she have a number that we can reach her on?"

"I'm not goin' to just give out her number like that. I'll let her know y'all stopped by and need to talk with her. I'm sure she'll give you guys a call."

"Okay, then we're done here. Again, sorry this happened to you."

"All right."

After they left, I locked door. I felt relieved that they were gone. Instead of helping me, them bitches were acting like *I* was the criminal. This place was a piece of shit. I couldn't wait to go home to my man and our new life that we were about to start building together. I rubbed my hand over my belly. "Mommy and Daddy can't wait to meet you, sugar."

Chapter Twelve

Naomi

After having sex that evening, it kind of lightened the mood between Trini and me, but it didn't last. On the way home, he was adamant about doing something bad to Yash. I tried pleading with him that he shouldn't hurt her.

"Listen, babe, I know you're angry, and I totally understand, but you have already killed yo' boy. You don't need to get yo' hands dirty again."

"Dirty? Ha-ha. You don't know the level that I'm on. All I have to do is make a phone call, and that bitch will be dead in seconds. She's a dutty gyal that don't need to breathe another second. Do you know how fucked up I feel inside knowing I didn't believe my nigga? I grew up with this nigga. He was the first dude I met when I come from Trinidad. He didn't make fun of my brightly colored clothes or my funny accent. He was a little brother to me. That's why I put him on once I started making major moves. This bitch fucked that up." He slammed his hands up against the steering wheel, and he almost lost control of the vehicle, but he corrected it before he slammed into a wall.

"You need to calm down. Look, you almost killed us," I spoke softly.

"My bad, ma. I'm just so fucking angry. I can't believe I killed my man all over a fucking lie." He reached for half of a blunt that was in the ashtray, took several pulls, and then started coughing.

"I'm sorry, babes. Look, we're leaving tomorrow, and you'll never have to see us again. I know that don't mean a lot or won't bring yo' boy back, but I'm begging you to let her leave with me. You owe me a favor anyway." I hated to take it there, but I was desperate. Daddy used to say, "Fair exchange ain't no robbery."

He looked over at me, then refocused on the road. A few minutes of silence passed by, and then he spoke. "You are not a easy gyal to deal wit', but you're right. I owe you one. She lucky she has you as a friend 'cause she would be one dead bitch if it wasn't for you. We're even then, right?" He looked back at me with seriousness in his voice.

"Yes, we are," I reluctantly said.

During the rest of the ride, we chatted a little about our lives. He kept warning me not to keep calling him Jamaican. It was an insult because he was Trinidadian. But to me, all Caribbean people sounded alike, so what was the big deal? By the time I finished my thoughts, he was pulling up in front of the hotel. As soon as I saw that, I started feeling sad. The week that I spent with him was one to remember, and I hated that this was it. He pulled the vehicle over and got out, not giving a damn that he was blocking the traffic behind him. I also got out of the car, and we started hugging.

"Listen up, B, if you ever need me, just hit my line, and I'll get to you. I hate that you won't give a real nigga a chance, but I respect it. Take care of yo'self, shawty. Here you go." He let me out of his grip and handed me a bundle of neatly wrapped bills. My eyes popped open, but my common sense interceded.

"What's this for?"

"It's yours to help you get yo' life started."

"I can't take this. I appreciate it, though." I tried giving it back to him, but he refused to take it.

"Yo, B, chill out. Put it in yo' purse before a nigga snatch it up or something. Take care of yourself, B. One love."

Before I could respond, he started walking away. I ran after him and grabbed him. I locked my lips on his and started kissing him passionately. "Goodbye, Trini. You're a real one," I said with my voice cracking. Then I backed away from him and walked into the hotel. I wiped the one tear that fell down my face. In another life and another place, I would choose him.

I walked into the lobby and waited for the elevator. When I checked my phone, I was shocked to see I had multiple missed calls from Yash. I wondered what the fuck she wanted. I guess I'd find out when I got up to the room.

I opened the door and walked in. She was sitting on the edge of her bed. As soon as I walked in, the smell of cigarettes hit my nose. I stopped in my tracks, trying to find the words I needed.

"Girl, tell me you weren't smoking up in here? You know what Daddy told us."

"Daddy didn't tell *me* a damn thing. He told *you,* and *what's* the big deal? The smell will be gone in the morning."

"You know what, Yash? I am tired of yo' fucked-up behavior since we got here. I'm tired of sparing yo' feelings and tiptoeing around you. Why don't you just let it all out? What is yo' fucking problem with me?"

"Problem with you? Different from the fact that my best friend is running around here with a dude who is the opp. His friend raped me, and he agrees with it."

"Bitch, you're delusional. He had nothing to do with that, and you know it."

"Hmmm, you're so naïve. Smart in school but dumb as fuck in real life."

"*I'm* dumb? *You're* the one who lied that a nigga raped you when he didn't. Listen, *I'm* the reason why you still breathing right now. So, instead of being a miserable-ass bitch, be grateful."

"Girl, fuck you. You have no idea *what* you talkin' about, but carry on, sis," she chuckled.

"Girl, it's late, and I'm tired, so I'm going to sleep. I got an early-morning flight to catch."

I wasn't going to entertain this chick a second longer. She could sit up here and pretend like I didn't hear her on the phone, but I knew what the fuck I heard. Plus, if she really got raped, why not push it harder? At this point, I just needed to get the fuck home. What was supposed to be a great trip turned out to be toxic and full of drama.

Chapter Thirteen

Naomi

The day I left New York, I was in my feelings. Part of me wished I could have some more time with Trini, and the other part was excited to be leaving the state. Too much happened too fast, and I wished I could put it all behind me.

Yash and I didn't speak any, and we went to the airport in separate vehicles. Trini dropped me off. When I got to the airport, she was standing outside, smoking a cigarette. When I got out of the car, she smiled at me and shook her head. By the time Trini hugged me and we kissed, she had disappeared behind the double doors.

I realized she changed her seat on the plane, and I didn't trip behind it. She was acting stupid as fuck, and I wasn't going to run behind her. My only fear was hoping she would keep her mouth shut about Trini and me, 'cause if she didn't, this could cause big trouble between Jerome and me.

It had been two days since I got back to the A, and Yash and I had not spoken a word to each other since we left New York. I guessed she was still in her feelings, and honestly, I didn't give a fuck about it. I was not sure what really happened in that room, but I knew what I heard when she was on the phone. Plus, her weird behavior after made me question everything about what really went down.

Since returning from New York, I had a few job interviews lined up, and I was feeling pretty good about that. Daddy was excited that I was following his recommendation by applying to Emory Midtown Hospital. He had some connections with them, but I was not sure 'cause he never really talked about it. But he often bragged about how it was the best hospital in Georgia, or he might take it as far as the best in the world.

It was early in the morning, but the Georgia sun was beating down heavily. It was nothing compared to the New York heat, but it was almost there. I stepped out of my ride and walked into the hair salon on Hairston. My hairdresser, Audrey, had a new shop by the Kroger store, and I was more than excited 'cause it was in my neck of the woods.

I rang the bell and waited for someone to let me in. The other stylist, Quiana, walked to the door and opened it.

"Hey, girly, come on in. You know Audrey's ass is a few minutes late as usual," she said while walking away.

"Girl, I know, and her few minutes be half an hour. I'ma sit my happy ass down and wait until she pop up."

There were a few other clients who were seated, so I took a seat in the only available spot. I pulled my phone out and started scrolling through social media. I was curious to see what, if anything, Yashira posted.

I got on her page, and right away, I noticed the "add friend" option. So, this bitch *really* took it there by unfriending me. I mean, this wasn't the first time that we disagreed, but we always bounced back. I scrolled down and noticed only one post was public, so I could see it. "So happy to be back in my boo arms," it read. That was strange 'cause I was unaware of her having a boo. I knew of her fucking some nigga from the East, but she never posted about him 'cause he was married, and like she claimed, he was only good for fucking when she got horny. As puzzled as I was, it was none of my business who she was fucking, so I hopped off her page. Still in my feelings that she had unfriended me, I called her number, and it went straight to voicemail. I tried a few more times, and the same thing happened. It didn't take long for me to realize that she blocked me.

I didn't have time to dwell on her reasoning 'cause Audrey walked in with a handful of bags. "Good morning, ladies," she said as she headed to the back office.

I got up and walked back there and knocked on the door. "Come in," she yelled.

"Hey, girl, what's going on with you?"

"Ain't shit. I wish I had another one of me 'cause a sister is tiredddd," she giggled.

"I feel you on that. That's why I'm enjoying my little free time before I step into the working world. I ain't goin' lie. It's kinda scary 'cause I've never had to do it on my own."

"It's goin' be hard at first, but hang in there. You'll get the hang of things in no time. How was your trip to New York? Did you enjoy yourself?" she asked as she bit through a biscuit and chicken sandwich that she was eating.

"Girl, it was a'ight. Some bullshit popped off with Yash, and that kind of ruined the rest of the trip."

"Really? Oh shit, I forgot, I ran into her yesterday at Publix on Panola, and I asked her for you. She gave me a nasty response, so I kept it moving. I should've known something had gone down."

"Girl, she showed me the real side of her. She almost got us in some serious shit."

"Hmmmm, I told you from way back when we were in school that she was not a good friend. She was always jealous of you, but you kept her snake ass around."

"I know you told me. Even my little sister told me, but we've been friends so long, it was hard to see the bullshit. Plus, I used to feel like as long as it's not me she fucking over, e'erything was good. I just can't believe that it took me this long."

"Listen, honey, these hoes are not loyal. Knowing a bitch for years don't mean shit. Remember the same mouth they praise you with is the same one they use to talk shit behind yo' back. Truthfully, her ass been a snake. She only hangs around you 'cause you had a nice-ass life. Be grateful that you finally see the real her before she crossed you in a deadlier way. Count it as a blessing."

I heard her words, and even though I agreed with her, I felt uneasy. This was my best friend, my partner in crime, and my sister. I wanted to believe that we could get through anything together. But the signs were there. How could I ignore the red flags?

"Come on. Let me wash you. I have a lot of heads to do today." She stood up and opened the door.

I stood up and followed her. I tried to push all negative thoughts out of my head, but it was hard. We continued talking until she finished washing my hair and placed me under the dryer.

I decided to dial Jerome's number. We only spoke briefly when I first came back. He claimed he was coming through to see me last night, but that was a lie. I waited up, and when I called, his phone kept going to voicemail. I was getting sick of his behavior with me. I'd rather he just say it was over and be done, but the thought of us being done put a hole in my heart. Regardless of what went down in New York between Trini and me, I still loved Jerome, and that was who I wanted to be with. After all, he was the one that Daddy approved of. Breaking up would devastate both families.

The phone kept going straight to voicemail, which was strange. His phone always stayed on 'cause he was on call at his second job at Grady Hospital as a resident doctor. His latest behavior toward me wasn't adding up. I needed to see him; I needed answers ASAP.

Last night was another night that I couldn't sleep, and to make matters worse, my phone alerted me that I had a text message, so I reached over and grabbed it. I barely opened my eyes to see who it was . . . It was a pic. I opened my eyes fully to see what I was really looking at. It was a pic of Trini and me kissing in the bar that first night. A second picture came in. I was in Trini's bed, sleeping in his shirt. More pictures continued coming in from Jerome's phone. I threw the phone into the wall, smashing it. "Yash, you stupid bitch. How could you do this to me?" I hollered out.

I jumped off the bed and grabbed the smashed phone. I tried to cut it on, but it was broken and wouldn't turn on. I started bawling louder. I wanted to catch this bitch and rip off her head. How could she betray me like this?

"Oh God, Jerome, baby, I'm so sorry. I swear I didn't mean to." I cried louder and louder.

I couldn't sleep the rest of the night. I thought of different ways to explain this to Jerome. How was I going to face him? I was waiting for daylight so that I could head over to his condo. I didn't care if I had to get on my knees and ask for forgiveness. I would do whatever it took. I loved this man, and I would spend the rest of my life proving it.

After I left T-Mobile at 10:00 a.m., I headed to Jerome's condo on Wesley Chapel Road. I thought about calling him again, but I doubted that he would pick up the phone this time around. I got to the apartment in less than ten minutes and found an empty parking space. As I walked to the entrance of his condo, I noticed his 2022 Dodge Challenger was parked in its usual spot. My heart started skipping beats. I was feeling nervous and scared. I didn't know how he would react, but I was hoping he would hear me out and give me a chance to explain myself. I hoped we could get past this foolishness, and we could have some makeup sex.

I made my way upstairs to his condo. I put my ears up against the door to see if I heard any kind of sounds, but it was quiet. Knowing him, he must be sleeping or playing his favorite Xbox One game on the console I bought him for Christmas. I knocked loudly, so I could get his attention, then waited. There was no response, so I knocked louder. I guessed I overdid it 'cause his elderly next-door neighbor opened her door and looked at me up and down before she slammed her door shut. I shrugged my shoulders as if she were still standing there. Jerome and I often joked about how damn nosy her ass was.

Back to the matter at hand, this was strange that he wasn't answering the door, and I was pretty sure he was there. I took my phone out of my purse and called his number. I placed my ear up against the door and listened. His phone was ringing loudly in the condo. Then I heard a movement inside. Good, I must've awakened him. I was excited and feeling confident that he would answer the phone, the door—something. But seconds turned into minutes, and I was standing there with the phone in my hand, feeling stupid as hell.

"Jerome, open this damn door. I know you in there," I yelled out while I banged on the door with my fist. "Open the fucking door, boy, and quit playing so much," I yelled.

The door flew wide open, and he stood in the doorway in his boxers, looking at me with anger plastered all over his face.

"What took you so long to open the door, and why you ain't answering my damn phone calls?" I questioned him while I shoved my way past him.

"Why the fuck you here, ho?"

"What the fuck you just call me?"

"Bitch, you heard me correctly. Shouldn't you be sucking that nigga, Trini's, dick?"

"What the hell . . ."

Before I could finish my question or get an answer, the proof was standing right in front of me. My best friend, my sister, my rollie was standing in my man's living room in her drawers and bra. Our eyes locked as my chest tightened. Confusion and anger washed over my body.

"Jerome, what the fuck is going on?" I turned my full attention to him.

"What's going on? Shit, you see what it is," he boastfully answered.

"You and him fucking around? How could you do this to me?" I turned back to her, hoping that one of them would say it was a sick joke they were playing on me.

"Bitch, don't act all surprised. Jerome and I been together. We was just waiting for the right time to tell you. But since you went to New York, being a slut and all, we figured the timing was right."

All sorts of crazy shit ran through my mind. I lunged toward that bitch and grabbed her fucked-up-ass weave and used all the strength that I could muster up and flipped that bitch on the ground. I started pounding her in the face while she threw blows back. However, they were no match for the ones I was getting in.

"Yo, yo, y'all bitches fucking up my shit," he yelled out.

Then he started pulling us apart. I let her ass go and started throwing blows at him. He grabbed both my hands and threw me up against the wall. I hit my head, but I didn't stay down. I jumped quickly to my feet, still trying to get at him. "Yo, you need to chill out before I call the police on yo' ass."

He backed up and grabbed his cell phone. "Say I won't. You need to just get the fuck outta my shit. You got yo' man in New York, and shawty and I are together."

His words were cold, and they chilled every bone in my body. I wanted to kill them both, but I didn't have a gun. So, I took one last look at them before I started walking away. I got close enough to gather all the spit I could and spat right in his face.

"You dumb bitch, I should beat yo' ass." He raised his fist at me.

"Go ahead so my daddy can blow yo' fucking brains out."

"Man, fuck you, slut, and yo' bitch-ass daddy. Now, get the fuck outta my shit before I call the police to do it."

I was tired of looking at them, plus my head was starting to hurt badly from the hit I took earlier.

"And you, scary-ass bitch, we not done. Every chance I get, I'ma beat yo' ass," I yelled before I dashed out the door.

I ran down the stairs and headed to my car, where I quickly opened the door and got in. That was when the gates opened, and the tears started flowing down. An agonizing pain shook my heart as it shattered into a million pieces. The two people I loved the most stuck a knife in my soul, and there was no coming back from that.

How could I be so naïve that I didn't see this coming? Then it hit me. I couldn't have. He claimed he hated her guts. There were times when he begged me to stop being her friend. She despised him, even encouraged me to talk to Trini. That was when it hit me. They set me up.

I banged my head up against the steering wheel twice, which only made the pain hurt more. *This is too much. God, please take this pain away.*

Chapter Fourteen

Yashira

This bitch had everything that I could only dream of having, but the one thing her ass didn't have was the man that she loved and adored. Here she was, thinking she had Jerome wrapped around her prissy little finger, but all along, his head was buried deep in my pussy.

I remembered two years ago when she introduced him to me. There was nothing special about him at the time, so I greeted him and kept pushing. It wasn't until she kept on bragging about how he could eat pussy really good that he caught my interest. I wanted to find out if his tongue game was on point like she claimed.

We were out one day, having lunch, when she excused herself to go to the bathroom. I decided this was the right time to make my move, so I used my foot and started moving it up and down his leg under the table. He seemed to enjoy it 'cause he sat there smiling while he bit down on his bottom lip. That was all the confirmation I needed, so I took the bold move of asking for his number. He quickly gave it to me right before Naomi made her way back to the table. The rest was history because, after that day, he was my man too. The days he wasn't with her, he was with me. That was, until I started falling hard for him. Then I wanted him for myself, but he was scared to tell Naomi and more scared of how his family would react since the two families were close.

Timing was everything. Who would've thought Little Miss Perfect would go to New York and give away the pussy to a nigga she just met? I couldn't have written the story better myself. I encouraged her along the way 'cause I needed proof that she was cheating, and I got everything that I needed—even got a pic of her kissing Trini in the bar. Later that night, I sent the pics to Jerome. I knew it would piss him off, but I didn't care about how he felt. I knew this would break them up for good, and boy, was I right. The entire trip, I kept him updated on everything that was going on 'cause I knew he was going to be my man when I got back to Atlanta.

When I returned to Atlanta, Jerome was feeling down, but that didn't last. I convinced him that ho wasn't good enough for him, and I would be a better woman for him. It didn't take much for him to see it from my point of view, especially when I showed him all the pictures that I had. He couldn't believe that she would do this to him, but then again, the proof was right in front of him.

"I can't believe that she really fucked that nigga. I should confront her now," he said as we lay in the bed, naked.

"I gave you all the proof. It's right there in yo' face. What else do you need? You know her ass ain't goin' admit nothing to you." I massaged his dick while I started licking it, trying to bring it back to life.

"Aweee, shit. Damn, that feels good. I feel what you saying. I just thought she loved me."

I removed his dick from my mouth and looked at him. His eyes were still closed.

"Jerome, you need to wake the fuck up. This bitch don't love you. She was in New York, telling this nigga how you was a fat, lazy nigga with a small-ass dick. She was happy she met a nigga from the islands that knows how to fuck good."

"That bitch said all that? Oh, hell nah. My dick ain't small, and I know how to fuck. Shit, what you think? Is my dick little?" He jumped off the bed and grabbed his dick.

I wanted to laugh, but I kept it in. Truth was, his dick *was* little, but his tongue game was fire, so he made up for it. But I couldn't tell him that. I could see in his eyes that he was in his feelings.

"No, babes. You know I love your dick, and I love the way you fuck me. Her ass been around so much. That's why she thinks your dick is small. But it's a good size, boo." I stroked his ego.

"Yeah, I know that's right. I fuck that bitch good. Shit, I fuck plenty bitches, and none had a complaint. You know what? Fuck her. I don't fucking need her. I got you, babes. I got you," he yelled out.

Those words were like music to my ears. I finally had my man to myself, and there was no way I was letting him go back to her.

I might not have gotten the money, but I got the man, and that was far more rewarding. I smiled as I looked over at Jerome lying next to me, butt-ass naked.

Epilogue

Naomi

It was never the stab that hurt the most. It was when I realized who was holding the knife to my back. I fed this bitch, gave her my clothes to wear, and gave her a place to stay when her own mama threw her out. But all along, she was waiting patiently to take my place.

Maybe it was God's way of showing me that there were snakes all around me. I just hated that I didn't find out earlier. My mind was thinking back on everything that transpired a week ago. As bad as it hurt, I was waiting for an apology from the man who claimed he loved me, but it never came, so I had to accept the fact that I cheated, he moved on, and no matter how much history we had, the betrayal outweighed that.

After catching Jerome and Yashira together, my world was shattered. I couldn't stop crying. That was . . . until Trini called my phone the next day. I was reluctant at first to talk to him, but he sensed right away that something was wrong. I broke down and told him everything that had transpired, and he listened and didn't interrupt me, not once. I bawled my heart out to him on the phone. Still, he remained quiet. When he felt like I was finished, he spoke. He didn't judge. As a matter of fact, he surprised me. He wasn't the arrogant Trini that I'd met. Instead, he apologized for the way they treated me, then he told me

the offer was still open to come live with him in New York.
I wasn't sure about that, so I told him I would think about
it.

After thinking hard and playing out everything in my
head, I decided to take him up on his offer. Only thing
was, I would get my own place. My heart was broken,
but my mind was still working. I still didn't trust him a
hundred percent; hence, my decision to get my own place.
Even though this was a difficult decision, I went to Daddy
and tried my best to convince him. At first, he wanted no
parts of it. He even threatened to take me out of his will.
I started crying. I just needed a clean start. As a little girl,
I knew Daddy never liked to see me crying, and this time
was no different. He walked over to me, wiped my tears,
and hugged me. Then he told me I could go, and he had
a realtor who could help me find a condo out there. I was
so happy that I just hugged Daddy. I was pleased that he
had my back, no matter what.

The traffic at the airport caught my attention. As usual,
Hartsfield Jackson was packed, even on a Sunday. Daddy
weaved his way through until he finally made it to the
Delta door. Police were motioning for us to move along,
but Daddy, being his old, unruly self, pulled over as soon
as someone else pulled off. He parked, then got out. I had
to love this man. He just didn't give a damn.

I grabbed my purse and got out. Daddy unloaded all six
suitcases, then loaded them on a trolley. I could see the
sadness written all over his face, and that made me sad.

"Baby, you know you still can change yo' mind. You be-
long here with us, not in New York. Your family is here."
His voice cracked. I watched as a teardrop fell from his
eyes. This was strange 'cause I'd never witnessed this
man break down or even show emotion before today.

"I love you, Daddy, and I'm just a phone call away. I'll come visit as much as I can." I hugged him tightly while I fought back my own tears.

We hugged so tightly that you could feel the love without words being spoken. My daddy was my world, and I hated that I decided to make this move, but I needed to do this for me.

With tears in my eyes, I made my way to E gate. I was sad that I was leaving Atlanta, but my heart was broken that I was leaving my family. I'd never been on my own, but with everything that happened in the last two weeks, this was the best decision for me.

The two-hour flight from Atlanta to New York seemed more like seven hours. My thoughts were conflicted, and at one time, I questioned my decision. Was this what I *really* wanted, or was it just me running from the truth? To be honest, it was a little of both. Deep down, I missed Jerome. He was all I knew. He took my virginity, and up until I let Trini fuck me, he was the only dick I ever had. At first, I felt guilty that I had cheated, but after everything was revealed, I discovered that they had been carrying on behind my back for *two years*. How ironic was it that they pretended that they hated each other's guts while, all along, they were together? The thoughts of everything left a sour taste in my mouth. I looked out the window and into the clouds. A tear fell down my face, but I quickly wiped it away.

"Baby girl, you're going to be all right. Be strong." A voice echoed in my head. Then I smiled and closed the plane window. That was all the confirmation that I needed.

Fifteen minutes later, the pilot announced that we should prepare for landing. I gathered my things and waited for the plane to hit the runway. After I disembarked,

I went to retrieve my bags. This was only a portion of my things; Daddy was going to bring the rest up the following week. He could've shipped them, right along with my car, but he insisted on driving up. I knew it was only his way of making sure I was good while I was in the Big Apple. I couldn't help but love that man 'cause he always made sure I was straight, no matter what.

Whitney Houston's lyrics, "Try It On My Own," rang out in my head as I pushed my trolley out to the common area of the airport. I glanced around, trying to get a glimpse of Trini. He said he would be here, so I prayed that he'd keep his word. My heart started beating rapidly, and my frown quickly turned into a smile. That NY Yankee cap with a fresh pair of tan Tims gave him away. I abandoned the trolley and ran up to him. He grabbed me up in his arms and spun me around in the air, then planted a big kiss on my lips as he held me tight. People stared at us, some smiling, while some looked angered 'cause we were in their path. We didn't care about any of that. All that mattered was that I found my way back to him. What was supposed only to be a summer fling in New York turned into me taking that leap, packing everything I owned, and flying out to start my life anew with the man who showed me that love still existed. After we had had enough of being all over each other, he grabbed the trolley. "Welcome home, love," he said.

"I'm happy to be here with you. All I ask is that you take care of my heart 'cause it's been through some shit."

"Nothing to worry 'bout, love. I promise I'll take extra care of it, just like it was my own."

He took my hand into his. We held on to each other as we walked out of the airport and into our next chapter. Two imperfect strangers writing the perfect love story. . . .

Thot Girl Summer in Chicago

by

Na'Cole

Prologue

Before this story goes further, allow me to introduce myself. Tisha Santana is my name, but you can just call me Santana. I have a best friend named Chi'Meka who goes by the name Meka, and a boyfriend named Marcel. They were the only two constant people in my life. That was . . . until my man got himself locked up.

My journey began twenty-one years ago when I was born to Tatiana Rodgers. I came sliding out of her nasty-ass pussy on May 23rd, 2000, at 5:59 p.m. She was a money-hungry bitch who married my sperm donor, a Dominican immigrant named Elder Santana, for his cash. So, I guess you can call me a mixed breed. And you can say she introduced me to the fact that money should always be the motive.

From what I can remember growing up, my mother kept me laced in the latest, and I honestly think it was because my father wasn't around. Their relationship lasted all of eight years of my life. My mother found herself having to pick up where he lacked, even if that meant working two jobs, just so I could keep up with the Joneses when all I really wanted was her attention.

Of course, I milked that shit for all it was worth. I preyed on the fact that my mother felt guilty about running my father away. Back then, I was Daddy's little girl, so when he abruptly picked up and left me without a goodbye, I vowed to make my mother feel my pain. As I got older, I became rebellious. By the time I turned 15, her ole trifling ass passed away from natural causes. From that day forward, I had to raise myself, forcing me to become the woman I am today.

Living a life of promiscuity, I was lost. With no mother to guide me and no family to love me unconditionally, I was out in this cold, cold world alone. But before we get all sappy and shit, here is a story of two girls from the South Side of Chicago. Shit might get a little crazy, or it may end up beautiful because when you know, you know. I've never been a soft, marshmallow type of girl, and I won't start today because life has taught me how to be a bitch.

Chapter 1

Santana

The Beginning

"Yes, Marcel, I love you. I told you I was going to be here for you and hold you down," I said through the receiver as I spoke to my soon-to-be ex-boyfriend, who I had been dealing with for the past four years.

When I met him, I was too young to understand what the words "I love you" meant. All I knew was that the attention I didn't get from my father, Marcel was giving it to me. All the material things I missed out on, Marcel spoiled me with. And the sex was intoxicating. He was an experienced man while I was just a virgin. After the first night with him, he had me wide open, and I had quickly fallen deeply in lust.

Marcel was a handsome man. A copper-tone nigga with a nose piercing like Tupac. He was even as gangsta as him. His lips were small, and I suppose that's because he never smiled with his mean ass. His beautiful eyes were almond shaped and almond colored. Everything about him made me want him. But that was back when I was young, dumb, and full of cum. It was the little things that made me feel like he was the one for me. Today, that's not the case. In fact, for the past two years, that hasn't been the case. Nowadays, he irked my soul. Although I promised I would hold him down, I didn't know how much more of being with him I could take.

Putting a shot of tequila to my lips, I threw it back. My nerves were shot. This shit he was on the phone talking about was for the birds. Listening to this nigga go on and on about the love he thought I had for him and me having to reassure his ego was starting to get old.

"You don't sound too convincing, shorty. The streets are talking, Tisha," he said, calling me by my real name. I just rolled my eyes and scowled. He knew I didn't go by Tisha.

"Marcel, you know I hate it when you call me that." My voice was dry and tired.

"Yeah, I know," he said sarcastically, laughing. Light-skinned niggas think everything is a fucking joke, but I always get the last laugh.

"Then why do you do it? Fuck, Marcel, call me Santana like everyone else does," I sneered, trying to stir up a bullshit-ass argument to turn the focus off me and my ho-ish ways. I should've gone to college to be a psychologist because I was definitely about to detour our entire conversation. At least I was about to try. It's no secret what my life consisted of, but Marcel was so stuck on his image that he didn't want to be embarrassed.

"Man, I'ma call you what the fuck I wanna call you, Tisha."

I huffed and sucked my teeth. This nigga better stop playing with me. All these little spats do is make me go out and play with a new nigga. And when I say play, I mean that in the nastiest way.

"What's the mufuckin' problem? You don't wanna be with me or some shit?"

"Did I say that?" I asked. This was my opportunity to tell him the truth, but I couldn't.

Marcel was currently serving a twenty-year federal sentence after being caught transporting guns and drugs. I thought our love story would never end. Marcel was supposed to be the love of my life. I swear, I loved his dirty drawers. However, after two years of being in love and fucking with him so heavy, he just had to go do some dumb shit to get himself locked up. Being faithful to a nigga while he's incarcerated, serving twenty years, just wasn't for me. I tried my best to be that woman, but I was still young, only 21 years old. Not to mention, I had just begun to live my life. Hell, I just became old enough to buy my own damn liquor. When I broke that down to Marcel, he seemed very understanding.

My pussy purrs too much for me to be saving myself for twenty more years. I might as well be reborn again. Fuck that and fuck him. I sat the last few summers out trying to be loyal to him, but now, that shit is over with. It seemed like the more he sat in jail, the more insecure he became. I've never been a reckless bitch, but in the past, the more he accused me of not being faithful, the more I wanted to be unfaithful. Eventually, I began fucking for money, and I wasn't afraid to tell him what I was doing. Shit, Marcel had pushed me into my current lifestyle, and at this point, I really didn't care.

I never told this nigga to sell drugs. Nor did I tell him I would waste my youth waiting for his ass to get out of jail, and he shouldn't want me to.

Yes, the money he made from his drug deals afforded me nice things. Still, I was not a kept bitch. That nigga hadn't given me his last name or a baby with his last name to sit me down. I watched my mother go through this same situation when I was a shorty, only for her man to get out of jail and do her bogus. Come to find out, the nigga had a whole wife and kids on the side. Although I knew Marcel didn't have a wife or anything like that because everyone knew he belonged to me, I couldn't stick around. I guess you can call me a disloyal-ass bitch, but it is what it is.

I still tried to be there for him whenever I could. But in my mind, he was no longer my man; his ass belonged to the Feds. Two years ago, I felt like I had to hold him down because of all the shit he had done for me. In the midst of me doing that, he tried to control my life, and that was where he fucked up. A nigga who can't provide me with money or dick cannot control shit over here. His money wasn't long enough to keep me content. I hadn't seen a dime of the money I knew he had ever since he had been locked up. So, I've been providing for myself, and pussy pays my way. That was the only job skill I had. Marcel had taught me very well when it came to sex.

"What's up, Marcel? Why are we always arguing every time you call?" I asked, yelling in his ear.

"Because I keep hearing shit about you. Things I don't like. You're supposed to be my bitch."

Here we go again. Here *he* goes again. Who was this nigga showing out in front of? Rolling my eyes, I took the phone from my ear and looked at it, silently fuming. Already knowing what the hell he was about to say, I just listened.

"Answer me this, Santana. Who the fuck was that square-ass nigga you had picking you up from the building last weekend?" he asked, and I smacked my lips. Bitches really need to mind their own business, and when I say bitches, I'm definitely talking about his fat-ass mama because she is the only person who told him that shit. Miss Big Bertha. She acts like she gets paid to watch my every move.

"I don't know what you're talking about."

I'm so over this shit, and I'm sure he could tell by my tone. When Marcel got locked up, he left me with nothing but a hundred thousand dollars. Back then, I was able to deal with his nagging. But after blowing through that shit in less than a year, and him never replenishing my funds, my feelings for him quickly began to trickle away. My rent ain't shit but twenty-four dollars a month because I'm not working, so I pay that shit up for the entire year in February after I file my bogus taxes. Still, I've become accustomed to a certain type of lifestyle, and money is needed to feel secure.

I used to think that dealing with a drug dealer would elevate my life. And for a good while, it did. Thanks to Marcel's drug money, I stayed rocking the latest expensive shit. My car was a Benz, and my pockets stayed on swoll. Then he just had to go fuck up everything. So, I put a price on this pussy. Still, I try to do my li'l shit on the low. I make sure my men pick me up down the street and around the fucking corner. It's crazy how he's calling me talking about a nigga picking me up. His mama talks too much, nosy ass. That bitch must have bionic eyes and ears. Wide-back whale.

It never fails, every other week his mama telling him my business and him calling me, trying to check me. But I'm uncheckable, boo, and that's what they fail to realize. The sooner Marcel gets it, the sooner he will stop wasting his breath. The nerve of him thinking he can run me and my life from behind bars.

"You know what, Marcel? Ain't nobody told you that bullshit but your mama. I'm sick of her."

"Santana, don't try to turn this shit around. Answer my fucking question," he yelled.

Sighing, I gave in and began explaining myself. Lying my ass off, of course, I said, "You know my car is fucked up. The transmission went out. I had to call an Uber to take me to Meka's house." I laid it on thick. He would for sure buy my explanation because Meka is my best friend and Marcel's favorite cousin. Her name will soften him up.

"Damn, Santana, I forgot all about that. Too much shit been on my mind lately. I'm tired of being locked down in this bitch away from you. You know if I were out there, you wouldn't have to worry about shit."

"Yes, Marcel, I know. Still, I'm out here alone, so I do what I have to do to make money." After drinking another shot, I opened up a pack of bubble gum. I put a piece in my mouth and began chewing loudly.

"I apologize, baby. Go upstairs to my mama crib and tell her to give you the money to get your car fixed. I can't have my girl riding around in Ubers and shit," he said, and silently, I laughed. He falls for my lies every time.

"Uhh-huh. Marcel, I can't keep doing this shit with you. If it's not one thing, it's another. We are always arguing about what she said or he said. Fuck what they said. We have an understanding. As long as I don't get pregnant or married on you, then we're good."

"Man, Santana, I know I'm asking a lot of you, but nobody knows about that. Just keep the shit you do away from the crib. What we have is between us."

"I got you, boo. And as far as your fat-ass mama, you already know I'm not asking her for shit. What you need to do is tell her to stay outta our business. Am I all y'all talk about when you call her?" My face, at this point, was scrunched up as I blew a bubble that popped in his ear. The sound echoed loudly throughout my all-white, spacious, fully furnished living room. I looked down mesmerized at my cocaine-white, polished, coffin-shaped nails. Ling Ling had done her shit.

"Nah. That's my mama, man. We're not gon' disrespect her. Whatever she sees, she's supposed to tell me, right?"

"Not when it pertains to me. That bitch is *your* mama, *not* mine," I said, and Marcel sighed.

He chuckled slightly before he began throwing out threats. I guess I went too far when I called his mama a bitch. Oh well, it's not like I'm lying. Her wide-load ass be doing too much for me. Yelling in my ear, Marcel thought he was snapping. His voice boomed through the receiver, sounding as if he were speaking through a megaphone. *OK, go off, sis!* I thought, laughing to myself. The nigga sounded like a whole bitch.

Nigga, you're locked down. You don't run shit but them fat-ass lips, I huffed, thinking to myself. I'm so done with Marcel and Miss Wide Back. Since Biggie Smalls is so important to him, he can be with her. After all this good coochie I done gave him, he wants to take his mama's side? Fuck him. She's a bitch. I hung up the phone and put the number on my block list. That nigga can serve the rest of his time alone. I hate when a mufucka kills my vibe. Geesh. He got me all the way fucked up. Don't get me wrong, he's a good man. Marcel was a great provider when he wasn't in jail, and to my knowledge, he wasn't a cheater. He was about as loyal as they came. Most importantly, he loved me so much. Right now, I just need a little excitement in my life. Not to mention, I have to make my own way through life now that Marcel is serving his time.

I was forced into this, forced to become a made bitch, so I have pussy for sale. No money, no service, and Marcel's time has run out. That nigga can find him someone else to play with. The summer is just getting started. Maybe I'll decide to entertain him in September, but for now, he can catch me in the wind. Nigga, play with your dick, not wit' me, is about to be a whole mood all summer long.

Chapter 2

Marcel

Locked Down

Hearing the dial tone go off in my ear let me know Santana had hung up. I love her, but at times, she made me want to wring her fucking neck. Ever since a nigga been locked up, shorty been getting beside herself with the disrespect. Talking about my mama. It's fucked up how comfortable she was calling my OG fat, wide back, Biggie Smalls, and shit. Santana be going too far. Especially since she knows my OG is my heart. Even with me knowing how much Santana despised her own mother when she was alive, I still would never say anything disrespectful about her. That shit ain't right. I might've sold drugs and shot niggas for a living, but I respected my elders.

Back when I was giving her this ten-inch pipe and throwing her a few thousand daily, she was very obedient. I could tell her to suck my dick in front of all my homies, and she would do it. Don't get me wrong, she's always had a smart mouth, but when I had my shit together, she listened to me.

The day I met her, I knew I would make her mine. Although she was only 17, and I was already 23, I was determined. I was on my way to the top of the drug game, and I needed a shorty who was gonna hold me down no matter what happened. I sensed she was the woman for the job as soon as I looked into her doe-shaped eyes. If I went to jail or got into a shoot-out, she would be willing to hide my gun when the police came knocking. She was just one down-ass chick. She was my bitch and my nigga. Shorty held me down, and I loved her for that. In return, I tried to give her the world, but giving shorty the world took away my freedom.

The shoot-outs never came, but a nigga did end up in jail facing a twenty-year bid. It feels like ever since I been in this mufucka, Santana has done a whole 360. She went from being my down-ass bitch to an attitude-having, shit-talking, disobedient asshole. It's true, we have an understanding. I mean, honestly, I can't control nothing from here. I gotta let her live her life as long as I continue to be her priority.

Back when I snatched her ass off the market, Santana was a hot commodity around the way. The entire South Side of Chicago knew who she was, even when she was a shorty. She's beautiful, not a regular face I usually see in my neighborhood. Her half-Black and half-Dominican features contributed to her perfection. She is like a chocolate goddess with long, thick, black hair. Her dark brown eyes are mesmerizing. It was as if they pulled me in every time I looked at her. I wish me being in her presence right now were an option. Every time she popped her shit over the phone with them thick-ass soup-coolers she called lips, I imagine myself kissing and sucking them. Santana is the definition of beauty, love, and loyalty. Well, at least she was when I was still out in the real world.

It wasn't long after I got locked up, I began hearing little things about her. Things that had me ready to cause a fucking riot. Word is she was whoring around Chicago. News out on the streets travel fast as a mufucka in the pen. In my heart, I knew I needed to let her go, but I loved her too much to let that happen. So, I figured if I can't beat 'em, join 'em. I spent the last two years of my life being in this bitch, missing out on living freely. But I had to let baby girl live as long as she didn't make me look like a fool. Honestly, I understood her plight. Twenty years is a long time to wait for love. Trust me, I know. Still, I'm doing the same twenty-year wait with her. Shit, I done fucked a few security staff myself, so I understood. I just didn't want to hear about the shit.

Shorty got my mind wondering. Every time we talk, we argue, and weeks later, we make up. It's like a never-ending cycle of back and forth between us. Prison has fucked up my entire life. It's always me calling her to inform her about the shit I heard, and her turning everything around. Money somehow always crept into our conversations, and she ends up forgiving me after I give her what she wants. I left Santana with money, but I know a hundred thousand doesn't last that long, especially since she had a spending habit. Without money being brought back in to replace the shit she already fucked off, by now, she is definitely asshole broke. I surmise that is where all our arguments came from. However, she should know I'm willing to do whatever it takes to make her happy, even from prison.

I'm still sitting on almost half a million, so why would I leave her out there broke and struggling? That piece of information I choose to keep to myself. I'm not willing to let her suck me dry. I could've just left all my shit with Santana if I were going to let her overspend the money I risked my fucking freedom for. I trust her to a certain extent. But with my dough, that's where I draw the line. Instead, I stashed my shit. My mama is one of the few people with access to it, as well as my best friend, who is more like a brother, Drip.

After finally coming to terms with her hanging up on me, I hung up the phone and put my forehead to the receiver, thinking. I closed my eyes. I had to get in contact with my nigga Drip. Since Santana had too much pride to go ask ma dukes for some money, I figured I would ask my bro to drop it off to her.

Sitting up, I turned to see if I could sneak in another phone call. The line was long as fuck. Still, I picked up the receiver and put the phone to my ear. Before I could dial Drip's phone number, I felt a mufucka breathing hard as fuck on my neck.

"Nigga, hurry the fuck up," a big, burly-ass nigga said into my ear.

I frowned, caught off guard, ready to shoot the fair one with this nigga. I'm not with all that gay shit, and dude was too close up on me. Now, usually, I'm with the shits, but when I turned to see who I was seconds away from manhandling, I realized who the nigga was. We both laughed and bumped fists.

"Damn, nigga. First of all, give me a few feet. You almost got these lethal mufuckas put on you," I said, showing him my fists while laughing and shaking my head.

"Yeah, a'ight," my nigga," Big Block said while laughing. "You lucky it was only me and not one of these other niggas. You know how they treat you light-skinned niggas up in here."

"Man, that's the last thing I'm worried about." I turned and began pressing buttons on the phone.

I met Big Block on the bus while we were being processed for transport to the prison. Me and that nigga had a lot in common. We were both known for running the cities we are from. Big Block is from New York, and just like me, he is serving twenty years. Our crimes are a little different. In my opinion, the nigga shouldn't even be sitting this bitch. The nigga drove all the way to Chicago to handle his sister's boyfriend. Finding out she was in the hospital because her boyfriend shot her caused Big Block to react off emotion. That shit should've never cost him his freedom, though. He got jammed up after the boyfriend was found with a gunshot wound in both hands and clinging to life. Big Block had beaten him to a pulp. I guess the judge wanted to make an example out of him. So, they charged him with assault and attempted murder. In this bitch, Big Block got my back, and I got his. We don't share cells or no shit like that, but when we have rec and free time, we kick it. I can't wait until we both get outta here and can kick it for real. I've always been curious to know what the Big Apple is all about. But I knew that shit wasn't coming anytime soon.

"Yo, son, Santana gon' be the death of you," he said, shaking his head at me, already knowing what my issue was. Like I said, this shit was the norm every time I talked to her. He folded his arms across his chest like a disappointed father. The nigga was like six foot and six inches tall, about six inches taller than me. He stood there looking like a damn bodyguard.

"I know." Sighing, I put my forearm up to the phone as the automated system told me to announce myself. I followed the prompts, and a few seconds later, Drip accepted my call.

"What's good, Jo?" Drip said.

"Shit, I can't call it. A nigga in a bind, though," I said. I was pressed for time with this call, so I had to skip all the formalities and get to the point. "I need a favor, bro."

"What's going on, G?" he asked with a hint of worry in his voice.

Darren Lewis, a.k.a. Drip, has been my nigga since the sandbox. Me and that nigga been through life together. From robberies to standing on the block selling weed and climbing our way to the top in the game. Now, he's running everything. Drip is holding shit down until I get out of the joint.

Me and Drip were actually together the night I was locked up. We had just come back from meeting up with our connect. Typically, we would ride together to re-up, but something about that day didn't feel right. It was my idea for us to take separate cars. It's as if I thought the bullshit into existence. It was also my idea to leave half the drugs in the car with me. As soon as we hit the highway, I saw lights flashing behind me. The shit was crazy. I didn't even put up a chase or nothing. I pulled over, hoping it was only a routine traffic stop. However, I was immediately forced out of my car and onto the ground. It took less than a minute for the police to locate all the drugs I had, not to mention the loaded nine hidden between the driver's seat and the armrest. I knew my ass was cooked. I just prayed Drip made it back to the Chi with the rest of the product. And he did. I took the wrap for everything. Now, here I am on the phone, asking another nigga to drop some money off to my woman.

"I need you to drop a few thousand off to Santana. You hear me? Shorty need that shit ASAP."

"Damn, G, you still fucking wit' ole girl?" Drip asked as if Santana were just any bitch off the street, and I frowned. I didn't question his question; I just let him finish his statement. "G, because you my nigga, I'm a let you know, shorty is foul. She been having all types of niggas picking her up and dropping her off at the building. Rich niggas driving all types of foreign whips."

"Nah, it ain't nothing like that. She's been using Uber and shit because her car is fucked up," I chimed in. I knew what Santana had been up to, but that was between me and her.

"Nigga, I ain't never seen an Uber driver tongue kiss a bitch as a form of payment."

"Fool, you trippin'. That wasn't my bitch you saw kissing another nigga," I said, but I knew Drip wasn't cappin'.

"Nigga, what I gotta lie for? Yo' girl out here bad, my G."

I chuckled slightly, not wanting to seem bothered. But the shit he was saying had me dying inside. Yet, what could I do? Feeling less than a man and dwelling on it was out of the question. I had no control over the shit Santana was doing. She was my woman, true enough, but I wanted to see her happy, even if that left me feeling like a damn fool. I just hung my head.

"Me and Santana got an understanding. You too involved in what she got going on. Just drop the money off to her." Man, I felt like a big-ass sucker, but I loved that damn girl too much not to help her out.

"G, you my mans a hundred grand. It's only right I look out for you. She ain't right, though, G, but I got you. I'll drop the money off in about an hour."

The entire time Drip talked, my heart raced. I knew how she was living. I didn't like it, but shit, I understood it.

"A'ight, G. I appreciate that."

"Marcel, G, you need to leave her scandalous ass alone. She ain't shit, bro. You need to do your time in peace. I'm a have to hook you up with a good girl."

"Nah, man. I'm good on that," I said, knowing it was time to let her go, but I couldn't help my feelings for her. At this point, I knew how bitches with low self-esteem felt. I would rather take half of her because that was better than not having her at all. When we are good, things are beautiful. Even when it's bad, she makes sure my books are straight.

"I'm not tryin'a hear that shit, G," Drip said, laughing. "Santana is a ho; ain't no way around it. I'm hooking you up."

"Yeah, OK," I said, hanging up. Just like with my mother, Santana and Drip didn't get along. They never have. That nigga couldn't wait to rub that damn rumor in my face. Goofy ass. That's my G, though.

Chapter 3

Sexy li'l bitch, sexy li'l ho
I love the way you walk, love the way you talk . . .

I jumped up outta my sleep and looked over to my left at the clock sitting on my nightstand. Feeling around for my ringing phone to turn off the alarm, I yawned and hummed along with the song. "Throat Baby" by BRS Kash was my shit.

After that argument I had with Marcel earlier, I couldn't function. I had to take a nap just to rejuvenate myself. I needed to rest my mind and start all over again because ain't no fucking way in hell a nigga that's locked up for twenty years is gonna have control over my mood. He may have been the best dick I'd ever had, but that dick no longer belonged to me.

My body was dripping wet from perspiring in my sleep, and I knew my body probably smelled sour as hell too. I wiped the sweat from underneath my neck and between my breasts before swinging the covers from my legs.

Knock! Knock! Knock!

I jumped and grabbed at my chest as the knocking got louder.

Bam! Bam! Bam!

Rolling my eyes, I took a deep breath. Who the hell was disturbing my peace and banging on my door like they were crazy? Almost made a bitch piss on herself.

"Bitch!" I yelled. "Stop knocking on my fucking door!"

Dressed in a silk nightgown, drenched in sweat, I stood up and took giant steps, rushing from my bedroom and into the hallway. Although I lived in the projects, and I was the only person on my lease, Marcel was able to get me a four-bedroom, two-bathroom apartment. So, the interior of these white-painted, gold-speckled brick walls was huge, and the front door seemed so far away.

"Wait a minute, dammit!" I seethed. My attitude was on a hundred. I hated when mothafuckas banged on my door as if they contributed to my rent. This had better be a damn emergency. *Somebody better be dead or half dead,* I thought.

Approaching the door, I heard a nigga's voice calling out my name, sounding just like Marcel's messy-ass best friend, Drip. He was a fucking lame, but the hoes loved him. I mean, he wasn't ugly. He was handsome. He was just an asshole, and I hated his ass. I looked through the peephole and saw his goofy-ass face. Now, this is one nigga I could not stand. He was one of Marcel's flunkies, another one of his messenger boys who was always in my business with his snitching ass. I had my reservations about him. I had a feeling he was the motherfucka who tipped off the police and set up Marcel. It was too much of a coincidence for me. I just had no way to prove it. Even with that being said, I didn't want to come in between Marcel and Drip's fake-ass friendship.

"Santana, open the door, man," he said, yelling like he was my nigga. I put the chain latch on my door and unlocked it. Twisting the knob, I cracked the door open slightly and peeped outside at him. He was not welcomed into my home.

"May I help you?" I asked, looking at Drip with a scowl on my face. The sight of him disgusted me. "Stupid ass," I whispered.

"Stupid?" he retorted, with his dumb-ass nostrils flaring. I pursed my lips, cocked my head to the side, and raised one brow. I wanted to laugh. I was a little embarrassed because I didn't think he would hear me.

"Yeah, stupid. Did I stutter?" I asked.

"I'm not even here to argue with you, G," he said. That nigga hated my guts too, so I was surprised when he didn't have a comeback.

"I know you're not. Punk ass, what are you here for? To run back and tell Marcel some more shit? How about I tell him you was tryin'a fuck me back in the day?" I asked with a slight smirk on my face.

"Man, I ain't never tried to fuck you. Lying, goofy ass," he replied, but he was lying through his fucking teeth.

Before I met Marcel, Drip stepped to me. He tried to spit his little game but came up short. His game wasn't wack, wack because I almost fell for it until he told me his name. Nigga, who the fuck names themselves some dumb-ass shit like Drip? Shit sounded like a venereal disease. Although he's a cutie, I just couldn't get past his stupid-ass name.

"Whatever, Drip Drop," I said, laughing at my own joke. "What the fuck do you want?" I still had the door slightly ajar.

Drip sucked his teeth and said, "Drip Drop . . . You got jokes, I see."

"I mean, I do what I can, when I can." I shrugged, still wiping sweat from my body.

"Fuck all that, Santana. Be nice for once in your life and let me in," he said.

"I think the fuck not. I can hear you just fine from here. What's up?" I asked, looking at him with one raised brow. I was not playing with his ass.

"Here, man," he said, reaching into his pocket. I watched as he pulled a rubber-banded bankroll out and peeled off a stack of one-hundred-dollar bills. "I don't like you for my nigga, Marcel," he said, looking down into his palm as he pulled the bills from his rubber band. "But he insisted on you having this li'l paper."

I saw the bills in his hands and beamed. My whole mood instantly changed. I was happier than a gay man in Boystown. Now, although I was done with Marcel, I wasn't going to turn down his money. Bitch, I was born at night, not last night. I didn't give a damn how much he pissed me off earlier.

"Give me a second. I need to get decent."

"Cool. Hurry up," he said.

My lip curled up on the left side. "Hurry up, my ass." He wasn't the boss of me, but for that green, at that moment, I would let him say what the fuck he wanted to say to me. He could call me a filthy bitch if he wanted to.

Shit, it was Friday Jr., almost time to live a little, and I needed to go shopping. I closed the door and ran to my bedroom to retrieve my robe. Quickly racing back to the door, I removed the latch. I was now willing to be cordial with Drip. Opening the door, I stood there in my cute little silk pajamas and robe, smiling, inviting Drip inside.

"Just like a money-hungry bitch. I bet that's all it takes to fuck too," he said, and I chuckled slightly. I wasn't impressed at all by his sarcasm. Nor was I gonna argue. He was right. That was all it took to fuck me, but he would never get the pleasure of finding out that shit for himself.

"Drip Drop, you don't have enough money to fuck me, baby. Just ask Marcel," I replied, giving him something to run back and tell his jailbird-ass friend. "Nothing in your pockets can afford a bitch like me, but that was cute." I pinched his cheek. He pushed my arm, and I held my hand out, awaiting my money.

"Thot ass," he scowled as I displayed a half-lip smirk.

"If I'm a thot, you'll never experience it." I snaked my neck and winked my eye. "I curve little drug dealers like yourself daily. Y'all ain't got shit I want. Marcel was an exception, but I didn't know any better back then."

"And you ain't got shit I want. Disrespectful ass."

"Yeah, yeah, whatever, nigga. Just give me my money, and you can leave. I got a long night of whoring ahead of me." I smiled. I knew his telling ass was about to run back to Marcel and tell him everything I said, but I wasn't scared of that nigga.

"Hooker," he said as he placed the money into my hand.

"Your nigga loves this hooker, though." I looked him up and down while smirking. He shook his head, and I shrugged my shoulders. "Thank you for the funds, Drip Drop. I didn't even have to fuck for this. You're the best," I said, laughing. It was time for him to go, and it was time for Meka and me to get out in these streets. Drip looked at me, and his facial expression was disgusted.

"You a mufuckin' disgrace, shorty," he said before opening the door and leaving.

Oh well, don't judge me; judge yo' baldhead, dead-ass mama.

Once Drip left, I slammed the door. Instantly, I began flipping through the hundred-dollar bills. It all added up to $5,000. This money wasn't going to get me too far, but it had to suffice.

Chapter 4

"Head fire, pussy good, and plus, I stay wet.
Just fuck me earlier in the morning, baby, that's the best.

I turned my radio up to the max as Trina's voice crooned "I Got a Problem" through the speakers. The bass from the beat was so loud that my living room walls shook. I had to agree with Trina. I honestly had a problem—a hood chick with a bad attitude and a bad body to go with it. Not to mention, I used everything I possessed to get what I wanted. By no means was any other woman fucking with me on any level besides my best friend Santana, but there was no competition between us. Santana and I were two bad bitches who fucked hoes up mentally whenever we stepped on the scene.

After losing my virginity at the young tender age of 9 to an older boy while playing boys chase the girls in the projects, I quickly began to develop ass, titties, and a huge sexual appetite. I honestly think I'm addicted to sex, and I know for a fact that fast money is my number one obsession. Sex and money just went hand in hand. I guess you can call it prostitution because I personally never left a man's hotel room or home with just a wet ass. Nah, these niggas had to pay to play. Nowadays, women like me aren't standing on corners looking for our next come-up. The internet and knowing niggas with dough were definitely booming in my line of business.

For years now, my cousin's friend Drip had been one of the niggas who tricked off with me. He kept my pussy content and my pockets happy. Still, his time was dedicated to the streets, not me. Nevertheless, we made sure to keep our dealings on the low. Although Marcel was in jail, I knew he would trip if he found out about us. I knew Santana wouldn't approve either because she and Drip couldn't stand each other. I never got the backstory on why, nor do I care to know.

Often, we would dip off to Calumet City, a suburb south of Chicago, to a nice hotel and have sex all day long. We never made love, though. Afterward, we would just lie up. With my head resting on his chest and his fingers roaming freely through my hair, we would talk about life. I might've slipped up a few times and told Drip about the shit Santana and I were getting into, but I wasn't on no shady shit. I just felt so comfortable talking to him when we were alone. Some people call that pillow talking, but that was only after he would confide in me.

"Meka," he would say. His saying my name in a low tone was how most of our conversations started off.

"Yes, Darren?" I would reply with my head still on his chest, listening to the beat of his heart, which always seemed to speed up its pace as if he were nervous to expose his deepest thoughts.

"Have you ever thought about leaving Chicago? Not on no vacation type of shit, but leaving and starting a brand-new life somewhere else? Like Africa or some shit where no one from your past can find you?"

"I can't say that I have. I love my city, and I love the money I make here. Picking up and moving would be too much for me. Especially moving to a foreign country where I don't know shit about the culture."

"I love my city too, but I honestly feel like I have nothing left here. My best homie is locked up for twenty years, and

I feel responsible. That could've easily been me. I just feel like death or jail is near as fuck. I'm tired of looking over my shoulders, wondering if a nigga gon' kill me behind some shit I may or may not have done. Marcel shouldn't even be in jail, bro." He sighed.

"What does that even mean? What have you done, Drip?" I would sit up, place my hand on his chest, and look him in his eyes. He was so hard to read, but his words always sounded as if he had something to do with my cousin's unfortunate luck.

"Nothing, man." He would grab my chin and peck my lips. That was all it took for me to shut up and mind my own business.

This was like a constant conversation, though. He was clearly harboring a lot. He would tell me about how he wanted to leave the drug game alone and how often he dreamed about his life coming to an end behind his street shit. I would always sit and listen without judgment. However, I would try to motivate him to do something different with his life. He was a good man, but his mentality was hood as fuck. And after Marcel was locked up, he became paranoid. Imagine that . . . A paranoid nigga with a gun on his hip. Together, we came up with ideas and ways for him to maintain a steady income while he slowly pulled away from the streets, although he wasn't entirely out of the streets. A new career as a party promoter definitely afforded him a great lifestyle, and I was here for it, considering he was partially responsible for keeping my lifestyle in order.

Drip was my one and only usual big spender, plus, our time together was always beautiful. No, we weren't boyfriend and girlfriend, but you couldn't tell us that, especially when we were alone. He didn't have a girl, and I didn't have a guy, but we knew a real relationship between us wouldn't be right. Drip was too deep into his business ventures, and I was too young to settle down. So, we never tried to push the issue. I wasn't done living my life. I wasn't built like Santana. I didn't know how to be tied down to one man, especially if he gets permanently displaced from my life. I would have to find ways to cope. Nah, fuck that.

The music from my cell phone silenced, and my ringtone began to blare through the speakers. I ran over to my phone and saw Drip's name on the caller ID. I smiled; it was almost as if we were spiritually connected. He always seemed to call me whenever I was thinking about him.

"Yo," he said as soon as I picked up. His voice was so deep and laid-back. He sounded like he was driving. From the way the wind blew through the phone, I could tell he was driving at top speed with his windows down, possibly on his way to some money.

"Yo," I replied softly. "You tryin'a spend some money today?" I asked with a slight smirk on my face.

"Damn, you don't waste no time, I see."

"Why would I? I know what you want, and you got what I need. Why play games?" I replied slyly.

"Is that right? That's crazy because I thought we were friends," he said, chuckling.

"Yeah, we're friends. Still, I know when you want some of this coochie, my love. I'm sure I'm not the only girl you're fuckin', just like you know you're not the only man I'm fuckin', but you're the only man I come back to consistently."

"You a fool, Meka." He chuckled nervously as I waited to get an honest reaction. I wanted to know how this man really felt about me. Did my saying I fuck other men strike a nerve? "I just came from dropping a little paper off to Santana." He went around the subject. Drip was from the streets, so I guess he wasn't going to tell me if I hurt his feelings or not. He continued. "She gave Marcel some li'l sorry-ass story about her car breaking down and shit."

"OK, and? Her car did break down," I said, going along with my friend's lie.

"I know that scandalous-ass ho a prostitute. She should have money to pay to get her own shit fixed. I don't like the way she's playing my nigga."

"Prostitute?" I asked, my voice in a surprising, questioning tone. Because if he thought that way about *her,* how did he honestly feel about *me?* Santana and I lived the exact same life, with the exception of being in a relationship. I was single and able to do me. Drip was paying me for my time and sex. I knew in the back of his mind he judged me too. Although I would've kicked it with him without the money, that still didn't negate the facts of the matter.

"You know what I mean."

"No, I don't know what you mean."

"Shorty think she slick, man. Marcel locked up, and she still finds ways to get financed by him. I'm not fuckin' her, so at this point, I'm done handing her money."

"Are you mad?" I asked because he sounded pissed the fuck off. "Sometimes, I swear you do too much, especially when it comes to my friend. Tell me something, Drip, what's the beef?"

"I'm cool, Meka. There is no beef. Santana is a ho, and Marcel deserves better. He needs a bitch who's gonna do that bid with him with her pussy closed, not leeching off him while he goin' through it. That bitch probably would've fucked me for that little-ass paper if I told her to."

"Marcel is my cousin, but he's also a grown-ass man. He knows everything Santana does, trust me. Between you and my auntie telling him all the negative shit she's doing,

I know Marcel be ready to break up outta that bitch and harm my friend. You be worried about the wrong shit. Sometimes you make me feel like you'd rather fuck with her."

"Never that! Man, Meka, I don't like shorty. I'm just stating facts," he said, and I sighed.

"She's a money-hungry, scandalous bitch. All the bull-shit she was saying when I dropped that money off . . . Shorty was *definitely* ready to fuck."

"Please let Marcel run his own relationship. You and my auntie keep running back telling him about Santana is only fuckin' with his mind. Just change the subject. Let's talk about us."

"What about us?" he asked. Drip just didn't know I ran the same game on niggas as Santana. So, cousin or not, I couldn't knock her.

"You haven't been over in a while. I know you miss this pussy," I said, but fucking Drip right now was the furthest thing from my mind. His words were a turn-off. I was tired of him talking shit about my best friend.

He told me to hold on while he answered his other line, and I said OK. I took the phone from my ear and put it on speaker. Then I clicked on my Instagram app and scrolled through. I hearted a few pictures and dropped a few fire emojis as I waited for him to click back over. As I scrolled, I saw that there was going to be a block party out west the following night, and I was down for whatever. I pulled up Santana's name in my text messages and typed in the location along with big dick baller alert, lol.

Santana: Aye! Aye! Aye! I'm wit' it. Let me go ahead and get my outfit together.

Meka: Yes, bitch, do that because we're out in these streets tomorrow.

"What color panties you got on?" Drip's voice boomed.

"Huh?" I was so focused on my conversation with Santana that I forgot all about him.

"If you can *huh,* you can hear, baldhead-ass girl. What color panties you got on?" I swear if shit were different, Drip and I would be in love, living the American dream.

Nonetheless, I wouldn't be true to myself if I didn't ask, "What color money do you have in your pockets?"

"All big blue faces, shorty."

"What a coincidence. My panties are the same exact color. How about we do an even exchange?"

"A'ight, I'm on my way."

Chapter 5

Santana

The following evening . . .

It was a perfect Friday night, right in the middle of summertime Chi. The sky was dark blue, the breeze was just right, and I had on a cute little Prada dress that I picked up from Swap-O-Rama flea market. Before leaving home, I checked my reflection in the mirror a thousand times and took a bunch of pictures. I was sexy as fuck, and my dress made my ass look gigantic. Tonight, Meka and I were on our way to a block party on the West Side. We were two girls from the South Side, the Englewood neighborhood to be exact, but somehow, social media had a way of forcing us out west, out of our element, where we had to be on constant guard because the West Side girls hated the South Side chicks and vice versa. But that was where all the big dick ballers were, so we weren't beefing. When it came to the nightlife, me and my girl played no games. And when it came to these niggas, Meka and I were cold at running game. Tonight was no different.

First, I had to stop at the liquor store to prepare myself for a long night in whatever direction the wind blew us. I was ready to pull an all-nighter. There was no better way to enjoy the evening. It was hot as fuck outside, so I knew we would definitely end up on somebody's block, in somebody's hood. Let the shenanigans begin.

I pulled up to the corner store and parked right in front, only turning my radio down several notches because Jazmine Sullivan's song "Bodies" was an entire fuckin' vibe. Before Marcel went to jail, I was a good girl with ho tendencies. Now that he was no longer around, I had all the time in the world to explore it. Although I catered to Marcel and only him, in the back of my mind, I always wondered what it would feel like to have a different man inside me every other night. And when I finally stepped out and fucked another man, I liked it. Hell, I *loved* it. Plus, the money was well worth it.

Before killing the engine and stepping out, I checked myself out in the mirror just to make sure my mink lashes, makeup, and nude lip stain were just right. Seeing all the small-time hustlers on the corner, I couldn't step out of my whip looking anything less than a bad bitch. Turning the interior light on inside my car, I recorded a quick Snapchat video of myself. From my mufuckin' face, I cocked my head to the side and trailed down my body, rolling my upper torso as I made my way down, showing off my cute outfit. I looked so fye. That little lie I made up about my car being fucked up earned me an easy five grand, and with that money, a bitch had to stunt a little. The Prada dress I bought from the flea market didn't look too counterfeit; it had me looking the part. It was a tube top dress that flared out into a tennis skirt at the bottom, which stopped right below my ass. My feet adorned a pair of authentic Prada slides.

"Santana, what's going on, love?" I heard as soon as I opened my car door and stepped out. My Benz was all black, and I had just gotten a car wash earlier that day, so my baby looked just as good as I did.

"Hey, baby, how you doin?" I greeted, slamming my door. I raised one brow and kept it moving. I really didn't give a damn about him or how he was doing. I was just a polite bitch. If I can be honest, I didn't even know who the kid was.

There was a group of guys standing on the corner shooting dice, looking like the typical hoodlums. So, I made sure to secure my purse, tightly clutching it in my hand. Back in the day, I was the bitch every dope boy was checking for, but after Marcel stamped his name on me, niggas became timid. Back then, seeing a group of hustlers congregating on the corner would make my coochie get wet, no lie. Nowadays, seeing so many over-grown-ass niggas with no future ahead of them, the shit just disgusted me. Still, I smiled and flipped my long, silk, pressed hair to the back, knowing all the men were staring at me as I swished my fine, thick ass toward the corner store's door.

I admit, I was so out of their league. Yes, I'm conceited, and I'm sure it was apparent. Their thirsty "let me holla" antics didn't move me. Plus, they knew not to fuck with me, considering who my man was. So, they would try to look at me discreetly. They for sure weren't my type. They were corner boys for a reason. Simply put, they couldn't afford me. I heard a "What's up, Santana?" and "What's good, shorty?" from some of the guys. Still, they knew I wasn't about to give them any play. I continued walking until I reached the door. I put my hand to the handle, attempting to walk inside, but I was suddenly caught off guard.

"What's good, li'l lady?" a deep, sexy voice said.

Now *that* was a grown-ass, mature voice. I stopped right in my tracks and turned around. He didn't have a Chicago accent, so I knew he wasn't from here. If anything, he was from the suburbs. I don't recall ever hearing his voice before, so I needed to see if his face matched his deep baritone. I looked from man to man, trying to see who this coochie whisperer was because the command of his voice almost instantly drenched my panties. He wasn't hard to separate from the rest, seeing as though he was one of the guys who stood off to the side watching the dice game instead of playing. He looked at me seductively. He had the biggest smile on his face, which made me blush slightly. I looked him up and down, taking a mental note of him, programming his entire being into my memory, from his complexion to his height, and especially his body build.

I couldn't front, he was fine as hell, but I wasn't into his type. A nickel-and-dime hustler who stood on the corner all damn day with no real money in his pockets and no future ahead of him. Still living with his mama or faking the funk with a bitch he didn't really want to be with just to have a roof over his head. Yes, I was able to create my own biased opinion about him that quickly. I absolutely hated his type. A cute face but dressed like a fucking thug. What a waste. I bet his pockets had nothing but lint in them.

His baggy shorts, wife beater, and Chicago Cubs jersey made him look so ghetto and broke. Cute or not, his appearance was too immature for me. So, I knew his pockets were sitting on Enfamil, meaning, I knew his cash was baby as fuck. His skin was to die for. He was so chocolate and dark that he almost blended in with the night's sky. His lips had the perfect tint of dark brown, and his teeth, God, his teeth were so white. If this were back in the day, he would've definitely been mine. He wore a fitted cap on his head that was conveniently pulled down low, covering his eyes slightly so that I couldn't see his entire face.

I smiled at him, licked my bottom lip, and pulled the store's door open. I had no words for him. Imagine me going from a nigga who provided me the world to a guy who couldn't even afford my twenty-four-dollar rent.

"Aye, where you goin', li'l lady?" I heard him, but I didn't respond. I just kept it moving. This wasn't that.

I could easily fall in love with another trap nigga because I happen to know that no other nigga does it better. However, they can't give me everything I want. I was already dealing with a damn jailbird. In a perfect world, Marcel would still be out here with me. He was from the streets and a hopeless romantic—all the things my heart desired. But nah, this isn't a perfect world, and I wasn't willing to replace my ex-love with Mr. Blue Black, even though he was fine as hell.

As soon as I entered the store, my cell phone began to ring. I looked down at it and smiled, knowingly. I flipped my long hair to the back, walking over to the freezers.

"Hello," I answered, and waited for Meka's response. Opening the freezer door, I grabbed a sixteen-ounce bottle of lemonade.

"Santana? Did I just see you walk inside Pop's store?" she asked.

"Yeah, that was me. I had to come get me a bottle of Don Julio before we headed out west. Where the hell are you?" I asked, looking behind me.

"Bitch, I just rode past. Me and my li'l friend."

"Your li'l friend?" I asked. "Who's the bitch? Because my friend ain't never got no other friend that I don't know about," I said, walking over to the counter.

"Girl, calm down," she said, giggling. "You know him, but we'll talk about that at another time."

"Hiiiim?" I questioned, frowning, doing my best Soulja Boy impression. I placed my juice on top of the counter and asked the clerk for a fifth of Don Julio.

"Girl, you are so dramatic. Just meet me back at my crib when you're done."

"Yeah, yeah. That's fine, boo. I'll be pulling up in about five minutes." I disconnected the call, looked at the cashier, and smiled.

Pop's store had always been my favorite store since I was a shorty. The owner, Pops, pretty much helped raise all the kids in the neighborhood. Especially those of us without our real fathers at home. He provided a warm, welcoming environment, along with guidance some of us kids needed. Nowadays, his son Josh was running things. He was just as welcoming as his father.

"What's up, Santana?"

"Hey, Joshua." I put my hands on the counter, looking at him with a massive smile on my face. Now, *he* was definitely my type. I knew this nigga had money, and he was making his shit in a legitimate way. Our only issue would be his family accepting a Black chick from the hood being in a relationship with their Arabic, suburban son. He spent so much time in the store and in the neighborhood that he spoke more Ebonics than me.

"How has Pops been?" I asked as he began ringing up my items.

"He's been OK. Him and my moms been traveling, seeing the world."

"That's what's up, Josh. When you talk to him, tell him I said, 'Hey,' and to come visit us soon." I had never met his mother before, but his father, Pops, was my nigga.

"All right, I got you, Santana. I'll let him know."

"So, what's my damage?" I asked, referring to the price of my drink. I bit the side of my bottom lip. Whew! This man could definitely get it.

Josh looked at me and smirked. He placed my bottle of tequila, along with my lemonade, in a bag. He also placed two plastic cups inside and read off the dollar amount.

"That'll be sixty dollars."

"Damn, y'all taxing shit around here," I said, but still pulled the three twenties from my purse. I started to hand the money over to Josh, but the voice behind me stopped me midreach.

"Aye, my mans, ring this up with whatever she has. I'm paying for everything," he said, reaching over my shoulder while placing a bottle of ginger ale on the countertop. "My bad for reaching over you." His tone was low.

"Yeah, that is your bad."

I turned to look at him and frowned. I guess I looked like a forty-dollar ho to him. Well, sixty dollars because that's how much my total was.

"I don't need you to pay for my shit. I got it. Keep your little dollars in your pocket," I said. I reached into my purse and grabbed a few more dollars. I handed them to Josh along with my sixty dollars. "Here you go, babes, and don't forget to tell Pops what I said."

Looking at dude again, I handed him his ginger ale and left the store.

A few minutes later, I was pulling up and parking in front of Meka's house. As I did in front of the store, I flipped my mirror down and checked my reflection.

"Cute," I said, puckering my lips together, and blowing myself a kiss.

I was ready for the night. I was ready to pull me a guy with a little bit of money. My pockets weren't in dire need, but honestly, that little four stacks I had left over from Marcel's generosity weren't going to last long.

I flipped my mirror back up and pulled a plastic cup from the bag. Blessing the bottle with a quick gang sign that I knew absolutely nothing about, I peeled off the transparent film and opened the top. The subtle aroma of tequila hit my nose. I took a deep breath, breathing it all in, feeling my body loosen up a little. I was about to get fucked up. I poured myself a cup with a swallow of lemonade juice inside. Putting the cup to my lips, I took a sip and frowned as the hot-ass liquor made its way down my throat.

"Aaahh!" I screamed and choked. This shit needed some fucking ice. I should've told that nigga to give me a bottle from the fridge.

I sighed and called Meka's phone. As it rang, I sat there still holding my throat, mad as hell. Her phone made me even more upset as it rang and rang until her voicemail finally picked up.

"If you a broke nigga, you know what to do. Hang the fuck up because, nine times out of ten, I've already blocked you. *Beep*."

"Bitch, come the fuck on and bring some ice with you." I laughed and rolled my eyes before hanging up.

Meka's ass was something else. I sat in the car for ten more minutes before I decided to get out and walk up to her front door. My lazy ass really didn't feel like it, but she was taking too long, and I was ready to drink and bullshit. When she called me earlier, she knew I was on my way to her house. As a matter of fact, she knew I was right up the street. I gathered my things and picked up my plastic cup. Opening the door and stepping out, I fixed my dress and sauntered up to the front door. I twisted the doorknob and walked inside. I was on the verge of calling Meka's name until I walked into the kitchen and saw Drip's punk ass standing between her legs while she sat on top of the counter, letting him kiss all over her neck.

"Meka!" I yelled, and she screamed as he jumped and turned to look at me. "I can't believe you're fucking the help, bitch," I said. My face had the ugliest grimace on it.

"Man, help these nuts," he spat.

"Very original, Drip Drop," I returned the sarcasm. "Ugh, Meka, I think I'ma be sick." I put the hand that held my liquor to my mouth and my free hand to my stomach.

"Bitch, what the fuck are you even doing in here?" she asked, hopping off the countertop. She began fixing her clothes as Drip stood there against the counter with a big-ass smirk on his face.

"Yeah, what yo' trick ass doing here? How much pussy you sellin' tonight?"

I stood there looking dumb as fuck. Why does his punk ass know my business?

"I like your li'l fake-ass, cheap-ass Prada outfit. That mufucka look cheesy as hell," he said, laughing.

"Boy, fuck you," I countered.

"OK, y'all, that's enough," Meka yelled.

"Oh nah, don't do that, Meka. You let him talk his shit, then want to cut me off? You already know I was about to get right into it with his ass."

"Man, yo' bucket-head ass wasn't finna do shit."

"You dusty-ass, dry-ass nigga. Meka, get rid of the help, please, and thank you."

"Hooker—" he began.

"Darren," Meka cut in, turning to him, stopping a brewing argument. "Thanks for bringing me home. I appreciate it."

"No problem." He stood from the sink, kissed Meka on her neck, and walked out. I followed him with my eyes. I mean, I turned my head and body to watch as he made his exit.

"Um, Meka, what was that about?"

"Nothing, Santana."

"Nothing? Bitch, I'm not stupid. You fuckin' that corn-ball-ass nigga?"

"Santana." She cut her eyes at me as she walked past me. "I have to get ready."

"I thought we were besties? I thought we told each other everything?" I asked, following closely behind her. "Your sneaky, pussy-having ass."

"Whatever, bitch," she laughed. "We *are* besties, and we *do* tell each other everything, but Darren is not up for discussion. Let's talk about getting some money from these niggas instead," she told me with a serious look on her face. I took that as my cue to leave that conversation where it was.

Chapter 6

Meka

I looked over at Drip and smiled. He was so sexy with his usual, serious expression. I never thought in a million years my heart could feel anything other than lust for a man. I never knew I could feel like I'm floating high in the sky, and a man would be the reason behind it.

We had just made it back to the city after spending the entire day cooped up in the Sibley Suites Hotel. That day, all we did was talk and fuck, never giving each other a break. Now, that right there was all it took to form a spiritual connection. Whenever Drip and I were together, he pleased my mind and body; my soul was just a casualty. I had the feeling Drip wanted to be more than just fuck buddies, but he didn't know how to approach the conversation, and I was going to stay far away from the thought. I had no real reason for not wanting to be in a relationship besides money, and the way I made my money was by fucking different men. Plus, I was still young, too young to settle down.

Nevertheless, Drip had it all, and he had the means to make me reevaluate my life. But I would be lying if I said I was ready to be exclusive. Plus, I didn't want to dedicate my life to a drug dealer and end up like Santana. After years of building a relationship, at the snap of a finger, his ass gets locked up, or I'm grieving over his dead body. It would be just my luck.

As we exited the expressway and on Forty-Seventh Street, the sun was beginning to settle. I could've stayed wrapped up under Drip all day and night, but what real bitch spends her summer nights caking with a man? I watched him smoothly nod his head to Lil Durk's "Backdoor." He seemed to be in deep thought, as if the song brought back old emotions and memories. With one hand resting on the armrest and the other gripping the steering wheel, he watched the road, staring straight ahead, rapping the lyrics. It was as if he studied these lyrics for years. Drip knew the song verbatim, like he wrote it himself. He didn't miss a beat as he and Durk rapped about not being snaked by his homies. On some for real shit, he didn't have many homies besides my cousin Marcel, so that made me question what he was feeling.

"Drip," I said, turning my body in the seat so I was facing him. "Can I ask you a question?"

"What's up?" he said, taking his eyes off the road for a second to look at me.

"Is everything OK?"

"Yeah, I'm Gucci," he said, but I knew he was lying. I lifted his hand from the armrest and placed it in mine. He gripped my hand, and our fingers intertwined.

"You just seem a little troubled. Every time I'm around you, it feels like you have something you want to say, but never say it, and your energy at times is negative."

"Of course, I have troubles. I'm human. I'm a Black nigga in America. Name one man who ain't got some type of issue. I'm not a perfect person, but my troubles are nothing personal toward you."

"OK, babe," I simply said and sat back in my seat. I guess his point was valid. I didn't want to nag him or make him discuss his feelings with me, but I knew shit had to be deeper than he was letting on. I picked up my phone and silently wrote a status.

How can a man without guidance lead you, ladies? Never mind, don't answer that. The male species is something else.

I typed that shit with conviction. Nowadays, Drip was the topic of all my Facebook statuses. No one knew who I was talking about but me. I really needed to stay off social media. Next, I'll be talking about how I love him. I set my phone on my lap and stared as it came alive. Notifications from social media began to fill my locked screen with "So-and-so liked your post" and "So-and-so commented on your post." I didn't reply. I just cleared my screen and focused ahead, deciding I wouldn't log back in until Santana and I were outside.

As we drove down Forty-Seventh Street, I saw Santana exit her car and walk toward Pop's store. My bitch was looking real cute and spicy. Her "come freak me" dress was sexy.

"Drip, pull over," I said, overly excited to see her.

"Nah," he said, and I knew why. There was way too many niggas standing outside, and he would definitely be jealous if one of them tried to holla at me. I wasn't his woman, so he couldn't really get gangsta with them over me.

"What you mean, no? Santana just went into the store. Pull over."

"You and that bitch can link later." He was so disrespectful.

"Drip, don't talk about her like that. Whatever happened to you respecting your best friend's woman? Niggas don't do that anymore?" I asked him.

"Santana don't give a fuck about Marcel. I been told him to leave that bitch where she stood. She don't give a fuck about you either. Shiesty ass."

"Whatever."

I waved my hand and dialed Santana's number. She picked up on the first ring.

"Was that you who I just seen walk into Pop's store?" I asked.

"You know that was that gold-diggin'-ass bitch," Drip said in a low voice, and I hit his arm.

"Where the hell are you?"

When I said I was in the car with my li'l friend, Drip leaned over and bit the side of my face, which caused me to giggle. I can't believe I was able to keep this thing between Drip and me a secret for so long. We had been fooling around for about two years now. Still, I tried to keep our business out of the public eye.

Santana and I talked for a few seconds longer, and afterward, we hung up. I looked over at Drip and placed my hand on his thigh, rubbing him softly.

"You don't wanna unleash the beast, baby. So, cut it out."

I was silent. He knew I was ready to choke and slob on his dick. My head skills were the absolute beast. By the time we were pulling up in front of my house, I was kissing his earlobe, and my hand was down inside his pants, jacking him off. His dick was on Debo; that motherfucka was swoll and cocky as hell. His body jerked as his car came to an abrupt stop right in the middle of the street. He took a deep breath, and I laughed.

"Stop." He looked at me with bedroom eyes. The seductive look on his face forced a smirk on my face as I released him. "Let me park first, Meka. You gon' make me crash this mufucka." The way he said my name . . . *mmm*.

"OK, OK, I quit. Go ahead and park your li'l funky-ass car."

I sat back in my seat as he parked. After fitting in between two other cars, he climbed from the driver's side, walked around to my door, and opened it. Before I could step out, he grabbed me, picking me up in his arms. Drip wasn't a fat nigga, but he wasn't a skinny nigga either. His size was medium build, just right to handle my 150-pound, five-foot frame. He carried me inside the house and into the kitchen, kissing and sucking my neck on the way there.

"Drip, I need my light bill paid," I said, moaning, making sure he knew he had to come up off some type of cash. I never purposely tried to make him feel as though he was paying for the pussy, but shit, a closed mouth won't get fed.

"I got you," he replied as he continued to kiss me. "What else do you need paid?"

OK, now *that's* what the fuck I'm talking about.

"My rent." My words came out lustfully. "My car note, and I need some pocket money."

He sat me down on the countertop and pulled a few hundred from his pocket. Although he was still tonguing my neck down, I had my eyes on him and his pockets. Suddenly, he pulled back and placed the money he pulled from his pocket inside my bra.

"You don't have to wait until we about to fuck before you ask me for anything. I got you. You're my best friend's cousin. All the fucked-up shit I've done . . ." He shook his head. "I like you a lot, Meka. Shit, I'm starting to think I low-key love you."

"Thank you, daddy," I beamed. Fuck that love shit because love does not pay the bills. Wait a second! Did he just say all the fucked-up shit he's done? That statement did not go over my head; however, I didn't say anything. Whatever that meant, I'm sure he would tell me sooner or later. I grabbed his ears and pulled him closer. I began passionately kissing him on his lips as his hands roamed my body. I allowed it, moaning as if his dick were penetrating me, and we were hunching. His lips moved down to my neck effortlessly as my head fell back.

"Meka!" I heard Santana's squeaky-ass voice yell.

We were caught. I'll be damned if my little secret with Drip is no longer between us two. Fuck!

Chapter 7

Santana

These Chicago streets didn't owe me shit but a good time. Living life on the edge with no regrets was how I wanted my evening to turn out. I was prepared to get wasted and cheese all up in a couple of niggas' faces. This cute little outfit and beat face wasn't for nothing. Plus, Meka looked cute as well. With a pair of high-waisted white short shorts that made her booty cheeks hang out at the bottom, and a simple lavender bralette, my bitch was looking too sexy. She had a pair of all-white Jordan 1s on her feet, and her accessories were real silver. None of that fake costume jewelry shit, but real, authentic silver. We were just two thick chicks ready for some real action and attention from an out West nigga.

As the Chicago-style mixtape blared through somebody's car speakers, and LilReco rapped about dancing on a thick bitch from behind, Meka and I slow whined our bodies. We were both hype as hell. Not really in the mood to be juked from the back, but we were definitely ready to get shit popping.

After we reached the West Side and parked, we decided to walk around just to scope out the scene. We didn't really know anyone out there, but we were acquainted with a few faces from social media. Did I mention this was also Drip's neighborhood? Most times, people from Chicago didn't venture outside their respective hoods, but Meka and I had kicked it with Marcel and Drip out here on several occasions. So, I guess we were safe or whatever. Now that I knew about Meka and Drip, I decided I would fall back on the insults. She was my best friend, and I didn't want her to feel uncomfortable. I didn't want her to have to choose between the two of us. I knew nothing was serious between them, though. Meka was afraid to love. Still, I decided I would make amends with him. Even if that meant apologizing to him for whatever I may have done to rub him the wrong way.

We walked over to a huge green box that sat right in the middle of the grass up against a row house. My legs were beginning to hurt, and I was growing a little bored. So, we climbed to the top of it and sat down. By this time, we had already finished off our bottle of Don Julio. Now, we were left with half-full cups of liquor. We sat there watching the crowd, vibing out to the music. Cars full of bitches and niggas drove through, dancing and acting a fool, and we cheered them on. It was definitely a sight to see.

"So, bitch, is Drip up for discussion yet?" I asked before putting my liquor to my lips. I knew what her answer would be, but I just had to ask.

"Girl, that nigga," she said, smiling and blushing. If I didn't know any better, I'd think my friend was in love. "He's cool peeps."

"Cool peeps?" I laughed. "Cap, cap, cap, cap. The shit that I walked in on tonight, that man is more than just 'cool peeps.' And from that smile and those flushed cheeks, I know for a fact it's more than just a friendship."

"I mean, he's nice. He pays my bills, and we have sex sometimes, but that's it. There is nothing special about what we have going on." She was downplaying their situation, and I knew it. "He's like a job. He's a stable income." She put her cup to her lips and smiled.

"Girl," I pursed my lips together, "why are we chilling in his neighborhood? Are we out here to keep our eyes on him?"

"Hell no," she said, frowning. "He ain't even out here. He doesn't even know we're here."

"Oh, how do you know that? That nigga checked in or something?" I laughed. "Come on, tell your best friend the truth. I'm not mad at it. I'm actually happy for you because you're the one who's always been against love."

"Nothing has changed, boo. My heart is still cold as ice."

"Mmm-hmm, I just bet it is." Putting my cup to my lips, I drank the rest of my tequila. Now, I was feeling tipsy.

"Believe what you want." She Kanye-shrugged my ass. Just like a nigga that had been caught up in his bullshit, she ran that "Believe what you want" line on me.

"Well, look, I've drawn my own conclusion, so I won't keep questioning your lying ass. There's a whole lot of flashy niggas out here; let's move around."

"Exactly. That's the only reason we're here, for the flashy niggas," she said.

We climbed from the green box, tossed our cups in the grass, and began walking down the block. I felt like a superstar, and I'm almost sure Meka felt the same way. Camera flashes came from all directions. Everyone around us was taking pictures and going live on social media. My fans were reaching out for me. My hand was getting grabbed by almost every nigga I walked past. I was definitely in my zone.

"What's good, li'l mama?"

"Shorty, you thick as fuck."

"Sheesh, baby got a body."

Those are just some examples of the compliments Meka and I were getting as we maneuvered through the block. Of course, we stopped for a second or two to exchange phone numbers and have conversations. Nothing too deep, just long enough to know if they were worth our time. Every nigga out there looked as if they had money, apart from a few stragglers. The thing is, who was going to be willing to fuck off a few thousand on me? As we approached the end of the block, I knew I had my victim. He was a light-skinned man with a few tattoos on his face, a cross between his eyebrows, a few teardrops under his left eye, his gang affiliation under his right eye, and the year 1995 on his neck. I was a sucker for a man who was inked up. Not to mention, he was tall as hell. He reminded me of Marcel. Damn, I missed that nigga. He had a big-ass Kool-Aid smile on his face and a double Styrofoam cup in his hand as we walked toward him and his crew. It's as if he were silently commanding my body with his eyes, forcing my feet to approach him. Instantly, I was infatuated. I wanted him and whatever he was willing to offer.

It didn't help that he and his friends were leaned up against a sexy-ass, champagne Audi R8 Spyder. That mufuckin' drop-top had to run him at least eighty thousand. He didn't look like a leasing type of man. I was for certain he owned whatever he touched. And I was ready for him to do me dirty and own this li'l pussy all over those leather seats.

"Money make the coochie go *whoop, whoop*," I blurted out, and we both busted out laughing hard as hell.

"Bitch, who you telling? My coochie doing summersaults right now," Meka chimed in.

"You know what that mean. Money is near and dear. Miss Puss is excited."

"I heard that."

We approached the guys, and I wasted no time walking up to him as if I knew him, while one of his friends greeted Meka. I smiled widely. He smelled just as yummy as he looked. The blue jean shorts he had on sagged off his ass a little. At the same time, they were fitted, making it apparent when he stepped outside that everything on his body had to coordinate. His underwear was Gucci, his shirt was a cream-colored V-neck with the word Gucci stamped on the front of it big as hell, along with the cream-colored Gucci sneakers on his feet. I loved niggas like him. The type that needed the entire world to know what he was holding.

I confidently took his cup from his hand. I was trying to see how far he would let me go. I put the cup to my lips, expecting him to cuss me out, but he didn't. He just watched as I stuck my tongue out. The entire time, I gazed at him. Licking the rim of his cup before taking a sip, he was now looking at me, confused. I was a nasty bitch, and I don't apologize for it. He tapped his friend's chest as he laughed.

"Here," I said as I handed his cup back to him. I don't know what the fuck he was drinking, but that shit was disgusting.

"Maaaan," his friend said. "Shorty done stuck her whole tongue in yo' cup, bro, and you gon' drink that shit? What the fuck type of weird, freaky-ass shit bitches be on nowadays?" I didn't say anything. I kept a straight face as I continued looking at my prey. His friend's words didn't make me no never mind. I wasn't concerned with how he felt.

"Santana," Meka said with her mouth wide open. She busted out laughing, which then caused me to smirk. "That's my best friend," she said proudly.

"Damn, love, what's to you?" he finally asked.

"Honestly, I'm not into beating around the bush. You want me, or no?" I asked, smiling. One thing about me. I went for what I wanted. He and his money are what I wanted.

"Daaaamn, G, I like her. She over here spittin' that hot shit. I wonder if a bitch will give me some play with that smooth-ass shit she just said," he said, and everybody laughed. "Man, real shit, say that line again so I can type it in my phone."

I chuckled slightly, looking at his six-foot, dark chocolate frame. He was a little bit on the hefty side with baby titties and a beer belly. I could understand why he would need a pickup line or two to attract a female. He was styled up, though. It wasn't like he was a fat, broke mufucka, but a shallow bitch would definitely look past him.

"Man, get yo' big, fat, funky ass on. She ain't spittin' shit hot but her breath," he chuckled, and so did everyone else.

"Aww, hell naw. Don't play with her like that. Right thought, wrong bitch," Meka said, laughing. His little joke was funny as hell, though. We slapped hands.

"Don't tell him nothing, friend. He gon' be stalking me by tomorrow," I replied, winking my eye.

"Nah, he needs to know to play wit' his dick, not my friend."

"Play wit' my dick, huh?" he asked. Looking at me, he said, "Do you wanna play wit' it for me, ma?"

"Maybe," I replied.

"Damn, shorty, y'all on some freaky-ass shit, bro."

"Man, stay outta grown folks' business," he said as he kept his eyes on me. I just smiled. He was feeling me, and I was about to smoothly get into his pockets. "So, your name is Santana? Like the Mexican nigga that play the guitar?"

"Yeah."

"Maria, Mariaaaa! She reminds me of a *West Side Story*, but shorty ain't from Spanish Harlem. She grew up in Chiraq." His friend began to sing and sway to his own rendition of "Maria Maria" by Carlos Santana.

"My name is not Maria." I laughed, turning my attention back to my prey. "What's your name?" I asked.

"The hood calls me Gucci," he said, pulling at his shirt, showing me the green and red wording. Afterward, he dusted off the side of his left shoe. "Because a nigga smell and look like money." He bit down on his bottom lip. "I provide the whole hood with a good time, you feel me?" He dug into his pocket and pulled out a wad of bills. I was all eyes and ears at this point.

"Liquor, weed, pills, it don't matter. Whatever you want, I'll pay for it. These li'l niggas look up to me. For me, life is real fuckin' Gucci, li'l shorty." This nigga was lame as hell. I frowned. He turned me off a little. Still, I was going to fuck him. I just wished he would shut the fuck up.

"That's what's up." I leaned into him and put my hand to his chest. He put one hand on my waist and took a swallow from his cup.

"What else does Gucci got going on?" I asked, licking my lips. I felt on his dick, and it was hard. It was an OK size, nothing to really brag or be excited about. With his bottom lip between his teeth, he looked me in my eyes and grabbed my hand. He leaned back a little bit more and put my hand down his pants.

"Oh my. Damn." I had to stroke his little ego and his medium-sized dick.

"Meet my li'l nigga, Guilty." I silently blew out a breath, then put on a phony smile.

"Gucci and Guilty, how cute." I pursed my lips together.

"Yeah, Guilty is very friendly. He likes to be licked." He smiled, and so did I. Now, I was about to milk him in more ways than one. That's all I needed to hear.

I turned to look at Meka. "Um, Meka, I'm about to ride somewhere with Gucci real quick."

"Where?" she asked, pretending to be concerned. She already knew what I was up to.

"I gotta show her something real quick," he said, grabbing a handful of his dick. "Parlay and the rest of my guys will keep you company."

"Yeah, I gotta go see a man about a dog," I winked.

"OK, boo, go ahead and do yo' thang. Gucci, be careful with my friend," Meka said.

A few minutes later, Gucci and I were pulling up in a secluded area behind an abandoned building. There was no talking as he pushed the driver's seat back. I wasted no time undoing his pants and pulling out Guilty. I got on my knees in the seat and commenced to fucking Guilty with my mouth.

"Shit, shorty," he moaned.

Grabbing a fistful of my hair with one hand and moving his hips back and forth to the rhythm of my mouth service, his other hand massaged in between my pussy lips. This right here was my specialty. I loved sucking dick. I often timed myself on how long it would take for me to suck a nigga dry. I relaxed my throat muscles and slid my mouth all the way down on him, licking his balls before coming back up. He hissed, sucking in air in between his teeth.

"Swallow this big mafucka." Gucci was very confident in what he was packing. I almost choked from amusement when he said that because it wasn't shit big about his dick. "Make Guilty explode, shorty," he said, grunting loud as fuck.

I moaned along with him for dramatic effect, getting him to a quick climax, sucking the skin off Guilty as I allowed him to beat up my tonsils, and hot fluids filled my mouth. I was ready to see what a medium dick could do in this pussy because I had never experienced anything like this before. And I was about to charge him an arm and a leg for my services. I sat up, looked out the window, and spat out his sperm. Then I turned to look at him as he caught his breath.

"What's up, Santana?" he said, turning his head to look at me.

"That dick," I said, massaging Guilty so it stayed erect. He grabbed at my waist and pulled me to him. I guess he was going to make me put in all the work. I was cool with it, though. The more work I put in, the more he would have to pay. I climbed on top of him, straddling him, and sliding my wetness down on him. No condom, no nothing. I lived on the edge and didn't give a damn about a baby or STDs. That's what the clinic is for. To get rid of anything medically that wasn't a necessity in my life.

"Fuuuuck," he grunted loudly as I rode him. His eyes were instantly rolling to the back of his head. "Give Gucci this pussy, baby," he said, panting loudly. I mean, for an irregular-sized dick, he was working with a little something. He even made my coochie stay wet.

"Yes, daddy," I replied. "You can have this pussy. Take it. It's all yours." I was just saying any-damn-thing—anything to make him feel like he was the man.

Roughly, he grabbed my waist and moved himself in and out. He and little Mr. Guilty were overly excited at this point. He began fucking me harshly, making me feel a little pressure down below. Within a few seconds, Gucci reached down, pulled his dick out of me, and I jacked him off until he busted. I watched the sticky, white substance squirt from the small hole in the tip of his erection—two orgasms for him and none for me. I calculated the cost in my head. Shit, this was going to run him about $1,000.

"Shit, Santana. You got a nigga tired now," he said as he adjusted his clothes, then his seat.

He looked at me and rubbed my thigh. Without me even asking for anything, he went into his pocket and peeled off a few bills. This hoeing shit was so easy. I didn't know niggas like him could be so generous. I took the money and put it into my purse.

"Thank you," I said shortly before sitting back in my seat and putting my seat belt on.

"No problems, love. I'ma need some more of that, though." He started the engine, and we pulled off. "I'll pay for that shit every time."

"I got you, boo." I smiled as the wind blew through my hair, and I focused straight ahead.

Chapter 8

Meka

Them niggas had to know they fucked up when they let me connect my phone to the Bluetooth. Although I was more of an R&B type of girl, Kash Doll was my bitch. Her song "Thumbin" seemed to fit the occasion and my current mood. She was my alter ego. I channeled her music, living by every word as if they were law.

After Santana and Gucci dipped off, I continued chillin' with his friends. I wasn't afraid of being left with them either. Them niggas were friendly and cool as fuck. Getting me situated with a cup of Casamigos and half a pill, I was now on chill mode and so fucking high. A little horny too. But I couldn't fuck none of these niggas from Drip's hood. That shit just wouldn't have been right. Plus, I had plans to get up with Drip later on tonight to put out the fire that was burning in between my legs. As the music played loudly, I stood on the block with Gucci's guys smiling, rapping, and dancing as I went live on Facebook. My eyes were low, and my mouth felt as if I were chewing on cotton, but I was feeling cute as fuck.

"What's up, liiiivvve!" I yelled, smiling wide as hell.

Through intoxicated eyes, I watched as my views went up. Parlay was standing behind me with one arm wrapped around my waist and his face in the crook of my neck. I was so fucking high that I didn't stop him. I just went with the flow. There's no way this man should've been all on me like this without putting a few dollars in my pockets, but the liquor, along with the drugs, had my mind a little impaired. I pictured Drip and me in this moment. How cute it would be to be out and about with him just like this. My mind was in overload, each thought fighting for my attention as they battled to be the one to stick out the most.

I had at least three hundred views, which was the norm for me. But when I saw his name, I almost immediately sobered up. Drip had that type of effect on me. Without him even being physically in front of me, he made me feel. I felt weak, like a teenage girl. I felt all giddy and shit. Like someone had just mentioned my crush's name in front of me. I was blushing, cheeks red and flushed.

I ran my fingers through my hair and slid out of Parlay's grasp. I didn't want no smoke.

"What's up, Drip?" I said casually into the phone. People didn't need to know our business, and I wasn't trying to be disrespectful. What Drip and I had going on was on the hush-hush, but I'm sure my viewers caught a vibe and felt our chemistry from the way I was smiling as I said his name. "What's the word, bro?" I asked. Inwardly, I laughed knowing that brother and sister word was a secret code for "Yeah, I'm fucking him or her." Drip never replied. He just continued to blend in with the rest of the viewers. A minute or two later, my phone rang. It was Drip. I quickly ended my live and answered my phone.

"Hey, love," I said. I was all smiles as I caked it on the phone with Drip.

"What the fuck you mean, 'What's up, love?' Where you at?" he asked, too serious for me, and my brows dipped low in confusion. He was trippin' for real.

"Damn, Drip, calm down. I'm outside. Why, what's up?" I could only imagine the look on his face as I spoke those words. He forced me to have the same energy as him.

"Man, you got that lame-ass nigga Parlay hugging all on you and shit while you on social media. G, don't piss me off. Don't make me come down there and blow that mufuckin' block down."

"Boy, he ain't no-mufuckin'-body to be pressed over. And you need to stop doing the most. We're just friends, *right?* You ain't my man."

"You funny, Meka. I don't give a fuck if I'm your man or not. You better put some respect on me, shorty."

"Whatever, Drip," I said, hanging up on his jealous ass as Santana and Gucci pulled back up.

The two exited the car. I watched as Santana and Gucci stood there talking to each other for a few seconds before she came walking up to me, smiling. She must've gotten some good dick and money, but I'm sure the look on my face worried her.

"Is everything OK?" she asked.

"Yeah, I'm fine." I shook off Drip's threat. Santana and I began walking away, toward the other end of the block.

"Y'all gone?" Gucci yelled out, stopping us in our tracks. We both turned around.

"Yes, boo. I got your number. I'll see you around the way," Santana yelled back at him.

I looked at my phone, disconnected my Bluetooth, and told Parlay I would be calling him as well. We continued to walk away, and that's when the questions began.

"Soooo, how was it?"

"Bitch, it was terrible, but I got a thousand out of the entire thing."

"Terrible?"

"Girl, yeah. That nigga dick little as fuck. All that height and big-ass feet for nothing."

"Well, bitch, I'm sorry to hear that. At least you got paid."

"Yeah, I'ma fuck that nigga again." She stuck out her tongue and began gyrating her hips. I laughed.

"Do you think his friend Parlay is just as generous?" I asked, but before she could answer, a dark car rode past us. For some reason, that made us both stop and turn around.

The car suddenly braked in the middle of the street. The windows on the passenger side rolled down, and seconds later, gunshots rang out on the side of the street where Gucci, Parlay, and the rest of their guys stood. Everything seemed to move in slow motion as Gucci's body jerked backward. There had to be at least four bullets that hit him in the chest. The other men tried ducking for cover, trying to retrieve their guns from their hips so they could return fire, but they were too late, especially Parlay. Seeing him being shot in the head and his body slumping to the ground afterward, terrified me. Santana pulled my arm, and we took off running in the opposite direction. The tires of the car were loud as fuck as it skidded off. I knew for a fact this was all Drip's doing, and my pussy instantly began to thump. Once the shock of this situation wore off, I was going to fuck the shit out of him. For sure, he wasn't lying when he threatened to shoot the block up over me, and I wasn't mad at it. Later, I was going to let him shoot up the club. If a nigga ain't killing niggas over me, then I don't want him.

As we turned the corner and walked down the next block, we were silent. Knowing Drip was the person behind the gun, I wasn't afraid. As we crossed the street, a horn beeped behind us, and we turned around.

"Meka," he yelled, and I squinted. I knew it was Drip. I knew his voice without a question. "Come on, hurry up," he demanded. Santana and I looked at each other and hauled ass to his ride.

"You crazy motherfucka." I slapped his arm as soon as I sat down in the passenger seat.

"You did not have to kill that boy, and how the fuck you get here so fast?"

"Fuck them niggas. They owed me some money. They ass was ready to die," he said, holding up a gun that had a long-ass clip in it as he drove down the block.

"Get that shit away from me." I pushed his hand.

"Scary ass," he laughed and put his gun on the side of his seat.

"Take me to my car, Drip," Santana said from the backseat. She was a little shaken up, and I could tell. She was too quiet, and she was never silent in Drip's presence. When they were around each other, they both always had something slick to say.

"Sit yo' punk ass back and chill. You can get that weak-ass car tomorrow."

I sucked my teeth and said, "Drip, don't start."

"I told Meka I was going to be nice to your weird ass, but fuck you. Take me to my car. You just shot ten niggas. Yo' ass is crazy, and I don't want to be around the shit."

"Yo' chump ass. If you was a good ho, you would've robbed they dead ass," he laughed, but that little joke didn't amuse me. "This car is too hot to spin down the block again. I'm about to take y'all fat asses somewhere to eat. We need to talk business real quick."

"I got your fat ass," Santana replied. "You limp dick bastard. Me and you ain't got no damn business to discuss, you fuckin' snitch."

"Man, ain't shit limp over here. And what I snitch about?"

"That ain't what I heard, bastard. You know you been telling Marcel all my fuckin' business."

"Whatever, Jo."

"Right!"

"Damn, Santana, calm down. That dick definitely stands tall," I said, smirking.

"Don't make me throw up," Santana replied.

"Naw, but seriously, we can come back tomorrow and get your car when it's light outside. Drip, stop being an asshole, and stay out of her business."

They both agreed to drop their petty argument, and within thirty minutes, we were taking our seats inside Golden Nugget Pancake House on the North Side. After placing our orders, we sat patiently waiting for our food. I sat next to Drip, who was all in his phone. Santana sat directly across from me, opening every single package of sugar and pouring them into her cup of ice water. She looked tired and a little traumatized. I grabbed her hand, cocked my head to the side, and smiled as her eyes slowly met mine.

"Are you OK, best friend?" I asked.

"So, this shit is normal for you? Y'all sitting in here all nonchalant, ready to eat and shit like this crazy-ass nigga ain't just went *Menace II Society* an hour ago."

I chuckled slightly. I mean, this wasn't normal, but the way Drip came through his own hood emptying clips on niggas over little ole me was a turn-on.

"No, it's not the norm," I replied.

"Marcel would've never put me in no damn predicament like that."

"That's my nigga and all, but he's not an angel. Never mind that, though. What I brought y'all here for is this," Drip said, turning his phone around, showing a pool party he was the promoter for. I'd seen the flyer on his Instagram page constantly because he was promoting the event, but I was confused about his angle. I wasn't sure what this had to do with us.

"Oookkkk," I said. "You're promoting a pool party."

Drip leaned into the table and motioned us to do the same. We did as instructed.

"This nigga is the reason Marcel is locked up," he said. "Mr. Yung Swag. I been looking for his goofy ass."

"I'm confused," Santana said. "What did he do? How is *he* the reason Marcel is locked up?"

"He used to be my nigga. Me, Marcel, and Yung Swag used to run the West Side a few years back. It's kind of weird how that nigga disappeared after Marcel went to jail."

"Wait a minute. I remember that nigga. He used to be at my auntie's house with you and my cousin," I said.

"I been racking my brain trying to figure out how the police knew to be right there at the wrong time. The mufuckin' streets recently started talking. He don't know that I know he set me and Marcel up. I been waiting to get next to this nigga for some time, but he was suddenly off the radar. His goofy ass been missing in action for about two years now. Then all of a sudden, I hear the nigga a rapper now, signed to Epic Records. That's when I knew I had him. I began hitting that nigga up on social media, tryin'a get in where I fit in, and I was able to hook up this li'l pool party."

"Mmm . . . So, what is it you want us to do? And what's in it for me?" Santana asked.

"Right," I chimed in.

"What I want y'all to do is attend this party. Wear the sexiest shit y'all can find. Real authentic shit, though, not that knock-off shit you be wearing, Santana," he said seriously, and she threw her straw at him.

"Fuck you, Drip. You limp dick bastard," she snarled. "Meka, get your man."

"Dammit. Can we have at least one conversation without y'all arguing?"

"I wasn't tryin'a be funny, shorty. I'm telling you to dress nice when you roll up in there. I need you to get him to leave the party with you, and then leave the rest to me. I need him in your face, offering you a good time. That nigga set yo' man up and went on with his life like it was nothing. This isn't for me. This is for Marcel."

"I'm down," I said. "Santana?"

She sighed and looked from me to Drip, then sucked her teeth.

"The nigga is a goofy and lame as hell. People who come from the hood and come up on a little cash love to stunt. And they choose bitches who love to stunt too. Whatever money you get outta him is yours to keep."

"Yeah, I guess you can count me in," she said after hesitating a little.

"A month from today is the party. Have y'all shit right and tight."

Soon after, our food came out of the kitchen. We sat breaking bread for an hour before Drip took Santana and me to my house.

Chapter 9

Santana

Exercising had never been a part of my daily routine, but this seemed to be the only way to calm my nerves. I was dressed in a pair of stretch shorts, a sports bra, and running shoes. I had pulled my hair back into a ponytail, and my AirPods were fitted snugly inside my ears. As Guy sang softly, I zoned out. With tunnel vision, I power walked down State Street, not even giving a damn about the people who spoke to me. I heard them, but they weren't anyone important. Watching a nigga I'd just had sex with minutes prior die right in front of me was fucking with my mind. Not to mention, the shit Drip wanted Meka and me to do was weighing heavy on my mind as well. I was ready to get all this shit over with. I needed to change my life and my lifestyle. Things just felt safer when I was in love.

When it came to the summertime, I always envisioned myself on the islands or in Miami, on the beach, living it up with a beautiful man. The run Marcel made with Drip before he got locked up was supposed to be his last one. We were only a few weeks away from vacationing for three months in the Bahamas. But just like that, he was snatched from my life. I hated Marcel and Drip for that. After we were done with this mission and got paid, I planned to leave. I was going to run far, far away from Chicago and the States.

It had been almost an entire week since I agreed to help set up Yung Swag. Although I currently had Marcel's ass on my blocklist, I still loved him. Plus, I hated a snitch bitch. So, this job was going to be my pleasure. I guess no one believed in the old saying, "Snitches get stitches." Or they thought they would never get caught. I figured getting a little revenge on Marcel's behalf was the least I could do. That nigga Yung Swag ruined my life, and now, I was going to ruin his.

I blew out a breath and wiped sweat from my brows. Standing in place, I put my hands to my knees and bent over. My head began to spin, I felt nauseated, and my body felt weak. I moaned. Suddenly, I began to feel sick. Not pregnant sick, but worried, mixed with a bit of thirst and hunger sick. I paused my music, put the back of my hand to my forehead, and attempted to stand straight up. I didn't want to fall the fuck out, but as soon as I stood up straight, I stumbled backward and fell on my ass.

"Whoa," I heard a crowd of niggas yell, but no one except maybe two people came to my rescue.

"You OK, shorty?" one of the guys asked as he knelt beside me. He began to fan my face with his hand. At this point, I was sweating profusely.

"Is she OK?" I heard another voice ask. This voice was that of a woman. My vision was a little blurry, and the faces before me looked distorted, so I couldn't tell who was trying to help me. The male voice sounded slightly familiar, while the female's voice was nothing I recognized.

"I'm OK," I said, trying not to be a bother. I placed my hands on the concrete and attempted to stand up, but I fell back down.

"Wait, shorty. Calm down. Just sit right here for a minute. You look flushed," the guy said. "Aye, run in the store across the street real quick and buy me a bottle of water," he said to the lady who stood there with him.

Feeling disoriented and fucking embarrassed, I began to weep. I mean, I was ugly as fuck, crying like a big-ass baby. Instantly, my head began to hurt. "I'm so sorry." Real fucking tears poured from my eyes as I held my head.

"It's cool, love. Stop crying. I got you," he said.

He was so gentle and understanding. Still, I felt emotional. Shit, I didn't understand what I was going through, and I didn't like it. I didn't know why I was on the brink of fainting. Truthfully, I hadn't been eating or sleeping much over the past few days. Maybe I was just hungry and exhausted. My face was wet with sweat and tears. It felt like a thousand niggas were in my head, foot working on top of my brain; that's how bad my head was hurting. When the lady brought the water bottle back over to us, he opened it and put the bottle to my lips. I took deep swallows, welcoming the ice-cold, refreshing liquid into my system.

"How you feel?" he asked. That's when I looked at him. As his entire face became visible, I realized it was that sixty-dollar nigga from Pop's store. Was this nigga following me? How was he even here right now?

"I feel a lot better," I replied, trying to move away from his grasp, but he had a tight grip on me. "Thank you for all your help. I think I'm fine now. You can let me go."

"No problem, Santana." He remembered my name. "I just want to make sure you don't fall."

"Thank you, sir, but I'm not gonna fall."

"Maaan, I can't be sure of that, so I got you. You good?"

"No." I wiped my eyes. I wanted to stop crying, but I couldn't. I felt helpless. Me almost fainting and needing help from a stranger has never happened to me before, especially not from someone I'd just treated like shit a week before.

"Where do you live? Maybe I can walk you home," he offered.

Honestly, my heart swooned. His gesture was unexpected and cute. I thought about how I would repay him. Still, my ghetto bougie ass was ashamed to tell him I lived in the projects.

"Um . . . I probably just need another sip of water, and I'll be OK," I said, but I was lying. I still felt terrible, but I had to keep up my rich bitch persona.

"Nah, G." He smirked a little as he spoke those words, and I licked my lips.

Damn, Mr. Sixty Dollars, Mr. Blue Black, Mr. Blacker-Than-Me was so gaddam fine. Today, he was dressed comfortably. His body looked like steel in a pair of grey joggers, a fitted, black V-neck shirt that was almost identical to his skin, and a pair of black Nike Air Vapormax gym shoes. Today, he didn't have a cap on, so I was able to see his entire face. He didn't have a full beard, just a mustache and a goatee. His hair was cut low in a fade, and his eyebrows were thick. He was slightly sweaty, and he looked as if he'd just come from the gym.

"I'm not letting you walk home by yourself."

He helped me stand up. Carefully, he wrapped his muscular arm around my waist. Damn, he smelled so good. At that moment, the whole thing with Yung Swag and Marcel was pushed to the back of my mind.

"No, seriously, I'm fine."

"That you are." He licked his lips, causing me to blush.

"That was nice of you. Thank you." I smiled. "But I know I'm looking all kinds of crazy right now." I took my AirPods from my ears as he continued to hold me up by my waist, keeping me steady.

"I mean, you do look crazy." He laughed, agreeing with me. I had to laugh too.

"Wow," I said, ashamed. I began fixing my hair and wiping tears from my face.

"So, which way are we walking?" When I realized the nigga didn't have a car, and we had to walk to my house, I was a little turned off. That right there just proved he was a broke nigga, and that was the type of shit I couldn't fuck with.

"Walking?" I asked, taken aback.

I didn't live far from the store, the next block over to be exact. Still, if he had paper, the nigga would've had a vehicle to take me home in. I was thinking about asking him to take me to Meka's house, but when he didn't offer to drive me home, I figured my apartment would be more convenient. *Broke ass,* I thought to myself.

"This way." I pointed him in the direction.

It took us about ten minutes, but we finally made it to my building. I stopped walking and took a deep breath.

"What's wrong?" he asked. I looked at him, smiling nervously. Knowing where I lay my head at night, I knew he would have him questioning a lot about me. From my Prada outfits to my Mercedes-Benz, and my snobby-ass attitude.

"I don't actually live here," I lied. "I'm not even from Chicago. I'm just here visiting my best friend for the summer."

"OK." He frowned, looking at me like he knew I was lying. "Should I help you upstairs, or are you good right here?"

"Yeah, you can help me upstairs. I mean, you came this far."

He held my right hand in his and held me around my waist with his left. We walked up the small step and up to the elevators. I lived on the seventh floor, so there's no way I was walking up the stairs. We stood there silently as the door opened and the smell of piss invaded my nose.

"Damn," he said, and I looked at him. This shit was so embarrassing.

"I know, right? I been trying to tell my cousin to move outta here for years now." He looked at me and smirked as we stepped on the pissy elevator.

"What floor does your cousin live on?" he asked, still frowned up.

"Seven," I said, putting my hand up, covering my nose and mouth, trying to block out the smell.

He pressed the button, then turned to look at me. He licked his lips as I, with everything in me, tried to avoid eye contact.

"So," he said, and I closed my eyes.

"So," I repeated after him and opened my eyes. Blushing a little, I turned my gaze from him and focused on the numbers, watching them count upward until we reached our destination.

"Who really lives here? You, your best friend, or your cousin?"

The elevator dinged.

"Huh?" I asked.

He reached for my waist again, and we exited the elevator. My apartment was around the corner and all the way at the other end of the hall from the elevator, so we had a little walking to do.

"If you can *huh,* you can hear. Who lives here?" he asked, and I laughed.

I could've continued with the lie, but I was already caught up. I didn't even realize I said my cousin and best friend lived here.

"OK, you caught me." I rolled my eyes. "I live here."

"I was gon' let you keep lying too. What, you embarrassed about your living situation?"

"I'm not a good liar," I said, laughing. "I'm kinda embarrassed. Most people think I'm stuck up, and I know I have a fucked-up attitude. Too fucked up to be living off government assistance."

"Nah, your attitude is like any other woman who has their guard up."

"I guess."

As we turned the corner, I saw a big-ass mass standing in front of my door, knocking.

"Fuck," I said under my breath.

"What's up?" he asked, looking from me then straight ahead at Big Bertha.

"That big-ass blob standing down there is my ex-boyfriend's mother," I said, and he chuckled a little. "Oh, and that's me, my cousin, and best friend's apartment," I laughed.

"Cool," he said shortly. "Should I leave, or is it cool that I walk you to your door?"

"No, I don't want you to leave." My voice was loud, louder than I intended. So loud that Biggie Smalls turned to the side and looked at us. "This bitch," I sneered.

"Are you sure? She looks pretty upset. She may not like seeing you with another nigga besides her son."

"Fuck her and her son," I spat. "Come on."

We walked up to Bertha and the door, and that's when I noticed she had her cell phone pressed to her ear. I knew for a fact she was on the phone with Marcel, and there was about to be some type of drama. Specifically, because he was about to try to show his ass in front of his mammy.

"Hey, Biggie, I mean, Bertha." I put on a fake smile. She looked at us both with a scowl on her face.

"Who is this?" she asked.

"This is my friend . . ." I replied, but I drew a blank, realizing he had never told me his name. I was really living recklessly. I was about to let this man inside my crib, and I didn't know anything about him, not even his name.

"Lorenzo," he cut in. Lorenzo . . . His name was fitting. "How are you?" he spoke smoothly.

"Marcel . . ." Marcel's bitch-ass mother said into the phone instead of speaking back.

I looked at Lorenzo and shook my head. He just smiled and nodded his head at me understandingly as she put her phone on the speaker. I pushed past her rude ass, attempting to unlock my door.

"My son, your *fiancé*, wants to talk to you."

I laughed the fuck out loud. Since when did he and him got engaged?

"Girl, you know your son is *not* my fiancé." I snatched the phone from her hand. I wasn't about to play these fucking games. I took the phone off speaker. This was a private conversation.

"Hello," I sighed deeply.

"Yeah, hello," Marcel said, and I rolled my eyes. I didn't feel like talking to him right now. Bad enough I just fell the fuck out from worrying about the bullshit I got myself wrapped up in on his behalf.

"Hey, Marcel."

I twisted the doorknob, opened the door, and we walked inside. Lorenzo stood back while Bertha continued to look him up and down. I frowned.

"You can come in," I said, looking at him, and Big Bertha was right on our heels.

I told Lorenzo he could take a seat in the living room, ignoring Marcel's mother as I walked into the kitchen and threw my keys on the table. I was so annoyed. I sat at the table and listened to Marcel talk.

"What's up, baby?" he asked. "What's been going on? I been tryin'a call you, but your shit been going to voice-mail."

"I haven't received any calls from you, Marcel."

"I left you a thousand voicemails, Santana. What's up?"

"Nothing. You must've called the wrong number be-cause I don't have any voicemails or missed calls from you," I replied. He was about to keep talking. The nigga was ready to start an argument, but I cut him off. "Look, I have company. I'ma have to talk to you next time."

"Company? Who the fuck you got in my crib?"

"Nigga, your name ain't on no lease. The last time I checked, *I* pay the rent. Your crib is in the fuckin' federal penitentiary."

I stood and took the phone from my ear. Walking out of the kitchen and into the living room, I handed back her cell, and she put it to her ear. Then she looked at me all funny and shit but didn't say anything. She knew not to play with me in my face. She might talk all that shit about me to Marcel, and I was fine with that, but she knew better than to come outta her face recklessly with me. I opened the door and watched her with pursed lips as she walked outside.

"Bye, bitch," I said, slamming the door in her face.

I knew I had her at a loss for words because before she walked away, I heard her tell Marcel, "This bitch is fuckin' disrespectful. Not only did she call me out my name and slam the door in my face, but she also walked into your apartment with some black-ass nigga."

I laughed, walked away from the door, went over to Lorenzo, and took a seat.

"Damn, mother-in-law wasn't feeling me," he said, and I laughed.

"Fuck her messy ass. What can I do to repay you for helping me out?" I asked, smiling and twirling my hair in between my fingers.

"Shit, nothing. I was just doing the right thing. I couldn't see you out there like that."

"I know you were being nice. Still, I want to do something nice for you. Maybe I can cook you dinner?" I asked.

"How about *I* cook dinner for you?"

"No, Lorenzo. You've already done enough for me." I smiled and stood. "Come on." I grabbed his hand, pulling him up.

He stood up and followed me into the kitchen. I prepared a kale salad with tomatoes, raspberry vinaigrette dressing, fried chicken, a baked sweet potato, and ice-cold water for both of us. Usually, I didn't invite strangers into my home, but Lorenzo made me feel comfortable.

Chapter 10

Marcel

Stop Playing Games

I heard about the shit that happened in the hood, and I felt bad for Santana. She had to witness gunplay up close and personal. No one knew who did the drive-by, but I was made aware that my girl was right there in the middle of it all. She'd never seen a nigga gunned down in the streets, and this is something I knew for a fact. I never allowed her access to that part of life. Shit, I didn't even know what she was doing over there. Plus, I heard about her and Yung Swag. Last weekend, when I talked to Drip, he told me she was fucking fam. That nigga was something like a business partner of mine back in the day, and now, I learned he was the reason I'm in jail. Shit just wasn't adding up. After Drip told me about Santana's new relationship with Yung Swag, I let him convince me to put these two li'l baddies on my visitation list. I mean, Santana wasn't giving me the attention I needed, but I was for sure they were. Honestly, it was truly over between Santana and me, but I needed to hear her voice one last time before I walked completely away.

I had been calling her phone relentlessly for some time now. After a week of trying to get in contact with shorty,

I realized she had me blocked. That was the craziest shit ever. She really was pulling a disappearing act on a nigga after all the shit I had done for her. The last time we talked, she broke up with me. That shit was normal, so I didn't take it seriously, but now, I see what it is. I ain't trippin', though. I wanted to be on some "if I can't have you, nobody else can" shit, but I understood she didn't want to be lonely. Santana deserved companionship, and that wasn't something I could give her at the moment. Still, me hearing a nigga's voice in the background as I talked to my mama on the phone had me in my feelings. It wasn't Yung Swag, though. Last I heard, that nigga was a rapper and doing big things. Niggas like him didn't chill in the jets. The nigga who was at her crib was named Lorenzo. I heard him say his name when Santana introduced him to my moms. Who names their son some fuck shit like that? Lorenzo? That soft-ass name.

"Did you hear what she said to me, Marcel?" My mama's voice was loud as she talked, shaking me from my daydream. I didn't know what Santana said to her, but clearly, it was disrespectful. She was notorious for that. Santana better be lucky I was still locked up, or I would've put some act right on her ass. All I know is whatever she said had my mama pissed.

"Nah, Ma, I didn't hear her. What did she say?" I asked. I was calm, not wanting to agitate the situation further.

"That bitch is fuckin' disrespectful. I told you before you got into a serious relationship with her to leave her ass alone. She's a money-hungry, triflin'-ass motherfucker. Not only did she call me out my name and slam the door in my face, but she also walked into the apartment you got for her with some black, midnight-looking-ass nigga."

Damn, Jo. Santana was in the outside world, making me look foolish. I should've listened to Mama a long time ago. I could kill Santana right now for the way she disrespected me in front of my mama. She was so reckless with her mouth and her ways. I had no words for shorty no more. I guess Drip was right. I needed to let her go.

"I told you that girl was no good, son. And she got your damn cousin out there whorin' right along with her."

I sighed. I didn't want to hear that shit. I was already mad, Jo.

"Ma, call Meka for me," I said with my arm resting atop the phone and my forehead up against my arm. I needed to know what was with Santana. Shorty was trippin'-trippin'. My mama clicked over, and I presumed she was calling my cousin. Any questions I had about Santana, I knew Meka could answer them. When ma dukes clicked back over, I heard her and Meka laughing. I quickly cut in.

"What's good, cuzzo?"

"Cousin? Oh my God, Auntie! Why didn't you tell me Marcel was on the phone?"

"It was a surprise."

"Man, cuz, what's been going on with your buddy Santana?" I asked, skipping all the casualties. I wasn't in the mood for small talk. Plus, I was only a few minutes away from my call ending.

"What you mean? She's been fine. Nothing major. We just been kicking it. You know, the usual shit," Meka said.

"The usual shit, huh?" I asked.

"Yes, cousin. What's wrong?"

"Stop playing games, Meka, and tell Marcel how Santana out here whoring and got you wrapped up in the same shit," my mama said. Ma dukes was bold as hell.

"Whoring? Hold up, Auntie, you outta pocket for that. Ain't nobody out here being a ho," Meka said, but that was none of my business.

"Ma, that's not why I asked you to call Meka. She's grown, so she can do what she wants to do. My concern right now is Santana."

"What about her?" she asked.

"Drip told me she's fucking around with Yung Swag," I said, accusingly.

"What? Never. He didn't tell you no shit like that."

As she said that, I heard a male's voice in the background asking about our conversation.

"Who is that?" I asked.

"Nobody. Look, cousin, I'm busy, so let auntie know to call me the next time you call her." Before I could respond, she hung up.

Chapter 11

Meka

My legs were spread wide open as Drip's head moved up and down, kissing and licking my pussy. I watched him through slit eyes. My thighs were on his shoulders, my nails were gripping the bed, and my toes were pointed to the sky as he savagely savored and lapped up everything this sweet pussy had to offer. To the sound of Drake featuring Givēon's song "Chicago Freestyle," Drip took his time with me. He was something like a gentle thug as he took control of my body one freestyle bar at a time. Drip and I had never made love, and today was no different, but the way he made me feel at this moment had my heart second-guessing shit. Moaning, I grabbed a hold of his head and bit down on my bottom lip. I was seconds away from comin' all in his mouth.

"Drip," I said his name pleadingly.

He was doing the most. Honestly, he was doing too much. What the fuck was he trying to do to me? He didn't have to put nothing extra into what we were already doing. I was already becoming a dummy for him, ready to do anything, and it was all for the sake of good dick. The head was just extra.

I had already agreed with him, convincing my best friend to help set up Yung Swag. I felt terrible about it for the simple fact that he had nothing to do with my cousin going to jail. But I knew Drip needed this. I let him tell Santana that bullshit-ass story, and I went right along with it. Next, he was gonna have my ditsy ass stabbing and shooting niggas for him.

"Move your hand," he said as I flinched and grabbed at his head. He reached over his head and took my hands into his. Drip was not playing fair.

"Please, Drip," I begged. If he wanted me soulless, that's all he had to say because I was almost dead from exhaustion.

"Shut that punk-ass shit up." He looked up at me, smiling. I breathed in and out as fast as hell.

"Let's just kiss or something." I was damn near in tears. I never wanted a man to make me feel this good, I swear. That shit had me so emotional.

"A'ight," he replied, but instead of kissing the lips on my face, he continued to kiss my pussy lips. I mean, the nigga was tongue kissing my coochie at this point. Before I knew it, my body was shaking and convulsing. I was dripping. I felt it sliding down my ass and onto the bed.

We were on the verge of fucking until my phone began to ring, and I saw my auntie's name on the caller ID. Auntie Bertha wasn't my favorite person in the world. I hated the way she treated Santana, but her son, my big cousin, was one of my best friends. If she was calling me, then it was because of him.

"I have to take this call," I said to Drip, still moaning and out of breath. Whew. That young man had worked me over.

"Go ahead," he said, standing up from the bed and walking out of the bedroom.

I answered, and right away, my auntie began talking shit and acting silly. We shared a few laughs before I heard Marcel's voice on the phone. I was so happy to hear from him. We talked for a few minutes, and it wouldn't be right if Auntie Bertha didn't say some disrespectful shit. Talking about me and Santana been whoring. I mean, we was out here getting paid for pussy, but shit, what grown-ass woman fuck with men for free? "Not I," said the cat. Auntie Bertha had me fucked up, but that wasn't for everyone to know. Drip reentered the room and decided he would make his presence known. When Marcel asked me who he was, I almost shitted bricks. My heart dropped into my stomach; we were nearly caught. Marcel definitely wouldn't have taken it as well as Santana. I came up with a quick-ass excuse. Afterward, my phone call with Marcel ended. I hung the fuck up, looked at Drip, and flared my nostrils.

"*Really,* Drip?" I asked.

"Man, how the fuck was I supposed to know who yo' baldhead ass was on the phone with?" He got back into the bed and lay down. Lying on his side, he pulled me to him, spooned me, and wrapped his arm around my neck.

"You almost got us caught up."

"So, we like each other, shorty. What's wrong with that?" he asked.

"A lot," I responded.

"I just want you to know I appreciate you and the shit you doin' for me." He decided to change the subject.

"Yeah, yeah, Drip. Just make sure my best friend doesn't get hurt."

"Her ho ass gon' be OK. This should be like a walk in the park for her sack-chasing ass."

I sighed and pushed at Drip with my ass. "Stop disrespecting my friend. She's nice enough to pull this off for you."

"I was just playing." He laughed but wasn't shit funny.

Chapter 12

Santana

Cater To You

"So, Mr. Lorenzo, what do you do for a living?" I asked as I sat across from him with a glass of water in my hand. I was curious to know. I was clearly dehydrated as I took a huge gulp from my glass and set it down on the table. After falling out earlier, I was done with liquor, at least for today.

Leaning forward, I smiled with my ears wide open, praying my theory about him was wrong. I liked him, but I couldn't deal with a man who was broke. I didn't give a fuck how strong my feelings were. I just prayed this man had some type of money and not no little-ass chump change. And I prayed he wasn't a drug dealer. I wasn't trying to fall in love with him, not this soon. But as I said, I liked him, and I didn't know why. This was only our second time bumping into each other. It was crazy. He was the total opposite of Marcel. Marcel was vanilla while Lorenzo was dark chocolate. I bet his dick was so chocolate that it would melt in my mouth. Marcel was six foot tall while Lorenzo appeared to be at least six foot and five inches tall. Marcel sold drugs while Lorenzo . . . Well, as far as Lorenzo went, I didn't know what the hell his occupation was.

"I work for a living," he said shortly, and I laughed. I didn't know if he was being sarcastic or not, but he spoke as if he were the wrong nigga to be questioning. I liked his attitude. Still, I wasn't trying to waste my time. This meal was free today, but next time, he would have to pay. "I'm not the type of man you think I am." I looked at him, frowning with a slight smirk on my face. He didn't know shit about what I thought about him . . . or maybe he did.

"What?" I picked up my fork and began to dig into my salad. Stuffing my mouth with kale and tomatoes, I was speechless, not wanting to say anything stupid.

"My lifestyle isn't something I just willingly tell every-body. Just know I'm not who you think I am. I don't sell drugs, I don't pimp women, and I don't fuck any and every woman I meet. I make my money and stay out the way," he said, now looking at me as he bit into his chicken. I watched him with admiration. He was a man's man *and* a gentleman. The way he explained it, he had his life together. He knew what he wanted. Still, I was a little confused why his occupation was a secret.

"You make your money, huh?" was all I could think to say. Shit, I made my money too, and my lifestyle wasn't something I was willing to tell everyone about either. But his explanation was a little fishy.

"Yeah, I make my money legitimately. My hours aren't from nine to five, but these hands here are the hands of a hardworking man."

"I see." I cleared my throat. His hands were big as fuck.

"The day I saw you at the corner store, you were a little harsh. You played me to the left, and you judged me." He chuckled. "Am I wrong?"

I laughed and sipped my water. After swallowing hard, I cleared my throat. "I did judge you, only a little, though." I used my thumb and index finger to emphasize how small my judgment of him was. But honestly, my assumptions about him were huge. "But you still haven't proven my judgment wrong. You said everything you said and ain't really say shit. The only thing I took from this is you work at McDonald's or some shit."

"What would be wrong with me working at McDonald's? It's an honest job."

"Nothing is wrong with it, but it wouldn't be enough for me. I'm used to a man making over a thousand dollars a day. It'll be dumb of me to fuck with a nigga who doesn't come close to a thousand dollars in two weeks. And you're too fuckin' old to be broke."

His eyebrows furrowed as he looked back down at his plate. I think I offended him, but I wasn't sorry. I couldn't apologize for how I felt.

"If that's your way of asking me my age, I'm 26. What if I owned my own McDonald's? Would you be interested in me then?"

"Hell yeah because I know the owners of Mickey D's are checking a bag."

"Damn, so you one of *those* types."

"What type? A brutally honest type?" I was getting heated. The look on Lorenzo's face made it clear he was disappointed. My eyebrows scrunched up, and my nostrils flared as I waited to hear what he had to say.

"No, a money-hungry, young-minded bitch who thinks a pretty face and possibly good pussy will pay her way through life."

"Bitch?" I put my hand to my chest, offended. His tone wasn't hostile or nothing, but damn . . . Once again, he had me speechless.

"Am I wrong, or am I right? Let me ask you something, Santana. What do *you* do for a living? How old are you?" I didn't respond. I just rolled my eyes down and looked at my plate.

"I mean, damn. You're living in the fucking projects. I bet your rent ain't shit but forty dollars, but *you* judging *me*. Whether or not I work at McDonald's, I can afford all your bills."

He scooted his chair back, and I looked up at him as he went into his pocket. He peeled off ten bills and threw them on the table. Yeah, he knew I was *that* type of ho, but I couldn't let him leave upset. And he was *not* getting his money back.

"Lorenzo," I said softly. But he was right. As he began to walk toward the living room, I scooted my chair back and stood up. I ran up behind him and grabbed his arm. "Lorenzo." He turned to look at me. "Don't leave upset."

"I'm not upset." He rubbed the top of his head. "Thank you for dinner."

"You're welcome," I said, looking up at him.

"I gotta go."

I released his arm and followed him as he walked to the door.

"Can we hang out tomorrow or something?"

"I don't know," he said. "I might have to pull a double shift at McDonald's."

I rolled my eyes. He was petty as hell for that.

"Well, can I give you my phone number so we can keep in touch?" I really felt like shit for making him feel the way I did.

"Yeah, that's cool."

He handed me his phone. I typed my name and phone number inside before handing him back his phone, and he left.

Chapter 13

Meka

Three Weeks Later

I hadn't seen my friend since the day we set up this entire thing. It was almost as if she were trying to dodge me. So, I decided to pop up at her house. It was exactly a week before we were set to pull off Operation Yung Swag. I pulled up to the building and parked inside the parking lot right beside Santana's car. I knew this bitch was at home, so there was no ducking and dodging me today. Maybe it was all in my head, but I felt like she knew I had a hand in this. Weeks earlier, Drip told me the same story he told Santana, and I was heated. I scrambled my brain on what we could do to cause havoc in a nigga like Yung Swag's life. Just like any other man, I knew he was a sucker for a pretty face and even prettier pussy. That is where I ran the whole setup by Drip after one of our many sex sessions. At first, I wasn't going to involve Santana, but Drip insisted. He wasn't with the idea of Yung Swag even touching a morsel of my body.

"We can get Santana to do it. She's a freak any-damn-way," he said.

But honestly, *I* wanted to fuck that nigga. I knew he was holding, and I wanted all that paper for myself. I didn't want to share anything with anybody.

"Nah, Santana ain't gon' be down with this shit." At least, I prayed she wouldn't be down with it.

He sucked his teeth. "Just let me do all the talking, shorty. I know how to get in her head. I study bitches for a living."

And that is what I did. I listened to him. I let Drip talk me out of my blessing, and that was fucked up. Especially when he got to popping shit about getting in bitches' heads. Did he mind-fuck me too? It didn't even matter, though. I had already agreed to it, and here we were, seven days away from the setup.

I stepped from my car and slammed the door. It was about nine in the evening, and a bunch of badass kids were still outside running around. I grimaced, looking at the ugly fuckers as they played dodgeball, almost knocking me down and hitting me with the ball.

"Y'all better watch where the fuck y'all throwing that ball," I yelled, not giving a damn whose kids I was talking crazy to. I fight kids and their pussy-ass mamas too. These parents these days didn't give a damn about their kids anyway, and that's why I don't have any—trifling asses probably too busy in the house sucking dick.

"Sorry." The little boy placed his hand to his mouth apologetically.

I didn't respond. I just walked inside Santana's building and up to the elevator. I pressed the button, and the door opened right away. I made a gagging noise, almost fainting as the smell of piss, Pine Sol, and ammonia hit my nose.

"Nasty, trifling-ass, project babies," I said under my breath.

Covering my nose, I stepped inside and pressed the seventh-floor button. I was about to get Santana out of the house one way or another. When I reached her floor and stepped off, I sighed a breath of relief. I didn't know how she did it day in and day out, living amongst the poor. Living here had to be like living beyond poverty. This shit was the gutter underneath the gutter. However, my bitch Santana's crib was decked the fuck out.

I walked up to her door and, instead of knocking, I used my key and unlocked the door. Cool air rushed my body, and the sound of R&B music soothed my ears. It was dark, except for a lamp that was turned on beside her couch. I began walking to the back, where her bedroom was. I smiled mischievously and walked on my tippy toes when I heard moaning. Not only was Santana moaning, but a guy was also moaning too.

"OK, Santana, get it, get it," I said in a low tone, and afterward, I laughed. My friend had that nigga moaning like a bitch. "That's right, friend, fuck that nigga like you mean it!" I yelled, busting into her bedroom, ready to watch a real live porno.

"Aaahh!" she screamed aloud and pulled her blanket over her body. I still heard a male's voice, but there was no one there but her. "You don't know how to fuckin' knock?"

"What'chu mean?" I heard a voice ask. "I thought I knocked that pussy out already."

I was flabbergasted. Was she really in here having phone sex? Was the nigga even paying her for her services? Have times really gotten that rough?

"He knocked the pussy out, huh?"

"Really, Meka?" Santana said, laughing,

"Bitch, I thought you was in here fucking that nigga senseless."

"She was," he said. His voice was deep and sexy as I realized Santana had her phone sitting beside her. She was on FaceTime with some dark-skinned nigga, but I could barely see his face.

"Daaaamn, Santana, who is he? He's kinda cute from over here."

"My friend," she said shortly. "Babe, we will resume this when she leaves."

"A'ight, love, call me later." Santana hung up, and I looked at her with pursed lips.

"So, who was he? I thought we told each other everything?" I repeated the same shit she said to me a month ago.

"We do, but he's not up for discussion." She threw the blanket off her body, exposing her bare assets. Sis definitely still had a cute body on her. She picked up a T-shirt from a chair in her room and put it on.

"Bitch. Don't use my words." I laughed and flopped down on her bed. "Anyway, I came over to get you out of the house. You been acting funny, and now I see why."

"I haven't been acting funny." Her tone was somber as she sat down beside me.

"Yes, you have, friend. But you know I'm not afraid to call you out on your shit." She looked at me. Her eyes seemed sad. It was like, all of a sudden, an emotional switch turned on, like she was bipolar.

"There is nothing to call me out on. I'm not in the mood to play."

"What's wrong?" I asked. This wasn't like her.

She sighed, closed her eyes, and said, "Bitch, I don't know if I can go through with this whole Yung Swag shit. I been racking my brain about it, and I just can't."

"What?" I looked at her, crazy as hell. There was no turning back from the agreement. I know she didn't think that whole ducking and dodging me shit was going to exempt her role in this.

"I'm not saying no; I'm just saying I'm afraid. That nigga gon' put a hit out on us."

"Whatever, Santana. I didn't come over here to talk about that. Put some clothes on. Let's go outside."

Santana didn't say another word. She just got out of bed and began getting dressed. While I waited for her, I texted Drip.

Me: Hey, boo. There may be a change of plans.

Drip: A change of plans to what?

Me: You know, Operation Yung Swag.

Drip: Why is there a possible change of plans?

Me: Santana is freaking out about this shit. She said she's not with it anymore.

Drip: Well, you better talk her into doing it.

Me: We don't really need her, Drip. I can do this shit myself.

Drip: Nah, I need Santana to do it. If not, I'm a shoot that bitch in her pretty little face. Believe that shit.

Chapter 14

Santana

Bare Wit' Me

I watched my phone as it danced around on the nightstand. I had been dreaming about Lorenzo for the past few nights, and that shit wasn't normal for me. Every time my phone rang, I grew super excited. That man had definitely gotten to me. This time was no different. My eyes lit up as my phone began to ring, and I heard Teyana Taylor's voice. I don't know if people still did this, but I made sure my love, Lorenzo, had his own special ringtone.

"I been tellin' niggas lies (Yeah)
Try to split up all my time (Yeah)

I snatched up my phone and smiled, fixing my hair, then pressed the talk button. I didn't give a damn how beautiful people told me I was. Whenever I interacted with him, I had to be totally perfect.

"Hey, boo," I said, cheesing hard as hell. "Did you make it to work yet?"

"Yeah, just got here. I'm sitting in the parking lot right now."

"Mmm, I wish you were here in Chicago. I miss you."

Several days after our disagreement, he called me, and I apologized to him. After that, we spent the entire day together, just hanging out at the beach. Ever since then, we'd been talking daily, but I hadn't seen him in about two weeks because his job had him so busy. We would speak mostly at night because that's when he was at work. It was always quiet around him, and he always sounded as if he were inside a car, so I assumed he had a bitch at home and was sneaking around to talk to me on the phone.

I would hear a woman's voice every now and again, but I had no real authority to question him. I hadn't even given up the pussy yet, and that definitely *wasn't* like me. Honestly, I hadn't fucked him yet because he hadn't tried to fuck me, but I still owed him for the thousand dollars he had given me.

"How much do you miss me?" he asked.

"A whole lot. I don't even be missing niggas, either. When am I gon' see you?" I asked. My voice was a little sad.

"When do you want to see me?" he asked. At this point, I felt like he was playing games.

"Now."

"A'ight, I'm at the crib. Put some clothes on . . . On second thought, leave your clothes off. Come pull up on me," he said, but I didn't know where he lived. I knew what building he lived in, but I didn't know his apartment number.

"What?" I giggled. "Pull up on you where?"

"Where you think? At the condo."

"Sir, you know it's not a problem for me to pull up on you, but what's the apartment number?"

"Let me know when you're downstairs, and I'll give it to you."

"Lorenzo, stop playing."

"I'm not playing, Tisha. Pull up."

Shit, I jumped my ass up out of the bed and started getting dressed. He didn't have to tell me again. I guess my assumption about him having a bitch was dismissed. Because if he did have a girl, he wouldn't have invited me to his apartment. I went into the bathroom and took a quick ho bath. You know, one of those really quick washcloth, soap, and bathroom sink baths. I propped my leg up on the basin and washed my cat just in case he felt like getting his grub on tonight. Afterward, I pulled my sundress over my head and let it flare out past my ankles without panties or a bra. Then I turned off the bathroom light and walked out. I went into my kitchen and picked up my keys and purse. I was about to spend the night at Lorenzo's house, and I was ready.

When I reached the door and opened it, I jumped, startled by Lorenzo standing there. He grabbed me, picked me up, and wrapped my legs around him as he walked inside, kissing and feeling on me. We were silent as he walked me over to the couch and laid me down. As he began to tear off my sundress, I tugged at his pants. That phone sex shit had my hormones going crazy. Plus, I was about to suck all one thousand dollars up out of that dick. That night we orally pleased each other, and I must say, Lorenzo was good at what he do.

After twenty minutes of our "I miss you" oral sex, my phone chimed. It was a screenshot of a text message between Drip and Meka. I lay my head on Lorenzo's back, as I read their words and knew I couldn't back out of this.

Chapter 15

Santana

Three Days Later . . .

Meka and I stood near the DJ's booth with a glass of Moët in our hands, babysitting it while we danced and rapped along to City Girls' hit song "Act Up." That night, the Radisson Blu Aqua Hotel's pool party was on the rooftop in downtown Chicago. The scenery was absolutely gorgeous from the big-ass pool to the city's skyline. This was my type of party, but I wasn't here for enjoyment. As loud Hip-Hop and R&B music blared through the speakers, Meka and I stayed strategically positioned where we could see everything and everyone.

Following through with Drip's plot, we were here to fuck over a nigga. Yung Swag was going to be in the building tonight, and I was determined to make him pay for the shit he had done to my ex-boo. Meka and I were down for whatever. At least, that's what I wanted my exterior to show, but deep down inside, I wasn't with this shit. After meeting Lorenzo and talking to him on the phone almost every single night, I realized I didn't owe Marcel shit, and I didn't need to avenge anything on his behalf because he was no longer my problem. Instead, I was ready to take Lorenzo's and my relationship further. I was ready to build something new with a new man. Still, here I was, ready to ride. I just prayed I made it back home in one piece because I promise you, I was scared as fuck.

We stood there scoping out the joint, trying to stand out without being the center of attention. It was like being a detective, undercover, on a secret assignment, silently watching everyone and their actions, dissecting them without them even knowing it.

Looking to my right, I realized how upscale and affluent this party was with all the bottles floating around and thick women in damn near nothing but $6,000 dental floss-looking bathing suits. Most of the women clearly had their bodies tampered with in some type of way. And don't get me started on the niggas. There were way too many big-dick ballers with high-quality, top-notch labels on who stunted on bitches for a living to count. If I were here for pleasure, I would've had every single nigga's phone number programmed in my phone.

The atmosphere was low-key and sexy as fuck. Nothing but beautiful women and men with money were sprinkled throughout the place. Meka and I just somehow seemed to blend in with the rest. There was no indication that I only had lint, a stick of gum, a sample bottle of YSL Black Opium perfume, and a couple of Magnum condoms in my little handbag. Dressed in a two-piece Gucci bathing suit and five-inch Gucci heels, we looked the part. We looked like we were well put together, Doublemint twins, including my natural, curly, long hair, and Meka's body wave, twenty-eight-inch bundles. We were sent here on a mission. The champagne we held in our hands, we paid for with our last few dollars. It was now warm, and the bubbles had deflated from us holding our glasses for the past two hours. With my back turned to the crowd, I smiled. Me not wanting to do too much, I looked at Meka as we two-stepped and snapped our fingers to the music.

"Have you seen him yet?" Meka asked, smiling. We were on some sheisty shit for sure.

"No, not yet," I smirked. Turning around, I backed my ass up on Meka, and she wrapped her arm around my neck as I took a baby sip from my glass and rolled my body on hers.

"Bitch, is there a plan B if you're not his type?" she asked, whispering in my ear.

"Hell naw, so let's not think negatively." I closed my eyes and smiled.

"What if he doesn't even notice you? Then what?"

"He will. All the big-dick ballers notice Santana," I told her, referring to myself in third person. That was a dumb-ass question. Meka knew all the men loved them some Tisha Santana. I talked with confidence, but inside, I was scared as fuck.

"You are too much, friend," she said, laughing. I removed her arm from around my neck and turned to look at her.

"And you know it. My confidence is on one thousand, period." I did the "cut it" motion with my hand and stuck out my tongue. We were here on business, and we weren't leaving or taking too many sips from these pissy-hot glasses until what we came here to do was accomplished.

All of a sudden, the City Girl's music faded out, and a song I'd never heard before began to play. The guy rapping on the track had a voice deep as hell. It seemed as if he could barely catch the beat as he rapped about shooting niggas in an alleyway and pissing on his grave while he laughed in the homie's face. This was some Chicago shit here. Ghetto as fuck.

"They just let anybody rap nowadays," I said to Meka, shaking my head.

"Bitch, that's Yung Swag's new song." As soon as she said that, the DJ's voice spoke over the music.

"My nigga Yung Swag just stepped into VIP. What's good, young killa?" Everyone around us went wild. Excitement filled the pool party as we looked over at the VIP section. Now, he wasn't much to look at, but his blinged-out smile was sexy.

"Bitch, now we need to get up in there," Meka said to me. I just smiled at her. We moved closer to his section so he would notice us, and we did just that.

Yung Swag was a straight goofy; at least he looked like one. So, I played him close, watching his every move as he maneuvered around VIP with his friends. My ho-dar could tell the difference between a real nigga and a foe. He was obviously a man who used his money to woo women. To be honest, it was the diamond smile for me too. I wanted to strut to him and tell him he could have me for the night. I had just enough confidence to pull that off too, but Lorenzo was seriously on my mind.

Soon enough, Yung Swag and his security staff were walking around the party, greeting his fans, and my eyes were still on him. I wasn't paying attention to the men who surrounded him, pushing the crowd to the side. A handsome face was a far-fetched compliment when describing Yung Swag, but his money definitely made up for it. The three platinum chains he wore around his neck, a diamond stud in his right earlobe, Red Bottom sneakers, Versace drawers underneath his denim shorts, along with the Versace button-up shirt that showed off his hairy chest, screamed he had more than chump change in his pockets.

Meka and I weren't fans of his, so we weren't falling to our knees like all the other women, and because of that, we stood out. I watched him until he made it back into VIP. We made eye contact for a second or two. He smiled at me with them shiny-ass teeth before turning around and joining his crew.

A few minutes later, I heard a deep, sexy voice behind me say, "Hello, my Black Nubian queens." He spoke with so much confidence, putting a little bit more emphasis on *Nubian queens.*

It was a weak game for me. I liked it but would never admit it, not out loud. No man has ever called me a Nubian queen. I was far from it. I was from the hood, where niggas called you "shorty" or "his bitch." I was tempted to turn around. Instead, I looked up at Meka with furrowed brows, just to get a "yay" or a "nay" before I wasted my time turning around to look at him. He sounded familiar, but I couldn't figure out where I knew him from since he spoke with a slightly proper accent. It was almost as if he were trying to disguise his voice because that proper shit sounded fake as fuck. I didn't want to unnecessarily entertain another man and miss my chances of getting to know Yung Swag, so I remained focused. Still, I wanted to know what he looked like and find out if the familiarity of his voice was that of a man I had grown to like over the past few weeks. Without a word, Meka grabbed me by my waist and pulled me closer to her. I took that as a "No, don't waste your time." I silently sucked my teeth.

"She's taken," she yelled over the music. "Ain't that right, shorty?" she said, laying it on thick, kissing my cheek, and palming my ass. I laughed and leaned my forehead into her shoulder.

"Damn, bitch, is he ugly?" I whispered.

She discreetly said, "Uumm-hmm," as she cleared her throat.

"Oh! I apologize," he said. His voice displayed a bit of shock.

"No apologies necessary, love. You didn't know." Meka's tone was now sarcastic.

"I didn't mean to be rude. That was my bad," he said, yelling over the music. "To show how apologetic I am, can I offer you both a drink?"

I felt Meka's chest heave slightly, so I removed my face from her shoulder and looked up at her. She smiled at me, and I smiled at her. Without a response, I was a little intrigued. He now had my attention. I loved me a thirsty-ass nigga with money. Excitement filled my body because this hot-ass champagne was nasty as hell at this point. He just offered to buy us a fresh drink. Maybe he was watching us the same way we watched everyone else.

"I can drink," Meka said.

"Yung Swag would like to bring you two ladies to VIP," he announced, and, biiiitch, my stomach instantly began to hurt.

Although I was now nervous, I was also relieved. We were in there, and I was about to do something I never thought I would have the nerve to do. My relief quickly washed away when he introduced himself as Lorenzo. I turned around to look at him and make sure my ears weren't deceiving me. Moving over to the side a little so that I was standing next to Meka, I was in shock.

"Wow," I said under my breath. "Lorenzo?"

What was he doing here? He told me he wouldn't be in town. He was a businessman who traveled to and from Chicago often. When we bumped into each other the first time, he was here on business and visiting a family member. The day I almost fainted, he'd just come back from Detroit conducting business. He was never home because his job kept him busy, but I still didn't know what he did for a living.

However, I talked to him earlier today and told him about the party I was going to. I never gave him the location or nothing, but somehow, he was here. Granted, he did inform me he would also be attending a party today himself to celebrate his cousin's record release, but I never put two and two together. I had no clue his cousin was connected to Yung Swag. Shit, he was being just as secretive as I was. My mouth fell wide open as I looked at him. He was so damn handsome with his dark chocolate skin. Lorenzo was one fine, suave-ass nigga. The crazy part is . . . He wasn't my type. I had always liked light-skinned men.

I never really did anything for love, not even with Marcel. Me watching my mother growing up, money had always been the motive, but there was something about him. My bottom lip was trapped between my teeth at this point. It was the gentleman for me. Lorenzo was just that. He never showed me anything less than a perfect man, even after we had our little "disagreement."

I shook my head at him and mouthed, "We don't know each other." He frowned. I guess he wasn't under-standing. I didn't worry about Meka catching on to the awkwardness of Lorenzo's and my interaction because she was too busy lusting over his body, considering he had on an unbuttoned white linen shirt, showing off his dark chocolate muscles and tattoos. The gold chain that hung around his neck seemed to accent his beautiful skin, and the shorts, bay-be, that man's dick print made me envision him without *any* clothes on. I'm sure Meka felt the same way.

"Hell yeah, Santana, gon' ahead and go to VIP with Yung Swag while me and Lorenzo have our own li'l party down here," Meka said quick as hell, breaking our silent conversation. He chuckled at her while I turned my head and looked at her, side-eyeing the hell out of her.

"Nah, it won't be any private parties going on. We can all kick it upstairs," he announced, and I turned my atten-tion back to him. I squinted my eyes.

"Um," I stuttered. "Yeah, upstairs is cool," I smiled.

The way he curved Meka without being disrespectful turned me on. Lorenzo was a real man. It's apparent he wasn't a hood nigga. I imagined myself sucking the skin off Lorenzo's dick as soon as I got him alone. I was still in my head about this entire situation. As far as Yung Swag went, I didn't know how I was about to pull this off, but I had no choice. I mean, honestly, I never had to be forced to fuck anybody, but this situation with Yung Swag had me uneasy. All I needed was a few shots, and I knew I would be at ease.

"Well, damn . . . It's like that, Mr. Black African American Man?" Meka asked. I couldn't do shit but laugh in my head. She was so fucking silly. She felt dumb as hell too. Women like us needed a man's validation. She wasn't used to a man telling her no.

"*Not* African American Man."

I was now laughing out loud, and so was Lorenzo.

Meka looked at me and rolled her eyes. I knew she was embarrassed.

"So, y'all ready?" he asked.

"Yeah, I'm ready to get up close and personal with you, Hershey's Kiss," Meka said, smiling as she wrapped her arm around his. I didn't like that shit at all. That bitch was pushing it. Mr. Hershey's Kiss, my ass.

I eyed him, and briefly, he looked at me. I wanted to curse him the fuck out and beat her ass. I wasn't in the mood to stand here and watch Meka try to get some money out of my soon-to-be man. Because after this was all done and over with, I was going to ask Lorenzo to make me his woman. Now, I have a whole attitude.

"Damn, bitch, let that man have his arm back," I spat, and he chuckled. Meka just looked at me, confused. She had no idea who Lorenzo was to me.

"Let me go talk to my friend for a second," she said before releasing his arm. She looked irritated as she stepped to me and took my hand into hers. We walked away, and she led me over a couple of steps from him and said, "Bitch, I know he doesn't like me, and I'm cool with that,

but you gotta chill. I know he's feeling you, and that's OK."
I didn't say anything. "Well, I can see it in his eyes. It's
almost like you two motherfuckas have a connection, like
y'all know each other. So, I figured I would take him off
your hands for a little bit while you get shit popping with
Yung Swag."

"Lies, bitch. You tryin'a get in that man's pockets."

"And your point is? You about to get paid, so why can't
I?"

I wanted to tell her so badly that Lorenzo belonged to
me, but I didn't want him in the middle of anything I had
going on. Plus, I didn't trust Meka at this point. She tried
to walk away, but I grabbed her arm.

"Bitch, we're not here for that," I said, and Meka rolled
her eyes. "Drip probably got his eyes on us right now with
his deranged ass. He's probably hawking us."

"Girl, fuck Drip. I wanted to fuck Yung Swag anyway."

"Nah, Meka, Drip is too fucking crazy to be playing
with him. You saw what he did to Gucci and Parlay. Bad
enough I'm nervous as hell." I looked at her seriously. "I
don't think I want to do this anymore. Marcel's ass is in
jail, and he ain't getting out. Me robbing Yung Swag ain't
gon' help him come home any sooner." I rolled my eyes.
"This shit ain't even about Marcel. Drip is up to something,
and I have a feeling you know what it is."

"Bitch, I don't know shit, so don't even come at me
like that. You actin' like a bitch, for real. This nigga just
invited us upstairs to kick it with Yung Swag, and instead
of us going up there, you want to stand here and start an
argument with me."

"Whatever, Meka," I sighed heavily.

Right in the middle of this luxurious party, my best
friend and I argued. I was trying to protect Lorenzo.
Drip was crazy as fuck. I didn't want him to shoot up the
damn party. I definitely didn't want him to do anything

fucked up to my new boo. So, hell yeah, I was going to talk my shit and keep Meka and Drip away from Lorenzo. I wasn't sure where Lorenzo went, but by the time Meka and I were done pointing fingers and getting loud, he had disappeared. I looked at Meka with my nostrils flared and excused myself to go to the bathroom.

"Bitch, I gotta go pee, and don't fucking follow me." I turned on my heels.

"Girl, fuck you," she said as I walked away, my ass jiggling and all.

As soon as I entered the bathroom, I ran into the first stall and slammed the door shut. My stomach was doing flips. Not just any flips, though. It felt like a thousand gymnasts were in my gut doing those difficult-ass flips they be doing on TV. Bending over, I opened my mouth, and vomit instantly spewed out. This was the worst feeling ever. Plus, I didn't know what Drip was about to do to Yung Swag, and I was walking him right into a booby trap. What if Drip kills him? That shit wouldn't sit right with me knowing I had something to do with somebody's death. My conscience would be so fucked up. After throwing up, I flushed the toilet, opened the door, and walked over to the sink. My mascara was smeared a little, and my nose was running as well. So I pulled a paper towel from the holder and wiped at my face carefully, not wanting to mess up my makeup.

Someone knocked at the bathroom door. I turned to my left. I didn't have to say a word. I just stood there and watched Lorenzo walk inside. He stared at me as I stared at him, both of us confused with each other's presence. I didn't understand why he was here, and clearly, he wasn't expecting to run into me at this party.

"Lorenzo." I took my eyes from his face and focused on the floor. I didn't know what to say besides his name, so I said nothing else.

"Why are you here?" he asked. "What's going on?"

"What type of question is that? I'm here to have a good time with my friend," I said shortly, still looking down. I didn't want to feel see-through, so I didn't look in his face. This nigga was tugging at the heart I thought disappeared when Marcel went to jail.

"That's it?"

"Ye-yeah," I stuttered as I felt myself becoming queasy again.

"Don't lie to me," he said, placing his humongous hand underneath my chin and lifting my face. When I looked into his eyes, tears began to pour from mine. Lorenzo was turning me into a sucker.

"I can't tell you."

"Tell me what? Why didn't you want your friend to know we knew each other?"

"No, Lorenzo. I can't put you in the middle of this."

"Tisha." He grabbed me and wrapped his arms around me. "In the middle of what? What the fuck is going on?" Being so close to him felt so good. It took everything in me not to lick his entire bare chest. He was so damn caring.

"I'm here on a secret mission," I finally said honestly. "Damn, Lorenzo." I sighed and looked up at the ceiling.

"A secret mission?"

I took in a deep breath and blew it back out. Then I pushed away from him, ready to spill my guts. I didn't want to talk about Marcel with Lorenzo, but for him to understand where I was coming from, I had to.

"My ex-boyfriend was set up by the rapper, Yung Swag. Several years ago, they sold drugs together. I was told that Yung Swag tipped the police off about a drug deal Marcel and his friend Drip had done, which is why Marcel is in jail. At first, I wanted Yung Swag and his woman to suffer the same way Marcel and I had. Not being able to be with each other . . . Me and Marcel have been through a lot. He was the love of my life, and after losing him to jail, I was left out here alone." Lorenzo just stood there listening to me talk. His eyebrows were furrowed, which meant he was listening hard as hell.

"No money, no job skills, hell, no real-life skills. I wanted to make Yung Swag pay. That was . . . until I met you." I walked back up to Lorenzo and put my hands on his face.

"How did you plan to set up Yung Swag?" he asked. His tone and face were serious. He had me feeling like he was either going to help me or fuck me up.

"I-I . . ." I stammered over my words, knowing I was about to admit to him that I was a fucking prostitute. Most women who fucked for money could never take that title and own it. They'd always say some shit like "I'm not fucking no man for free." But I just call it what it is. It is definitely prostitution. "I'm supposed to get him to leave with me, have sex with him, and leave everything else to Drip."

Lorenzo stepped back and frowned. He and I had yet to have sex. We'd had plenty of phone sex, and he'd even eaten my pussy. I had sucked his dick, but there hadn't been any actual penetration.

"And fuckin' him is that simple for you? Setting men up sits well on your conscience?" he asked with his eyes squinted.

"No, it doesn't sit well, and that's why I feel sick to my stomach. I don't want to go through with this, but Drip threatened to hurt me if I don't." I broke down crying, thinking he would try to comfort me. "A few weeks ago, he shot up a whole block right in front of me."

"You do know Yung Swag is my cousin, right?" My eyes grew big as hell, and now it was my turn to take a step back. Now that I told him what I was sent here to do, I knew he was about to fuck me up. I'm not gonna lie, but a bitch was scared as fuck.

"I didn't know. I don't want to hurt him, though. I don't want to be a part of any of this," I said frantically. My lips were moving a mile a minute.

"You are going to go through with this. I don't want that nigga to hurt you. I actually know Marcel. Me, him, and my cousin all grew up together. I don't know Drip, but I've heard of him. I moved away to the suburbs when I was in the fifth grade, and we lost contact. My cousin was supposed to be putting Marcel down with his record label before he went to jail. Word around the hood is his so-called best friend Drip set him up, and that's why Swag stopped fucking with both them niggas altogether. My cousin was working too hard building an empire. He didn't have time for the fuck shit."

I blinked, almost in tears all over again. I knew Meka had to be just as oblivious as I was; she just had to be. There was no way she knew this information. Marcel was her favorite cousin. Drip played us both.

"Follow through with your plans. I got something for that nigga."

"So, you want me to fuck your cousin?" I asked.

"If that's what it takes. Whatever you need to do, do it." Lorenzo was visibly upset, but I didn't want him to be mad at me. I was sucked into the lifestyle. Whether I was selling pussy or trying to set up a nigga, I didn't choose this. This isn't something I just woke up one day and decided would be my life. At least in my heart, I didn't feel like this life was by choice.

"Lorenzo." I pulled his face to mine and kissed his lips. I didn't know how to feel about him being OK with me fucking his cousin.

However . . . Minutes later, Lorenzo escorted Meka and me into VIP. He walked us over to Yung Swag and the rest of his entourage.

"What's good, cuz?" Yung Swag said as he shook hands with Lorenzo. The entire time, he had his eyes on me. "Shorty finally decided to come up here, I see." He looked at me and bit down on his bottom lip. Damn, his teeth were icy.

"Yeah, shit. Shorty said she didn't know you or none of your music, so I had to make sure she got a chance to meet you."

"Is that right?" He looked at me like I was a piece of meat. He was definitely ready to eat up my entire body.

"Yeah," I said, looking him up and down. He ran his hand down from my breasts to my navel, and I caught his hand before he could go any further. "Nice to meet you, Swag."

"Hell yeah."

"Aye, me and Meka will be over here." Lorenzo gestured his head in the direction of the bar. After he and Meka walked away, Yung Swag and I continued our evening.

"Yo' body tight as hell, shorty, and yo' pussy fat too." He walked up on me and rubbed up against me. Running his fingers across my pussy print, I grimaced.

I felt like shit making Lorenzo watch me have an intimate moment with his cousin. I guess men were different from women when it came to emotions because I could never. . . My face was already scowled as I was silently suffering on the inside, watching him talk to Meka. The phony bitch had her hand all on my man's chest.

"Can we take a few shots?" I asked, and he agreed.

We took a few shots together until he was bent, and I was semi-tipsy. When I walked into VIP, he had a cup of brown liquor in his hand, so I assumed that's why he was so easily wasted. I wasn't complaining, though.

The rest of the evening was filled with me dancing on Yung Swag. He even forced me to play with his dick in the corner. I admit, he was definitely packing, and I offered to service him when I got him alone. After he said he was with it, I gave Meka the eye, and that was all she wrote. I was about to bring him to Drip. Yung Swag was willing to leave with me, no security, no nothing.

Chapter 16

Santana

Fuckin' Wit' Me

Passionate moans and throaty grunts echoed throughout the spacious Range Rover. In the backseat, I squatted over the girth of a man I'd just met hours earlier. He had a face only a mother could love, but that was neither here nor there.

My "yes, daddy" and his "fuuuucks" were so loud, for moments at a time, we drowned out the sweet melody of a few chirping birds that sang beautifully, welcoming the already risen sun. The potent smell of brown liquor and sweat seeped from our pores, penetrating my nostrils, forcing me to grimace. After the ten shots I'd had at the party, I felt as if I would vomit, but I continued to go with the flow. I couldn't fuck up the plan. After officially meeting Swag and dancing with him for hours, not to mention how he made me play with his dick in the club, I was ready to get paid for my time.

"That's right, baby, ride this dick," he said drunkenly as he whispered in my ear.

Feeling his warm breath on my ear forced goose bumps to form on my skin instantly. I moaned, pulling my ear away from his lips as I sat up. I had to think about all the beautiful evenings with Lorenzo, whether that was phone sex or just a simple conversation, to get me in the mood. Because there was nothing beautiful about the way I was fucking this man. And it was all for the sake of money and me fearing for my life.

Looking down at him, I kissed his lips softly, shushing him. I usually didn't kiss men who weren't mine, but I'd never been with a nigga with diamond teeth. As I ran my tongue across them, I tasted nothing but money. *What if Lorenzo can't take care of me the way I need him to?* I thought. I would be giving all this hoeing up for nothing.

Morning dew covered the windshield as fog from our gyrating bodies graced the tint of the side and back windows. We were both intoxicated and working hard, both racing toward a climax, but I was determined to put him into a deep coma with all this pussy power. With my arms hugging the headrest and his face planted deep in between my breasts, I rotated my hips back and forth. Euphoria covered my whole body, causing me to shake and shiver. I was almost there. Like Megan Thee Stallion, I worked my legs and knees, never taking a break or missing a beat. The birds' "one band-one sound" orchestrated this entire thing, rhythmically forcing my body to move to their tune.

It was six something in the morning. Too late and too early for me to still be awake, doing the nasty with a man I didn't know. Honestly, I didn't know this man from a can of paint. Shit, I don't listen to his music or nothing. Hell, I don't even remember his real name, but I'm sure he told me. Well, I think he told me. Even if he didn't, the big-ass knot I felt in his pocket while he grinded up against me all night long at the party made little trivial things like that not even matter. The whole time we danced, I discreetly searched his body. I was so extra, touching him and laughing at his weak-ass jokes, looking for everything I could steal.

Some good dick, check! His wad of money, double check! His three chains, triple check! His Red Bottoms, Versace shirt, hell, I'm even stealing this nigga's drawers. *Check, check, check, check, bitch,* I thought to myself.

Shortly after, I felt his body convulse, signaling he had ejaculated. His head fell back against the headrest as I slid off him. His eyes were closed, and without a word, he began to snore. The nigga was knocked out. I removed the condom from his dick, careful not to lose any of his sperm. I tied a knot in the rubber. I planned to freeze his babies and attempt to sell his shit to the highest bidder on eBay or Craigslist.

Buzz, buzz. I heard my cell vibrate in my purse and gravel on the other side of the window as a vehicle came to a complete stop. I looked over at him and took a deep breath. I began to slip back into my little-ass bikini, and I put his babies inside my bra for safekeeping. He was out cold, so I didn't worry about moving around too much. Sighing, I put my hand to the window and wiped away the smog.

"Bitch, come on!" Meka yelled as Drip exited her passenger side and walked over to the truck.

My head was on a swivel as I searched for something to put his items inside. *Fuck,* I thought to myself. My heart was beating fast as hell, feeling like I was pressed for time. I needed to get up out of this jam ASAP. I looked under the seat in front of me and sighed in relief as I pulled a black plastic bag from underneath it. I began picking up all Yung Swag's possessions and tossing his shit into the bag. I didn't even bother going through his shorts to see how much money he had on him. I knew he was paid, and I knew his pockets were stacked. I made sure I didn't leave anything behind. After I had everything I came for, I reached forward and popped the locks to the Range before making my exit. I opened the door, still dressed in my bathing suit, as I ran over to Meka's car and got in. My heart was beating so fucking fast. Robbing Yung Swag was so fucking fun, but what we didn't know was that he had eyes everywhere. Meka and I clapped hands.

"Bitch, what's in them pockets?" she asked as she put her car into drive. I reached inside, pulling out his money. I flared the bills out and was fucking disappointed when I saw a one-hundred-dollar bill on top and the rest were singles and fives.

"Bitch!" I yelled. "That nigga played me!"

"What? What happened?"

"Look!" I showed her the money.

Before we could react, Meka's car was suddenly riddled with bullets. We both screamed as hot metal penetrated the doors, windows, and our bodies. I looked over at Meka as a bullet blew through the driver's-side window, right into the side of her head. I cried so hard after witnessing my friend taking her last breath. Now, it was my turn. Another bullet rapidly made its way into the side of my neck and then the passenger's seat headrest. I absolutely knew I was dead. I closed my eyes as my adrenaline calmed the pain of my leaking bullet wound. As the gunfire ceased, a serene feeling took over my body.

These mufuckas really took us out of our glow, and the shit wasn't even worth it. The summer for us came to an end with a bang, and I mean that shit literally. This was supposed to be my last hurrah before I got back to what I thought was everyday life. I had found someone I really liked. Someone I was trying to build with. I even let that man call me Tisha. Shit was crazy. Although we were brand new to this, I wanted to see where this love thing went. Lorenzo wasn't no thug-ass nigga, nor was he a drug dealer. He was a real man.

But it was too late for should've, could've, would've. So, as I lay here next to Meka, almost breathless with my eyes wide open, I couldn't wait until death finally took me away.

Epilogue

Drip

I was a master of manipulation. I needed a motha-fuckin' award for the shit I pulled off. I ain't never have shit growing up. So, now, I was determined to have it all. What people didn't know about me is that I don't give a fuck about nothing or nobody. If it didn't benefit me, I stayed away from it.

For example, Meka . . . I had that ho wrapped around my finger. I was fucking her so good that I had her thinking I was in love, which, in return, made her fall for me. She wasn't shit but a prostitute in my eyes. Always begging for money every time we fucked like I was a trick or her personal bank account. Nigga, I was a player, and I never did shit without a motive. So, I decided to use her the same way she tried to use me. Money wasn't shit to me, especially not the little paper I was giving her, so I was willing to fund her lifestyle as I worked my way to the bigger picture. That weak-ass hundred-dollar rent and eighty-dollar light bill didn't put a dent in my cash, especially since I was living off the rest of Marcel's money.

I needed shorty to trust me. She believed in me so much that she didn't even question if I had anything to do with her favorite, bitch-ass, big cousin going to jail. Instead, I had her feeling sorry for me and the fact that my ace was locked up doing twenty years. The bitch really believed I missed that soft-ass nigga. Yeah, I let CPD know about the drugs and shit. I needed Marcel out of the way so I could be on top. I did just that, but somehow and someway, word got back to the hood that I was the reason he was locked up. Still, Marcel didn't believe a word the hood was saying. He knew I was a loyal nigga . . . or so he thought.

Them niggas ran me out of the hood quick as fuck. That shit didn't matter, though. I still had a few niggas ready to ride for me without a question. I was on to bigger and better things, especially after I decided to rob Marcel's business partner and newest Chicago rap mogul, Yung Swag. And Marcel's ex-bitch, who played me to the left back in the day, was going to slut for me and bring that nigga to me.

Santana and Meka were some dumb-ass bitches. I never had love for a ho or nigga. So, after I was in Yung Swag's Range Rover, I gave the signal for my li'l homies to air them bitches out while I rode off with Yung Swag knocked out asleep in the backseat. I was going to torture his ass until he led me to at least a million dollars. I needed to make Chicago, hell, Illinois, a distant memory.

As I pulled into an abandoned warehouse, I parked and pulled my gun off my hip. I got out, walked to the passenger's side, opened the door, and smacked the fuck outta Yung Swag with my pistol. He screamed and tried to cover his face in defense, but I was all over that nigga. He was clearly disoriented and confused as I savagely yanked him from the backseat, asshole naked and all.

"What's going on?" he asked repeatedly. This shit was too easy. He still had a hood mentality, thinking his city loved him so much that he could just ride around without protection.

"You know what this is," I stated. I dragged him over to a pole where there were twist ties laid out on the ground.

It's crazy how everything I needed was laid out for me. I guess after he heard my voice, he realized who I was, and he began to come to.

"Drip, G, what the fuck is you doin'?" he asked as I finally got him to the pole and began trying to tie him up. I felt like an officer as I held the nigga down while he resisted. But I didn't even get a chance to tie up the nigga as I was hit from behind. I took a blow to the back of my head with the butt of a gun. Falling to the floor on my hands and knees, my gun slid away from me. I looked behind me and saw the face of a nigga I'd never seen before.

"Yo, cuz, you good?" he asked as Yung Swag slowly nodded his head. Soon after, I felt a size 14 boot kick me in my side. I fell to the floor, coughing and choking, trying to catch my breath. Dude's big-ass boot had me winded.

"Man, fuck you." I rolled on my back and held my side. I saw the gun in his hand. I was ready to die. I wasn't ducking shit. I had done too much dirt in my life to fear a nigga pointing his gun in my face. "You pointin' that gun; you better use it," I warned.

Yung Swag stood to his feet, holding his face. The whole time, I was surprised I didn't knock none of them cubic zirconium teeth out of his damn mouth, but he was bleeding like a mufucka.

He spat on the ground before saying, "Nah, Lorenzo, G, he ain't even worth yo' bullets. Let that nigga breathe. Life killing that nigga slowly anyways."

As the two began to walk away, I tried to stand up. I needed to get to my gun. I wasn't letting him leave with his life or without me getting paid. That just was *not* in my plans. As soon as I was on my feet, men dressed in all black with police shields, body armor, and guns came rushing into the warehouse. I knew this was it for me. I wasn't about to go to jail. Being caged up like an animal just wasn't for me.

"Put your hands up," I heard a voice say as I watched Yung Swag's cousin pull a dog tag-looking badge from underneath his shirt.

I laughed slightly. Damn, I didn't think this shit through, man. I tried to dive for my gun and was instantly shot multiple times. Bullets rained down on me from all directions, hitting me in the chest, legs, arms, and forehead. I fell to the ground, lifeless, as a pool of blood quickly began to surround my body. Fuck, I guess in the end, Karma found a way to take me out.

Santana

Beep! Beep! Beep!

I heard monitors going off in my ears as my eyes began to flutter open. It was like walking into the light as the sun beamed down on me. I never knew hell could be so bright, or was this heaven? The room was white and smelled sterile, but I knew I had done too much wrong for the Lord to welcome me through the pearly gates. This couldn't be heaven.

The last thing I remembered was robbing Yung Swag and being in the car with Meka, counting up all the cash I had stolen from his pockets as she pulled away from the scene. The next thing I knew, bullets flew through the window like pellets. I remember seeing Meka getting shot in her head, and I remember screaming and crying, knowing my friend was gone. Shit, after taking a bullet to the neck, I knew my life was over too. In the back of my mind, I couldn't help but think Lorenzo had sent me off. Because where the hell was he to protect me and Meka? But when you're a money-hungry bitch, you had to take life for what it was. Although I hooked up with Yung Swag to avenge Marcel's incarceration, and because

I was scared as fuck of Drip, I was also in it for the money. Still, I ended up with nothing.

As I focused my eyes and began to cough up phlegm, the monitors beeped faster. Nurses quickly filled the room, smiling, excited to see me awake. I was obviously still alive.

"Detective White!" I heard a staff member yell out. "Miss Santana is awake."

I tried to sit up, but my body was weak as fuck. I put my hand to my neck, and a big-ass bandage was stuck there, protecting and healing my wound.

Detective White? I thought to myself. Why is there a detective here? I began moving around, wanting to get the fuck up outta here. I couldn't go to jail.

"Just relax, Miss Santana, lie back," a nurse said. I tried to speak, but I had a tube stuck down my throat.

A few seconds later, Lorenzo came running into the room. He looked at me, and I sighed in relief. The sight of him was soothing. He was familiar. I was excited to know he had been by my side this entire time. Lorenzo was here to save me, I thought . . . until I saw the police shield around his neck. Tears began to rush from my eyes. He was a cop, possibly investigating me—or worse, here to lock me up for the shit I pulled on Yung Swag. I had no one to help me get out of this. I had no clue what Drip had done to Yung Swag.

"Are you guys able to remove the tube?" I heard him ask. I just knew he was about to question me. I needed to get my story together.

"Yes, she's breathing just fine. The tube can come out now."

Ten minutes later, the tube was removed, and I was laid up on Lorenzo's chest, no longer afraid. Of course, he questioned me about my lifestyle, and I decided to keep it all the way true with him. He deserved that much.

Lorenzo explained that the shit Drip told me about Yung Swag was untrue. He used Meka and me to do his dirty work. I could've beat the hell out of myself, believing a sucka-ass nigga like Drip. At that point, I knew he had set up Meka and me. And Lorenzo confirmed it when he told me Drip was behind the shooting of Meka and me. He also let me know that Meka and Drip were dead. I cried so hard for my friend. She didn't deserve that shit. She was like a sister to me and the only person I had left. It has been three weeks since the shooting, and, of course, I missed my friend's funeral. That shit fucked me up, but life had to go on.

The rest of the day, Lorenzo and I hung out, cuddled up, loving on each other. A few days later, I was out of the hospital. Instead of going home, Lorenzo took me to his condo. He decided to stay in Chicago until I was well enough to take care of myself. I love him for that. Being with him was like a love I had never felt before.

He pampered me like a little baby, and when I was well enough, he finally made love to me. He laid me down gently. He told me how much he loved me and didn't give a damn about the life I lived before him. With slow strokes, he kissed my lips as I scratched his back, marking my territory. The shit was magical. I could've sworn I saw the sun, the stars, and the damn moon. No lie, I think I saw heaven when he made love to me. I'm being silly, but on some real shit, Lorenzo now had my heart and soul wide open. If only Meka could see me and the smile this man was putting on my face, she would probably say, "Fuck love, make that nigga pay you." But he loved me, and I loved him. He had the type of love money couldn't buy. His heart was pure and giving. After dealing with Marcel, I wasn't sure if love was what I really wanted. However, Lorenzo forced the feeling on me. He never brought up the shit about me fucking his cousin, Yung Swag. We put that day behind us and moved forward with life. I think, more than anything, Lorenzo was just happy I was still alive.

After two months of him taking care of me, we decided we would be together. I said deuces to the projects and moved into the condo permanently. That is when we became a family. Lorenzo was that nigga. He took me from poverty to luxury within the blink of an eye. As soon as he gets time off from work, we plan to take a much-needed vacation. It's crazy how I went from wifey to a ho and back again. Honestly, I don't even want the wifey title. I prefer wife. There's a big difference. I went from being with a jailbird to being with a detective, from a Marcel to a Lorenzo. This time, I wasn't going anywhere, and neither was my man. This summer has taught me a lot about life. Specifically, you don't always have to use what you have to get what you want. Sometimes, your heart is enough, and it'll attract that one special person when the time is right.

Thot Girl Summer in Detroit

by

T. Friday

Dedication

This book is dedicated to the five most important people in my life, my brat pack: Jordin, Jacob, Jacory, Jakayla, and Jalisa. Please understand that everything I do and every struggle I overcome is so that you guys don't have to worry about a thing. I love you guys, and don't ever forget it.

Acknowledgments

To my Blunt, you have been in my corner and stood by me for the last fifteen years. Although I be getting on your nerves, you never switched up on me. Our bond is unbreakable.

To my publisher, Racquel Williams of RWP, you rock! People always say make your first choice your best one, and I can say making you my first and only publisher was the best decision I could have ever made. Over the past few years of working with you, I have learned so much in this industry. No matter what the situation is, you have had my back every time. You have shown me nothing but love, and for that, I truly appreciate you.

Jasmine Moore and Jennifer Dinwiddie, I appreciate you two for always being my listening ear when I talk about my characters as if they are real people. Y'all's time is just around the corner.

To my Pen Sister Christine Davis, it's because of you that I'm doing something I love. I really appreciate you and your grind.

To my wonderful readers and my supporters, I'm nothing without you guys. For the last four years and twenty-five books later, you guys have read and reviewed all of my books, and I appreciate every one of you. I just want to say thank you from the bottom of my heart. It really touches my heart when I hear some of you say I have become one of your favorite authors. You all make me keep going stronger.

Acknowledgments

To my dearest baby sister, Amanda Jordin Hollis, my white chick, I love and miss you so much. I swear, fifteen years wasn't long enough to have you here with us. I'd give anything to hear your voice again.

To my mom, Lisa, and dad, David, I wish you guys were here to see that I'm finally doing something I love and know for a fact that you two would be proud. I love and miss you guys so much. Please continue to watch over the family.

Chapter One

Trina McKnight

As I lay on my back with my legs resting on this fat nigga's shoulders, all I could think about was how this turned out to be my life. I couldn't lie, the money was feeding a bitch, but I was tired of using my pussy to make a living. I constantly told myself this would be the last summer I sold pussy to pay for my classes the following fall.

"Who pussy is this, bitch?" Reggie growled in my ear, like a wild animal.

Hearing that shit was irritating to my soul, but I fucked with him before and knew this fat nigga paid more when I boosted his ego. I took it as either he knew his dick was trash and needed that boost, or he really thought he was killing the pussy.

"It's yours, daddy. Yes, fuck your pussy, daddy," I moaned out with a fake, screwed up face just in case he was watching. Like I said, this nigga loved for me to play roles.

Truth be told, I couldn't feel shit, and this is why every time I fucked with him, I always went home to finish what he started. Shit, I had toys that made me wetter and fucked me better than this fat muthafucka.

"Aww, shit, I'm coming," he moaned just after a short seven minutes of hard pumping.

Lord knows I tried so hard not to laugh in this nigga's face, but that ugly-ass expression he makes when he's about to release is comical. I just couldn't hold it in any longer.

Reggie must have caught an attitude because as soon as I started laughing, he pulled his little shooter out and aimed straight toward my fucking face.

"You disrespectful, nasty-ass muthafucka!" I yelled, snatching the sheet to wipe off my face.

Reggie was the one laughing now. "Is it still funny, bitch?"

I wanted to yell out, "*Hell yeah, fat, little-dick bitch*," but he looked like he was ready to beat my ass. My gun was on the other side of the room, in my purse, on the dresser.

I watched as Reggie picked up my shirt to wipe off his dick. This fat muthafucka then had the nerve to toss the nasty shirt in my face like I wasn't shit. I guess, in my line of work, I wasn't.

Shit only got worse from there. Can you believe he had the nerve to walk out the door without even leaving me gas money to get home?

I got in my car feeling like I was playing the game all backward. Instead of selling pussy, my stupid ass was handing the shit out like free candy on Halloween.

No money, no nut. I was all fucked up.

On my way home, I prayed I'd be able to leave this bullshit-ass way of living for good. This couldn't be the life the Lord intended for me.

Growing up, I always wanted to own a soul food restaurant. I remember being in my grandma's kitchen, cooking with her. I've always been book smart. I guess I just picked the wrong road to travel down.

I came from nothing but wanted everything. After high school, me and my bestie Eve attended community college, taking out student loans and shit, thinking we were gonna live our best life. But shit got hard, and with no support team behind us, we were all we had, so we had to do some shit we weren't proud of.

I was the brains behind the two of us and made money by doing papers for some of my classmates while Eve worked in the school library. That helped with rent and bills in our small apartment, but at the end of the day, we were starving. Truth be told, we were some ramen noodle-eating muthafuckas until the New Year of our freshman year.

A hot shower and some leftovers were all I needed before climbing into bed.

It's crazy how just last night, I came home with several hundred, then tonight, I brought home nothing. For now, I was only gonna do business with certain muthafuckas. Not no little-dick muthafucka that couldn't even make me come. For now, it was all about me and what makes *me* happy.

"Turn that shit down, bitch!" I yelled, trying to bury my head in my pillow.

I loved my best friend Eve, but this bitch woke up too fucking early, blasting her music. After the night I had, I wasn't in the fucking mood to hear shit, but a deposit hitting my account.

Eve popped her head in my bedroom door. "Good morning, bitch. Get dressed so we can go to breakfast."

This bitch had the perfect shape but stayed eating.

I rolled my eyes before responding. "I'm tired and don't feel like leaving the house."

"You went out with Reggie's fat ass last night. What the fuck you tired from faking a nut?"

Although I was still pissed about being played, I had to laugh. Eve was the sillier one out of us.

"Oh my gawd, bitch, don't even remind me about last night. That's a whole 'nother story."

I watched as Eve walked in, then flopped her ass down on my bed. "Let's talk about it at breakfast. Come on, my treat."

Hearing that this bitch was gonna pay this time, I jumped my ass up. "Give me a minute to get dressed."

That minute of getting ready turned into two hours, and then more time picking somewhere to go. Eve and I ended up at Applebee's, eating lunch.

"So, what the fuck happened last night?" she asked, all in my business. Since this was my day one, I was ready to tell my story, *Surviving a Fat, Small-Dick Nigga.*

"Now, you know how I always told you he wasn't working with shit, and I always had to fake it, right?"

"Yeah," Eve quickly replied, ready to hear my story.

"Anyway, he was making this ugly-ass face, and I couldn't hold my laugh in. Fat muthafucka was mad and skeeted on my fuckin' face. Then his nasty ass picked up my shirt and wiped off his dick."

Eve's face told me she was just as pissed as me, if not even more.

"Eww, bitch. I would have popped his fat ass."

"That's not even the fucked-up part," I had to warn her.

"Damn, bitch, there's more to the story?" she questioned.

I hated to tell her, but I had to. "Yes, girl, there's more. Tell me why this muthafucka walked out of the room without paying me."

"Oh, hell nah, bitch. Where was your gun? I know you ain't let him play you like that."

"My shit was in my purse on the fuckin' dresser. I'd dealt with him a few times before, so I didn't think to have it near me," I tried to explain.

I knew Eve was disappointed in me by the way she shook her head. Shit, I was disappointed too.

Let's get this straight: I wasn't a twenty-four-hour, seven-day-a-week ho. I was actually paying my way through college. I thought I had a good plan to make easy money without working too hard to get it, and shit would be a straight shot to success. But I ended up hitting a few bumpy roads on the way. A bitch was tired, but I wasn't giving up.

"Now what?" Eve asked, still looking disappointed.

"To be honest, I'm sick of doing this shit anyway. If I wanna stay in school, I need to find a real job. If not, I'll be back at home with my mama, and you know I don't want that. I'm not trying to give her a reason to laugh at me."

I had so much love for Eve, and every day, no matter what, she showed me why I should love her.

"You're not dropping out of school. Even if I have to double up on my dick intake, I got you."

We laughed, but she was my ride or die for real.

Candy

Although I never sold my pussy, I hated hearing bitches talk about mismanaging theirs. I don't know why, because it wasn't my business, but it irked my nerves so badly. I wanted to go sit at their table and put these little hoes on game right then and there, but there's a time and place for everything.

I had finished with my salad, but I sat there a little longer, sizing up these girls. They were pretty in the face with nice tits and ass for days. I knew if they fucked with me, they could make some real money. And from the sound of shit, they needed my help.

Once I saw one chick pay the bill, then stand up so they could leave, I did the same. I didn't want to come off as a creep, so I tried to play it off as soon as we got to the parking lot.

"Excuse me, do one of you beautiful ladies have a lighter?"

The one named Eve shook her head no while the one who was giving out free pussy looked in her purse.

As I waited, I noticed they were label hoes from the bags to the shoes. Yeah, they had good taste, but they were rocking shit from three years ago, and it all screamed Goodwill. They needed my help to play catch-up on the latest shit.

"Here you go," she finally said, handing over her red Bic.

I took the lighter, then lit my blunt. "Thank you, girl. After that meal, I needed to hit this a few times. Y'all smoke?" I asked, handing over my blunt.

They stayed in the parking lot smoking with me, and just by that very action, I saw why niggas played their asses. These young hoes didn't know me from a can of paint and were cheefing my shit. What if I had laced my shit so I could kidnap they dumb asses or something?

From there, I knew how to play them.

After introducing ourselves, I pulled out my business card. "It's always nice to meet new people. I'm actually having a party this coming Saturday and wouldn't mind you two showing up. Why don't you guys call me, and I can go over the details, then send you my address?"

Eve was all in. "Sure, I'll be there."

Bitch was too excited, but I waited to see how Trina would respond. She seemed to be the chill one out of the two.

"What about you? I promise you're gonna have a ball," I said, trying to convince her.

It was just my luck that the dingy one of the two was on my side. "Come on, bitch, this gonna be fun. How often do we meet a cool female?"

"A'ight, girl, I'm down," I heard Trina say.

Before jumping in my Range Rover and driving off, I overheard Trina tell Eve she better have fun. I smiled, knowing they were gonna have fun . . . and much more. I was about to put on my cape and save these hoes.

Eve Santana

I searched through my closet trying to find something to wear to this weekend's party. I wasn't sure how it was gonna be, but I sure didn't wanna look like a bummy bitch in that muthafucka. I was known to be a bad bitch and needed to look such at all times.

I'd worn most of the shit I owned and needed something new. Frustrated and tired of being broke, I ended up with all my clothes in a pile on the floor.

Rushing into Trina's room, I started raiding her closet. "What the hell are we gonna wear tomorrow for this party?"

"I'm thinking about that short red dress that hugs my ass. Maybe I can pull a nigga or something 'cause a bitch broke."

I smiled at her decision. I felt a little jealous but smiled knowing that red dress was the shit. "Bitch, I don't have shit to wear. I wore all my sexy shit already," I whined.

Trina got up from the bed. "You the one who got a date tonight. Buy you something to wear in the morning."

I shook my head no. "I'm going out with Marcus, and you know he pays well, but I really wasn't trying to dip into my school money. Remember, we're trying to stack this summer, not spend."

Trina gave me a strange look. "Yeah, you right. Damn, what you gon' do?"

Turning my back to finish searching her closet, I let her know I would find something.

***

At eight o'clock on the dot, Marcus was outside waiting for me to come down like clockwork.

Since he was married and all, this man made sure to come out to play with me at least twice a week. He kept my pockets right and stayed telling me how much he loves me. I constantly told him not to do that shit. Not only was it weird, but also because of his wife. Strange thing is that shit didn't stop him at all.

Some probably question how I'm fucking a married man for money, but he brought up his wife when he expressed his feelings. It's simple. Business is business, and feelings are never to be mixed in.

He was in love with my sexy ass and the way this little black dress fit me. I could see why. I walked out the door and found Marcus standing with the passenger-side door open, waiting for me. He was a true gentleman when he wanted me to ride his face all night.

Before getting in, he tried to kiss me on the lips, knowing I don't play that shit.

"Marcus, what did I tell you about that shit?" I yelled, jumping into the car.

He got in the driver's seat. "What's the problem, baby?"

"You're married. Save those kisses for your wife."

He sat there for a minute before driving off. "I don't see why you be trippin' all the time. I love you, Eve, and ain't shit fake about that. Truth be told, I fuck you more than I fuck Tammy."

Shaking my head, I couldn't allow myself to fall for his shit. "We do business together, Marcus; that's it."

The way he started to breathe heavily, I could tell he was getting pissed. "What I gotta do to have you for myself? I'll leave her and take care of you and all your problems."

I sat there thinking about the game this white dude was trying to run on me. It all sounded good, but he was married. He wasn't gonna leave that bitch for me for real. He just talked a good game. I saw this shit on TV too often.

"Let's do what we're gonna do so we can call it a night. All this shit you talkin' about makes me wanna go home."

I was lying my ass off and wouldn't dare miss out on his money, but I needed him to understand where I was coming from.

Marcus was pissed, which meant he was about to pin me down to the bed and beat this pussy up. I smiled as my pussy thumped, thinking about his pink dick.

That's right. I was fucking this white man, and the sex was great. I was the first Black girl he'd ever been with, and he cherished my pussy. Truthfully, if he weren't married and could see me more than twice a week, I would only do business with him. This man paid good money and tipped even better. Sometimes, I wondered what he had to offer his wife because I was getting mine.

As soon as we got into the room, Marcus pulled out a tittie and started sucking and licking all over my nipple.

"I miss you so much, Eve," he moaned out between each suck.

His using one hand to pull my thong to the side so he could play with my clit had me dripping on his hand.

"You so fuckin' hot and wet, baby. Don't come just yet. You gotta let daddy taste that muthafucka first."

He was so nasty, but I loved it. "Yes, daddy, come eat on this forbidden apple."

Marcus picked me up to place me in the bed, and just like that, he was eating my pussy and ass like it was his last supper.

I tried so hard to leave before it was too late, but after that beat down, we were walking out at check-out time.

"What are you gonna tell your wife?" It wasn't my business, but I was curious. Marcus fucked me up with his answer.

"I'ma tell her I was balls deep in the one I love."

"Stop playing with me, Marcus. I told you before that we just do business together. You keep being on that bullshit, and I'm gon' cut you lose."

"I'm sorry, baby; please don't do that," he begged.

Although I hated to see a grown man beg, I could tell by the look in his eyes that he was hurt by my threatening to cut him off. It was apparent this man needed my pussy to breathe.

Marcus must've been caught up in his feelings because it took him extra long to drop me off at the apartment complex.

"Damn, we finally here. Thanks for the ride, Marcus."

"Anytime, my love."

I smiled as I watched him dig through his wallet.

"I hate that I'm married and can't have you completely to myself. I swear, just tell me when and I'll leave her for you."

With that being said, he handed over a knot of hundred-dollar bills. Keep in mind, he'd already given me $2,000 just to spend the night with him.

"Thank you, baby."

"Baby? I knew you'd come around," he jokingly teased.

We laughed together before I got out of the car.

Going into the house, I saw Trina was still in bed, knocked out. I didn't want to wake her, so I went to take a little nap myself. We had a big day ahead of us, and I needed all the energy in the world for tonight.

I lay there thinking about Marcus. I constantly told myself not to fall for his shit because, in real life, what man has left his wife for a bitch who sold pussy on the side?

After a good fuck, we'd cuddle in bed, and he'd remind me he was in love with me and only married Tammy because he got her pregnant and her dad sort of forced him to marry her ass. Now that the dad is dead, he feels like he doesn't have to stick around any longer. I wasn't sure if he was just saying what he thought I wanted to hear, but I knew deep down inside that Marcus would take care of me and everything. But something told me I didn't want the drama that would come with him. Other than cheating with me, Marcus seemed to be a good man, and Tammy wasn't gonna let him go without a fight.

Chapter Two

Candy

"I hire you fools to do these parties twice a month. There's no way y'all should be fucking up this bad!" I yelled at the party designers.

I wasn't your average female boss, and I was the best at what I did. Jasper left my boss ass in charge for a reason.

Looking back, I wasn't a wild child growing up, but I knew what I did and didn't want. When I turned 17, I learned the true value of my pussy. Daddy wasn't in the picture, and my mama didn't give a fuck about me for real. When her boyfriend at the time tried to stick his dirty dick in me while I was sleeping, I kicked his ass. I busted that muthafucka's head open with the lamp that rested on my nightstand, then ran into my mama's room looking for help. This bitch was sitting on the edge of the bed smoking a cigarette. She actually got mad because I didn't let him fuck me with his dirty dick. She cried, saying he was gonna leave her because *I* wouldn't act right. I had to whoop her up too before getting the fuck on. Mama or not, I didn't play that shit. If her pussy wasn't good enough for his bum ass, then he just needed to leave. I ended up on the streets for about a month before I met Jasper.

Jasper was way older than I was. I'm talking about twenty years my senior, but at the time, he was my savior. He fed me the night he picked me up from the bus bench and invited me to his home. I was scared, but it was the end of November, and it was cold as hell outside. For a week or so, I lived a good life in his baby mansion and felt like a queen. After that short period of time, I knew I never wanted to go back home or be on the streets again, and he made me feel like that would never be an option.

One night, after I got out of the shower, Jasper came into my bedroom. That night, he talked to me about the type of business he was involved in. At first, it scared me, but he promised nothing would happen that I didn't want to happen. After getting deeper into the conversation, I told him I was scared because I was still a virgin. He was shocked because at 17, most females had already been fucking, and some were mothers. He told me I would make even more money because I wasn't ran through, and they loved fresh meat the most. I needed the money, but selling my pussy to a bunch of weird muthafuckas wasn't my thing.

Jasper thought I was stupid because I was young and had been sleeping on the streets, but I wasn't a dumb bitch. That night, I lost my virginity to him, but only after making the deal of a lifetime. He was allowed to have my virginity if I could stay there and only be his. He tossed in me helping him find other girls to work for him, and that's how I made my own money. Once his tongue touched my pussy, the deal was sealed.

Turning 18 and finally grown, Jasper asked me to marry him. He was the only man I had been with and loved, so I said yes. When I turned 22, Jasper died but was generous enough to leave everything to me, even his business. Over the years, I've been the one helping these hoes make money by throwing these parties twice a month.

My parties weren't for the broke. I had the politicians, rappers, football players, doctors, and even lawyers attending, paying top dollar to fuck one of my girls. Every month, they sent a payment to my account simply to enter my home. They paid the girls whatever they worked out, and I didn't give a fuck because I got my money off top. I did have meetings to remind these girls to never lowball their pussy because these muthafuckas were paid, and after a good fuck, they should be as well.

"Why aren't the bottles on ice?" I asked the bartender in disbelief.

Just as I was about to pop off, my phone rang.

"This is Candy," I softly spoke into the phone.

"Hey, this Eve. Remember you smoked some weed with me and my homegirl Trina?"

I shook my head, hearing Eve's ghetto ass. If I decided to keep her around, I was gonna have to work with her ass, for real.

"Oh yes, I remember," I quickly said, hoping she would get to the point.

She started ranting about them coming and trying to see what type of party it was, so they could dress appropriately.

"Love, just dress your best. I must also mention that my pool and jacuzzi will be open for use tonight, so feel free to bring a swimsuit."

"OK. This party sounds like it's gonna be off the hook. We'll see you tonight."

"All right, come prepared to have a ball." With that being said, I quickly hung up.

Then I went to my office to check out things. My account was extra fat, and my clientele list was popping for the night. With these two new girls, I knew things were gonna get better for me *and* them.

"Ma'am, I made sure each room has clean sheets on the bed and towels in the bathrooms," Sarah informed me.

"Thanks, hunny."

Sarah walked away, leaving me to my thoughts.

I often sat at this very desk where Jasper fucked me after looking at his account. I missed the fuck out of him every day and knew he would be so proud of me and the way I was keeping his business going strong. Sometimes, I wondered if he put a curse on me. Still, to this day, he is the only man I have given my heart and pussy to. Like I mentioned before, I wasn't into selling my pussy, although I was a beast at selling the next bitch's pussy. All the rich dick that swung in and out of my home didn't do shit for me. Every night, I went to sleep with a rubber dick vibrating in my pussy.

Eve

"What about this one?" I asked Trina, holding up a pretty yellow dress.

Trina gave me a strange look. This is why I hate going shopping with her. Her ass was too picky for me.

"What's wrong with it, bitch?"

"Only get that dress if you gon' walk into the party rapping, *'I got an ass so big like the sun.'*"

I couldn't help but laugh. "You a petty bitch."

"I'm just saying, pick something a little safer. We don't know these people for real," she tried to explain to me.

At the end of our shopping trip, I ended up getting a little black dress. I guess black was the safest color to wear. Since I mentioned to Trina that this was also a pool party, we picked up a new bikini just in case we got in the mood.

We weren't sure how the party would turn out, but we still wanted to look our best. We never knew who we could run into. The way we looked at it, there was money to be made everywhere.

***

Later that night, as Trina drove to the location of the party, we couldn't help but wonder exactly where we were going. Looking at the expensive houses, we knew for sure we were no longer in the hood. Even with our funds combined, we could never do it *that* big.

"Oh my gawd, bitch, that is the house right there."

Looking over at the baby mansion, I was shocked. "This can't be it. Maybe that bitch gave us the wrong address and got us on a dummy mission. I know she don't stay out here."

Trina started to point. "Look at the cars pulling up over there. That has to be the party. Let's go have some fun."

After parking, we stood outside the car, making sure we were both on point.

Trina looked good in her famous, fitted red dress. And, of course, my ass was looking plump in the black dress I found at the last minute.

"We're gonna be the baddest bitches in there tonight."

She giggled. "Ain't we always?"

"Cause *periodt.*"

Stepping in, we were like kids in a fucking candy store. The layout of the house was so beautiful, and everything looked so expensive.

"She must have rented this bitch out," Trina whispered.

Before I could agree with my girl, Candy snuck up behind us.

"Actually, my late husband left it to me."

Trina was embarrassed that Candy heard her and quickly tried to apologize. "I'm so sorry, girl. I just assumed that because you're our age, this couldn't have been your house."

Candy smiled. "It's OK, girl. Trust me, many don't believe me when they find out this is my house. By the way, I got y'all beat by a couple of years."

"Damn, bitch, you look good."

Candy smiled in between sipping on her drink. "Thanks, Eve," she responded.

We stood there for a moment just looking around at the party guests. There were a lot of females who I had to admit were all bad, but it was the male guests who caught my attention.

"Oh my gawd, is that Big Rob, that rapper from 7 Mile?" I asked.

"Yeah, that's him. Do you wanna meet him?"

"Hell yeah, I love his music," I said, too excited.

Candy grabbed my hand, then walked me across the room.

"Look, these niggas don't like all that groupie shit, so you gotta calm down. Treat this nigga like he a regular-ass nigga."

"All right, I got it," I said as I tried my hardest not to be geeked up about meeting a celebrity.

"Hey, Robert, so glad you could make it. This is my new friend Eve, and she's dying to meet you."

I stepped up so that I could say hi as she walked away.

"Hey, I'm Eve, and I love your music. Been a fan since day one," I admitted.

"How are you doing, Eve? I must admit that I have some beautiful fans."

This man was running game, and I knew not to take his words to heart. I pretended whatever he was saying to me was only for me and not a repeat from the last bitch. We sat at the bar to continue our conversation. He was trying to impress me by ordering the most expensive bottle they had. He was good for it, so I didn't stop him.

"How long have you known Candy? I've never seen you at one of her parties before."

"I just met her the other day, and she invited me and my girl to this gathering."

"So, this your first party?"

I giggled at the way he asked me that. "Yeah. Didn't I tell you I just met her like two days ago?"

Big Rob's hand left the bar top, then found its way to my leg. My legs were crossed, but that didn't stop him from sliding his hand up the split in my dress. I couldn't believe my favorite rapper was trying to get fresh with me, a local nobody. Pulling me up from my seat and onto his lap, Big Rob whispered in my ear as he placed small kisses on my neck.

"Let's go somewhere quieter."

I knew what *those* lines meant. He was tired of the small talk and was ready to fuck. I started to wonder if Big Rob was really big like the way he rapped about in his songs. Standing up, I was ready for whatever. I allowed him to get up and lead me to one of the million rooms upstairs.

Big Rob didn't even try to get me into bed. This nigga picked me up and sat me on the edge of the bathroom sink before quickly pulling out his dick. Having no panties on made it easy for him to reach this pussy that was dying to feel him inside of it. Moments later, he was jamming that bitch into my pussy. No foreplay, no pussy eating—nothing. This nigga was a whole fraud behind his music because his dick wasn't even that big. While his ass was rapping about ten inches, my guess was a good seven with a slight curve, but he was working that muthafucka.

I couldn't lie. This nigga had me folded up on the sink, beating up my shit, but my thoughts were everywhere. I couldn't help but wonder why the fuck I didn't make him wear a condom. My dumb ass wasn't that damn starstruck. Or was I? As he sped up his pace, I started to push him back.

"Wait a minute."

"Damn, shorty, what's up?" he said, slowing down just a little.

"Don't come in me."

Big Rob started laughing. "Trust me, I won't. I'll never get caught up in all that baby mama bullshit."

Without saying shit else, he yanked me up before turning me around so he could feel this wet pussy from the back. This nigga didn't know me, and I didn't know him in real life, but the way he was fucking me made me feel used and cheap. I made up my mind that once we were done, a bitch was gonna make him pay for this pussy.

"Oh shit," he yelled out before pulling his dick out and rubbing his nut all over my ass cheek.

"Damn, I hope you didn't get that shit on my dress," I said before realizing he had pulled my dress all the way up to my titties.

"Nah, shorty, you good."

As I started to stand up, Big Rob stopped me. "Wait a minute."

He turned on the water in the tub and grabbed a washcloth from the shelf. I felt the warm washcloth wipe up his mess. At least he was thinking of me, but he still had to pay. Once I stood up to fix myself, Big Rob grabbed another washcloth so he could wash my pussy.

Next, he dropped both washcloths down the laundry chute.

I wasn't sure how to ask for a payment, but I couldn't afford not to get anything out of the deal but a wet ass.

"So, about what just happened . . ."

He didn't even give me a chance to finish as he pulled out a knot from his pocket.

"Here you go. Maybe we can hook up at the next party."

With that being said, he walked out, not bothering to look back.

I held the money for a hot second before counting the hundred-dollar bills.

"$10,000?"

Trina

Eve had left me, but I wasn't too worried because she was still at the party somewhere. Besides, after talking to Candy about taking up a business management class in school, she introduced me to this guy named Gerald. He was an older guy but owned his own barbershop, two to be exact.

I knew of him from the news before. Every year, for the last three years, he had been doing those back-to-school giveaways in the hood. He would even cut the little boys' hair for free.

"So, what type of business were you looking to get into?"

I couldn't help but smile. Besides sitting around, talking to Eve about my dreams and goals, I never had anyone ask about me.

"Although I have a few tricks up my sleeve, I wanna open a soul food restaurant."

"You must throw down in the kitchen."

"Hell yeah, I'm a beast," I said, tooting my own horn.

He smiled. "Maybe one day you can cook me dinner, and I'll be the judge of that."

"Slow down, playboy. Didn't I see you on the news with your wife and four kids?"

Gerald felt the pressure and took a sip of his drink. "What that got to do with you makin' me a meal?"

"I never met a wife that would allow another bitch to cook for her husband."

I knew Eve fucked with married men, but I didn't.

"You lookin' too much into it, baby girl. You show me a good time with a meal included, and I'll show you how much I appreciate you with a large tip."

I sat there looking foolish. For some reason, I felt like I had the word *trick* written on my fucking forehead.

"Are you new to this type of party or something, baby girl?" he questioned.

I took a minute to look around. This shit wasn't a fucking party. It was a meet-and-get-fucked type of party. Everything was clear now, and I understood why there were all these bad bitches talking to these older, rich-looking dudes. I was in the middle of a fucking whorehouse.

"Excuse me for a second," I said as I walked off to find Eve.

I was searching for Eve but bumped into Candy first.

"Hey, girl, can I talk to you for a second?"

"Sure, is everything OK? How are things going with Gerald?" she questioned.

I didn't say a word until we were alone in a room.

"What type of party is this?"

She played dumb. "What's the problem?"

"Is this some type of whorehouse or something? Did you invite us here to sell pussy?" I yelled in her face.

As she giggled, she pushed my hand out of her face. "Listen, little girl. I'm not forcing you or your girl to do shit y'all weren't already doing."

"What?" I asked, confused.

Now I was wondering if this bitch had been following us because she was all in our business.

"Look, y'all trying to get paid or played? Y'all both too cute to be fuckin' for pennies."

I stood there looking stupid. She did have a point.

"Look around my shit. I got all this shit and only a good few years over you. The *real* power is in the pussy. Take note and learn that shit."

With that being said, Candy walked out of the room, leaving me to my thoughts. I thought about what she said and fixed myself up before returning to the party. Once back downstairs, I saw Candy walking away from Gerald and wondered if they had been discussing me. With a smile on his face, Gerald walked toward me.

"I hope you have a better understanding of things now."

"Yes, everything is clear."

"So, what's the best dish you can whip up?" he asked, jumping back into the conversation we were just having.

I smiled, trying to feel completely OK with what I was doing. "I love soul food, but breakfast is my favorite."

"Mine too. You know that's the most important meal of the day?"

I nodded my head.

Gerald grabbed me by the hand. "Let me see your moves on this dance floor."

As we danced, Gerald made sure to keep his dick pressed against my body. He wanted to fuck bad as hell.

"I can't wait to have you alone," he whispered in my ear.

I didn't say shit as I was grinding my ass on him. If there was money to be made, I was ready.

Once the song was over, I turned to face him. "I'll be right back."

He grabbed my arm to stop me. "I hope you don't get lost. I got good money for that pussy tonight."

I walked away with a fake smile on my face, but really, I just wanted to talk to Eve.

"Hey, boo, you havin' fun?"

I could tell she was buzzing, which meant she was having a really good time.

I pulled her out to the patio. "Do you understand what type of party this is?"

She looked at me with a straight face as if she were trying to sober up. "I didn't at first, but Candy pulled me to the side and kind of explained some things to me."

"So, how do you feel about everything?"

"Girl, just have fun and make that bread. I went off with Big Rob, and that nigga threw me $10,000 just to pop this pussy over on the bathroom sink. Bitch, I ain't never made that type of money in one night. This old-ass lawyer paid me $15,000 just to eat my pussy and ass. He said he had a thing for Black bitches with a fat ass."

"Really, bitch? Are you *serious?*"

"Bitch, I had to ask him how much I could get to fuck him. Shit, a bitch needed all her funds."

"What did he say?" I asked, laughing.

"He said his dick didn't get hard. That's why he could only tongue fuck me."

Now we were both laughing, and I actually felt a little better about things, knowing these men had real money.

"You hooked up with anyone yet?"

"Not yet, but that guy Gerald, that be all on the news, wants me to leave with him tonight. What do you think?"

It didn't take Eve a second to answer. "Be careful and go make that money. I'm going straight home and will see you in the morning."

I passed over my keys to Eve so she could leave. After hugging each other, Candy walked her ass over to us.

"Hey, ladies. Tonight might've been different from what you two are used to, but I'll be calling you both tomorrow to give you a better understanding of everything."

"Maybe you should've done that first," I said, still kind of pissed that she was on some sneaky shit.

"I do apologize about that. I didn't wanna scare you off when we met at the restaurant. Please forgive me, and know I just wanted to help after hearing about the fat nigga running off without paying. These guys in here are paid, and if you two continue to fuck with me, you'll never have to worry about money again. Trina, I had Gerald talk to you because I knew y'all could connect with the same business mind. Play your cards right with him, and he can help you out in the long run."

Candy then looked over at Eve. "You met and fucked one of your favorite artists out. Like I said, my best interest is helping you guys out."

"I'm tired and about to head out," Eve told Candy.

"How are you getting home?"

"Since Trina got a date, I'm driving her car home," Eve replied.

"OK, just be safe."

We watched as Eve walked off.

Then Candy hugged me. "I promise those days of mismanaging your pussy are over."

By the time she walked away, I felt different about her and saw things her way. I turned to look for Gerald, who wasn't hard to find. He was close by, waiting for me to return.

"You ready to get out of here?"

I nodded. I didn't have any problem selling pussy. My thing was he's married. As he led me to his car, I was nervous as fuck.

"Where are we going?" I asked. I didn't want this man to take me to the house he shared with his wife and kids.

"I got a spot," he said.

"Oh, OK."

"I know you're new to this, and probably don't know all the rules, but families are off-limits to discuss. Really, besides names, any personal shit isn't important. So, don't speak on my wife or anything else about my family," he said with a little attitude.

"OK, I got it."

We both were quiet for a minute.

"You know, besides hearing that you were into being a business owner, I thought you were beautiful. I was happy when Candy introduced us."

I knew Gerald was trying to have a normal conversation to calm me down. He must've known I was worried and nervous. I appreciated that so much. Finally getting to the condo where I assumed he took all his side bitches, I was ready to make my money. Walking in the door and looking around, "bachelor pad" screamed through my head.

"Nice crib."

"Thanks," he said, pulling me in for a hug.

This dude had to be in love with my ass 'cause no matter what was going on that night, his hands always found a way to squeeze an ass cheek.

"You can follow me so that we can get a little more comfortable."

I started to follow him into the bedroom before he stopped.

"Damn, girl, you got my mind gone. My ass almost forgot something."

"What's that?" I questioned.

Gerald held out his hand. "You gotta hand over the cell phone."

"What?"

"Yeah, it's to protect me and my family."

I nodded in agreement before pulling my phone out of my purse. I wasn't the type to fuck and run my mouth, but I understood that he had a lot to lose if it got out that he wasn't shit.

Entering the room, Gerald picked up his remote, and music instantly started to play. He was some type of old-school playboy, and you could tell. Gerald slowly pulled my dress down to the floor so I could step out of it.

"Spin around for me, baby girl. Let daddy see all that ass," he ordered.

Like a good girl, I did what he asked. I turned around a few times just to tease Gerald. Finishing my final twirl,

Gerald grabbed me by the waist before pulling me closer to him. I usually didn't allow kissing on my dates, but the man had his tongue so far down my throat, I could barely breathe.

"You all right?" he asked once I finally broke free from him.

"Yeah, I'm good."

Gerald walked me over to the bed. He took a seat, but wanted me to stand up.

"You gotta work for this money. Strip for me, baby."

I slowly danced and grinded my ass in his face, causing his dick to poke out of his drawers. Next, I tossed my bra across the room.

"Damn, baby girl, you got me ready to empty my account for that ass."

I learned when I first started this lifestyle that muthafuckas would say anything for the pussy, so his words didn't mean shit to me. I was gonna do what I had to for my bread, then dip on his ass.

That night, I learned Gerald was an old-ass freak. That man sucked and fucked on every inch of my body. Just looking at him, you'd never guess he had it in him.

Feeling the sun burn down on my naked body, I jumped up.

"Damn, I gotta go," I mumbled.

Gerald must have felt me get up because his ass jumped up too. "Where do you think you're going?"

"Home," I simply answered.

He chuckled. "Nah, baby girl, you owe me breakfast."

That man spent all night and half of the early hours pinning me down on the bed, fucking the shit out of me. I don't know how he thought I had the energy to cook breakfast too. I wasn't a fucking robot.

"Are you serious?"

"Hell yeah, I'm serious. After tearing up that wet pussy, I need food to build up my energy. I got an interview in a few hours."

After showering, Gerald gave me a T-shirt to put on so I could cook his breakfast. Tired and all, I took my ass in that kitchen and slaved over the hot stove. I needed money for school, and couldn't be picky on how I was gonna make it.

I got in my Uber, leaving Gerald's stomach full of cheesy eggs, grits with shrimp, and fish. He enjoyed his meal, which got me a bonus. Arriving home, I counted out $35,000. I know I didn't wanna do this shit at first, but the money was just right, and a bitch couldn't complain.

Chapter Three

Candy

Maybe I was wrong for the way I just tossed Eve and Trina into the jungle, but I bet those hoes made more money than they ever did on their own. The night of the party, Eve is the one who jumped right into it. She had no idea what type of party this was, and she didn't care to find out. Eve wanted to get fucked, and she got just that; any payment was extra.

Truth be told, I liked her because she was true to herself. Now, Trina, on the other hand, was different. She tried to act like she was mad about the type of party I invited her to, but she left with a muthafucka. Most girls who were nervous or whatever would have made their money in one of the rooms upstairs and called it a night. Bitch acted like she was too good for my party but went off to get dicked down. I bet her ass was gonna be at the next party as well.

Today, I was gonna call the girls and invite them to dinner or something so I could see where their heads were after their first night of doing one of my parties. The guys were digging the newbies, and I knew there was money to be made. Seeing that it was now 2:30 p.m., I decided to give them a call. I was pretty sure they'd slept off the night before and were ready for a new day. After the fourth ring, Eve answered her phone. I decided to call her first because she seemed a bit more down-to-earth.

"Hello."

"Hey, Eve, this is Candy. I wanted to invite you and Trina to dinner at my place tonight. There's no secret agenda behind this, and it will only be the three of us outside of my staff."

I could tell over the phone that Eve was all smiles. Little bitch was down for whatever.

"That sounds like a great idea. I'll talk to Trina about it and see what she thinks. I'll call you back a little later."

"That sounds like a plan."

Once we got off the phone, I went into my office to check on my bank account. Last night's party was a success, and from the early deposits that were hitting my account for the next party, I knew it was gonna be even better.

Knowing these girls weren't about to turn down a free meal, I let my cook know we were having extra guests for dinner that night.

After logging out of my account, I made my way downstairs to get my daily massage. This was one of the best moments of my day, aside from watching my account grow.

Maria had been around since Jasper was alive, and I understood why he kept this bitch. Every day, after a long, hot shower, I would put on my robe, just to take it off and have her massage my body. I know I mentioned before that I hadn't been with a man since Jasper died and that I used toys, but Maria was the best head doctor ever. That bitch could suck all my stress away out of my asshole.

I didn't have to say shit to her. I simply dropped my robe and climbed onto the massage table. Maria liked to rub me down with this hot oil that felt so good sinking into my skin. While massaging the oil on my juicy booty, she always managed to slip a finger or two inside my pussy. I can't lie. That shit turned me completely on. Enjoying her hands on my body, I thought back to the first time she turned me out. I was 17, and she was probably about 29 at the time.

I had been staying with Jasper for a good two months when he introduced me to his personal massage therapist, Maria. Later that night, Jasper went out claiming he had some business to handle, but whatever. It probably had something to do with another bitch, but that's a whole other story. Maria met me in the kitchen and suggested I let her give me a massage since I looked stressed out. I had no idea what she had in store for me that night.

"Just lie flat on your back, and I'll make you feel better," she ordered.

After removing my clothes, I did as told. Being broke and from the hood, I never had the pleasure of getting an authentic massage. Truth be told, I never had anyone touch me the way I allowed Jasper to touch me. Everything was going well . . . until I felt Maria's oily fingers slide in my pussy.

"What the fuck!" I yelled, causing her to panic.

"I apologize, ma'am. Please don't tell Mr. Jasper about me. I just couldn't help myself. You're just so beautiful."

I wanted to slap that bitch 'cause I wasn't into bitches, especially older, Mexican bitches. Still, she kept playing with my pussy as she apologized, making me wetter than I'd ever been before.

Once she flipped me over on the table, Maria buried her face in my pussy, making me moan out. If anyone had heard me, they would've thought I was downstairs taking a ten-inch pipe.

She eased up a little, then whispered, "Don't run, ma'am, I'll make you so happy, just like I do for Mr. Jasper."

Did this bitch really just admit to fucking around with Jasper? Yeah, she did, but I couldn't get mad. I opened my legs wider, so she could dive right back in. I wanted to feel as good as Mr. Jasper's cheating ass.

I lay there, letting this lady have her way with me and never told a soul. It was our little secret . . . or so I thought. The next morning, Jasper was up in his office. I thought he was going over some work, but to my surprise, he was watching Maria suck on me.

"Candy! Candy, get your ass up!" he yelled, standing in the doorway.

I jumped up, not knowing why he was pissed off. I followed him as he stormed out of the bedroom and into his office.

"This the type of shit you doin' in my house?" he questioned as the video played out on the computer.

I'd never been in this type of situation before and didn't know what to say, so I stood there like a fucking mute.

Jasper was pissed and jumped up, slapping the shit out of me. "Bitch, do you hear me talking to you?"

"Sorry, I didn't know that was gonna happen. I just wanted a massage." I let those words come out as soon as the video showed me on all fours, spreading my ass cheeks open for Maria to fuck my ass with her tongue.

Jasper laughed at me. "I don't own you, but if that's what tip you on, let me know something. In this house, I have two rules for you to follow. One, never give my pussy away to another nigga, and two, never lie to me."

I was still quiet and embarrassed.

"So, was it good?"

I was scared to tell him it was the best head I'd received knowing he and Maria were the only ones to ever do that to me, so I lied. "No, I didn't like it."

Jasper chuckled before slapping me again. "You're still lying in my face."

I watched as he stepped out of the room. I could over-hear him telling someone to send Maria up to his office. I was so scared and just knew he was about to beat both our asses before putting us out on the street. Lord knows I wasn't ready to go back home. Maria walked in with Jasper right behind her. She was scared and never looked me in the eyes.

"Maria, Candy said she didn't enjoy the massage last night."

I couldn't believe how he put me on spot like that.

"I'm sorry, I tried my best, I really did."

Jasper walked over to me, making me flinch, thinking he was about to fuck me up for real. Instead, he lifted my head to kiss me.

"Take off your clothes," he whispered in my ear.

I was scared but obeyed. As I undressed, he stood there next to Maria, watching my every move. I saw him whisper to Maria, and she started to undress as well.

"Maria, go ahead and show me how you did her last night. Candy, I want you to tell me what you didn't like."

"Jasper, this is crazy."

"Shut your ass up before I take you back to the bus stop!" he yelled.

Scared of going back to being homeless, I lay on the couch in his office and cocked my legs open for Maria. Just like last night, she drove me crazy and had me moaning out. Jasper sat in his seat watching with his dick in his hand. This nigga was turned on and couldn't control himself.

"All right, Maria," he called out as my legs began to shake. "Candy, did you enjoy that?"

This time, I decided to tell the truth. The way my legs were still shaking after the fact, there's no way to say I didn't. "Yes, I did."

*"Good. Maria, for now, your job is to make sure me
and Candy are completely satisfied."*

*Even though he saw me on tape enjoying Maria's work,
he still made her do that shit in front of him. Jasper could
be such an asshole sometimes. I thought I was gonna be
able to leave, but he made me sit in his chair to watch
Maria suck his dick until he nutted down her throat. I
now understood why he got daily massages and never
asked me for head.*

Now, years later, she has always been my go-to person.
She would massage me until I dozed off, then eat me until
I woke up. Whenever I needed a little extra attention, she
was there to save the day. Maybe I'll let her give Eve and
Trina a massage as a thank you for all the hard work she
put in over the years.

Eve

"So, how was your night?" I asked, taking a seat on
Trina's bed.

"Bitch, I made just about enough to pay for my first
semester with that guy Gerald. At this point, fuck all my
old clients."

I was surprised to hear Trina say that shit, but she
was right. One night, we put the amount of money in our
pockets that we were probably making in months doing
our own hustle.

"I think I'll keep Marcus around, but fuck everyone
else," I had to admit.

We both giggled.

"Bitch, if we keep doing this, we can finally move into a
better place and get a new car," Trina pointed out.

I agreed with that. We were sharing the car she had, and it worked out a little, but having my own shit would be cool.

"So, Candy called me earlier."

"What the fuck did she want?" Trina asked.

"She wants us to come over for dinner. She said she wanted to talk to us about last night. Do you wanna go?"

"I do wanna go. I know I was mad at first, but she was right about some stuff. Last night, we did what we were used to doing, but only for muthafuckas with *real* money."

I was happy she was seeing things my way. "Girl, that's what I'm saying. We were just fuckin' a nigga for a hot $200. Dealing with her, I made bread, letting an old muthafucka lick this pussy. Ain't no way in the world I'm going back to the old days."

"So, is this what we gon' do?"

"Hell yeah, bitch."

Trina gave me a serious look. "If you down, I'm rolling too."

After taking a shower and getting dressed, Trina and I decided to go shopping. We wanted to look cute for dinner with Candy. She claimed there wasn't a hidden agenda, but there's no telling with her ass. That day, we were finally about to walk into the store and pay for whatever we set our eyes on without looking at a price tag. If this is how our life was gonna be from now on, I had no problem dealing with Candy.

"Bitch, you look good in that dress. I swear red is definitely your color."

I turned to face Trina. "Thanks, boo. You look good too."

We stood in front of my full-size mirror, examining ourselves. We were both two bad bitches, but now with money.

"You ready to go see what our boss wants?"

"Hell yeah, but I got a feeling she just wanna make sure we're still on good terms after her little party."

"The way I look at it, that bitch just put us on," Trina added.

"You right, bitch, but let's be on our way. You know this bitch live far as fuck."

I now understand how she could afford this big-ass house and shit. That bitch only had a few years over me and Trina, but I wanted to be like her. We stepped in, then heard someone call out to Candy that her guests had arrived. An older white guy approached us.

"Please follow me."

We did as told and followed him into the dining room. Candy was seated at the head of the table, so Trina and I sat on either side of her.

"Welcome, ladies. I'm so happy you could make it. No hard feelings, I hope?"

I was the first to speak up. "Hell nah, girl. You really looked out for us."

Trina took her turn to speak up. "Although you could've been straight-up with us, I did end up making more money than I've ever made in one night, so I can't be mad about that."

"To be honest, when I overheard you two talking over lunch about niggas running off with pussy money and how broke you two were, it was only right to help out. I hate seeing women in this game being oversexed and underpaid. I do apologize for misleading you two, but I wasn't sure how to be up front with you."

I understood where she was coming from 'cause I wouldn't have known how to ask someone if they wanted to attend a party to sell pussy either.

We sat around eating fat, juicy steaks and drinking some of the best champagne there was. I felt if Trina was down and saw no flaw in this shit, then I was down for the ride right by her side.

Trina

After dinner, a bitch was buzzing and full. I was ready to take a nap. While I chilled in the recliner, I watched Candy and Eve dance around, just enjoying the night.

"Come on, Trina, come play with us!" Candy called out.

"I'm good. Besides, I'm really not a big drinker, and I'm fucked up right now."

Candy walked over to me. "I know what you need," she said with a grin.

If that bitch knew what I really needed, she'd pull a nigga with a big dick out of her pocket, but instead, she left, then returned to the room with this Mexican chick.

"Trina, this is Maria. She is my personal massage therapist, and trust me, she will get you together."

Maria reached out her hand to help me out of the chair. To be honest, I could go for a good massage. A bitch never had a real one before.

"Come with me, ma'am, and I'll make you happy."

I turned around to look at Eve, but that bitch was dancing and drinking from the bottle. I knew I was driving home that night.

"Go ahead and undress, I'll give you a second," Maria ordered.

Getting undressed was easy since I was only wearing a dress. It was too fucking hot for anything else. Just as promised, Maria returned to work her magic.

"This oil is a little warm but will relax your whole body," she warned.

"Okay, I'm cool with that."

Maria got to work on my legs and feet, and that shit alone had me dozing off. What made me try to get up was when my toes felt wet. I know this bitch *wasn't* sucking on them.

"What the hell?" I yelled out, trying to sit up.

"No, no, no, ma'am. Lie back down. I'll make you happy," she said again.

Not sure if what happened was for real or if it was just me dozing off that had left me a little clouded, but I lay back down.

I wasn't sure how long I had been asleep, but I woke up hearing myself moan out. "*Mmmm.*"

"Yes, I can make you happy," I heard her whisper.

"What the fuck are you doing?"

Maria continued to suck on my clit as if I weren't even talking to her. As I tried to get up, I could feel her hand holding my lower back down on the table.

"Maria, stop," I finally called out.

Maria was undoubtedly enjoying herself. She had one finger in my pussy while sucking away my soul.

"I'm sorry. You're just so beautiful, and I couldn't help myself."

I sat there confused. Never in my life had I been attracted to a female. I still wasn't, but damn, she knew what the fuck she was doing, and I liked it. Instead of going off or getting up to leave, I lay my ass back down on the table, but this time, I flipped over on my back.

Maria opened me back up and didn't hesitate to finish her job.

Chapter Four

Candy

Now that Trina was out of the picture, I could play with Eve. During dinner, Trina seemed to be cool with everything, but I still wanted Eve's sexy ass to myself.

"Damn, girl, do I need to go get another bottle or what?" I asked, knowing damn well she didn't need shit else to drink.

"Oh my gawd, bitch, no," she said, stumbling to the couch.

I sat next to her. "You are very beautiful."

Her words slurred, "Thanks, you are too."

I still had my glass in my hand, taking sips, watching her slowly doze off. "Aht, aht, bitch. You're not about to go to sleep on me. Get up and play with me."

She sat up a little, giggling. "I'm buzzing like a muthafucka right now, Candy."

I wasn't trying to hear that shit. I've wanted her since day one, and I *always* got what I wanted. Sliding my hand under her dress, I smiled seeing the bitch wasn't wearing any panties.

"Oh, so that's what tip you on tonight?" she said with a grin on her face.

"That's only if you're down for a good night."

I stood up from the couch and helped her drunk ass get up. I never fucked any of these bitches in my room, but with twelve other rooms in the house, space was never a problem.

Picking Eve out of the two was the best decision I ever made. She was a real-life freak and not scared to be herself. Not only was she open to fucking around with me, but she also didn't mind me using my strap on her. This bitch took it in every hole, and that's something most hoes were against. I couldn't wait to add that to her profile. These niggas were gonna have to double up on my money for this one.

"Oh shit," I heard her moan out.

I had her bent over on all fours with my strap in her ass while having her hold a vibrator in her pussy. I giggled as this bitch squirted all over the bed. She was going crazy like a raging bull.

"Next time, I gotta try that on you," she said as we climbed out of the shower.

I was blushing. "So, there's gonna be a next time?"

"That's all up to you, Candy. I mean, you the one who started this shit," she responded.

"I would like to see you before our next party later this month. If you have to bring your friend, I'll have a way to keep her out of our way."

When we finally made it back downstairs, Trina was coming back from her massage.

"Damn, girl, you look so stress free. That massage must've been magical," Eve teased.

Trina had a slight grin on her face. "Yeah, it was. Are you ready to go because it's late as hell?"

"Yeah, I'm ready if you are," Eve responded.

I walked them to the door.

"It was nice of you to invite us to dinner. We appreciate it."

I hugged them both. "I'll be reaching out to you both about the next party, and I hope to see you both there."

"For sure, girl."

Eve

The car ride seemed awkward. We usually talked about everything, but that drive home was too quiet. I wasn't sure how to tell her what happened between Candy and me.

"What's on your mind?"

"Life," she simply said, very dryly.

"You know you my bitch; you can talk to me," I assured her.

"Eve, tonight, I allowed some shit to happen that I really don't think I wanna do again. I'm not happy with myself right now."

She was getting on my nerves playing around instead of just coming out and saying what she gotta say. "What's wrong, bitch? What the fuck happened?"

"When I went downstairs for the massage, that Maria bitch ate my pussy."

I tried not to laugh, but the way she said it tickled me. "What?"

"Bitch, I'm serious. That bitch was rubbing me, and when I woke up, she had her face buried in my pussy, going to work."

"I'm confused. Are you complaining or did you enjoy the shit?"

Trina started to laugh. "Bitch, I don't know. You know I don't fuck with bitches, but I can't lie, that shit felt good. She just kept saying, '*I'll make you feel good, ma'am.*'"

I kept laughing. "So, did she?"

"Hell yeah, and I came all over that bitch's face," Trina said, laughing.

"Was she mad at you?"

"Hell nah. That bitch kept sucking on me like a fucking pacifier."

"Bitch, are you *serious?*" I asked, laughing.

She stopped laughing for a second. "As soon as I realized what had happened, I jumped up from the table. Bitch caught me slippin'."

For the rest of the ride, we talked about how Maria got down, but I couldn't tell her what happened between me and Candy. For some reason, I thought she would judge me or something. I usually didn't care 'cause we thotted together many times, but this time felt different.

Trina had been my bitch since day one. We were always about getting our money together. I remember when we went out with these two brothers. These niggas didn't even care enough to get separate rooms. Me and my bitch were getting fucked on the same bed by these brothers and didn't give a fuck when they switched up on us. We took both dicks and enjoyed our night. We did a lot of thotting together, but still, something was different about this night.

The next afternoon, after a hot shower, I lay across the bed thinking about Marcus's ass, but only because he'd been blowing up my phone like crazy. This might sound strange, but I was all fucked out and not in the mood to fuck with him that night. Now you know something had to be up if my ass wasn't in the mood to fuck.

"Damn, dude, give me a fucking break," I bitched as I finally answered the phone after seeing he wasn't gonna stop calling.

"Hello," I said, giving much attitude.

"Good afternoon, my beautiful queen. I can't wait to see you later."

I rolled my eyes. He knew how to kiss ass for sure.

"Good afternoon, Marcus. How can I help you?"

"Marry me, my love."

I started to laugh. This man didn't give up, knowing he was married, and we were only "business associates." "Marcus, stop playing with me before I tell Tammy on your ass."

"Go ahead, I'm begging you. Maybe then, she'll leave me for good. I went home the other morning smelling just like your sweet pussy, and she didn't say shit. I didn't shower until that night, and nothing happened."

"Marcus, you're crazy. I swear you have a problem."

"I'm only for you and your love. I have a surprise for you tonight."

I hated to burst his bubble, but I wasn't in the mood to hook up with him. "Marcus, about tonight, I'm so tired. I think I'm gonna have to reschedule."

"Nah, that can't happen. I'll pay you double just to chill with me tonight. To sweeten the deal, you won't even have to fuck me. Just let me taste my forbidden apple."

How could I turn down double pay just to get sucked on? I wasn't that type of dummy.

"What time are you coming to pick me up?"

"How does 7:00 p.m. sound?"

"All right, just call when you're outside."

Since I didn't have shit else to do, I decided to nap until it was time for me to get ready.

Just as I was dozing off, Trina came into my room. "Move over, bitch."

"Girl, you see me trying to rest, so go get in your bed," I said playfully, pushing her away.

Trina's irritating ass held on to me. "But I love you, bestie. I'm not going nowhere."

We both laughed.

"What do you want, girl?" I asked.

"The school is starting to drop classes on their site. Let's get ahead of these muthafuckas and find our classes now."

"Girl, I'm not in the mood for that school shit right now."

"Okay, I'm about to handle my business, but don't be mad when all the good classes are gone."

After she left, I closed my eyes. Truth be told, if this party shit worked out over the summer, my ass wasn't gonna stay in school. Candy was living the dream, and that bitch wasn't giving a school her hard-earned money, so why should I? That's another thing I didn't wanna talk to Trina about. It seemed like we were going in two different directions now.

Like clockwork, Marcus was in front of the building, waiting for my sexy ass to come down.

"Damn, you look so good, I just wanna bite your ass," he said, rubbing my ass as I got in the car.

"So, what's my surprise?" I asked as he drove off.

"I'll tell you when we get downtown to the room."

Marcus never took me anywhere cheap. He would never pay for one of those seventy-five-dollar rooms. When it came to me, he didn't mind spending whatever. I played it off, but I couldn't wait to see my surprise. Marcus could be so romantic, and that's one of the reasons I kept coming back to him, besides the money, of course. I never had a real boyfriend who did romantic shit with me. These niggas only liked to fuck on me and cheat.

The room was filled with rose petals and candles. I couldn't help but blush.

"You're so sweet, Marcus."

"Anything for you, my love."

Marcus had a problem remembering he was married with all that love shit.

"What's my surprise, Marcus?"

"Calm down, baby, it's coming," he said, undressing.

I know for sure he remembered me saying I didn't feel like fucking tonight. My face must have said a lot because Marcus caught on really quickly.

"No worries, I know you're tired and don't wanna fuck, but as promised, I just wanna please you tonight."

After taking off my dress, Marcus ordered me to lie on my back so he could make me happy. This man licked and sucked on every inch of my body. That night, he was my personal washcloth.

"Damn, Marcus, you got me about to come again."

Saying that only made him suck on me even harder. This man really wanted to eat me alive, and if there were a way, my ass would've been gone.

"Marcus," I moaned out as I came once more.

"I love you so much, Eve."

I didn't care how good he made me feel; I wouldn't allow those words to come out of my mouth. I loved Marcus's money, dick, and head, but I couldn't love a married man. In my feelings, I finally pushed his head away from me.

"What's wrong, baby?"

"Marcus, you gotta stop telling me that shit."

"I can't help the way I feel about you, Eve. I love you and want you to be mine."

I couldn't deal with the shit any longer. I climbed out of bed and put on my dress. I found a way to get money and didn't have to deal with Marcus's ass any longer. I was trying to be nice and keep him around, but he was getting on my nerves, trying to pressure me into being his girl.

"What are you doing, Eve?"

"I played this game long enough with you, Marcus. Yes, I was wrong, but I can't keep sleeping with you. Go home to your wife tonight."

"Wait, Eve! What about your surprise?"

My greedy ass turned around to face him. "What is it, Marcus?"

I watched as he walked over to his pants on the chair. He pulled out a ring box while dropping down on one knee.

"Marry me, Eve. I promise I'll take good care of you."

"Marcus, get up. I don't know why you don't understand that I can't marry you while you're still married. Just go home to your wife, and let's say this was a freebie. I gotta go."

Marcus sat on the bed crying while I got myself together. I hated to leave him like that, but he was doing the most.

"Eve, please, just give me one more chance," he begged.

"I'll catch an Uber home. You need to go home to your family and forget about me."

As I shut the door, I could hear him screaming like a madman and throwing things. I hurried to the elevator to set up my ride. I needed to get away from him by any means.

In the lobby, while waiting for my ride, I prayed Marcus didn't come down there and make a scene. I'd hate for him to embarrass both of us. Once the Uber arrived, on my way home, I deleted his number from my phone. At this point, I had no choice but to cut him entirely out of my life. The money was always good, but he broke the number one rule of mine because he fell in love with me. I was a thot who sold pussy. I wasn't brought into this world for love.

Chapter Five

Candy

I had a longtime friend who came into town with his buddy at least four times a year, and they needed some excitement in their life. I know from the videos that I secretly recorded and watched that these men were lovers and loved dicks with a dash of pussy on the side. They paid top dollar for the nastiest, freakiest ho I had. Since I had already tested out Eve, I decided to call her up instead of using her to entertain me. I told them I had a girl on deck that was down for whatever as long as they had their bread stacked, and, of course, I needed my finder's fee up front. Everything was good on their end; now, I just had to pull her in. She answered the phone on the third ring.

"Good afternoon, sexy."

I could tell I had woken her up, and she was blushing. All my girls were happy when they thought they were my favorite.

"Hey, Candy. What's up, boo?"

"Listen, I have a job set up with an old friend of mine and thought that it would be perfect for you."

Eve hesitated to respond as she gave it a little thought.

"If you're not ready to be a big girl and make this money, just say that shit. I can always call one of these other bitches that's been in the game a little longer, but they'll pay more for a fresh face," I said just to see if I could get her to break.

"What time and where?"

I smiled, knowing my plan worked. "Just come to my house in the next hour or so, and I'll help you get prepared for them."

"Them?" she questioned.

I didn't have time for her bullshit and her trying to pull out now. "I'll see you in a few."

I hung up before giving her all the facts. I always allowed my closest friends to use one of the many rooms in my home. I got a kick out of going back and watching their fuck sessions when I was bored.

Laughing to myself, I realized Jasper had turned me into some type of pervert. I had to admit that something was seriously wrong with me. It had to be because I'd rather watch people get fucked than let another man touch my body in any way. Thank God for Maria.

Eve came to my door in exactly one hour, looking nervous as fuck.

"Hey, I just wanted to say thank you for calling me. I need this extra money, but what's this shit about? You said *them,* not *him.*"

I walked back to the couch. "Follow me, sweetie."

After we took our seats on the couch, I ordered Jessica to bring us a bottle of champagne.

"Tonight, one of my old buddies will be in town with a close friend of his. These guys are major freaks and only like to be hooked up with freak bitches that can handle multiple dicks at one time. Are you the right girl for this job?" I questioned.

"I'm not no amateur at taking dicks, Candy. I can handle them."

She looked scared, but I wasn't about to let her ass back down now.

"Don't disappoint me, Eve. These guys spend good money every time they come to Detroit for business. If you do well at pleasing them, they'll always ask for you and keep your pockets right."

I could tell that she was still a little nervous and probably felt she might have bitten off more than she could chew, but she was a bitch who was about making her money. Yeah, I could have dismissed her and found one of my regulars, but since she wanted to play this game, I was about to deal her in.

Eve

Candy had me shook. I have let two niggas run a train on me before, a few times, but she was talking like these niggas had dicks the size of a tree trunk or something. That afternoon, I made sure to show up to her house a little early so we could talk about my date for the night. As she spoke of her buddy and his friend, I sipped on my drink. Being drunk always brought out my alter ego and made the scared, young girl disappear. After another shot, Candy walked me upstairs to one of the bedrooms.

"For your protection and privacy, I've allowed you all to use this room for your date."

I looked around at how nice the room was set up. "It's nice in here. I can't wait to get my money together so I can get a nice house like this."

I noticed the strange look on Candy's face, but she didn't say shit. "The connected bathroom is right over here."

I peeked into the bathroom and instantly fell in love. This bathroom was so much better than the one Big Rob fucked me in. Stepping back into the room, I watched as Candy pulled out a shopping bag.

"These items are for you. Please use everything in here tonight."

She left the room so I could have some privacy. I shook my head, looking at the bullshit in the bag. Inside were handcuffs, a dildo, a butt plug, and some anal ease.

"Hell nah, what the fuck?"

Now I was thinking about backing out and taking my black ass home. I paced the floor, debating if I really wanted to go through with this shit. Her buddy was gonna have to find another bitch to bust open. I'd had my fair share of dicks, but from the shit in that bag, these muthafuckas were on some other shit.

Candy walked back into the room. "Hey, don't be nervous, boo. I know you're the best bitch for this job."

I nodded in agreement.

"This right here is your new best friend. Take this bitch, and the rest of the day will go smoothly."

She stood there waiting for me to take the pill with the rest of my champagne. I usually wasn't into taking drugs, but with her watching me like a hawk, I tossed it into my mouth and swallowed it down with my drink.

"Good girl. Now, after you freshen up, relax, and they'll be here in no time. Show my friend how Detroit bitches get down."

Relaxing in the tub, I started to feel how Ebony felt at Junior's bachelor party. In the pit of my stomach, something told me it was gonna be a crazy night. Feeling faded and ready to lie down, I finally got out of the tub. I swear I didn't feel like doing shit but go to sleep. I guess the pill was starting to work. I lay across the bed, praying I get a nap in before these muthafuckas get here.

As soon as I felt my body slip into a sound sleep, I was awakened by two Black guys tapping me. I knew it was time to get to work by the way they were both butt-ass naked, stroking their dicks. These muthafuckas ain't come to play. I checked out what they were working with before looking over at Candy, who was standing there with a smirk on her face.

"James and Thomas, this is one of the new beautiful girls I was telling you two about."

"Yeah, she is beautiful, but I'm trying to see what that mouth do," James said, rubbing his dick across my lips.

I felt so disrespected but smiled like everything was OK. Even the hood niggas I dealt with in the past never just slapped my lips with their dicks before.

Candy must've seen I didn't like that and tried to make sure I didn't fuck up what she had going on.

"OK, y'all, play nice."

"For sure, love. You know we're good guys," Thomas assured her.

Candy leaned over, placing a kiss on my lips. "They're gonna take good care of you as long as you play fair."

After that, Candy walked out of the room, leaving me with these guys who acted like they hadn't had pussy in years. I knew they were about to fuck the shit out of me with they thirsty asses.

"What you waitin' for, girl? Wet them lips up and suck this dick," James ordered.

Trying to act like I wasn't uncomfortable, I did as I was told. I slowly took it in, inch by inch. This man was packing, but I was about to show this nigga they weren't about to "little girl" me. I was a whole, grown-ass woman.

"That's right, bitch. Suck that dick, you nasty ho."

James talked too much shit for me, but he turned into a little bitch when I was sucking him up, and Thomas started eating his ass. Never in my life had I fucked with two nigga that fucked on each other too. At first, I was disgusted, but after a while, that shit was lit. Having two guys cater to your body just as much as they catered to each other was something new for my ass. But once it was all said and done, I walked out of the house the next morning feeling refreshed and with a fat pocket. I couldn't wait until they came back to town in a few months.

Chapter Six

Candy

I was somewhat crushing on Eve when I first met her, but now, I feel sorry for her. I had every intention of helping her make money. I really did, but she was too eager to do whatever for money, and the shit was low-key sad.

I watched Thomas and James double dick this thot down, then dick each other down. She didn't have a care in the world as long as she knew she was gonna make money. Not only was she quick to jump on this opportunity too fast, but she also never even asked how much she was gonna get paid to be these muthafuckas' sex slave overnight. James handed over a total of $150,000, and Eve walked away with only $50,000.

The next morning, after watching their sex tape and coming multiple times, I took a long shower, then got dressed. My goal was to go out and find some new girls for the next party. I had a good feeling Trina was gonna stay strictly business while Eve was gonna crash and burn pretty soon. I hate to speak so negatively about a bitch that I once put my lips on, but she was the type of thot bitch to do a line if a nigga had the right amount of money in her face. In my line of business, I'd seen it all and knew niggas would turn a bitch out on that dick and nose candy just to have something to brag about.

My first stop was this ghetto-ass mall. From what I learned, bitches loved the mall. They all loved walking around, looking, and dressing the same. This shit always reminded me of when Jasper had my ass in these malls picking up bitches that were looking to make some money.

The first few times I did it, I was scared shitless. I just knew a bitch was gonna think I was weird or something. I called myself being a boss bitch, stepping to this one chick in the shoe store. She was really tall and slim, but very pretty. She went the fuck off on me so bad. I still remember running out of the store, scared to get my ass beat.

I went home with no new pussy to offer, and Jasper tore up my ass. His favorite shit to yell at me when he beat my ass was that he would send me back to the streets or sell my pussy to the highest bidder. After fucking up two more times and getting my ass beat, I was tired and knew I had to find a way to pull in the perfect, vulnerable female to do some work. After practicing for a week straight, I went out one day and had three bitches ready to come to the party. I think one of them still works for me after all this time.

One day, I must've had a higher power on my side. This pretty, chocolate bitch fell straight into my lap, basically begging for help. Long story short, I found her in the restroom crying, so I played the concerned big sister role. She cried about losing her job, and when she told her boyfriend, he broke up with her, and kicked her out of the house, saying he only dated chicks with money. I felt bad for her and wanted to take her to that nigga's house to beat his ass myself.

After getting her to calm down, I played Jasper's role. I treated Tamia to a meal, and then I took her home that night. She stayed there with me and Jasper for a whole week before he was in her room, breaking down the rules for her. She didn't act too scared or nervous to pop that pussy for some money. To my surprise, she was working two days later at the party. Tamia worked for us for three months before she was able to get her own place and move out. She worked for us for a whole two years before a local ballplayer killed her. He had paid for Tamia at every party, and one day, his wife found out about him banging her young ass. His wife threatened to divorce him and take everything. He was so fucked up that he ended up killing Tamia.

Let me just say this, and this will be my first and last time talking about it. I found out Tamia and this particular ballplayer were hooking up behind my back and cutting me out of the deal. I was pissed but laughed, knowing I was going to get the last laugh. I never called them out on their betrayal. But one day, I just so happened to run into his wife at their family boutique. I might have asked if they were separated because I had seen him downtown with some young chick. She went the fuck off, and while her family and friends tried to calm her down, I snuck my ass right out of the shop. Two weeks later, Tamia was found dead. I never saw *that* shit coming, but how long did Tamia think she could get away with being sneaky? That's it; that's the story.

That afternoon, I went home with two new, pretty faces for my party.

Trina

It had been two long weeks since we did that party at Candy's house, and I'd only been on two dates since then. The money I made at the party helped out so much, but after paying for my classes, I was dead broke again. So, doing the next party was a must because I still needed my books for these classes. Since meeting Candy, I had slowed down with these dates after seeing how much I could really make in one night. Truthfully, for some reason, I just wasn't in the mood to continue with this lifestyle any longer. I planned to do just a few more parties and get the fuck on. I was using this Candy shit as a stepping-stone.

I noticed things had been changing around here, and I wasn't sure if it was my attitude of doing something I didn't wanna do anymore or Eve's new attitude, but she really had been getting on my nerves. Lately, her new best friend was Candy, and I didn't like it at all. She said fuck school and was out here tricking just to shop. I wasn't sure if Candy was playing in her head or what, but she was doing too much, just not enough. I wasn't jealous that Candy was using her as her go-to girl for extra jobs, but the way I looked at it, Eve jumped headfirst into the game, and it wasn't a smart idea. Yeah, we were both selling pussy, but she had Candy hooking her up on private dates and shit with all these weird-ass men. She was doing too much, and I hated to see her like that. Just the other night, she came home and could barely walk. She had to soak in the tub for hours just to reduce the swelling. The crazy part is that Candy called her the next day. Not to make sure she was all right, but to trick her out again.

Out of curiosity, one day I asked Eve how much money Candy made off her dates, and she couldn't even tell me a straight number. I always tried to be straight-up with my girl, but when it came to Candy, she was blinded by her bullshit.

"Where are you headed?" Eve asked, standing in my doorway.

"I wanted to go get my nails done so I won't have to rush at the last minute. Party in a few days," I said dryly.

"Damn, bitch, what's the fucking problem?"

"Nothing at all."

"It doesn't seem that way. Say what you gotta say, and say it with your chest."

I had to laugh at her ass. "OK, Ms. Big Badass. You wanna know what's the problem? Come over here to see."

I led her over to the mirror.

"Bitch, look at you. *You're* the problem. I think you're really losing focus on what's important in life."

Eve turned to face me. "Getting money is what's important to me. Bitch, you trippin'. What happened to my bitch who wasn't scared to get these niggas' bread?"

"I'm still that girl, but you've been on some wild shit lately."

"Whatever, girl. You ain't nobody fuckin' mama. Matter of fact, I do believe that all good things must come to an end, and the way shit looks right now, we're outgrowing each other. Things are only gon' get worse if we continue to be friends."

"What are you talking about, Eve? We've been girls since forever. Fuck wrong with you?" I questioned.

"You're jealous of me because Candy fuck with me the long way. Then she hooks me up with muthafuckas that are cashing me out."

I couldn't help but laugh at her, although I was dead-ass serious. "Jealous? *Really*, Eve? Did you forget we both were doing the same shit? You wanted those extra dates, while I decided not to do all that. I was the one who only wanted to do the parties. And as far as you fuckin' with Candy the long way, I already know y'all fucked. I just thought you didn't wanna talk about it because you were embarrassed or something, so I never brought it up."

"Whatever, bitch," Eve said, walking out of my room.

I didn't even wanna be in the same house as that stupid bitch. I couldn't believe she thought I was jealous because she fucked Candy. I was pretty sure Candy fucked a lot of hoes that she pulled in to work for her. The way I was feeling, I didn't even wanna be bothered with Candy *or* Eve, but I knew I would be a fool not to do this party this coming weekend. This one weekend could either make me or break me.

Being pissed off, I didn't even leave the house. I spent the rest of the day lying in bed, watching old love movies.

The next day, I got up to handle my business. After getting my nails, lashes, and eyebrows done, I felt pretty again. I was ready to go home and relax, but I still needed to find a sexy outfit for this weekend. I swear it felt weird doing all this shit without Eve by my side. We'd always been each other's support system, and now I wasn't even sure if we were friends after our last argument.

Since she recently bought a car, I knew she was probably out and about and could pull up. I sat on one of the benches in the middle of the mall to give Eve a call. Having beef with someone that I called a sister for years was lame as hell to me. We had a bond that should be able to overcome anything. At least, that's what I hoped. After the third ring, she finally picked up. "What's up?"

"What are you doing?" I asked.

I knew she had an attitude when I heard her breathing hard as if I were bothering her.

"I'm actually waiting on my date to show up. What's up?"

"I was about to look for an outfit for this weekend and was just trying to see if you were available to shop with me."

Eve laughed. "Girl, you kissin' ass better than the nigga from last night. You was on that bullshit, talking to me like you were better than me when you out here sucking and fucking for money just like me. I don't do fake shit, bitch."

Eve hung up after that. Before she did, I could hear Candy's stupid ass laughing in the background, and that's really what pissed me off. I wasn't worried about her talking shit. It was the fact she had a fucking audience that I didn't like.

"Trina," I heard someone call out.

I turned around to see a guy named Jarrod walking my way. I really wasn't in the mood to be bothered with anyone at the time, but since I had a crush on his sexy, black ass, I waited.

"Hey," I said softly.

This man did something to me that I couldn't even describe. No matter how many men I slept with throughout my life, Jarrod was the one who could've gotten it for a freebie.

"Hey, girl," he said, pulling me in for a tight hug.

The smell of his cologne instantly turned me on. I always had a thing for a nigga that knew how to dress and keep up with their personal hygiene.

"What you up in here, grabbing?"

I couldn't tell him I was on the search for a ho outfit, so I lied. "I was looking for an outfit for a friend's birthday party."

"I bet whatever you find, you'll look good in it."

This dude knew what to say to make a girl blush. Everything was perfect, but he was barking up the wrong tree. Yeah, I wanted him, but Jarrod deserved someone without a large body count. He didn't seem like the type who wanted to wife a ho. He deserved much better, no matter how much I liked him.

"I gotta go," I said, getting in my feelings.

"Aye, wait a minute," Jarrod said, grabbing after me.

I stopped to see what he had to say. It's clear that we liked each other, but I couldn't be the bitch to bring him down.

"I was thinking that maybe we could grab something to eat since we're both here."

Maybe next time. I thought it was cute how he was trying to get on. I pretended to give it some thought before telling him a bold-faced lie.

"I'm sorry, Jarrod, but I have somewhere to be."

The look of disappointment was all over his face, but I needed to push away.

"Why don't you give me your number so I can call you? Then maybe we can see what day we both are free and can go out."

I didn't wanna get him caught up in my lifestyle, but at the same time, I didn't wanna just shoot him down, knowing we were feeling each other. I needed to get my shit together, and soon. After letting go of my hand, we exchanged numbers. I walked away feeling like shit. I kept telling myself that after a few more parties, I would be straight, and then I'd be able to live my life for real.

I left the mall without an outfit after all that shit. Between Eve's bullshit and feeling embarrassed talking to Jarrod, I just wasn't in the mood anymore. Honestly, I was ready to slap some fucking sense into Eve's childish ass. And if Candy had something to say, I'd slap her ass too.

After getting home, I was still pissed. I found myself pacing the floor, questioning my whole life. I fucked around and made a living out of selling pussy, but I was old enough to know it was wrong. Then I had the nerve to be embarrassed about something I could have easily changed. I was a fucking mess. I sat there for a whole ten minutes looking at Jarrod's number, trying to build up the courage to give him a call. Truthfully, I would have loved to have a life outside of selling pussy. Here was a guy who truly liked me, and I was trying to push him away. I couldn't help but shake my head at my damn self.

I gave his number one last look before pressing talk on the phone.

"Hello," I heard him say after the third ring.

"Hey. Are you busy?" I asked, using my sexy voice.

I could hear him moving around as if he were leaving one room and entering a new room for privacy.

"Not at all, what's up?"

"My plans fell through at the last minute. Did you wanna meet up somewhere?"

He paused for a minute, but I could tell he was smiling. "Yeah, that sounds like a plan."

We decided to meet downtown at Hart Plaza. In the hood, Detroit wasn't really shit, but there was always something to do downtown. Once downtown, we met up just in time for things to start popping off for the African festival. We walked around holding hands and talking about life. I had to keep the conversation on my future because talking about my past or my life right now would scare him off.

Feeling my phone vibrate, I stopped midconversation. "Hello," I dryly said, seeing it was Candy calling.

"Hey, Trina, have you heard from Eve? I have a client here waiting for her ass. She was supposed to be here twenty minutes ago and isn't answering her phone."

Rolling my eyes, I quickly said no before hanging up. Candy then texted my phone.

Candy: There's no beef between us, sweetie.

I quickly texted back.

Trina: Of course not. See you this weekend.

I put my phone back in my pocket, feeling Jerrod's eyes staring at me.

"You don't have to go, do you?"

With a warm smile, I told him no.

At the end of the night, he was nice enough to follow me home, but we didn't do shit but kiss each other good night. That night felt magical without all the sex and everything. I knew that I needed more nights like that in my life.

Eve

The last time I talked to my best friend Trina, I was such a bitch to her. Now here I was, lying on this floor, bleeding out, praying I make it out alive.

Earlier that day, I had been talking my shit to Trina, and then I decided to be a bigger bitch and go to the apartment. I knew that she wasn't there, so I wasn't worried about shit popping off between us. After tearing up the apartment, I packed my shit to move out. I had already talked to Candy about crashing at her house for a minute until I could find a nice place to live.

Not thinking clearly, I tore up her room looking for her stash, but only found seventy-five dollars in her dresser. That bitch was broke, broke. She wasn't even on my fucking level.

I had just placed my last bag in my trunk when I heard a familiar voice call out my name.

I shut my trunk, then turned around, rolling my eyes. "What do you want, Marcus?"

"You've been on my mind. I just had to come see you since you blocked my calls and texts from your phone."

I shook my head at this man. He just wouldn't give up for shit. "I told you I was done with you. Now, go home to your wife."

"I'm trying to make you my fuckin' wife. Why can't you see how much I love you?"

"Marcus, I don't have time for this shit," I said, turning to get back in my car.

I intended to drive away from him so I could make it to my date that night, but Marcus had other plans for me.

I felt a cloth suddenly cover my mouth and nose, then everything went black. I didn't even have time to fight his ass back.

When I came to, I didn't even remember what the hell happened or where I was. That was . . . until Marcus walked into the room. This crazy muthafucka had me tied to a chair in his fucking dining room. Across from me was a heavyset, older, white lady tied up. I assumed it was his wife, Tammy.

"Marcus, what are you doing?" I asked.

"We need to get some shit together tonight. I refuse to continue to be unhappy."

Tammy tried to wiggle out of the rope that held her down, but, of course, she wasn't going nowhere. Shit, neither was I.

"Marcus, what is this all about?" she asked as if she weren't scared.

Marcus paced the floor. "Tammy, I tried to do this the easy way. I told you I didn't love you, and I wanted a divorce, but you wanted to make shit harder than it had to be."

"You're my *husband,* Marcus. We took vows to stay together until death do us part."

I sat there wondering why I was the only one really freaking out. This shit was nowhere near normal.

"Marcus, this has nothing to do with me. Please, take me home."

"That's where you're wrong, Eve. This shit has *everything* to do with you."

"Untie me, Marcus," I demanded.

"I can't do that, love. I know you'll run away without letting me explain everything."

I was scared and instantly started crying. "Marcus, I wanna go back home."

"Shut the fuck up, Eve. You know how much I love you. I'm not gonna hurt you."

Us being tied up didn't seem to piss Tammy off that much, but him saying that shit drove her over the edge. She started acting like a mad bull, trying to get out of the chair. This bitch was ready to kill me.

"You love this black bitch? Is *this* why you want to divorce me, Marcus?"

"Yes, Tammy. Damn, just sign the fuckin' papers so me and Eve can live our fuckin' lives in peace!" he yelled.

"Marcus, we can't be together. I told you that before."

Marcus walked over to me and placed a kiss on my lips, something I'd never allowed him to do. "You said we couldn't be together because I was married. I'm showing you that I'm trying to get rid of this bitch right now for you. I love only you, Eve."

"Untie me, Marcus, I'm getting scared."

Just as he started to free one of my hands, Tammy began yelling again. "Marcus, you have lost your fuckin' mind. Untie us and take that little bitch home!" she demanded.

Marcus untied one hand before he walked over to Tammy.

"Eve, will you marry me? I'll get rid of her just like I promised."

"Can I go home?" I cried.

Marcus surprised the fuck out of me, and I felt so bad for Tammy.

"Tammy, if I untie your ass, are you gon' sign these divorce papers?"

Tammy was a bold one and didn't fear this crazy muthafucka. "I'm not signing shit so you can be with your little whore."

Marcus didn't hesitate to pick up the butcher knife that was on the table. He looked me straight in my eyes before slitting her throat. Her blood was everywhere, and I lost it. After a loud scream, my tears poured out.

"What the fuck, Marcus?"

He walked toward me holding the knife. "We can get married now, Eve. She's out of the picture."

"No, Marcus." I continued to cry.

"I can take care of you now. It's just us now, love. I'm gonna take good care of you," he said, giving me another kiss.

Hearing noise coming from the back room, Marcus ran over there to see what was going on. Because one of my hands was already free, I quickly freed the other. This man was crazy, and I didn't want to end up like his wife, Tammy. Just as I hit the living room, I heard Marcus call out my name. Instead of stopping, I took off, trying to make it out the front door.

I never reached the door. The last thing I remember before everything went black was hearing the gunshot . . . before it hit me.

Chapter Seven

Trina

I guess Eve was really pissed at me because she had moved out. I tried calling and texting her ass over the last few days, but she wasn't reaching out to me. I wasn't about to beg the bitch to come back home or anything, but I was gonna let her know I was gonna fuck her up for fuckin' up this apartment. I honestly felt like if she wanted to move out, she should've just done so instead of touching my shit. Bitches be petty as fuck when you call them out on their shit.

Suddenly, my phone started going off. Me thinking it was Eve, I quickly answered, ready to go the fuck off.

"Hello."

"Turn on the news!" Candy cried into the phone.

In my gut, I started to feel sick and didn't want to see what Candy was talking about, but I turned the news on anyway.

As I listened to the reporter discuss the story of the murder/suicide involving three adults and one child, my heart dropped, and I couldn't stop crying.

"I'm so sorry, Trina, I really am," Candy said in between her cries.

I didn't want to hear shit from her, so I quickly hung up.

After the story went off, I understood that the white dude who was in love with Eve had kidnapped her. His sick ass killed his wife in the dining room. Then he went into another room to kill their child. Eve was found dead at the front door, so the police thought she was trying to escape when he shot her down. Marcus loved Eve so much that he lay next to her before blowing out his own brains.

Eve was all I had in this world, and now she was gone. I couldn't do shit but cry my eyes out. What was I supposed to do now without my sister by my side? We might not have been on good terms when she was murdered, but she was and would always be my fucking sister, blood or not.

I eventually cried myself to sleep, and when I got up, it was already dark.

I felt like someone was watching me 'cause as soon as I got up, my phone started going off.

"Hello."

"Trina, where are you?" Candy asked.

"I'm at home, just got up."

I heard her smack her lips. "The party has started, and you're late. With Eve no longer with us, I have something lined up for you."

I shook my head. "Bitch, are you fuckin' crazy? My fuckin' sister was just murdered, and you actually think I give a fuck about your damn party? Fuck you, bitch."

"I was only trying to help your broke ass out, but fuck you, broke, stupid, loose-pussy thot."

I wanted to go off again, but she hung up.

I sat on the couch and cried my eyes out again. Life wasn't fair at all, and this was a hard pill to swallow. Hearing my phone go off again, I decided to ignore it. I figured it was Candy calling back to talk more shit. She must've really wanted to get shit off her chest because she called right back.

"Hello."

Then I heard Jarrod's voice. "Hey, Trina, I just heard about your friend. I wanted to call and check on you."

I couldn't even respond. All I could do was cry into the phone as he listened. He stayed on the phone with me the whole time I had a breakdown, which I appreciated so much.

"I'm outside your apartment if you need a listening ear or just a shoulder to cry on."

I took him up on his offer and went downstairs to talk to him. I liked him, and in a way, I was using him as an escape from reality. I think he knew it, but didn't mind as long as he could be up under me. We sat in the parking lot just talking, but mostly, he held me as I cried over Eve.

Just as I decided it was getting late and I needed to go in, I noticed Eve's car parked a row over. Her keys and purse were still sitting on the seat.

"This shit so bold, Jarrod. She didn't deserve this shit," I cried.

He held me in his arms, repeatedly telling me to be strong and that everything was gonna be all right.

"Before I leave, I'll help you bring her stuff into the house, if you like."

I nodded in agreement. Jarrod did as he said he would do before leaving me. I spent the rest of the night going through her things and playing a memory game in my head. Everything that she packed up reminded me of the good times we shared. My tears turned into giggles as I thought back to all the crazy shit we'd been through together.

The last bag I needed to go through was smaller than the rest. Unzipping the bag, I found the rest of the money she had left over. Knowing she didn't have a family, I was gonna use the money to have her cremated. Something in me wanted my sister with me at all times.

Two Weeks Later

I was able to put together a small service for Eve. The little family she did have didn't show up, but some of the students from our school came to show some support, which I really appreciated.

One day, Jarrod called me out of the blue to check on me and to get me out of the house. I had been in the house depressed and in my feelings. I wanted to shoot him down, but I could hear Eve telling me to get my ass up and go see what that man wanted.

I got dressed and met him downtown. As we walked around Hart Plaza, he held my hand and just listened to me vent about everything that I was feeling.

"You still plan on attending school this fall?"

"I thought about taking the semester off, but I know Eve would haunt me every night. I was the one damn near forcing her to be in school. She wouldn't want me just to quit," I said, giggling.

Jarrod smiled. "I'm happy to see a smile on your face. You're truly beautiful, Trina."

"Thank you, Jarrod. I appreciate you being there for me during this shit."

"You know I like you a lot, and I know some shit about you, but that's not pushing me away. I don't want you ever to think I'm judging you on anything."

I stood there in disbelief. I wasn't sure how he knew, but the fact that he still wanted me is what puzzled me.

"Jarrod . . ."

"You don't have to say anything about that shit if you don't feel comfortable about it. I only brought it up since I felt like you were pushing me away because you were embarrassed about that part of your life."

I was embarrassed now and couldn't help but put my head down. Jarrod lifted my head, placing a kiss on my lips.

"It's time you be with a real man who's gonna help you overcome whatever had you doing what you were doing. You too fuckin' smart to be out in these streets like that."

As he held me, I cried tears of joy.

Over time, things were going good between Jarrod and me. That fall, we walked to class hand-in-hand. I was happy with him, and he was the best thing that'd happened to me in a long time. He'd been there for me whenever I had a breakdown, thinking about Eve. What I loved about him the most is that, although he knew about my past, he never brought it up or even wanted to talk about it. He loved me for me, and that's exactly what I needed in my life.

One night, while doing homework, my phone went off. Thinking that maybe it was Jarrod calling to tell me he was downstairs, I quickly answered.

"Hello."

"Party starts at 8:00 p.m. I expect to see you there."

"Candy, I'm not doing no fuckin' party. I'm no longer in that type of lifestyle. Bitch, stop calling me!" I yelled into the phone.

"I have men who paid for new faces, and you didn't show up. And we both know why Eve wasn't at the last party. Bitch, you owe me."

I gave it some good thought. "What time did you say it was starting?"

"I said eight. Bitch, be on time and be ready to work." That said, she hung up.

I had no plans on showing up to that bitch's house. I waited for Jarrod to show up so I could go over my plan with him.

"Babe, that sounds like a good plan. You ready to get this show on the road?"

With a smile on my face, I quickly said, "Yeah."

After making my important phone call, we chilled, waiting for everything to unfold.

It took some time, like a whole four days, but I was happy with my work. Jarrod and I lay across the bed watching the Channel 2 Breaking News.

Reporter Shelia Smith reported on the bust of a prostitution ring that was raided just days ago. Then she talked about all the lowlifes who were cheating and spending all their money on a good night. Candy's picture flashed across the screen as the madame who ran everything. She had a few charges against her ass, especially when they took out some underage girls at her last party.

I couldn't help but laugh. Hopefully, these women could find a better way of living.

"Good job, baby," Jarrod said as I lay on his chest.

"Thank you, baby. I couldn't have done this without you. I love you, Jarrod."

"I love you too, baby."

Chapter Eight

Candy

I sat in this cold room, listening to Johnathan, my lawyer, yell at me about my case. Muthafuckas were trying to give a bitch years for running a prostitution ring. Then on top of that, they were coming down on me because of those underage girls I had picked up at the last minute when Trina's thot ass decided she was done fucking with me after Eve got killed. I hated that I was so desperate to replace Eve and Trina with a pair of fresh faces that I didn't even check them li'l bitches' ages. They had ass and titties, and that was all I was looking for at the time.

Although I could never take a muthafucka seriously who begged to eat my whole ass on multiple occasions, knowing that I was facing time, I tried to let him feel like he had complete control of the entire situation. I was putting my life in this man's hands.

"This shit is really out of my hands. My name, like so many others, has been leaked to the public. It's a fucking surprise that I even still have my fucking job. Your case itself is opening up many other cases, and shit is not looking pretty for you at all."

I quickly looked over at Johnathan, then rolled my eyes. I was tired of his bitching and was about to let him have it. "Do your fucking job and get me off. Like I said before, yes, I threw those parties, but I never forced any of them thot bitches to sleep with anyone. They left with whoever they wanted to fuck. I never forced shit. If anything, I provided a safe environment for people to meet and mingle."

This fool looked me straight in the face and said, "I don't know how you think that's going to work. Look at your accounts and all that money. Did you even stop to think about what was gonna happen when them women testified against you? Bottom line, you're gonna have to do some time."

"We're gonna have to kill them young hoes before court," I yelled, meaning it all.

I was told that there were a few witnesses to testify against me, and I knew for sure that it had to be the young hoes. I knew my regular girls weren't turning their backs on me for shit. Some of those bitches raised a whole fucking family off money they made doing business with me.

I must have shocked him because he quickly covered his face before shaking his head.

"I'm *not* hearing this shit."

I saw that nothing I said was working, plus I was desperate. With a seductive look in my eyes, I started to slowly rub my hands up his thighs before they landed on his dick. This square muthafucka quickly removed my hands from his lap.

Although his dick jumped in excitement, Johnathon knew me well enough and knew better than to fall for my bullshit. "Stop playing with me, Candy. I've known you long enough to know that you ain't giving up no pussy."

I couldn't help but giggle. "Shit, I had to try my luck at something."

He chuckled as he shook his head.

Honesty, at this point, I was scared. It was a damn shame that even my lawyer was doubting his skills, and my chances of getting out weren't looking promising. "John, I'm not built for prison. I need you to make something happen," I pleaded with him.

"Hold on tight. I'll see what I can do. You know, with these names being leaked, there's a lot of happy homes being torn up, and folks are blaming you. Right now, things are not looking too good, Candy, inside and out."

"I never force anyone to do shit. Think about it. Why is it that everyone was getting fucked but me? It's simple because they wanted to fuck. You gotta get me out of this shit. Tell Judge Harris that he can get a sample of my pussy if he gets me out."

My lawyer, Mr. Johnathan Tucker, stood up and then walked out the door. He was trying his best to defend his client—me, Mrs. Candace Richardson-Porter—but only because of his dealings with my husband, the late Jasper Porter.

Walking out without saying shit, indeed, said a lot. John was tired of my shit.

I had heard that Johnathan's name had also been damaged. His career was on the line, and his wife was leaving with the kids, but his loyalty to a dead man was stronger than anything, and that alone was the only reason that he stayed by my side.

"Come on, Ms. Lady. It's time for you to go back to your cell."

I looked up to see the guard standing over me. Although I felt like I was about to do this time, I fixed my face. I refused to let a bitch see me sweat.

When the guard cuffed me to take me back to my cell, I had a plan and knew how to play the game. So, I made sure to back up my ass against his dick. Just to make certain he understood that what I was doing was flirting, I did it again.

"I don't think you want these problems in your life," he whispered in my ear.

He was right. I didn't want anything to do with a dick, but I wanted my freedom. Y'all remember the old saying,

"Desperate times call for desperate measures"? Right now, I was desperate as hell.

I turned to face him. Me pretending to blush had this man all caught up in my manipulative ways, and I could tell that he was ready to risk it all for a sniff of this pussy. He was just the right fool that I needed for my Plan B.

"Damn, I see you packing. These ho-ass cuffs the only thing that's keeping me from grabbing that muthafucka and stuffing it in my wet-ass mouth."

"Damn, shawty, you trying to get me caught up and fired?"

"Nah, I'm trying to get my soul snatched out of my ass, then nonstop rounds of back shots. Can you manage that?" I asked, licking my lips.

He gave me a look of confusion.

"If I'm barking up the wrong tree, let a bitch know something."

Then I watched as he licked *his* lips. "Nah, shawty, you good with your li'l sexy ass."

I wasn't feeling this man in no type of way, but he was so easy to pull in. I knew for sure that working with him, I would have him exactly where I needed him to be.

Usually, I would have been talking big shit on my way back to my cell to get the girls excited, but I didn't even have it in me. I had a plan that I needed to work out in my head before I put it into full motion.

This jailhouse shit wasn't something that I was trying to get used to and had no plans to try. Plan A had failed, and my lawyer seemed not to understand how bad I needed to get out of this bitch, so I had no choice but to start working on Plan B.

I knew the role I played in everything, but they were trying to put Eve's death on me. That thot freak bitch was dead because she was too fucking money-hungry while fucking with random dudes. I wasn't even the one who introduced her to that crazy-ass white man. She and the rest of them girls were grown and responsible for their own actions when dick and money were around.

Trina's stupid ass left me high and dry after Eve's death. After fucking with that nigga, Gerald, that first night, that muthafucka went crazy and kept popping up at my crib, looking for her raggedy ass. I promised him that she was gonna be at the party, and that bitch never showed up. Even after introducing him to the new girls, that man was ready to beat my ass cause that bitch wasn't there. I had to refund him his money and have him escorted out of the party, but fuck her too.

She was acting like she couldn't make money because her li'l friend was dead. I never understood what she wanted me to do. Was I supposed to hug her and become her crying shoulder? I thought I was being a real friend by letting her know that money was on the floor. Her roommate was just killed, and I knew she was gonna need every penny to cover that rent in them bum-ass apartments.

Enough of them bitches for now. I needed to get out and build up a whole new team of the baddest thots ever. I was even sure that some of my old bitches were gonna come back to work for me.

Entering my cell, I flopped down on the bullshit that they called a bed. "Fucking bullshit."

"With those charges against you, it's best that you get used to this fucking bullshit," I heard my cellmate, Denise, suggest.

That made my attitude ten times worse. "Bitch, please. This lifestyle will *never* be the right way of living, and it ain't shit anyone can tell me."

"Yeah, okay, princess," Denise teased.

"It's *queen,* bitch," I barked.

Over the last few weeks of sharing a cell with Denise, I had to teach her that I wasn't one of these friendly bitches in here. I might joke from time to time when I was bored, but I would hand out ass beatings if needed. She got the point, and honestly, she has been good ever since then. Every chance she got, Denise tried to be friendly. I loved a bitch that kissed ass.

"Ms. Candy, can I ask a question?"

I rolled my eyes. I was sick of her with this "miss" shit. "What the hell I tell you about that *Ms.* Candy shit, Denise? I'm not an old bitch."

"My bad. I'm just not understanding why these folks want you locked up anyway. I know what they are saying on the news and stuff, but even Ray Charles could see that you're too fancy for a place like this."

"Girl, there you go in my business again. I'm not trying to clear shit up with nobody but that judge. Whatever you see on the news, run with *that* story."

Denise laughed. "It seemed like you were only helping those girls make money, if you ask me. You weren't taking money from them or beating they ass like a pimp or anything. I heard them girls were making bread. I probably would have worked for you too if I knew you on the outside world."

I gave her the side-eye but noted to offer her a job when she got out. This minor downfall wasn't about to be the end of my hustle.

"Denise, how old did you say you were?" I curiously asked while plotting.

"I'll be 22 years old in a month."

"Damn, you are young. Why are you here anyway?" I questioned, finally realizing that she had been there for a few weeks, and I hadn't really had a chance to get into her business.

Denise's whole face changed. She looked sad, and I knew that there was a story to be told.

"I was out stealing some food and diapers for my daughter and got caught again."

"Again? Where's her daddy at?"

Denise giggled. "Now *you* in *my* business, girl."

"I was just asking. Maybe I can help you out when you get out. That's *if* you can help me while I'm here."

Denise sat up in her bed with a curious look on her face. She knew that working with me would bring out the opportunity that she'd been waiting for. "What do you have in mind?"

"Let me get some shit in order, and then I'll let you know."

Seeing that she was just as desperate as me to get out made it even easier to pull her into my plan.

After eating the slop that they called dinner, we returned to our cell. I wished that I could have reached out to Maria to put some of that money that I hid in her account on my books so that I could eat better, but I knew the smartest thing to do was to keep her in hiding. I wasn't about to fuck up what I had going on.

I lay in bed, thinking about my life and how I never really had a chance at being anything else but a bitch as I grew up. Being a manipulative bitch was in my blood, and I had my mama to thank for it.

At first, my mom was the type who would do whatever it took to make sure that we never wanted for shit after my father left us. My mama, Terry Richardson, was a hustla up until she started feeding her nose and shit. She no longer boosted clothes to make a profit to take care of me and the house. She was boosting to chase a high, her very first high to be exact. Even as a kid, I understood that the first high would never come back, and by the time they realized it, they were already hooked.

As I lay there, my thoughts went back to when my mama was on that shit and tried me for the first time. I had no problem showing her that I was indeed her child—one band, one sound.

"Candace, baby, stop all that damn crying. I told you all you had to do is make Mr. Johnson happy. He is not gonna hurt you, girl."

"Mama, I'm 10 and not a baby. I know what men want, and I don't wanna be his girlfriend. You old enough to be his girlfriend. You do it."

Then she slapped me, her baby girl.

"If it was that fucking easy, I would have been handled my business. You doing all that talking back and having a smart mouth is exactly why your daddy left us. Don't nobody like no smart-mouthed-ass child. Now, fix your face and get your ass out of this room," she yelled before leaving me to fix myself up.

Although I could remember hearing my mother tell Mr. Johnson that he was not to hurt me, I still didn't like being in the middle of this shit. I was far from being stupid and knew that whatever they wanted to happen was wrong.

There was also something in me that didn't want my mom to be mad at me. Her telling me that if I didn't go through with this, we were gonna be put out was a lot of pressure on a 10-year-old, and I didn't want to be homeless.

After fixing my face like my mama had ordered, I walked out of the room, wearing the pink training bra and panty set that she had just stolen earlier that day.

I couldn't help but wonder why my mama couldn't just give him them couple of dollars in her drawer, then pay him the rest when she got it instead of making me do this bullshit.

With the look of guilt, my mama walked out of the living room, leaving me to deal with that nasty-ass pervert, Mr. Johnson.

"Come sit down, baby girl," he said, patting a spot next to him on the couch.

Scared and all, I did as I was told.

"My mama said you weren't gonna hurt me," I said, acting shy.

Mr. Johnson placed my hand on the small bulge in his pants so that I could feel his goodies. "I'm not gonna hurt you, baby girl. I promise you're gonna love this."

I gave him a strange look, but he clearly didn't understand it.

"It's okay, baby girl. I promise you'll be able to get more of it after today."

I felt disgusted and tried not to throw up in my mouth. At this point, I didn't care about having a roof over my head. Being homeless didn't sound too bad after all.

Then he pulled his dick out and tried to grab my hand so that I could play with it. I quickly snatched it away, but he wasn't having that. This time, Mr. Johnson grabbed my small hand with a firm grip. I knew for sure that my hand was gonna go numb from him squeezing the life out of it.

Then I started to cry as he moved my hand up and down his dick.

"Aww, cut that shit out, baby girl. There's no need for all that. Go ahead and wake that muthafucka up," he moaned out with his eyes closed and head resting on the back of the couch.

After a minute, I stopped satisfying that dirty bastard, realizing they both had me fucked up.

"What the fuck wrong with you, girl?" he asked as he opened his eyes and sat up.

"I'm cold. I'll be right back."

Walking out of the room and past the kitchen, I could tell that my mama was wondering what was going on, but the guilt wouldn't let her ask me anything.

After putting my dress back on, I snuck into my mama's room to use the government phone that she put up for emergencies.

"Terry, where's that little girl of yours?" Mr. Johnson yelled out.

"She in the bathroom."

Mr. Johnson got up and then went into the kitchen, his penis still out and everything. "I hope you and that little bitch not trying to play me. You're about to be sucking this muthafucka in a minute if she don't come on."

My mama now had an attitude. "Damn, give her a fucking minute. She new to this shit."

"I hope so 'cause you promised I'd be the first to have a turn with her," Mr. Johnson said, still jacking himself off so that he didn't go soft.

As I whispered on the phone, I kept peeking out into the freak show that was taking place in the kitchen.

"Candace, come on, baby."

I didn't reply quick enough for Mr. Johnson, so he took it out on Mama.

"Fuck it. It's your turn," he said, trying to stick his dick into her mouth.

She hesitated to open her mouth, and that led to him slapping the shit out of her. "Get to work before I go fuck that little bitch and hard. It's her first time. I'll split that little bitch in two."

Just as she started to suck him up, the police burst through the door. "Put your hands up, you sick bastard," I heard the male officer yell out.

The female officer left her partner in the kitchen while she went to look for the little girl who had called them to that house. I swear this had to have been the fastest they ever came to the hood.

"Candace, it's me, Officer Howard. Please come out."

I ran out of the bathroom, crying to Officer Howard. "Thank you for saving me."

I was a little dramatic, but so what? I had every right to be. What the hell did I look like, letting Mama and his nasty ass take advantage of me?

Mr. Johnson was placed under arrest while I cried, telling my story about how he had tried to rape me, then assaulted my mama when I ran and hid from him. My mama was shocked but knew that if she fixed her mouth to say anything other than what I was saying, then she would have gotten locked up too.

After it was all said and done, I laughed to myself, realizing that I was just like her . . . manipulative as fuck.

That night, after the police left, my mom fixed dinner as if nothing that she did that day was wrong. I knew that she was gonna be a problem. Mama or not, I was gonna have to fix that.

Later that night, after she had fallen asleep without a care in the world, I walked out of the kitchen with the biggest knife that I could find. After climbing into her bed, I sat right on her fat, baggy titties so that she would be able to look directly into my eyes.

"What the fuck, Candace?"

She looked as if she wanted to say something else, but the sight of the knife stopped her.

"Let me make this quick so that you can continue getting your beauty sleep. If you ever in your fuckin' life try some shit like that again, I'll split your fuckin' throat in your sleep."

She saw the look in my eyes and knew that I wasn't the one to be fucked with. It wasn't until years later that she tried me . . . and got fucked up.

***

I hated not being able to sleep at night, but who in their right mind could ever get used to sleeping in a cold cell? Another thing that kept me up, besides my thoughts, was Denise crying herself to sleep every night. She never wanted to talk about her problems, but they were there. I knew that if I was gonna use her to get out of this bitch, I was gonna have to get her to trust me completely and open up.

Trina

"Aye, bro, ain't she that thot bitch whose friend got killed by that white dude a few months ago?"

"Hell yeah. That's her, dawg. I wonder if she was running around, tricking like her friend, 'cause I'll for sure pay for that shit."

They both laughed before the guy in the red shirt responded. "Go ask her if we can get a date later on. I got a hot forty dollars. That bitch is pretty."

I turned around to see two dumb-ass niggas all in my fucking business, being disrespectful as hell. My evil stare caused them to turn their backs on me and walk away as if they had never said anything in the first place. I could never understand how someone's pain could be a whole joke for someone else. Shit was mad weird to me.

It had been a few months since Eve was murdered, but I wasn't over her death, and these muthafuckas at this school weren't gonna allow me to be. As badly as I wanted to cry and go back home, the feel of Jarrod's arms wrapping around me from the back made me smile just a little.

"Damn, this line long as hell."

I turned to face him. "Yeah, it is."

The look on my face must have told him that something was bothering me.

"What's wrong, baby?" he questioned, full of concern.

My silence was enough for him to assume I was thinking about Eve again.

"You know we still got a few days to do this. If it's too soon for you to be here, we can go back to the crib and try again a different day."

I wiped away my tears. "I'm good. Let's just get this over with."

I wasn't gonna lie. After Eve's death, it was hard for me to do anything but cry about losing her. That crazy-ass Marcus didn't have to do my baby like that. I would never stop hating him. What hurt the most was that we were arguing and shit when all this shit happened. I could only wish that she left this earth knowing that no matter what hurtful shit we said toward each other, she was my sister, and I loved her.

Dealing with her untimely death, there were times that I didn't even want to live anymore, but Jarrod had been there for me every step of the way. After her funeral, everyone who said that they were gonna be there for me went on with their lives, but Jarrod was there with me every day to make sure I didn't end it all.

Since Eve's death, our relationship had moved so quickly. We weren't even in a real relationship when he helped pack my stuff and moved it into his house. Seeing that I was stuck, he had been there to pull me out that dark hole. Honestly, over the last few months, this man had shown me what being loved was all about, and I never felt so wanted in life before him.

The semester was getting ready to start up for the fall in two weeks, and that day, we were up at the college to pick up our books. All the strange looks and whispers were getting to me. I couldn't understand how people could be so fucking insensitive, including the news reporters.

Eve's business had been painted all over the news, and they had no problem dragging her. She had gone from being a murder-suicide victim to a prostitute who fucked around with a married man and got caught up in his madness. I sometimes found myself crying and blaming myself. If I hadn't told on Candy, then no one would have connected them and found out about Eve's true lifestyle. It was both of our lifestyles, but since I was still alive, of course, my shit was still somewhat on the low.

"Baby, I know Eve was your best friend and all, and I'm not judging you at all, but I think that maybe you should go talk to somebody about how you been feeling lately."

"I keep telling you that I'm good. Besides, Black people don't talk to shrinks and shit."

As Jarrod drove, he shook his head. "Nah, baby, you are not all right. I hadn't said shit before, but sometimes, I hear you crying in your sleep and shit. Why you think I be holding you so tight while you're asleep?"

A smile snuck across my face. "I thought it was because you loved me."

"I do love you, and that's why I'm worried about you."

He parked the car in the driveway, and I quickly got out. "I don't need to talk to nobody," I said, slamming the door.

He got out and followed me into the house. "I wasn't trying to fight with you, Trina."

"Who's fighting, Jarrod? I just don't want to hear that shit. Let me deal with this the best way I know how."

Jarrod tried to hug me, but I wasn't in the mood. I pushed him away before going upstairs to the bedroom.

I knew I was being a bitch, and he was only trying to help, but feeling like everyone always had something to say, I was feeling smothered.

After a long, hot bath, I planned on making it my business to apologize to Jarrod. If he didn't act like he cared, then I'd have a good reason to trip on him, but I needed to show him that I appreciated him for everything.

Putting on a T-shirt and a pair of black boy shorts, I went back downstairs to Jarrod. I stood in the living room doorway, watching him. He was so caught up in the football game that he didn't even notice me at first. I had to admit that not only was this man so good to me and for me, but he was also fine as fuck. The earth knew I needed a fine-ass man with the perfect dick to get me back on track.

After a minute, he finally looked up. "You hungry?"

I smiled. This was why I loved him. No matter what, he put me first, and for that very reason, I needed to get my act together.

Without answering, I walked over to the black leather recliner chair that he was seated in and slowly climbed and straddled his lap. "I'm so sorry for tripping earlier. I know you only want what's best for me, and I appreciate you so much, Jarrod."

Jarrod pulled me closer to place a kiss on me. "I'm not tripping off that, Trina."

"You still love me?" I questioned, already knowing the truth.

"You already know I do. Stop asking me silly shit like that."

I couldn't help but giggle. He was so lovable, but talked shit so smoothly.

As our lips locked, I started to undo his belt buckle.

"What you doing, girl?" he asked with a sneaky look on his face.

"Didn't you just ask me if I was hungry?"

He knew what time it was and quickly picked up the remote to turn off the TV. The next thing I knew, he was carrying me back upstairs.

When it came to this lovemaking shit, our asses barely made it to the bed. Most days, just like today, we ended up fucking on the steps. Jarrod had me pinned on the wall with my legs wrapped around his waist, all while he filled me up with dick.

"Fuck!" I heard him moan out.

I might have had more than a few bodies under my belt, but I still had that gripper.

Y'all knew about my past and knew I wasn't a stranger to taking dick, but this man right here was a straight-up beast. All these niggas had dick, but he knew exactly how to work it. The deeper he went into me, the more he made me feel like it was my first time being with a real man.

Round two started on the top of the stairs but finished with me squirting from back shots all over the bed that we now shared.

"Damn, girl, you wild as hell."

I rested my head on his sweaty chest. "Nah, it was all you this time, baby."

I was feeling so damn good that I couldn't stop smiling. Our love was real, and the sex was great. I couldn't lie. I was happy with him.

"I love you, Trina," he whispered before placing a kiss on my forehead.

"I love you too, baby."

Those words escaped my lips so easily, and I swore I meant them.

"Tomorrow, I want you to go to this thing my auntie throwing for her husband. He just expanded his business, and they're celebrating."

Without overthinking the situation, I whispered, "All right," before drifting off.

The next morning, after a long, hot shower, I went downstairs to fix breakfast. I didn't work or contribute to any bills, so I felt like I could at least cook and keep the house clean. Don't get me wrong, I had been looking for a job, but nothing was working out for me. Jarrod constantly told me not to worry about it, but I never liked living off anyone.

"Good morning, my love."

Jarrod wrapped his arms around my waist before placing a kiss on my lips. "Morning. You got it smelling good as hell in here."

"Don't I always?" I jokingly teased.

He stole a piece of bacon before sitting down at the table. "My auntie Sandy said we should be there by 2:00 p.m."

"Okay, that's cool. What type of business do her husband have anyway?"

"He has a few barbershops around Detroit, but he just opened up a new one out in Taylor."

Hearing that brought back bad, old memories. I just knew for sure my face turned pale.

"Huh?"

"Yeah, Uncle Gerald owns a few barbershops. You might have seen him on TV a time or two. He always having events. Him and his team do free haircuts for the kids and shit. Matter of fact, he got something coming up for the schoolkids next week."

Fuck responding, my ass couldn't even move. *Why me, Lord?*

"Damn, Trina, where you go that fast?" Jarrod yelled, pushing me away from the stove.

I still couldn't snap back to reality when I saw Jarrod rushing the pan over to the sink. I had burned breakfast with the news that I was going to have to face my past today. Don't get me wrong. I had run into a nigga that I might have fucked with before, but nobody related to a guy that I dated. This was the exact reason why I was so against dating in my line of work. I was trying to forget about all that thot stage in my life and fucked around and cuffed one of my trick's nephews. If it weren't for bad luck, I wouldn't have none at all.

"Damn."

I still stood there, dazed, as he rushed to open the side door so that the house could clear out.

"What the hell is wrong with you, girl?" Jarrod yelled, giving me a little shake to snap me back to reality.

"Huh?"

"You burned the food, baby. What's going on with you?"

I couldn't even look him in the eyes. With my head hanging low, I whispered, "Sorry," before running upstairs to the bedroom.

Jarrod was right on my ass. "Let's talk, Trina."

"I'm all right. Just give me a minute, please."

"I wasn't asking. I was telling you that we needed to talk. I don't know what's going on, but whatever it is, we need to work it out now."

I knew I had to get myself together now. The way that I reacted screamed that I was guilty of something. I told myself that if I wanted to keep my secret safe, then I had to act normally.

"I'm sorry, baby. Maybe you were right about me needing to talk to someone."

I never wanted to pour my heart out to a stranger, but I knew bringing it up would make him forget about me tripping and burning the food.

"It's all right, baby. I'll support you every step of the way," Jarrod said, pulling me into a hug.

Thinking about actually doing this made me decide to change my mind. "Wait, baby, we can't afford this shit right now. You already paying for everything, and I haven't found a job yet. Maybe we should wait."

"Don't worry about that right now."

"All right."

Jarrod laid me down in the bed. "Look, I'll go get us some breakfast. I want you to get some rest."

I nodded my head in agreement. Then I watched as he threw on some clothes before walking out the door. Once I heard the door shut and his car start, I cried and cried hard. This type of shit made me realize just how much I didn't deserve Jarrod. He was a good guy who deserved nothing but the best, and that, for damn sure, wasn't my thot ass.

After beating myself up and playing it cool for Jarrod, we were dressed and headed toward his auntie Sandy's house. I could feel my stomach knotting up every time the GPS announced that we were closer to our destination. I had to keep telling myself to calm down, which wasn't easy when it felt like I was going to shit on myself at any moment now.

"Two minutes away," I heard the GPS announce.

"Jarrod, I need to tell you something."

"Hold up, baby. Let me do this. I haven't been out here in a long time," he said, listening to the GPS call out the address for the last time.

As he parked in front of the large home, he killed the engine, then turned to me. "What's up, baby?"

At first, I thought I had it in me to tell him that I had tricked with his auntie's husband, but with his handsome face and loving eyes staring me straight in the eyes, I just couldn't bring myself to do it.

"I just wanted to tell you that I really do love you and appreciate you so much."

Jarrod leaned over to kiss me. "I love your mushy ass too."

We both laughed as we stepped out of the car. I couldn't change the past, but I could pray that it didn't fuck up my future.

Jarrod grabbed my hand, then led me into the backyard where his family was spending time together.

I had already had the opportunity to meet his mom, dad, and a handful of other family members, but today, I saw a few fresh faces.

"Hey, Auntie Sandy, this is . . ." With a huge smile on his face, Jarrod paused.

"Well, who is she?" his auntie Sandy teased.

I couldn't help but giggle. He was in love, and I was the lucky girl.

"My bad, this my girl, Trina. Trina, this is Auntie Sandy."

I reached my hand out to shake hers, but she looked as if I carried a dangerous disease. I started to wonder if "thot" was written across my forehead.

"I don't know why my nephew didn't tell you, but I don't shake hands. I'm a hugger type of lady," she said, quickly pulling me into a hug.

"Dang, Auntie, can I have her back?"

We all laughed while she released me.

"I'm sorry. It's just been a minute since Jarrod brought someone around. I was starting to believe that he had given up on love."

Her words had me blushing so hard. For some reason, being accepted by a nigga's family seemed just as important as having his heart.

"Oh, shoot, the man of the hour has arrived."

For a moment, what awaited me in the dark had slipped my mind, but her announcement had the butterflies in my stomach instantly attacking me. I had damn near choked on my juice.

Gerald walked straight over to us. I knew by the devilish smile that he wore that he was gonna be on some bullshit.

All while hugging his wife, he stared a hole right through me. I tried not to look his way and talked to Jarrod.

"Baby, can you show me where the bathroom is?"

"Yeah, come on."

Before walking away, Gerald rushed over. "Hey, Nephew. I know you and this pretty little lady wasn't about to leave before eating and chilling with the family?"

"I was just about to show her the bathroom. I'll be back."

I thought we were free until he caught up to us.

"I'll show her because I wanna change into something a little more comfortable. I don't wanna spill any of that barbecue sauce on my suit."

I squeezed Jarrod's hand, trying to give him a signal, but he wasn't catching on.

"All right, cool, Uncle. Good looking."

Jarrod gave me a peck on my lips before joining a cousin in conversation.

"Come on, girl. It's this way."

Only because I really had to pee, I followed.

"What the fuck are you doing?"

He was an asshole and wasn't trying to act normal. "I miss you. Let's have a quickie right quick in the bathroom," he ordered, snatching my arm.

I pushed him. "Get the fuck away from me before I cause a fucking scene," I warned him.

"You won't, and I'm willing to bet any amount of money on that. Besides, I'm quite sure my nephew doesn't know anything about us."

He was right about that, and I never wanted him to find out, but I wasn't about to play this game with him.

"There's nothing going on with us. Just leave that shit alone."

Seeing that the bathroom was right there, I rushed in, making sure to lock the door. After washing my hands, I peeked out the door and saw that Gerald was waiting for me. I quickly texted Jarrod and told him that I wasn't feeling too well and was ready to go. A few minutes later, I heard him outside the bathroom door, talking to Gerald.

I slowly walked out.

"Hey, baby. Unc was just telling me how he needed someone to help with the shop. You interested?"

"No," I responded a little too fast.

Jarrod looked confused. "What's wrong with you?"

"I'm just not feeling well. Sorry."

Jarrod set down his can of beer. "Let me use the bathroom, and then we'll be out of here."

After he shut the bathroom door, with a devilish smirk on his face, Gerald jumped right back in that bullshit. "You don't wanna come to the shop and help me with some paperwork? I'll even eat on that pussy just the way you liked that night."

"That was the old me. I'm not on that bullshit anymore. Please just leave that shit alone," I begged.

"Same thot, same pussy."

We both heard the toilet flush.

"Please, Gerald, or I'm gonna tell your wife."

He chuckled. "Let's go tell her! She might just want you for herself, and my nephew can beat your thot ass for being a fucking ho. From now on, that pussy is gonna be mine."

Just then, Jarrod walked out to join us.

"As I was saying, it's not a lot of work. I really need someone to file some paperwork and organize a few things. I'm sure you can handle it."

I couldn't believe how he was doing this shit to me.

"Damn, baby, you gonna make my uncle beg for your work?"

Jarrod and Gerald both laughed, but wasn't shit funny.

"We should be going now."

Jarrod thought I was being rude, and his face said it all. He gave his uncle a high five before walking away. Gerald quickly snatched me up for a hug. I tried to free myself, but he held on to me tightly.

"I'll see you tomorrow," he said as he squeezed my ass.

I finally caught up to Jarrod, but he wouldn't let me hold his hand as we walked to the car. He was pissed at me, but he had no idea how I felt inside. I wanted to scream out and cry. Honestly, if I had dropped dead in front of that house, I wouldn't have cared. This was my Karma catching up with my ass.

For the rest of the night, I thought about how and when I was gonna tell him the truth, but my mind kept drawing up blanks. Situations like this never had a happy ending, and I was scared to lose Jarrod. For once in my life, I had someone who loved me and didn't care about my past. Honestly, knowing that should have made it easier to tell him the truth, but it didn't.

My past was fucked up, and I could admit that I wasn't shit for some of the stuff that I had done. I always thought that whatever was done in the past was gonna stay there because he never asked questions, but damn, was this *really* my Karma? Did I *honestly* deserve to have Gerald thrown back in my face like this?

Since we arrived home, he had stayed downstairs, watching TV and ignoring me. I had embarrassed him in front of his family, but if we had stayed any longer, then shit would have been worse. I thought I was doing him a favor.

Thinking that I had finally fallen asleep, he crept back into the room.

I turned to face him. "Jarrod, can we talk?"

"Nah, you not feeling good. Go back to sleep," he said, trying to be a smart-ass.

"Jarrod, I need to talk to you."

"I have to get some sleep. I have something to do in the morning."

I turned to face the window. I didn't want him to see me crying.

The next morning, I lay there, pretending to be asleep so that I could listen to Jarrod on the phone with Gerald. I hated how Gerald wouldn't just give up and let me be. And why the hell couldn't Jarrod magically read my mind and see that I was bothered by his uncle?

"Unc, she wasn't feeling too good yesterday. I'm not sure if she'll be up to stopping by the shop today."

Gerald must have been trying to talk him into waking me up because I finally heard Jarrod tell him that he was gonna get me up and see how I was feeling.

"Trina, Trina, how you feeling?" he called out as he lightly shook me.

I swore I wanted to continue to lie there, pretending to be asleep, but Jarrod started to place these small kisses on my lips before making his way to my neck. He knew exactly how to get some shit started.

"Baby, I'm up," I responded with a Kool-Aid smile spread across my face.

I wanted to play with him that morning, but at the same time, I had to pretend that something was wrong with me. "Come on, Jarrod. I'm still not completely feeling too well," I lied.

He ignored my fake ass and kept kissing on me. "Ain't shit wrong with your ass."

"Whatever, boy. How you figure?"

"'Cause you telling me to stop, but got them legs wrapped around me. Stop playing and take this shit off before I have to leave."

Jarrod knew me better than I thought, but I still needed a way to get out of this shit with his uncle. Yeah, telling the truth would have been the smart thing, but I didn't want to hurt him. Besides, the confidence that I had last night had flown out the window. Then I started to think about Eve. What if Gerald was crazy like Marcus's white ass? The hole around me was getting bigger by the day.

I watched as Jarrod went to the drawer to grab a condom. Like I mentioned before, we never really discussed my past like that, but I understood why he strapped up when we were together. What surprised me about him was how yesterday, and a few other times, he fucked me raw without hesitation. I wondered what that was all about.

"Why you still dressed?"

"Bae," I whined, still faking it.

He was getting irritated with my fake ass, and although he didn't say it, his face said it all. At that point, Jarrod tossed the condom on the bed before walking out of the room. It was just seconds later when I heard the shower water running.

Waking up to good sex was our thing, and I was on pure bullshit this morning. Feeling guilty, I jumped out of bed to join my baby in the shower. If I wanted things to continue to work, I needed to act normal, no matter how abnormal things were about to get.

"Why the hell you be playing so much?"

I couldn't answer the question, but I made sure to make him forget he even asked me anything. I was always taught that you shouldn't talk with a full mouth, so inch by inch, I took his dick into my mouth. Just like that, he had forgotten about being mad at me. Over the years, I had picked up on some skills and wasn't afraid to use them, especially on the man whom I loved.

Eventually, our session came to an end, and we returned to the room. I sat on the bed with my towel wrapped around me.

"What you about to do?" I asked, seeing Jarrod getting dressed.

"I gotta go shoot a few moves. Once school starts back up, I'm not gonna have no spare time to do shit. Oh yeah, my uncle wants you to stop by the shop and check things out today. Can you do that?"

I just knew that after my performance in the shower, he was for sure going to want to spend the day up under my ass.

"I'll stop by, but I'm not making no promises about working there. Besides, school is about to start back up, and I need to focus on that, just like you."

"He said he only needed some little shit done, nothing serious that would take up too much time. Maybe he could give you a few pointers on starting your own business."

My face turned up, listening to him sound just like Candy on the night that she introduced me to Gerald.

"You good?"

"Yeah, baby," I lied with a fake half smile.

In no time, Jarrod was completely dressed and ready to walk out the door. IIe had no idea how badly I wanted to scream out and beg him not to leave me. I hated myself for not being able to tell him that I didn't trust his uncle or myself, at that. I never wanted to hurt Jarrod in any type of way, but I was a thot at heart that loved doing thot-girl shit. I wanted so badly to put my past completely behind me, but his uncle was the type that didn't give a fuck about shit but getting his nut, and I didn't trust myself at times. I was fighting my own demons.

This was the exact reason why I never dated when I was out making money. Dating has always complicated my lifestyle.

After getting dressed, I checked my purse to make sure I had my taser, just in case I grew the balls to tell Gerald to go fuck himself. Honestly, I didn't need anybody holding shit over my head, especially when I was trying my best to do right.

Jarrod had left the address on the dresser for me. I was planning on showing up, but only to put an end to all this bullshit. If Gerald decided to tell Jarrod the truth, then I could easily explain to him that he knew what I did in my past and that he needed to understand that weird shit happened every day in that field of work.

It was crazy how, away from Jarrod, my mind told me that I could tell him the truth, but, in his face, I couldn't hurt him like that.

When I pulled up to the shop, I could see that it was still early, and there was only one other car parked out front. I knew that it was Gerald's.

Once out of the car and at the door, I tried to open it, but the door was locked. Instead of knocking, I took it as a sign to get the fuck on. Maybe the big man upstairs was on my side, after all.

"Aye, girl, where you going?"

I turned to see Gerald standing in the doorway with a smile on his face. "Come on in, so we can get to work."

I knew he wasn't talking about the job but some sexual shit.

After shutting the door, he locked it again. I was gonna have to fight if he tried something stupid, but I was ready. My hand stayed in my purse, gripping my taser.

"Follow me," he ordered.

I followed him to his office, which was located near the back.

"Look, I only showed up so your nephew wouldn't think I was acting funny. I have no plans on sleeping with you again. I told you yesterday that I'm a changed woman."

"Blah, blah, blah. You don't have to fuck me today, but you gonna suck this dick the same way you did that night I paid for it. Do you know that I came back looking for your ass, and Candy said that you hadn't shown up that day? Why the fuck you never came back to see me? A nigga was real-life searching for your ass. I even popped up at the school you told me you went to."

I wasn't trying to hear all that bullshit. "You do understand that I'm with your nephew and love him deeply."

"Thots like you don't love shit but money," Gerald yelled, taking a seat in his desk chair.

"That's not true. I love Jarrod, and I know for sure he loves me," I said, believing everything that came out of my mouth.

While pulling out a knot of money, Gerald laughed at me. "I'm pretty sure that if my nephew knew how you made your money, he would have never looked at you."

"See, that's where you're wrong. Jarrod knows about my past and still loves me regardless."

Gerald pulled out his dick midconversation.

"Look at him. He's waiting on you, Trina."

"Fuck you!" I yelled, turning around to leave.

Gerald jumped up, grabbing me by my hair. "Bitch, you gonna suck this dick, or I'll be making *that* call to Jarrod, letting him know how I had your freak ass bent up like a pretzel just a few months ago. I found your thot ass in a fucking ho house. Let's see if he *still* want you after that."

I stood there, trying not to cry. I wanted to laugh in his fuckin' face, but he made me believe that he could convince Jarrod to stop loving me anymore.

Not only was he putting me in a situation that I didn't like, but Gerald was also now kissing all over my neck while jacking off his dick.

I was a thot, and certain shit did turn me on, so was I wrong for liking this? Hell yeah, I was, but I couldn't turn off my pussy. That bitch was getting wet, even when I didn't want her to.

When I was finally able to push him off me, he slammed my head back into the office door. "You still the same thot. Now, get your ass over here," he ordered, taking a seat at his desk.

Like he ordered, I went over toward the desk and slowly dropped down to my knees to please this old bastard. I didn't know what came over me, but I craved the feel of a dick in my mouth, even after having some that morning.

"Don't be scared, baby girl. Eat up this dick so that you can win your prize at the end."

I couldn't lie; I was sucking that muthafucka like I was on the clock and rent was due.

A burst of guilt came over me, and I started to cry, thinking about Jarrod.

"Okay!" I yelled, trying to get up. I couldn't do this shit anymore.

Gerald grabbed my head. "Bite me if you want to. I'll kill your thot ass."

I cried while doing something that I once loved. I hated myself.

"Damn, this is exactly why I could never get over your ass," he teased.

I kept going, but with his tight grip on my head, it was hard for me to relax.

"Can you at least let go of my hair?" I mumbled.

Gerald never answered but instead pushed my head back down on his dick. Muthafucka didn't care about me gagging or throwing up on his suit pants. He was gonna get his nut at any cost.

"Keep going, bitch. I'm about to come," he yelled.

I tried my hardest to get up. There was no way I was gonna swallow his nut. Truthfully, I barely enjoyed swallowing my man's shit.

With everything in him, he held me down, and you could guess what happened next.

Once he was drained, he slowly let me up. I was just about to go the fuck off, but he stared at the door, and his face was pale, as if he had seen a ghost. I turned around to see what or who he was looking at, but there was nothing there to see.

"Fuck, who was that?" I yelled.

He grabbed me. "Stop tripping. The doors are locked. It wasn't nobody."

I didn't want to believe him, but he was too calm for someone who had been caught with their pants down.

Feeling disgusted, I rushed to the bathroom to clean myself up. I had still planned on cursing out his ass when I got out.

What had just taken place was so wrong, and all I could think about was how I was a fucking thot ho who didn't deserve Jarrod.

When I walked out, he was standing at the front door, holding a stack of money. Although I claimed to be done with that lifestyle, my eyes lit up. What could I say? It was the thot in me.

"Go buy you something nice."

The hesitation caused Gerald to pull the money away. "What? This was a freebie?" he questioned.

I quickly grabbed the money and tossed it in my purse. "Ain't shit in life for free."

I had no idea that I had just signed a deal with the devil.

"Tomorrow, I'm gonna need you to be here bright and early, and make sure that tight-ass pussy is freshly shaved."

"No, today was the end of all this, Gerald."

He chuckled. "I don't think so, Trina. Besides, if this tape gets out, and my nephew sees it, your ass will be on the streets. I hope you stacking just in case he leaves your ass."

"Tape?"

"This is a place of business, girl. Matter of fact, I was thinking about playing it next week when I open the doors."

"Gerald, please, don't do this to me," I begged.

"It might bring you some more customers. Just look at it as me giving you free promotion. Fuck working for Candy. You can work for me now, baby."

My tears didn't mean shit to this bastard. Everything was a game for him.

I pulled the money back out of my purse. "Look, take your money back and give me the tape. I can't hurt Jarrod like that."

He tossed up his hands, as if he were giving up the war. "Just do what I want, and Jarrod will never find out about us. Now, I'll see you tomorrow."

I walked out, crying, but I couldn't blame anyone but myself. I had played myself like a dumb ass. It wasn't even about making money because Jarrod had me covered. I was just a thot.

On my way home, I couldn't help but cry. I was dead wrong for what I allowed to happen with Gerald. Yeah, he was wrong, but I knew he didn't give a fuck about Jarrod or me from jump.

When I arrived home, Jarrod was still out, which was a good thing. That gave me time to jump in the shower and scrub my mouth out before he returned.

The way I looked at this fucked-up situation was that I had not only played myself while betraying Jarrod, but I had also dug myself in a deeper hole.

Chapter Nine

Denise Michelle Williams

Bedtime was the worst for me, and it usually left me up in my feelings every night. It was bad enough that I was locked up and away from my 2-year-old daughter, Destiny, but at night, when it was silent, I found it the hardest time because all I could do was stay up and think about how fucked up everything was going. I cried thinking about how I had once again failed my daughter. I was not the perfect role model, but I loved her to death and tried to be the best mother that I could be. I wanted nothing more in the world than to go home to my baby girl. I knew the role that I played, but honestly, I would have been out by now if my baby daddy, Red, had come through with the money for me. But instead, he folded and left me for dead in this bitch.

The day of my arrest, I was halfway out the door with the diapers and can of ravioli when a security guard called out to me. After hearing him yelling for me to stop, I ran as fast as I could, only to be tackled to the ground. Soon after, I looked up to see Red pulling off with our daughter, Destiny, in the backseat. I had let him down, and the way he shook his head said it all. Since then, Red's slick ass had been dodging all my calls. To make matters worse, my mom's phone had been cut off, and I had no idea if Destiny was still with her daddy or now with her grandma.

Every night, I promised myself that I was done with him for good, and whenever I did get out of here, I wasn't going to fuck with him anymore. Baby daddy or not, he was trash. I needed to work on bettering myself for my daughter. Truth be told, we wouldn't have been in that situation if he hadn't been on no fuck shit in the first place. He tried to sell weed, but his habit was bigger than his hustle. With that being said, any extra money that I came across went back to his plug so that he wouldn't get his ass beat. It was fucked up how my stupid ass had always come to his rescue, and he was so quick to run off on me. I swore he was a fucking embarrassment around the hood, and I was the dummy for letting him turn me into his baby mama.

Ms. Candy had been my cellmate for the time being, but I knew that once she was sentenced, she would be sent to the big house. These muthafuckas wanted her head for helping some thots make money. It was crazy, but they only wanted to make an example out of her because she wasn't breaking bread with them muthafuckas. I didn't even think they honestly cared that they had found out about the underage girls being at her house.

I wasn't gonna lie. At first, I thought she was a stuck-up bitch, but after talking to her, I realized that I could learn from her. Sorry, but not sorry, she had been like a big sister to me, giving me all the advice.

Being embarrassed about why I had been locked up, I tried to keep my personal business to myself, but when Candy started talking about helping me in the outside world, I opened up. She promised to help if I helped her out while we were roommates.

"Denise, you awake?"

I turned to face Candy's side of the cell. "Yeah, what's up?"

"I pulled some strings, and your mom's phone should be on later today. Make sure you call and check up on her and baby girl."

I wanted to cry. "Thank you so much, Candy, but you still haven't gone into any details on what you needed my help with."

"When it's that time, you'll know everything."

I didn't respond because my mind was on talking to my people later that day.

After lunch, I made sure to be the first in line to use the phones. After my first two weeks here, and realizing that I had no one to talk to, I had stopped getting in line, and now, I was back.

"Mommy!" I called out, full of excitement after she finally accepted the call.

I was not surprised at all that she jumped straight to the point.

"Denise, when you coming to get this damn baby? Red dropped her off and hasn't been back since."

"Ma, I have to wait until I go back to court. Red never produced my bail money, and now, I gotta wait. Ma, I promise I'm gonna look out for you when I get out of here. Just make sure Destiny is all right for me."

The phone got quiet, and I knew that only meant that she was holding her tongue. Usually, we always fought over my loving Red a little too much. She knew he wasn't shit, but it had taken me a minute to see it for myself. Well, I saw the shit, but loving him was a hell of a drug. That saying, "Love is blind," was for sure the damn truth.

"One minute remaining," I heard the recording call out.

"Ma, I gotta go, but I love you and Destiny so much. Can you please tell her that I love and miss her so much and kiss her for me?"

"Yes, I'll tell her. You know, Denise, when you get out, I want you to do better. Do you hear me?"

I knew and understood exactly what she was talking about and promised myself to make her proud.

"Yes, Ma, and I promise you that I'ma do better."

The phone disconnected, and I returned to my room.

Just hearing how disappointed my mom sounded brought tears to my eyes. I lay across my bed, crying my poor little heart out. This couldn't have been the life that I was supposed to live. I was broke, with a broke baby daddy, trying to raise a li'l girl.

"Fix your face, Denise. Better days are coming."

I looked up to see Candy returning to the cell. For a woman who was about to serve some real time, I never saw her break down about shit.

"I talked to my mom. Ain't shit new. She is disappointed in me, but the good news is that she got Destiny. She said she hasn't seen Red since he dropped her off. I'm starting to hate the man who gave me the best gift in the world."

Candy took a seat on my bed. "It's gonna be all right. We both are gonna get out of here and live our best life, trust me."

"You think so positively. I like that," I said, trying not to laugh, although I didn't want to cry anymore.

Then Candy got up to make sure no one was in our business. "I think it's time to fill you in on my plan."

I was all ears. I had a lot of faith in her, and I knew that being friends with Candy and following her lead was my only chance out.

"First, when do you go back to court?"

"I meet up with my lawyer soon, and I'll find out then. This my second time getting in trouble, doing the same shit. I'm not sure how shit gonna work out."

Candy shook her head. "I talked to my lawyer today. He's gonna take over your case instead of that whack-ass lawyer you got. He's for sure gonna get you off with probably probation for a minute."

"Hell yeah. That's better than doing time. At least, I'll be home with my daughter," I admitted.

"I have a plan, but I need you to be down, no matter what. This shit will play out correctly if you don't back down. Can I count on you?"

Without even completely hearing out her plan, I agreed to be her right-hand man.

That afternoon, Candy went over her foolproof plan, and although I was scared, she promised that no matter what, I was gonna be good.

With desperation in her eyes, Candy looked intently into my eyes. "Denise, you're not looking at no real time, and I'm gonna make sure my lawyer gets you home, no matter what. It's time for you to put your big girl panties on and do this shit for your daughter."

Just like that, she had pulled me in, and I was ready to have her back. With the promise of me walking out to a large deposit, it was like I had no choice. I knew that money could help out my mama, Destiny, and me in a major way, and I couldn't afford to turn down this opportunity. After talking to Candy that afternoon, I felt that my chances of finally making my mom and daughter proud were greater than ever.

"Fuck you, stupid bitch!" Candy yelled, jumping up and tossing her lunch tray at me.

I jumped up, ready to fight, but the guard grabbed me, pushing me down to the ground.

"I'm gonna fuck you up, stupid ho. Just wait until I get loose."

Then I saw the other guard grab Candy to walk her out of the cafeteria. I hated how I was on the ground, and that bitch was getting treated like she wasn't the one who just assaulted me first.

"Let me up!" I screamed.

That was when I felt her knees in my back and the handcuffs going on me. "I'm gonna need you to calm the fuck down."

"I'm calm. I just can't breathe like this," I said.

Being an asshole, the bitch made me stay down on the floor a little longer, even though I was completely chilled out.

When she finally let me up, it was a relief. "Thank you."

"I don't need y'all bitches fucking up my day with all this unnecessary bullshit. Do you think you can go back to your cell and behave?"

"Yes, just take these cuffs off me, please."

Instead, she snatched my arm and damn near dragged me all the way back to my cell. To my surprise, Candy wasn't back in the room just yet. The way the guards reacted, I knew her plan was working, and everyone would believe that we were beefing.

Candy

Plan B was in motion, and after our little show in the cafeteria, they pulled my ass away to the hole for an overnight visit. At first, I thought I was gonna lose my mind in that bitch because of what I saw on TV, but I was straight, especially when Officer Daniel Fisher came to visit me later that night. I had been flirting with him hard and needed him in on my plan for my grand escape. After walking me to the hole that evening, I promised him some pussy. Maria wasn't around, so he was gonna have to do. Besides, how else was I supposed to pull him in? I learned years ago that niggas would go against their mama for some WAP, and that was precisely what a thot bitch had.

"You knew I was coming. Why you still got that shit on?" he asked while undoing his pants.

I needed to get things clear with him. "I'm not a huge fan of dick," I bluntly announced.

"Fuck you mean? You got me sneaking around, putting my job on the fucking line, and now you talking about you don't like dick. How the fuck you gonna try to play me?"

"I was thinking that maybe you would love to suck on this muthafucka," I said, giving him my best seductive look.

He stood there for a minute, as if he were thinking about what I said. His pants were down to his ankles, and his dick was in his hand. This man was ready to fuck. Too bad I wasn't giving up shit.

I was nervous, but I couldn't let this man feel like I wasn't the one in charge. I had to remember who the fuck I was. "How about this time, we take things slow since we're still trying to get to know each other? I'm a little nervous and don't want to disappoint you, baby."

He started to smile, and I knew I had him from there. Honestly, the only thing that I was happy that my mama passed down to me was my mouth. I swear, a bitch could sell ice to an Eskimo. I had the gift of gab, and anyone who was ever around knew that shit.

"Go ahead and lay your sexy ass down. Let daddy get a taste of this sweet shit."

I listened, and he had no problem pulling my pants down to eat on this pussy. Not being able to get a wax or even shave had me a little embarrassed, but he parted the hair down the middle and got to work.

Daniel ate this pussy so good that I knew he wasn't getting shit at home.

Before, my husband, Jasper, and Maria were the only ones in the world who could say that they ate my pussy, and now, I had to add his ass. Wait, I'm lying. I forgot that stupid bitch, Eve, ate my pussy before I turned her completely out. Damn, she did make me some money, and, for that purpose only, I missed her.

Anyway, back to this muncher I had now. He was freaky and wasted no time shoving his tongue in my ass. If only I had plans to stay here any longer, I would have loved to let him eat on me every night.

"Damn, Daniel." I moaned out, but not too loudly. I still had to be mindful about where we were.

"You so fucking wet, girl. I gotta feel this shit."

Before I could stop him, he had slid two fingers inside of me, roaming around.

He had me so turned on that I genuinely thought about letting him fuck me. I hadn't had real dick since Jasper, and it took me by surprise that Daniel's mouth and hands alone made me feel like I had been missing out on men all these years. I couldn't fucking lie. He had my mind gone for a minute. I felt like I was supposed to confess a love for him that I knew wasn't there or something. I started laughing at myself because I began to feel dick whipped and hadn't even had no dick yet.

Daniel got up, wiping his mouth off on his T-shirt. His grin was bigger than a badass kid getting everything that he wished for on Christmas morning.

"You know I'm gonna need some more of that good shit. Ain't no way in the world this was a one-time thing."

I smiled, opening up the invitation for him to continue to flirt with me. I still needed him for something other than letting my cum glaze up his face.

"Whenever you can find a way to make it happen, it's yours."

"Just like that, huh?"

"Yeah, but I'm gonna need your help with something."

By this time, I was standing in his face, playing with his dick, making him feel like he was the man.

"Anything, love. Just let me know what you need; I got you."

While helping him fix up his uniform again, I decided not to tell him my plan because I thought he might need another session before I let him in. Besides, it was hard to trust muthafuckas nowadays.

"We'll talk again."

With that being said, he snuck out, leaving me to my thoughts. First thing I was gonna do when I got out was take a shower. This juicy pussy of mine was still soaked, and I felt stinky. Having good pussy and not being able to share it with anyone was one of my problems, and that was why I came so hard on that man's face.

After a shower, I joined everyone for breakfast. Everyone was staring at me, and it had me wondering if they had beef or what. Then I remembered that I had just had my soul snatched, and the smile on my face was noticeable. These bitches probably thought I was friendly now or something.

During breakfast, me and Denise had to play it cool and sit at opposite tables, but we kept rolling our eyes at each other and talking shit, just to play it off.

"Damn, Candy, why that bitch over there looking at you like that?" white girl Kimberly asked.

I wanted to tell her to mind her own fucking business because I didn't like her goofy ass anyway, but I couldn't afford to fuck up my plan. I did one of the hardest things to do, and that was to bite my tongue.

"I don't know. Maybe she wanna suck on my pussy or something."

I didn't know why I said that goofy shit, but having my pussy munched on was heavy on my mind since Daniel had put in that work.

I was caught off guard when a guard came into the cafeteria to take Denise away. I couldn't help but wonder what that was all about. I could tell that she was scared and nervous as hell herself. As she turned around to look back at me, her face said it all. She didn't have a clue about what was going on.

Going back to my cell after breakfast and not knowing why Denise wasn't there was killing me. I was wondering if they knew about my plan and were squeezing her for information to get me jacked up. I also started to wonder if I could really trust her ass. Just thinking about that shit made me laugh. I would kill that bitch if she were a rat. I didn't trust too many, and if I opened up to the wrong person, I would have to make an example out of them. There was nothing like beating a bitch to death to let the next bitch know that I was *not* the one to fuck with.

"Oh my gawd, bitch. Guess what?" Denise joyfully sang as she entered the cell.

"Calm down, bitch, before you fuck up shit. I'm getting the fuck outta this bitch. Anyway, what's up?" I questioned, needing to know what was going on.

"So, Mr. Tucker came to see me today. You were right. He seems to be the top dog."

I sat up in my bed. "What did he say?"

"He gonna take over my case, and he might be able to get me out of here on probation. I can't believe this shit. I'm so happy."

Johnathan was the best at what he did, and since he hadn't been able to deliver any good news to me as of yet, I knew these people were about to bury me under the damn prison. I couldn't even get mad knowing that my freedom was riding on hers.

"You know that after your court date, we're gonna have to put my plan in motion. We both about to be out of this bitch."

I didn't like the facial expression she was giving me. I prayed this bitch wasn't trying to play in my face, or that was gonna be her ass.

"What's the problem, Denise? You need to speak up now before I have to fuck you up for real. I'm not for no games."

She giggled like everything was all right. "Damn, girl. Calm down. I was just going over your plan in my head, and I think this shit can work. I got your back, girl."

Hearing that made me feel a little better, and I was able to calm down.

"Tonight, at dinner, we gotta push this shit up a notch before we have our showdown."

Denise nodded in agreement, but something still didn't sit right with me.

"Matter of fact, we need to get shit jumping right now."

I guess she didn't realize what I was talking about until I snuck a punch at her. It connected to the right side of her face perfectly. I was surprised that the li'l bitch swung back, but then again, she was from the hood.

We were in the cell, fighting like some bitches straight off the streets. This bitch was giving me a run for my money, but she wasn't beating my ass. I hadn't fought in years, and it felt good to have my fist connect to a bitch's face.

"All right, break this shit up!"

We weren't fighting for a real reason, but it took four muthafuckas to pull us apart. We were throwing down in that bitch. As they pulled me off Denise, I could hear the girls in the other cells screaming and cheering us on. Them bitches loved drama.

"Damn, Candy, you didn't have to do that girl like that," I heard someone yell.

Little did they know, I really did. I needed them to see just how and why she would hate me enough to try to kill me.

***

"You girls gotta calm the fuck down," Daniel whispered as he walked me down to the infirmary.

"I keep telling you I'm good and don't need to be looked at."

Without paying me any attention, he continued to walk me into the room.

The nurse down there shook her head before telling him to cuff me to the bed on the other side of the room.

"Y'all young ladies stay fighting and messing up y'all pretty faces. I can't wait for you all to understand that them white folks don't give a fuck about y'all. They are entertained when y'all beat on each other. You fuck up out there in the real world, then come in here and do the same. Learn to sit yo' ass down and do your time."

I wanted to respond, but decided to just shut the fuck up and let her talk since she seemed to know everything. Me opening up my mouth would have only made her preach about respecting my elders, and I wasn't in the mood for that shit.

Danial moved out of her way so that she could clean my face.

"She gonna be all right?" he finally asked.

She gave him a dirty look. "Just a few bumps and bruises. She'll be all right."

There was some commotion outside the room loud enough to make Daniel walk out to investigate.

"He's too much in your face. You gotta watch these muthafuckas in here. To be straight up with you, most of these men only get pussy when they at work. Why do you think they work here and not at the men's prison? They nasty asses be trying to fuck on you young girls."

I didn't say anything but took in everything that she said. This bitch must not have known who I was because she had no idea that I was the one pulling the strings around here.

Daniel returned.

"What are you waiting for, sir?"

"Well, if you really wanna know, I had orders to take her to the hole after you finished with her. Is that a problem?" he asked with an attitude.

"Nah, I should be done in a minute, but you can have a seat over there by the damn door and out of her face," she ordered.

Daniel looked over at me before walking toward the door. I could tell that he didn't like how she was acting like I was a 13-year-old virgin, and he was a creepy old guy in a white van following me home from the store.

Waiting on her to clear me, I could hear Denise in the room next door. I really couldn't make out everything that she was saying, but she was doing a lot of crying.

"You all set to go to the fabulous hole. Hopefully, I won't see you in this place again."

I gave her a fake smile. "I'll try to stay out of trouble."

Daniel walked over so that he could cuff my hands back together and take me to the hole.

"You too fucking pretty to be fighting. I don't like seeing you like this."

I wasn't sure what to say to him. I was only using him, and he was acting like we were in a loving relationship. After a quick minute, I decided to use that to my advantage.

"I'm sorry. I just hate being messed with."

"I understand, but you gotta calm down before you get hurt for real."

As we continued to walk, my mind started racing.

"If I were to get hurt seriously, they gonna have me cuffed to the bed downstairs?" I asked, hoping not to make him suspicious.

"Nah, if it's too bad, they sending your ass straight to Receiving Hospital. Your ass gonna be cuffed to a bed in that muthafucka," he responded.

We had finally reached the dark, cold, quiet hall where the hole was located.

Daniel opened the door before uncuffing me. "I gotta go fill out some paperwork, but I'll be back later tonight."

Before I could say anything, he placed a kiss on my lips, then walked out the door. I couldn't believe how he was acting. This dummy didn't see all the red flags waving in his face. I was a fucking inmate, for God's sake. Since he was acting goofy, I was gonna play him as such. That night, while he ate my pussy, I was gonna talk to him about my plans and have his ass.

As I lay down, I thought about Denise. I hoped I wasn't too hard on her and that she still was gonna be down for my plan. The way shit played out in my head, we needed to fight just one more time before I let her get the best of me. Now, I usually was the type of bitch who was somewhat up front with a bitch, but because of my situation, now, I had to keep some shit to myself.

I initially told Denise that once everyone believed that we were beefed out because of the fighting, she was gonna have to stab me. At first, I thought I would be downstairs, and Daniel was gonna have to sneak me out, but he had just told me that I would get transported to a hospital, which was gonna work out better for me. He was gonna help me get the fuck on. Now, I did promise Denise that John was gonna get her out, but I never told her that if she went through with my plan, her ass wasn't gonna get out. That there was gonna be another charge against her ass. I only felt bad because of her daughter, but since she liked to play stupid for a nigga, why couldn't I play her ass too?

I knew what y'all are thinking. Candy, you're such a bitch. Well, I did send her mama some money for the baby. Damn.

Anyway, Daniel was gonna lose his job and probably serve some time, but I'd be long gone with Maria and my money before I would be able to find out shit. All I could think about was that in just a few days, my sexy ass was gonna be on an island with my pussy lips spread wide.

"Yes, baby, right there," I moaned as Daniel's tongue dove deeper into my spot.

I couldn't lie. This man was touching me in all the right places, and moaning out his name didn't bother me as much as the first time.

"Daniel, do you want me to be your girl?"

He lifted his head for a second. "Hell yeah, I would love that shit."

I allowed him to continue to work before hitting him with the next question. "What would you do if I were free and could go home to you?"

Daniel quickly answered. "I'd eat on this pussy and make love to you every night and probably marry your sexy ass. What's up with all these questions, Candy?"

"I wanna get out of here and live my life. These mutha-fuckas not gonna let me out on their own, and I gotta get out of this bitch before I get shipped out to prison. Daniel, I need your help," I cried.

I wasn't a crier for real, but I knew when and how to fake it.

"How the fuck am I supposed to get you out of here?" he questioned.

Daniel was now sitting up in the bed next to me, look-ing crazy.

"Baby, I got a plan, but I need you to promise that you'll have my back, no matter what."

I could tell that he was nervous, but with my hand jacking him off, he wasn't able to think straight.

"What I gotta do, Candy?" he asked before kissing me.

I took that moment to smell the sweet aroma of my pussy on his lips before pulling him in even more.

"Tomorrow, me and Denise gonna fight again, but this time, she gonna stab me. I need you to be the one to get me out of this bitch. Instead of going to the hospital, my maid will be waiting for me."

"You know shit is mad wild, girl? How the fuck am I supposed to play this shit off? What am I gonna say happened? Will your maid beat me down before snatching you?"

His laughing was pissing me off. My plan was flawless, and his goofy ass was laughing.

"She not gonna be alone, but you don't have to worry about being hurt. I *need* you, Daniel."

Thinking I had him hooked, I was surprised when he looked me straight in the face and asked, "When am I gonna get some pussy?"

I was such a stubborn bitch because I couldn't give him a straight answer. "Baby, what happened to us taking it slow?"

Daniel shook his head. "Bitch, you must think I'm crazy or something. I'm gonna need some pussy if I'm gonna go through with this shit."

I had to think of something quick, and the first thing that came to mind was Denise.

"Look, that girl, Denise, is in on this plan too. You can go to her, and she'll give you all the pussy you want. Even when we get out, you can have both of us by your side. Isn't it every man's dream to have two bad bitches at once?"

Now, Daniel was all smiles. He never had a baddie, let alone two at once, and he couldn't wait to brag about it to his friends.

"Both of y'all, huh?"

"Yes, Big Daddy. We gonna suck and fuck you so good, daddy."

He stood there for a minute, taking in what I was saying, while I prayed it worked.

"Let me go to where she's at. Then by tomorrow night, you'll finally be mine."

"Yes, baby, that's the plan."

Chapter Ten

Baby, I'm Sorry

Trina

"Baby, get up. You going to the shop today?"

I was sleepy as hell, but sat up to look at my man. He was fresh out of the shower, smelling good as fuck, with a towel wrapped around his waist. Last night. I played the sick role to keep him away, but only because the guilt was killing me.

"I was supposed to, unless you need me around the house."

I was hoping he would ask me to stay home, but he declined.

"Nah, baby, go help out his ass. I'm supposed to be meeting up with the fellas anyway to play some ball. Besides, my uncle already called, looking for your ass. Your work must have blown him away the way he was acting."

"What?" I questioned, not liking his choice of words.

"What I was trying to say is that he was acting like he really needed your help, like he ain't got other shops up and running."

I gave him a fake smile. "Oh, okay."

"You feeling better this morning, baby?"

I shook my head before speaking. "Nah, not really. I'm not sure what's wrong, but I'm gonna try to go help your uncle, then come straight home to cook dinner."

"What about you come home and get some rest? When I get home later and shower, I can take you out to dinner if you're feeling up to it," Jarrod said, placing a kiss on my lips.

I wanted to cry, but didn't want him looking at me all crazy and asking questions. "That sounds like a plan, baby."

Jarrod continued to get dressed as I went into the bathroom. I felt like shit about everything, but I was too afraid to call Gerald and tell him that I couldn't deal with him anymore. My mind was fucked up, and I couldn't decide if I was supposed to stay a thot or become a wholesome young lady.

Standing under the shower, I thought about the first time I called myself making easy money.

I was about 15 years old and called myself running away from home. I was chilling with my homegirl, Toya, and her boyfriend, Fred. He was an older nigga with money, so when he said his homeboy, Keshawn, was gonna stop by and chill with us, I didn't think twice about saying I was cool with that. Keshawn showed up and decided that him and Fred should go to the store and get some drinks. Right off, I knew what tip these niggas were on, and Toya was also hip.

"Aye, bitch, that nigga gonna try to fuck, but make sure you get a couple of dollars from his ass. And when y'all done, tell him you hungry, so they can go get us some Coney."

"All right, bitch, 'cause I am hungry as fuck."

Then I went into the bathroom to make sure my pussy was fresh for this nigga. I knew that older guys had no problem eating a bitch's pussy, especially a young bitch like myself. I was told that they did shit like that, thinking they were turning a young bitch out and could control her like that.

When I came out of the bathroom, Fred was sitting on one couch with Toya straddling his lap. They already had cups in their hands, drinking and feeling all on each other. Keshawn motioned for me to sit on the other couch with his ass. I didn't mind because he was fine and fresh as hell. I knew this dude had money and would break me off some.

"Move a li'l closer, shawty. Don't be acting scared of a nigga."

Trying to act grown, I slid over. "I'm not scared of shit."

Keshawn poured me a cup of the liquor they had just brought. Not wanting to be a baby, I took the cup and drank it down some. My throat was burning like a muthafucka, but he smiled, showing me that he liked that.

"Damn, you sexy as fuck. Why your girl ain't never brought you around before?"

"I don't know," I lied.

Truthfully, my mama kept my ass in the fucking house and away from niggas, and that was the main reason I left her home. I wanted to know what the hype of being a teen with no rules was all about.

Keshawn wasted no time feeding me the rest of my drink. I guess he didn't have any more conversation in him.

"Wait a minute, boy."

"Let me just pull out one of those titties."

I instantly started to giggle as I felt him pull off my shirt. Then he pulled my right tittie out of my bra and began to suck on it.

I couldn't do shit but giggle and enjoy his mouth on me. I wasn't a drinker, so I knew the liquor had taken over me.

"Damn, freaks, get a room." I heard Toya jokingly tease.

"I don't feel like moving, girl." My words slurred.

"It's cool. We about to go into the bedroom anyway," Fred said, picking up Toya and carrying her into the back room.

Keshawn wasted no time trying to undo my bra.

"Wait a minute."

"My bad. I thought you were a big girl and ready."

"I am, but I need to get some shit straight first."

He pulled out a rubber. "Don't worry about shit. I got us covered."

I had never put myself in this situation and wasn't sure how to come out and tell him that I needed some money if he wanted to fuck.

"What's wrong with you, girl? I thought you were down."

"I am. I just—"

He pulled out some money. "What? You need a couple of dollars in your pocket?"

I shyly responded. "Yeah, I do."

"Damn, shawty, that's all you had to say," he said while peeling off two one-hundred-dollar bills.

After he stood up to put his money back in his pocket, I watched as he set my money on the table. I smiled at the two crispy hundred-dollar bills. All I could think about was getting my nails done the next day.

Keshawn helped me undress, then wasted no time jammin' his dick into my pussy—no head or nothing, not even the rubber that he probably stuffed back into his pocket.

He knew I wasn't used to shit like this for real and took advantage of me. He showed no mercy as his dick stabbed at my guts. It was like the louder I moaned out, the harder he fucked me, and I didn't like it at all. Honestly, if it weren't for the money, I would have made him get the hell off me.

"Aww, shit. I'm about to come."

"Please don't come in m—" I begged in between my cries.

He started to fuck harder while holding me down on that couch. This man wasn't trying to let me move for any reason at all.

The sound of him grunting let me know that he had dropped his load in me. Next, he pulled out with the biggest smile on his face. "Get up and go pee. You ain't gonna get pregnant."

Not knowing no fucking better, my stupid ass got up to go pee. In the bathroom, I used a hot washcloth to clean myself up. When I came out, Keshawn was sitting on the couch, fully dressed.

"Aye, you good, shawty?" he asked, making me feel like maybe he wasn't an asshole for real.

"Yeah, I'm good. Just a little hungry," I said, remembering what Toya told me.

He quickly stood up. "Tell me what you want, and I'll go get it."

Thinking I had a new friend, I jumped up. "Can I ride with you?"

"Nah, shawty. You young as hell, and if the police pull me over, it wouldn't look good with me riding around at one in the morning with you. I promise I'll be right back."

Everything that he said made sense, so my dumb ass took a seat back on the couch. It wasn't until half an hour later that I decided to grab my money off the table. I wanted to fucking die at what I saw. Instead of two crisp hundred-dollar bills on the table, now, two one-dollar bills were there. I had let this nigga fuck for two dollars.

I turned off the water so that I could get out of the shower. I had a long day ahead of me, and I hated it.

I was happy that Jarrod was gone so that I could get my head together on what was happening. I could have sat there and pointed out how all this shit was Gerald's fault, but my thot ways had clouded me, and the love of money caused this damage. At this point, I figured that maybe I could stack this bread and keep shit on the low. I just had to learn how to hide my emotions when Jarrod was around. If I smiled and loved on him even more, he wouldn't notice nothing.

After getting dressed, I jumped in my car and headed toward the shop. To my surprise, a different vehicle was parked outside, and the door was unlocked.

I walked in, trying to play off the shit. "Good morning. I'm ready for work."

Jarrod's Auntie Sandy came from the back. "I'm glad you're ready to work, young lady. I need you to ride with me."

"My car's outside."

"I need you to ride with me for a second."

She did this little smile to cover her attitude. I wasn't sure what the problem was, but I followed her out the door.

"Jarrod hadn't brought a female around in years. You must got that platinum pussy between your legs."

Her statement caught me off guard, and I couldn't help but choke.

"Huh?" I asked, shocked and confused as hell.

She giggled. "We family, girl. We can talk about shit like this."

I still wasn't sure what to say, but that didn't stop her from continuing this weird conversation.

"My nephew be tearing that pussy up, don't he?"

"I'm not comfortable talking about my sex life with Jarrod."

She started to laugh. "Well, bitch, let's talk about your sex life with my fucking husband."

I damn near shit on myself but tried to cover it with a lie. "I'm not sleeping with your husband," I stuttered.

"Bitch, don't lie to me. I knew y'all fucked when you first came to my house. My husband got a type, and you it. I saw the way his eyes lit up when he saw you."

"I don't know what you're talking about, Sandy," I said, trying not to cry.

I knew if she knew the truth, Jarrod would know soon, and that only meant that my life was over.

"There you go again, playing in my fucking face again, girl. I saw you deep throating my husband yesterday at his fucking desk, ya wide-mouthed bitch."

Now, I was crying. "I'm so sorry. Please don't tell Jarrod," I begged.

She didn't respond, but she didn't mind laughing at me. At this point, I thought she was about to kill my ass or something.

I was surprised when she pulled up to her house. "Come on, girl. Ain't nobody about to hurt your ass."

I stepped out of the car, not knowing what the fuck was about to go down, but I felt like this was the end for me.

"Fix your face, girl. You too fucking pretty to be crying like that. You a grown-ass woman. Own up to your shit."

I tried to fix my face as I followed her into the house.

"Damn, Trina, yo' good-ass pussy done got me in trouble with the missus," Gerald yelled, pouring himself a drink.

Now, I really was confused. What the fuck did she want us to do? Sit around and talk about us fucking?

"What's going on?" I questioned.

"Baby, go ahead and talk to this girl," Sandy ordered.

"Hell nah. You the one who brought her here," he said, sipping on his drink.

"This is your fucking thot, fool. *You* talk to her," she responded while grabbing the drink out of his hand.

They passed the cup back and forth before Sandy finally said something. "Look, I'm gonna be straight-up with your ass. We have been in an open marriage for years, and I wanna fuck you with Gerald."

Today was one of those days that was full of stupid surprises because, boy, was I surprised.

"Hell no, I can't do that. I already fucked over Jarrod enough."

Sandy laughed. "You don't have a fucking choice. Besides, my husband already told me how good your mouth is. He even said your pussy was sweet like honey."

"This shit is crazy, and I'm not about to get involved in this bullshit," I yelled, standing my ground.

Gerald got up from his seat and disappeared into the back. When he returned, he was carrying a black brief-case. I watched as he opened it up on the table.

"Look at how your eyes light up when you see this paper. That's *exactly* how my husband looks at you. Come fuck us, and this all could be yours."

I couldn't answer because Gerald had come over to me and had already begun to kiss and suck on my neck. That man knew that shit woke up the thot in me from the first night we were together.

I was in big trouble when Sandy started to rub her hands across my breasts. My ass was stuck. I had my eyes closed and mouth open, enjoying four hands undressing me.

"Wait, I can't do this shit. I love Jarrod so much, and that's y'all nephew."

My words went unheard, and the next thing you knew, I was being carried off to their bedroom. They both sucked all over my body, and it was hard not to enjoy the shit. As I got into it and started to kiss them back and feel on them, I told myself that this was just another thang that Jarrod didn't have to find out about. I even decided that I was gonna buy him something nice with the money I was about to make.

Gerald had enough dick to satisfy both of us, but she was a big freak. This bitch pulled out a dildo bigger than Gerald's and Jarrod's dick put together.

My eyes bucked at the sight of it.

"Calm down, little girl. This dick ain't for sharing like my husband."

While Gerald fucked me from the back, Sandy arched her ass up in the air next to me and allowed him to ram that big bitch right up her ass. I shook my head, telling myself that this was gonna be the first and last time I entertained them.

After a shower and redressing, Sandy dropped me back off at the shop to get my car.

"Now that that's over with, my husband will no longer need your help at the shop, but I will call you if I need a repeat of today," she said, rubbing up my leg.

I clutched my purse as I got out of the car and got into mine. I watched as she drove off like shit hadn't just happened, and then I cried. I sat in my car crying because I really didn't know what the fuck was wrong with me. I had a good man at home, and I couldn't stop fucking for money, even when he gave me the world.

Finally making it back home, I was happy to see that Jarrod hadn't returned yet. Although I bathed there, I needed to take a long, hot one to soak my body. I was sore all between my legs. It wasn't long before I was so relaxed that I started to fall asleep.

"Trina, wake up."

I jumped, surprised to see Jarrod standing over me.

"Hey, baby."

He didn't respond, only walked away. I didn't know what his problem was. Maybe he lost the game or something.

With my towel wrapped around me, I went into the room. Jarrod was sitting on the bed, looking lost in his thoughts.

"What's wrong, baby?"

As I took a seat next to him, he jumped up. "It takes a lot for me to love someone, and that's why my family always say I never bring nobody around them. So, do you know how fucking embarrassing it is to bring you around my fucking family and friends, and you out here fucking my family?"

My mouth dropped, and the tears instantly began to fall. "Jarrod, baby, I'm so sorry. Baby, let me explain."

"You're right. You is a sorry-ass bitch, but it's my fucking fault. I don't know how the hell I fell for a known thot. I knew you liked to get fucked from jump. What the fuck was I thinking?"

"It's not like that, Jarrod. Please, let me explain," I begged.

"Ain't shit to explain. I rushed out so fast this morning that I forgot to tell you that I loved you. My dumb ass went to the shop to surprise you, and you wasn't there. I saw your car and thought the worst. I was worried about you and ended up tracking your phone. I was all right seeing that you were at my people's house, so I decided to pop up over there—only to find you in the fucking bed fucking my damn auntie and uncle."

I couldn't do shit but cry and beg for forgiveness, but he wasn't trying to hear shit I had to say. "Jarrod, it's not my fault, baby. I swear. Please just listen to me, Jarrod. There is something wrong with me. I need help."

"Yeah, Trina, you do need help, but I can't be the one to help you anymore. You gotta go, so I hope you was working today and not doing shit for the freebie."

"Where am I gonna go, Jarrod?" I cried.

"That's not my fucking problem. I gave you the world, and you didn't appreciate it. You on your own, Trina."

This man hated me so much right now, but I knew he still loved me deep down inside because he wasn't beating my ass like any other nigga would have done.

"I'm so sorry, baby."

Jarrod walked over to the dresser. "Remember, we were supposed to have dinner tonight?" he asked, pulling out a small box.

I slowly nodded my head.

"I was gonna ask your ass to marry me. I'm so fucking stupid. I swear. Girls like you don't want a fucking ring. Y'all want dick and shit."

As he talked his shit, I could hear his voice cracking, like he was trying not to cry. I had broken this man, and I had a feeling that he would never love again.

"I never wanted to hurt you, Jarrod."

At this point, he was tired of hearing me talk. He started pulling out the drawers that held my clothes and started throwing them at me. "Shut the fuck up. I don't wanna hear none of that shit. Get the fuck outta my shit," he yelled.

Scared, I grabbed whatever I could before going over to the closet. I got the purse that I had stashed all the money that Gerald had given me over the last two days. I didn't want to leave Jarrod, but he was so pissed that he couldn't even look me in the face. I could tell that it was hard for him not to explode, so I tried to leave him in peace.

Before completely walking through the bedroom door, I turned to give him one last look. This man had been there for me since day one, and my stupid ass fucked it up.

"Jarrod . . ."

He punched the wall before turning my way. With tears rolling down his face, he mumbled, "Get the fuck away from me."

Not wanting to hurt him anymore, I walked away from the only man who had ever loved me.

I wasn't sure where I was gonna go, but I knew Detroit was no longer a place I wanted to call home. Wasn't shit here but bad memories.

Chapter Eleven

Denise

Candy had me fucked up. I was ready to ride and be by her side, but that bitch really *did* beat my ass. I was pissed, but couldn't blame anyone but myself because I was warned before this shit even happened.

When I went to see my new lawyer, who was also her lawyer, he did tell me that my case was easy to beat and that I'd be going home real soon. What I didn't tell Candy was that he told me not to be so quick to trust her ass. He told me that she was a snake and wasn't to be trusted at all. Let him tell it, Candy had a way to make folks believe that she was there to help, but in the end, it was all about her. She never gave a fuck about anyone else but herself. He even went as far as saying that his friend, Jasper, had married her just to keep her ass around. He knew she would be dangerous on her own. Jasper had left her his business not because he loved her, but because he knew she was the right bitch for the job.

I sat in the hole, thinking over everything, and realized just how stupid I was. This girl was using me to help *her* escape, so basically, it was fuck *my* freedom. I wasn't even facing any real time, and this bitch was trying to get me caught up with a murder charge or something.

Being so quick to call a bitch a friend or sis, I had played myself. Although I got my ass beat, I still felt like

I had the last laugh. Not caring about being labeled a snitch because I was only gonna be there for a few days, I told. After the fight was broken up and they pulled us in different directions, instead of going straight downstairs to get checked on, I went upstairs to snitch. I told them her whole plan and all.

Now, from my understanding, I was in the hole to stay safe while they figured out how they were gonna stop her crazy ass.

"Aye, I came to collect," I heard a man say as the door opened.

I sat up, then realized that it was Candy's little friend, Daniel.

"What the hell are you talking about?" I questioned.

He began to undo his belt. "I told Candy that I was gonna help out with that crazy-ass plan that she came up with."

"So, I'm still trying to figure out why the fuck you in here."

I didn't know what Candy told this man, but his mind was gone, and he clearly wasn't thinking right, being all in my face.

"Candy said you was giving up some pussy for me help-ing out," he said, not realizing how crazy he sounded.

"Look, I don't know what the fuck she told you, but I'm not fucking nobody. I'm not even in on no plan to help her out either."

I didn't know why, but the more I tried to get him to leave, the closer he got to me. "I'm not helping you bitches out if I can't fuck. One of y'all gotta pay up, and she said it's you."

I wanted to laugh in his face and tell him to get the fuck on, but he looked like he was already tired of Candy's bullshit and wasn't in the mood for my shit. I had already had my ass beat earlier and didn't need it beat again.

"Look, you gotta get the fuck up out of here before you get in trouble," I yelled.

Daniel paid me no mind as he grabbed me by my shirt before tossing me back down on the bed. "Y'all bitches about to stop playing with me."

He pulled out his dick, not caring that my ass was crying and begging him to leave me alone.

He was bigger than Red, so I knew that he could beat my ass if he wanted to, but that didn't stop me from trying to get his big ass off me. "Get the fuck off me, muthafucka!" I yelled.

I fought hard, but once that man slapped the shit out of me, it was a wrap. I felt my head spin right off my shoulders before feeling him jam his dick into me.

"Shut the fuck up, bitch!"

I cried, begging him to get off me, but he refused to stop. This man had a buildup and was taking it out on my little ass, all because of that bitch, Candy.

"Y'all stupid bitches need to learn not to fucking play with a nigga like me. I should kill both of y'all hoes," he whispered in my ear while still fucking me.

I felt defeated and knew that he had won this battle, but when he started talking that shit about killing me, a super force kicked in, and I started to fight back. I already looked bad in my daughter's eyes. There was no way I was about to die in jail over nobody else's bullshit.

I went wild, kicking, screaming, and fighting back.

"Shut the fuck up, bitch!" he yelled, wrapping his hands around my neck.

This sick muthafucka was trying to choke me out.

I guess it was just my fucking luck. Right before everything went black, I heard someone yell out, "What the fuck is going on in here?"

I wasn't sure what was happening in the world at that moment, but as I lay there, blacking out, I couldn't help but think back to the first time I was raped.

I was only 16 when it happened, but the situation still fucked with me now. Well, not only me, but also Red too.

I was on my way home from the store. My mama had just got her stamps that day and let me use the card to get a few snacks for the night before she went out.

"What's up, Denise? Where you on your way to?" Steve yelled out from the opposite side of the street.

"Boy, you all in my business. I'm going home."

"I'll walk you the few blocks if you wait a minute."

Him being an older street nigga made me stand there and wait on his ass. Back then, having a dope boy walk with you boosted your reputation. I wanted a bitch to see me with his fine ass.

I watched as he served his last customer. He was so smooth with it. I swore that if you didn't know what he was doing, then you would have missed it.

"Aye, come here for a minute," he called out.

"What you want, Steve? I'm ready to get back to the house."

He grabbed my hand. "Chill out, beautiful. I got you."

I blushed as he caressed my hand.

"Aye, how old are you now?"

"I'm 16 but will be 17 by the end of summer," I proudly said.

"Oh, for real? You out here fucking these niggas yet?"

I rolled my eyes at the question. "That really ain't your business, but if you really wanna know, then no, fool."

Lord knows I should have left then, but something wouldn't allow me to pull my hand from him.

"Boy, you ready to walk me home now?"

"Stop calling me a boy. I'm a grown-ass man out here in these streets," he barked.

His change of attitude caught my attention, and then I was ready to go.

"Look, I gotta go."

I tried to snatch my hand from him, but he wouldn't let it go.

I tried again. "What the fuck is you doing?"

That whole time I was standing out there, I never noticed until then that he was stalling until no one else was out on the block. He quickly grabbed me before covering my mouth.

"Get your ass in here, bitch."

He forcefully dragged me to the side of the vacant house before pulling me through the door. I tried to fight off this dude, but I was so little that it was hard to defend myself. I ended up crying on a dirty-ass mattress in what was supposed to be the dining room. What a hell of a way to lose my virginity.

"Please, Steve, please, stop," I cried.

As he pumped harder, he responded. "Just shut the fuck up, and you bet not tell anybody."

"I won't tell. Please, just let me go home." I continued to cry.

He didn't give a fuck what I was talking about. He was getting something that he had been plotting on for a minute now. This grown-ass, 27-year-old man had had his eyes on me for years, and I never knew it.

"Please, get off me. Please."

"What the fuck, boy?"

Steve stopped for only a minute to see that it was his best friend, Red, walking into the spot.

I didn't give a fuck who it was. I wanted this nightmare to be over. "Please, help me. I wanna go home," I cried.

"Steve, what the fuck I tell you about this shit? Get the fuck off that girl, and let her go home," Red ordered.

About this time, Steve was back fucking me. "Nah, this that virgin pussy. I had to get this."

I continued to cry and pray that Red would save me.

"Get the fuck off her, bro," Red said, now trying to pull Steve off me.

Steve wasn't budging until Red placed his gun to his head. "Nigga, I said get the fuck up—now."

Steve slid right out, ready to fight. As he fixed his pants, he started to yell in Red's face. "Man, fuck this li'l bitch. I was gonna let you have some. What the fuck you tripping for?"

"I told you about this shit, nigga. You making shit hot over here."

While they talked, I was putting my pants on so I could run the fuck out of the house. I knew my mom was gone by now, so I wouldn't have to answer any questions about what took me so long.

"Nigga, you wanna fight over a bitch? Oh, this the shawty that your bitch ass was crushing on? My bad, bro."

I guess that was the last straw because Red swung at Steve. I took that moment to run away. Once I hit the side door, I heard a gunshot. Without turning around to see who got shot, I took off running home.

I raced home, crying my ass off, and only stopped when I hit my front door. That night was mad crazy, and I had already made up my mind to just forget about it. I couldn't be in this neighborhood with everyone thinking I was a snitch. I could only pray that he never came back for more and that he never hurt another girl again.

"Ma," I said, shocked to see her on the couch.

She could tell that something was wrong because I had never seen her jump up and move so fast in my life.

I cried as she wrapped me up in her arms.

"Denise, what the fuck happened to you? Come on, baby, talk to me."

We stood there for a minute, just crying and holding each other, but neither of us spoke. Honestly, I was scared to tell her because she would have wanted to get the police involved.

After a while, she walked me over to the couch. I sat down, but she went to the bathroom. I could hear water running in the tub. I got in the tub, sipping on the hot tea that she had made me.

"I know you don't wanna talk about this right now, but no matter what, I'm gonna have your back."

I nodded, letting her know that I understood her.

The next morning, I had to damn near beg her to go to work. I told her that I had no plans to leave the house or invite anyone in.

It was around twelve that afternoon when I received a text telling me to get my shit on the porch. I didn't recognize the number, so I peeked out the window to see if anyone was around the house.

Noticing that no one was there, I opened the door. On the steps, I saw that someone had brought home my purse and replaced all my snacks. It wasn't until I was about to shut the door that I saw Red standing across the street. He gave me a little wave before getting back into his car and driving off.

Sitting on the couch, I put together that he had killed Steve, and he let me know that I had nothing to worry about. He returned my stuff. I picked up my phone to text him thank you. That was the start of our relationship.

I grew to love him over time, and that made me put up with a lot of his bullshit. He was my hero. How could I ever turn my back on him?

***

"Denise, Denise, baby, wake up."

I slowly woke up, not knowing where the hell I was, but I knew who I saw. "Mama," I cried.

"Them people told me what happened in that jail. Baby, you gotta fight this time."

I was listening, but at that moment, all I wanted to do was hug on her forever.

"It's okay, baby. They letting you go home."

Hearing that made me cry even more. All I ever wanted was to go home.

"Ma, where's Destiny?"

As soon as those words left my mouth, Red walked in, carrying Destiny in one hand and a group of balloons in the other hand.

I knew I said I was done with him, but I still loved his ass.

I had been home for a week now, and I couldn't have been happier. Red even was acting right for the moment.

"Aye, a few days before you came home, this package came in the mail for you."

I grabbed the package from my mom. "You sure this mine?"

"Yes, girl, your name is on the damn package. It's from somebody named Maria. Who the hell is that?"

I slowly opened the package, surprised that her nosy self hadn't opened it yet.

"Oh my God," I mumbled with my mouth wide open.

"What is it, girl?"

I turned around so that she could see what I was holding. "Ma, we about to be set for life."

I hated Candy and promised myself not even to bring up her name once I got home, but that bitch had my money sent to the house before the task was even done, and for that reason alone, I thanked her. I knew she was mad that her plan didn't work, and she was still locked up.

Just in case you were wondering, I went through with pressing charges against Daniel, and he will be going to prison very soon. Also, my lawyer, Johnathan, took on my case against the jail, and a bitch was about to get paid.

Chapter Twelve

Candy

So, both Denise and Daniel folded on a real bitch. I waited in that hole for days, ready to bust the fuck outta that bitch, and Daniel never came to help me.

When the doors finally opened, I wished it was Daniel to save me, or at least give me some more head, but instead, it was two different officers whom I had never seen before. I guessed the other bitch was the head bitch in charge or whatever.

Without saying a word, they snatched me up and out of that room so fast.

"What the fuck is going on?" I yelled.

"Shut the fuck up," one of the officers barked.

I thought they were taking me to my cell, but they took my ass straight out of the building. I knew then that I had fucked up somewhere down the road, and my ass was about to pay.

It felt like I sat in that room for hours before finally asking for my lawyer. Once that was said, they left me alone, and I knew that I only had so much time before I got my shit together. They weren't about to pin shit on me. From what I understood, they were saying that Daniel raped Denise, and I sent him after her. That bullshit reminded me of that Eve bullshit all over again. When they brought up my plan to escape, I damn near blacked out 'cause what the fuck?

It took Johnathan a good hour to finally show up, but I was happy to see him. Well, I thought I was happy, but this man started talking, and it seemed as if everything that came out of his mouth was a different language.

"Instead of sending someone in to tell you the news, I decided to come down here to talk to you on my own."

"Fuck all that, John. I need you to get me out of here. These crazy muthafuckas trying to blame some more shit on me. Please—"

He shook his head. "Look, Mrs. Porter, I can no longer represent you in any situation that you've gotten yourself in."

Forgetting that they had one of my hands cuffed to the table, I jumped up, ready to fuck him up—only to be snatched back down to my chair. "What the fuck you mean you can't represent me anymore? What about your promise to Jasper to look out for me?"

"Jasper who?"

"Don't fucking play with me, John!" I yelled, not believing how he was playing in my face.

My tears didn't mean shit to him, and those who knew me knew it took a lot for a thot like me to break down and cry. As John walked out the door, I cried even harder, knowing that I really had no one in my corner. I was about to be just another pretty face in prison, probably for the rest of my fucking life. I couldn't believe that this was the end of me, Candace Richardson-Porter.